# Yitzhak's Escape

## The Jewish Flight to Uzbekistan

# Sandor M. Lubisch

This book is a work of fiction inspired by actual historic events. Names, characters, places, and incidents are used fictitiously.

Photo credits:
    Book cover photo: Sandor M. Lubisch collection
    Title page photo:  Sandor M. Lubisch collection
    Family photos:     Bracha Alterovits, Sandor M. Lubisch
    Profile photo:      Sandor M. Lubisch collection

# Definition of a Holocaust Survivor

(From the book: <u>Shelter from the Holocaust</u>)

"Jews who lived for any amount of time under the Nazi domination, direct or indirect, and survived"
- *Yad Vashem*

"Any persons, Jewish or non-Jewish, who were displaced, persecuted, or discriminated against due to the racial, religious, ethnic, social, and political polices of the Nazis and their collaborators between 1933 and 1945. In addition to former inmates of concentration camps, ghettos, and prisons, this definition includes, among others, people who were refugees or who were in hiding."
- *United States Holocaust Memorial Museum*

# Glossary

*abba:* The Hebrew word for father.

*aliyah:* (pronounced *ah-lee-yah*) The Hebrew word for immigrating to Israel.

*Bar Mitzvah:* The Jewish religious ritual recognizing a Jewish boy's entrance into adulthood, usually when he reaches the age of 13.

*Blitzkrieg*: (pronounced *Blitz-kreeg*) The German word for a highly organized and fast-moving military operation to quickly defeat the opposition.

*Bolechov:* (Yiddish pronunciation *Bol'-le- guttural chof)* Also known as Bolechow, Bolekhiv (Ukrainian spelling), Bolekhov (Russian spelling). A small town located about 64 miles south of Lviv in today's Western Ukraine. It is on the banks of the Sukiel River at the foot of the Carpathian Mountains. In 1938, 77% of the population (3000) was Jewish. Only 48 of the town's Jews survived World War II. As of 2022, it had an estimated population of 10,000.

*Bubbie:* (pronounced *Bub'-ee*) The Yiddish word for grandmother.

*CKZP:* The Central Committee of Polish Jews was established on November 12, 1944 and discontinued on October 29, 1950.

*Dzierzoniow:* (pronounced *Ger-zorn'-no)* A town located in Southwestern Poland in the Lower Silesia region. Prior to 1946 the town was known as Reichenbach or Rychbach.

*eretz:* (pronounced *air-etz*) A Hebrew word meaning "the land of".

*Galicia:* A region in today's Western Ukraine that was once part of the Austro-Hungarian Empire and Poland, where many Jewish people lived.

*imma:* (pronounced *e - ma*) The Hebrew word for mother.

*Kiryat Ono:* A city in the eastern section of the Tel Aviv district in Israel.

*kolkhoz:* A Soviet socialistic collective farm agricultural settlement.

*Kristallnacht (The Night of Broken Glass)* This occurred on November 9, 1938, when Nazis killed or injured many Jews, destroyed Jewish properties and businesses, and burned synagogues and homes in Germany, annexed Austria, and the Sudetenland in Czechoslovakia.

*Luftwaffe:* (pronounced *looft-wah-fah)* The German name for their air force during World War II.

*mensch:* The Yiddish word for a person, often a man, who is decent, mature, responsible and a person of dignity.

*minyan:* The quorum of at least 10 adult participants for a Jewish prayer service.

5

*oblast:* (pronounced *ah-blast*) An administrative region in Russia, the former Soviet Union, and in some of the previous Soviet-controlled countries, including Ukraine.

*pogrom:* (pronounced *po-grahm*) An organized massacre of helpless people; a massacre of Jews.

*PZPR:* The Polish United Workers' Party was Poland's communist political party, founded on December 15, 1948, and dissolved on January 30, 1990.

*rynek:* (pronounced *rye-neck*) An eastern European name for a town square or public market area.

*Shiva:* The Hebrew word referring to the seven-day mourning period observed by the immediate family of the deceased.

*shosse:* (pronounced *sha'-sea*) Russian word for highway.

*shul:* A synagogue.

*Stanisławóv (Stanislaviv)* (pronounced *Stan'-is- law'-vov)* The former name of today's provincial capital city and province, Ivano-Frankivsk. The name was changed in 1962 during the Soviet era.

*Stryi:* (pronounced *Stree)* A large city along the left bank of the Stryi River located about 15 ½ miles north of Bolechov.

*tallis or tallit:* A Jewish prayer shawl.

*Taniava*:  (pronounced *Ta-knee'-a-va*) The name of a small village and a forest near Bolechov.

*Torah*:  (pronounced *Tor-ah*) The Hebrew scroll of The Five Books of Moses.

*ulitsa:*  (pronounced *u-lit-za)* Russian word for street.

*Zaydie:*  (pronounced *Zay'-dee)* Yiddish word for grandfather.

Polish currency:
  *zloty:*    (pronounced *zlot-'ee*)
  *groszy*:  (pronounced *grah'-she*)
    1 zloty is divided into 100 groszy

Soviet Union currency:
  *ruble:*  (pronounced *roo'-bol*)
  *kopek:*  (pronounced *koe'-pick)*
    1 ruble is divided into 100 kopek

For Aunt Rose and Uncle Dan

Their love of reading inspired my writing endeavor.

This book is dedicated and written to preserve the memory of my mother's paternal family who perished during the Holocaust by remaining and facing the invading German army, and those family members who survived by fleeing eastward with the Soviet evacuation.

# Prologue:
## Zaydie's Metal Box
### Kiryat Ono, Israel
### May 2000

"Moishe. Shayna. When you finish changing your clothes and putting them in the hamper, come to the kitchen. Your mother and I want to talk to you."

I could sense the seriousness of my father's voice. He rarely called for us to come to the kitchen. My mom was usually the one to interrupt my sister and me from doing our homework, playing games, or even reading to come to the kitchen to eat lunch or dinner.

This day was different. My parents, younger sister, Shayna, and I had just returned home from my Bubbie Jenny's funeral. Our mom cried the whole time knowing that her mother had died and would no longer be with her.

Even though Bubbie Jenny's real name was Gania, she always preferred to be called Jenny. She had been ill and spent the last couple of weeks in the hospital. Zaydie Yitzhak immediately called my mom when Jenny fell in their apartment. An ambulance arrived and took her to the hospital. Since my sister and I were home from school, we went with our parents as my father hurriedly drove to the hospital, first picking up Zaydie. When we all arrived at the hospital, the attending doctor told us that Bubbie Jenny had suffered a serious heart attack. She had another heart attack at the hospital two days later and died.

While my Bubbie was in the hospital, my Zaydie Yitzhak came to stay with us in our apartment and

10

slept in my bedroom. I didn't mind sleeping on the sofa in the living room. I loved both of my grandparents very much and knew this was a very difficult time for him and my parents knowing that Bubbie was very ill. Plus, Zaydie Yitzhak and Bubbie Jenny were my only grandparents. My father's parents died when he was a young boy.

This January morning at her graveside funeral at the cemetery was a dreary day with dark clouds hovering above and thrusting a constant downpour of heavy cold rain onto us. Even though we carried umbrellas at the cemetery, our clothes got soaked and all of us needed to change clothes once we got home. Even our parents' friends and the members from Zaydie's shul who attended got drenched.

About 15 minutes later after being summoned by our father, I joined my sister and parents and sat at the kitchen table. I glanced at my mom and noticed she was still using tissues to dry her eyes.

My dad spoke up. "Both your mom and I want to thank the two of you for your solemn attention and quiet behavior at the graveside funeral. It is very difficult to lose a family member and know they will no longer be physically with us. We also want to thank you for not complaining about Zaydie staying with us while Bubbie Jenny was in the hospital."

He continued. "Before I leave to bring Zaydie back to our home, both your mom and I need your cooperation. First, do either of you know what we mean by sitting Shiva?"

Shayna shrugged her shoulders and remained silent.

I went ahead and spoke up. "I think I know, Abba. I think this is when friends come to your home to tell you how sorry they are about the death of your family member and to pay their respects."

11

"Yes, Moishe. You are correct. People come to the family home for seven days after the funeral. We, as a family, will observe the Shiva period for the seven days at our apartment. Therefore, it will be more convenient for Zaydie to continue to stay here with us. This means, Moishe, you will need to continue to sleep on the sofa."

"I don't mind, Abba. Anything I can do for Zaydie Yitzhak is fine with me."

"Thanks, Moishe. You're a good grandson. Even though we will observe Shiva, your mom and I want the two of you to continue to go to school and complete your homework assignments. We don't want you to get behind with your classes. I've made arrangements with my office staff for them to assume my grocery store responsibilities so I can remain at home with your mom and Zaydie.

"There's one more thing we want to explain to the two of you. And this is a big one. We have asked Zaydie to move in and live with the four of us permanently and he accepted our offer."

Shayna and I glanced at each other with a surprised and confused look.

"Years ago, when your mother and I wanted to get married, I was renting a small room in a friend's apartment. Zaydie Yitzhak and Bubbie Jenny offered for the two of us to live with them when we got married until we could find an apartment that we could afford. Now that Zaydie is alone, I feel it is my obligation to invite him to live with the four of us. He is 76 years old. It is best for him not to live by himself. He needs to be surrounded by family and not become lonely. Our apartment is close enough for him to continue to walk to his shul to join the minyan with his friends at the shul's Morning Prayer services. We know he likes to go there and socialize with his shul friends after the prayer service. He can also help your mom by warming up the evening meal before she gets home from working at the grocery store. Do you both understand why this is best for Zaydie?"

Shayna and I both nodded our heads affirmatively to indicate we understood.

"I'm going to call my friend who owns a furniture store and order two matching beds and mattresses, two small nightstands, and two matching dresser cabinets for your bedroom, Moishe. There will be enough room to keep your desk and chair in your room since your bedroom is much larger than Shayna's. I'm going to need you to be very kind and patient to your Zaydie since the two of you are going to share the bedroom. For you, Shayna, it's time that you had a bigger bed. We will move Moishe's current bed and mattress, nightstand, and dresser into your bedroom. We know a family who has a young daughter who could use your current bedroom set. I think we can get everything delivered by the end of next week. In the meantime, Moishe, please remain sleeping on the sofa."

"As I said before, Abba. I'm okay with doing this."

"Good. Thank you to both of you for your understanding. I'm now going to drive over to pick up Zaydie. Your mom is going to cover the mirrors and prepare for any visitors who may come this evening for Shiva and join us with reciting some prayers."

This news about Zaydie Yitzhak coming to live with us was a lot to comprehend. But I knew it was best for him to come and be with us, and I really didn't mind sharing a bedroom with him. He always told me jokes when he saw me, and I laughed even when the jokes weren't funny or didn't make any sense to me.

Our apartment was quite large, with three bedrooms, two bathrooms, a living area, dining room, and a kitchen large enough to have a small dining table. My dad made a good living working in the executive offices of a large chain of grocery stores in Israel. When Shayna and I were old enough to walk to and from school on our own, my mom started working at the grocery store located near the shopping mall close to our apartment building. My mom and Bubbie Jenny rotated the location where our family's Friday evening Shabbat meal would be held. This was one tradition I really valued. We were all together as a family at the end of the week to greet Shabbat.

We were a small family. Both of my parents were the only children in their family and we didn't have any relatives living near us. My mother's younger brother lived in the United States and could not attend the funeral. I recall hearing about my mother's aunt, who lived in Canada. But not much was ever mentioned to Shayna and me about her.

My grandparents and my family lived in an eastern section of the Tel Aviv area called Kiryat Ono. My grandparents' apartment wasn't too far from ours. My parent's apartment building had four stories and overlooked Reisfeld Park where my sister and I often played. We could see the park from our living room window since our apartment was located on the building's fourth floor.

Shayna and I had a few friends from school that also lived in the apartments near ours. Some of their parents were our parents' friends and also attended the Great Synagogue Karon. Zaydie Yitzhak and Bubbie Jenny were more religiously observant than us. They attended services at the smaller Ohel Yaakov Synagogue. Very observant people their age, who were originally from Eastern Europe, went there and many of them were their good friends. Depending upon our parents' work schedule, we didn't always attend the Saturday morning Shabbat service at the

Great Synagogue. The only time when we went regularly to all of their services was during the High Holy Days.

Once Shiva ended, my mom helped Zaydie determine the clothes and personal items he needed to bring to our home. My mom selected some kitchen items she could use, along with some family heirlooms to place inside the curio cabinet in our living room. The remaining furniture and other items were donated to a Jewish charity to disperse them to needy families.

As the new bedroom furniture was carried into our apartment, my father showed the movers where to place everything. My father was correct. Everything fit perfectly in the bedroom that Zaydie and I would share without it looking very crowded, and I could continue to use my desk to complete my homework. The bedroom closet was adequate to hang Zaydie's dress shirts, dress pants, and suit coats on the left side. My mom moved my shirts, pants, and sport coats to the right side. My mom followed the same pattern and placed boxes and other items on the closet's top shelf and put our shoes on the floor. There was enough room in the hallway closet to hang our coats and jackets.

After a few days, I became aware of my Zaydie's daily routine and habits. Shayna and I were the first ones to take a morning shower in the hallway bathroom and get dressed, while our parents used the bathroom adjacent to their bedroom. While we were all getting ready for the day, Zaydie would go into the kitchen wearing his white terry cloth robe and slippers and turn on the coffee pot. He also toasted and ate a bagel and drank his morning cup of coffee. Once Shayna and I and our parents came into the kitchen to eat breakfast, it was Zaydie's turn to prepare for the day. Before leaving for school during the work week and on those Saturdays when we all went to Shabbat morning service, Zaydie came out of the bedroom wearing a freshly pressed white shirt, tie, neatly creased dress slacks, and his black slippers. This was his daily attire.

When I first saw him dressed this way, when I had a private moment with my mom, I asked her, "Why does Zaydie dress up every day?"

"Moishe, he always dressed up as long as I can remember, even when I was a child. He must have liked to look very dignified and professional at the barbershop where he worked. I often heard comments from his customers that he looked like the perfect mensch!"

I also noticed that every evening before he and I said "Good night" to each other, he would remove a black metal box from the top shelf in the closet. Once seated on his bed, he turned away from me and held the metal box and remained silent for many minutes. I couldn't tell if he opened the box and looked inside.

I thought to myself:  *What is he doing?  What is this all about?  What is so special about this metal box?*

After witnessing him doing this every night for a week, I had enough nerve to ask him, "Zaydie, why do you look at the metal box every night before you go to bed?  Why is this box so special to you?"

He raised his head and turned and looked at me with a big smile.  "You are a very insightful and curious young man, Moishe.  Nobody has ever asked me about the metal box. I don't think I ever showed it to anyone except your grandmother.  You are the first one in your family to see it. Yes, it is very special to

16

me, and now that Bubbie Jenny is gone, it may be a good time for me to tell someone about it."

He returned the metal box to the closet and then sat at the end of my bed and continued to smile at me. "Since you are interested, I'll tell you everything. It is a very long story. I think it will be best for you and me to have a long talk after you complete your Bar Mitzvah in July. That's four months from now. Go ahead and continue to prepare for it. I'm very pleased your mother and father decided to have it at my small shul. I'm very proud to show my shul friends what a wonderful grandson I have. Once your celebration is over, let's spend a Sunday afternoon together, just the two of us. Is this all right with you?"

"Sure thing, Zaydie. I can wait. But I know I'll become even more interested in hearing your story as I see you look at the box every night. Good night, Zaydie. Sleep well."

"You too, Moishe."

Once my Bar Mitzvah ceremony was over, I reminded my Zaydie about his promise to tell me about his black box.

"I haven't forgotten, Moishe. The past few months gave me time to think about how I will tell the story to you. I went ahead and found some maps to help me explain everything. Most of what I will tell you I have never mentioned to anyone other than your grandmother, not even to your mom. It is too painful for me to remember and to talk to anyone about my life. I always wanted to focus and enjoy our current life together as a family. I think it is finally time for me to do this and you are the perfect one for me to tell. I was very proud of you at the shul during your Bar Mitzvah and I heard many compliments from the shul's rabbi and my shul friends.

17

"Before I begin, you have to promise me something."

"Sure, Zaydie."

"You must promise me that when you feel the time is right, that you will share my story with the rest of the family, especially your and Shayna's children and grandchildren. You must promise me that you will keep the memory of me, our family, and this story alive."

"I promise to do this, Zaydie".

"Good. How about this Sunday, let's go over to the park where we can sit and be alone?"

And on that Sunday, Zaydie Yitzhak and I walked over to the park and sat together on one of the park benches. The first thing he pulled out of the metal box to show me was one of the maps. "I drew this map to show you. There are also some old photos and documents in the box that I've saved. Now I am ready to tell you my whole story."

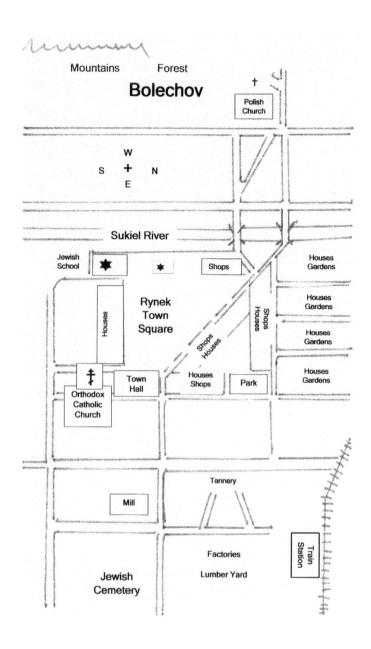

Mountains  Forest

# Bolechov

Polish
Church

W
S + N
E

Sukiel River

Jewish
School

Houses
Gardens

Shops

Rynek
Town
Square

Houses

Houses
Gardens

Shops
Houses

Shops
Houses

Houses
Gardens

Orthodox
Catholic
Church

Town
Hall

Houses
Shops

Park

Houses
Gardens

Tannery

Mill

Factories

Train Station

Jewish
Cemetery

Lumber Yard

20

# My Bolechov Childhood
## 1929-1932

I have very fond memories of my early childhood in Bolechov. For many centuries, Bolechov was part of the Austro-Hungarian Empire and ruled by the Hapsburgs. After each war, the borders changed. In 1991, when the Soviet Union was dissolved, the country became independent Ukraine. Bolechov is located in the southwestern part of Ukraine about sixty miles south of Lviv. When I was young, the Jews referred to Lviv as Lemberg.

I remember when I was probably four or five years old, I often followed my father, named Meir, when he left our house in the morning to go to work in his barbershop. This must have been around 1929, since I was born in 1924. I always preferred to be with my father instead of staying home with my younger sister, Leah, and my mother, named Rifka. I found his barbershop to be more interesting and entertaining than watching my mom doing housework, gardening, or cooking. I was a very inquisitive young boy. I constantly asked him the typical childhood 'what, why, and how' questions.

"Papa, what is that metal tool that you are holding?"

"Yitzhak, it is a hand clipper that I use to cut the hair at the back and side of a person's head."

"Papa, why do you always dress up every day when you come to the shop?"

"These clothes make me feel and look like a real professional and dignified person. Being the town's barber, I like to be a good example of what a well-groomed man should look like. It is best for me and the other Jewish shop owners to look secular to blend in with the local Ukrainian and Polish community. We all want everyone who lives in Bolechov to feel welcomed in our stores."

The Saturday Shabbat services at the synagogue were the only time that I noticed my father, my uncle, and the other Jewish shop owners wearing the Jewish kippah on their heads and the tallit prayer shawl draped over their shoulders. When I entered the synagogue, my papa placed a small kippah on my head for me to wear. I always sat next to him in the men's section, while my mom and sister, Leah, sat upstairs in the women's section. Only the very religious elderly men regularly wore Jewish attire on a daily basis, particularly the tillit katan undergarment that has the exposed fringes.

My father often reminded me, "I don't mind you being here with me in the barbershop. When I'm with a customer, you need to sit quietly in your chair and not disturb me. Besides cutting hair, I need to have a good conversation with everyone who comes into the shop and treat each one like a good customer. I want them to feel at home and comfortable."

"Oh, I see. Okay, Papa. I'll remember and be good and behave."

"Thank you, my son."

"Papa, is this why you open the shop on Saturday afternoons for your Polish and Ukrainian customers?"

"You are very insightful for a boy your age. The answer is, 'yes'. Some of the Jewish shop owners remain open on Saturday afternoons and close on Sundays. It is good for business, since on Sundays our Christian customers go to church and then stay home with their family."

Even though I didn't understand everything my father and the other men talked about, I could tell something was funny when they all roared with laughter. I was amazed that my father could speak so many languages. His Jewish customers spoke Yiddish and I could understand most of what they were talking about. His Polish customers spoke Polish, while his Ukrainian customers spoke Ukrainian. A few of them also spoke Russian. My father tried his best to initiate a friendship with each new customer in order for them to be relaxed and happy with their haircut or shave and return again. Many of the fathers often brought their sons to the shop for a haircut, and sometimes a mother would bring a daughter to have their bangs cut or her long hair trimmed a bit. It seemed that everyone in town knew and liked my father. When people saw the two of us walking down the street, they would greet him by saying, "Hello, Meir. How are you today?" or "Hello, Mr. Barkan and you, young man." My father always slightly tipped his hat when he greeted the women.

I started attending the town's secular primary school in 1930. All of the Polish, Ukrainian, and Jewish children in my first-grade class were very friendly. I became good friends and hung out most of the time with two Polish boys named Krzysztof and Marek, along with a few Ukrainian boys named Artem, Igor, and Danylo. Krzysztof and Marek's fathers worked in the town's Polish-controlled government offices, while Artem and Igor's fathers were farmers. All of their fathers came to my papa's barbershop for haircuts, shaves, and, if they had a moustache, a stylish trim. My father thought it was a good idea and encouraged me to become friends with their sons.

Before school and during recess the six of us played together. We formed our own volleyball team and often practiced during recess out in the school's courtyard when the town had warm weather. At the end of the school day, the six of us regularly walked from the school through the park that was in the

23

middle of town. The park was called the Rynek and served as our town square, even though a main dirt street on the east side of the park went in a diagonal direction. On warm days we would run after each other and play tag. But I couldn't stay in the park for a long time, since my afterschool chore was to go to the barbershop across the diagonal street to help my father clean up at the end of the day. My job was to sweep the fallen hair and any debris and empty the trash in the bin in the alley behind the shop. I was always happy to help him.

I think it was a year later during second grade, when one day during recess, Artem asked all of us, "Have any of you ever climbed up one of the hills to see our town? My father took me up there last weekend and there is an easy path to follow to get to the top. I can show you how to get there. All of the snow has melted and it is an easy hike. There is even a clear landing at the top where you can get a good view of Bolechov. Want to come with me? How about all of us meet at the park on Saturday, say about one o'clock?"

My family often went to the synagogue on Saturday mornings to attend Shabbat services that ended around 12:30, and then we went home to eat lunch. I told my friends I would be able to meet them in the park by 1:30, and we all agreed.

When my father, mother, sister, and I got home from services on that Saturday, I asked my parents if I could play with my school friends in the park. I didn't tell them we were going to take a hike. They probably would not allow me to venture so far away from the town without any adult supervision. Our house was very close to the park and my parents gave me permission to meet my friends after I ate some lunch, as long as I helped sweep the shop floor before it closed.

Artem, Krzysztof, and Igor were waiting for me at the Rynek. Marek and Danylo couldn't come. They had to remain home to help their parents with some chores.

Artem led the way northward through the park to the town's main eastern diagonal dirt street and then over the narrow bridge that crossed the Sukiel River. Shortly after walking past the Polish church, we turned left onto another dirt road that led into the Taniava Forest. As we climbed up the hill, I asked Artem, "How did your father know about this spot?"

"My father and some of his friends often come up here in the winter time to go skiing. The clear area up ahead on the top is where they put on their skis to ski down the hill."

In unison, the three of us said, "Oh!"

After walking a few kilometers, Artem pointed to a path on the left side of the road for the hike up the steep hill. It took us about a half hour to get up to the top. Artem pointed to a clear spot where there were no trees blocking the view of the town. "Let's go over there. There's a good place where we can sit and view all of Bolechov."

Artem was right. There was a great view of Bolechov from the top of the hill.

Bolechov was a nice small town and had about seven thousand people in the 1930s, with a very large number of Jews who lived there. Many of the Jewish men, like my father, were businessmen. Some, like my father and my Uncle Anshel, who was the town's tailor, were merchants and shop owners. Some owned land with dairy farms, cattle, and grain fields on rolling green pastures. Others owned many of the town's timber and leather goods factories. Most of their employees who worked at the farms and factories were Ukrainian.

From the top of the hill, we could clearly see that Bolechov was nestled in a valley surrounded by the gorgeous Carpathian Mountains' forests of tall pine and spruce trees. The Sukiel River gently flowed through the northern part of the town. During the summer, many families would go swimming in the river. The town's dirt streets added to its quaintness.

Only the wealthy and the Polish government officials drove cars or trucks. Others used horse drawn carts and small carriages. The town often got dusty during the windy winters, and we could often smell a dense musty odor coming from the chemicals used at the tannery factories.

When we all sat down at the spot that Artem showed us, we all proclaimed together, "Wow! What a view!"

I added, "You were right, Artem. We can see everything, even all of the people walking along the streets and in the park. They all look so tiny!"

Igor immediately yelled and pointed, "Look at the Rynek. I can even see the lime trees. There is a group of women walking through the park and holding their parasols to block the sun!"

Krzysztof also pointed, "Isn't that our classmate, Adrianna, holding a parasol? She must be walking in the park with her mom." We all laughed at his comment.

With great excitement, Artem pointed. "Do you see the building with the gold onion-shaped domes? That's the church that my family attends."

Since he mentioned his church, I felt comfortable pointing out the synagogues that we could see on the street next to the park. "Do you all see the synagogue on the right that looks like a big concrete fortress? That's the one that I go to. If you look to the left, you'll see the smaller synagogue. If you look to the right of the big one, that's the Tarbut School where we learn Hebrew."

We all took turns pointing and mentioning the sites of Bolechov, including the Austrian-looking town hall next to Artem's church, the various shops that lined the streets surrounding the Rynek, and even the factories. We all liked going to the small candy shop that was run by an old Jewish lady named Mrs. Gorbich. She lived with her adult daughter who took care of the house and family garden, while the daughter's husband worked at one of the dairies.

Many of the one-story concrete family houses and their gardens were clustered together along the dirt streets in view. Most of them looked like my family's house. They were painted white with steep gabled thatched or tin roofs, depending upon the family's economic status. My family's house had thick concrete walls, wooden floors, and a trap door. When opened, one of us would climb down a ladder to get to the cellar where my mom stored preserved food in sealed jars.

The town's train station, which was located about half a kilometer from the Rynek, and a portion of the train tracks were also visible from this viewpoint. Those attending high school had to ride the train for a short ride every day to a small town called Stryj, since Bolechov didn't have its own high school.

After spending about an hour on the top of the hill, I mentioned to Artem, Igor, and Krzysztof that I needed to go to the barbershop to help my dad. Artem mentioned that he also needed to go home. The three of us carefully hiked down the hill. I found it was more difficult to go down the steep hill than it was to climb up.

It was about 4:30 when I entered the barbershop. I think my father looked a bit upset. "Where were you? When I finished my last haircut, I went outside to see if you were still playing in the park, and I didn't see you. I thought you were going to play there with your friends."

"I was there, Papa. I really was there for a while. After playing tag, Artem suggested that we climb up a tall hill in the forest to see Bolechov from the top. He knew how to follow the path. It was one that his father showed him."

"Did Artem's father go with you and your friends?"

"No. Artem, Krzysztof, Igor and I went up there by ourselves."

"Yitzhak. I don't mind you being friendly with some of the Ukrainian and Polish boys. It isn't a good idea for you to wander off on your own at such a young age. It is just too dangerous. Something could happen to you since you are Jewish."

"What do you mean Papa? What could happen to me?"

"There are things going on in the world right now that you don't know about. Listen to me very carefully. Just promise me that you won't do anything like this again."

"Okay, Papa, I promise."

"I also think that it will be a good idea if you became better friends with the Jewish boys who go to your school. In two years, your sister and cousin, Mindel, will go to school with you. It's probably best for all of you to hang out with the other Jewish students."

"But Igor, Artem, Krzysztof, Danylo, and Marek are my best friends."

"You can still be friends with them as long as they treat you nicely and don't call you any names. Okay?"

"Yes, Papa."

My father was correct. In 1932, my sister, Leah, and my cousin, Mindel, started to go to school with me. They were in first grade, while I was in the third

28

grade. My mom walked us to school in the morning, while our Ukrainian housekeeper, Aneta, was at the school's gate waiting for the three of us and walked us home. I felt that I was old enough and responsible enough to take Leah and Mindel to school on my own. Even so, my parents insisted we needed to be escorted to and from school by an adult.

Aneta had been working for us for many years and she fit in like she was part of our family. She always addressed my parents by their first names, and likewise, my parents addressed her in the same manner. She encouraged my sister and me to also call her by her first name. She was never treated like an employee by my parents. When Leah and I were young children, Aneta would attend to us, wash the family laundry, help clean the house, and help my mom in the kitchen. When Leah and I no longer needed her constant care, she helped my mom work in the garden, prepare the family meals, and preserve food in jars to place them in our basement. Our garden had a variety of vegetables and fruit trees. My mom often served our family very delicious borscht, also known as beet soup, and stuffed cabbage. I often told my mom that her stuffed cabbage was my favorite. She responded by saying that she just followed her mom's recipe. Aneta also helped my mom bake bread and fruit-filled pastries called rugelach, particularly on Fridays for the family's Shabbat dinner.

Aneta and my mom regularly went together on Mondays to the market day held at the Rynek. Both of them went there shortly after all of the vendors set up their stalls in the mid-morning. Leather goods, sacks of flour, poultry, and pastry items, along with all sorts of fruits and vegetables and other food items, and even timber for wood burning stoves and fireplaces were available and plentiful.

Often, my mom sent Aneta during the week to the town's grocery store to buy flour and canned goods and to the kosher butcher to buy slices of beef and a whole chicken.

Aneta and her husband, Ivan, lived south of the Rynek in the Ukrainian area and not too far from us. Ivan worked at one of the meat-processing factories. Their grown daughter, Maria, was married to Borysko. They lived in a neighboring town, called Dolina. It was located a few kilometers from Bolechov. My mother greatly appreciated Aneta's help and regularly sent her home with loaves of the baked bread, pastries, and jars of the preserved food.

When I started the third grade at the school, I recognized two Jewish boys from our synagogue. Their names were Zalman and Feivel. I became friends with them, as my father requested, and often hung out with them at the Rynek after the synagogue Saturday morning services. Like my father, both of their fathers owned businesses in the center area of Bolechov and also came to the barbershop for their haircuts.

Things started to feel different in Bolechov in 1932. I noticed a bit of tension in the town. When I walked to and from school, the other people that I saw walking on the streets did not look very happy. In the past, everyone seemed friendly and greeted each other with a friendly "Hello". It didn't matter if you were Polish, Ukrainian, or Jewish. Everyone was respectful and kind to each other. Now, starting in 1932, people were looking down at the ground with scowled faces as they were walking. There were no more friendly greetings spoken to anyone, unless you knew the other person from your church or synagogue. When my father's Ukrainian and Polish customers came into the barbershop, they rarely initiated a greeting with him. He still greeted everyone who entered. If one was a regular customer, he always called them by their first name.

Also, beginning in 1932, I started noticing that during the evenings after our family ate dinner, my father often went next door to the house where my Uncle Anshel, Aunt Gital, and cousin, Mindel, lived. Aunt Gital's elderly mother, Feiga, also lived there. My Uncle Anshel was one of the few men in the town who owned a radio. Mindel once told me that her father liked to listen to the news stations from the nearest two big cities, Lemberg, and Stanislavov during the evening before he went to bed.

One evening when my father and mother went into their bedroom, I heard him speak to my mom, very softly. The only words that I overheard were, "Germany", and a strange word, "Hitler." I wasn't sure what he was talking about. I knew Germany was the name of another European country. The word, Hitler, was new to me. I had no idea what it meant.

My father and mother never said anything to Leah and me about Germany or the word, Hitler. Nor, did Aneta mention these words to us.

I thought: *Is there some secret that our parents are keeping from us? What's the big secret?*

I also observed something very strange going on at the synagogue on Saturday mornings. Before and after the services, the adults in the congregation turned close to each other's ears and whispered privately to each other. Some type of message was spreading among the adults. Their faces had alarmed facial expressions when they turned around from their private conversation. They looked like they heard something terrible.

*Something concerning is definitely happening. I just didn't know what was going on. I'm now very curious and determined to find out.*

# *You're Just a Dirty Jew!*
## Bolechov
## 1933-1937

Later in the school year while I was still at the secular school in the third grade, the spring weather was warm enough for our class to go outside and enjoy an outdoor recess period in the school's courtyard. Krzysztof, Igor, Artem, Danylo, and I quickly formed our volleyball team to play against another team of boys from our class. As hard as we played, the score kept being tied. We were used to winning all of the time. This team surprised us as to how good they were with their forceful hitting.

When we all heard our teacher's whistle signal announcing the end of recess, we knew our game would have to immediately stop. The other team had the serve and their server hit the ball to barely come over the net. My position was to stand next to the net on our side. When the ball came over the net, I missed hitting it back to the other team. The other team won the game.

Krzysztof loudly yelled at me very angrily so everyone out in the courtyard could hear him. "Yitzhak, you made us lose the game. You're just a dirty Jew!"

Igor added his yell. "Yeah. Why don't all of you Jews just leave? You aren't welcome here anymore!"

I was stunned. These were two of my best friends.

*Why are they yelling at me and saying these terrible words just because I missed hitting the ball?*

As we went back into the school from the courtyard, I looked at my other classmates. The Jewish students looked terrified as the other classmates stared at us with jeering and angry looks.

I enjoyed going to school, not only because I got to play volleyball, but also because I enjoyed learning new things. I was very studious and received good grades on my assignments and exams. I was often the only one in class to raise my hand to answer the teacher's question. The teacher, Mr. Novak, would smile at me when he called on me to explain to the class why my answer was correct.

Today, I noticed a difference. Mr. Novak never called on me when I raised my hand, even when I was the only one. He wouldn't even look at me, nor did he look at any of the other Jewish students in the class.

*Why is Mr. Novak ignoring me? I didn't misbehave in class today.*

I just had to tell my father about what happened today when I got to the barbershop. I didn't want to say anything to Aneta and frighten Leah and Mindel, as we all left the school at the end of the day.

When I went inside the barbershop, my father was cutting hair for a customer that I didn't recognize. I waited until the customer left before I said anything.

"Papa, some things happened today at school that upset me and I don't understand."

"Tell me what happened, Yitzhak."

"Well, first of all, my teacher, Mr. Novak, never called on me when I raised my hand to answer a question. He always called on me in the past, because he knew I could explain the right answer to the class. He also did not look at me, or any of the Jewish students all day. He never called on any of us. I don't understand why Mr. Novak is ignoring us all

34

of a sudden. He often told me that I was his best student."

I couldn't help it. I started crying since I was so upset.

"But there's more, Papa, that happened today. When I was playing volleyball with my friends, Krzysztof and Igor said terrible things to me."

My father handed me a tissue to dry my eyes and put his right arm around me. "What did they say to you?"

"Krzysztof called me a 'dirty Jew' and Igor yelled 'You Jews are no longer welcome here'. Why are they saying these things to me? I thought they liked me and were my good friends."

"Yitzhak, let's wait until we get home to talk about this. Your mother and I need to explain things to you and Leah. Okay?"

"Yes, Papa."

"Let's clean up the shop as soon as we can and go home to talk with your mom."

Once my parents, my sister, Leah, and I finished dinner and we were still sitting at the kitchen table, my father spoke up.

"Rifka, I think the time has come for the two of us, along with Anshel and Gital, to explain to our children what is happening in Europe. Yitzhak was called 'a dirty Jew' at school today, along with being told that 'Jews are no longer welcomed'. We can't keep avoiding having this talk with them anymore. I'll go over and tell Anshel and Gital that the four of us are coming over, while you, Leah and Yitzhak, clean up, wash the dishes, and put everything away."

My mom replied, "You are probably right. The time has arrived for us to have this talk with our children."

About half an hour later, my mom, sister, and I went next door and entered my uncle and aunt's home. Chairs from their dining room were already moved into the living room for all of us to sit together. As we were all getting seated, Uncle Anshel turned off his radio and sat down with us. Uncle Anshel, Aunt Gital, her elderly mom, Aunt Feiga, and my parents all looked at each other. None of them knew who should be first to speak.

After a long silence, my father spoke up.

"Mindel, Leah, and Yitzhak, I'll try my best to explain all of this in a way that I think that you will understand.

"There is a new chancellor in Germany named Adolph Hitler. He hates Jewish people. He calls us terrible names, like vermin, and tells the German people that the Jews are the ones to blame for the current hardships that the German people are experiencing. Many German men are out of work and the price of food and everything else keeps rising at an alarming rate. He has a large group of thugs who wear brown shirts with black ties. They go around beating up anyone who disagrees with Hitler and any Jews who they see walking alone. Hitler now has a large group of followers that are called Nazis. They are now the largest political party in Germany and have taken control of the country with Hitler as their leader. They are calling him the German word for leader, the Führer.

"The main German government building was recently burned down, and many people think that Hitler's brown shirts set it on fire on purpose. Hitler used this incident to convince the German president to end people's freedoms and allow people to be arrested for any reason. The country is now under Hitler's control and the German people and the rest of Europe are now afraid of him. They are afraid they will be murdered or beaten up if they speak up against Hitler."

36

"Papa, why do people hate us so much?"

"Yitzhak, that's a good question. There are many possible answers. Many Christian churches teach that the Jews are responsible for the killing of Jesus. You may have heard Jesus being called 'Christ' by your Christian friends. The truth is that Jews as a group did not kill him.

"Jews have often been the ones being blamed when things go wrong or when people are experiencing a hard time. Hundreds of years ago, Jews were forced to leave Spain and Portugal. Many found their way to come to Bolechov to help develop the town's salt industry and become merchants in the center of the town. This may have been when our family ancestors arrived.

"Even though Jews suffered difficulties through the ages, we always found a way to survive and prosper. Other people who live around us, who are not Jewish, become jealous of our prosperity and start to hate us.

"Just look at Bolechov. The three of you may not realize that the people who live in our town are divided into three groups. The Jews who live here are the majority. Many of the Jews own the shops, the farms, and the factories. Since 1919, the Polish government has controlled Bolechov. Most of the Polish men work in the government offices and many are in charge of the town. They are regarded as the town's aristocrats. The Ukrainian men work in the factories and at the farms. All three groups tend to get along. The Poles and Ukrainians need the Jews for the shops. The Jews need to rely on the cooperation of the Poles who work for the government. The Poles and the Jews need to rely on the Ukrainians to do the work at the factories and farms.

"Hitler's rise to power in Germany has rekindled the hatred of the Jewish people. The boys who made those awful statements to you most likely were repeating what they heard their parents say about Jews.

"Is this starting to make sense to the three of you? Do you have any questions?"

I looked at Leah and Mindel. They didn't look confused, so I spoke up. "I think you are telling us we need to be on guard when we are around anyone who isn't Jewish. Am I right, Papa?"

"That's a good way to put it, Yitzhak. This is the reason why your mom and I encouraged you to become friendlier with the Jewish boys in your class.

"We don't know what will happen in the future. Hopefully, Poland and Bolechov will remain a good place for Jewish people to continue to live.

"Anshel, I think that you and I should speak with the other Jewish fathers that we know and the officials at the Tarbut Hebrew School next to the synagogue. It may be time for the school to serve as the primary school for the Jewish children and have our children stop attending the secular school.

"Yitzhak, your Bar Mitzvah is getting close, in about four years. I think it is best for you to begin your preparation at the Tarbut Hebrew School during the afternoons after you are dismissed from the primary school. I'll have Aneta take you there. Since you have become friends with Zalman and Feivel, I'll speak with their fathers and ask them if either of their sons attend the classes at the Tarbut Hebrew School. If so, I'll ask if they or their wives would walk you to the barbershop after the Hebrew classes end. It is best that from now on that the three of you need to be with an adult and not be out on the streets on your own."

38

"If that is what you think is best for me, Papa, I will do as you say." Leah and Mindel nodded, indicating they understood.

"Thank you, my son."

A month later, I started going to the Tarbut Hebrew School to learn how to read, write, and speak Hebrew. Eventually, I wanted to learn how to chant like the rabbi when he read the Torah passage during the Saturday morning Shabbat service.

The Tarbut Hebrew School opened their primary school the following September. Many other Jewish children transferred. Their school hours were adjusted for the students to arrive half an hour earlier and end a half hour earlier than the secular school in order for us to avoid hearing derogatory remarks yelled at us by the Polish and Ukrainian children who attended the secular school.

Two years later on September 15, 1935, when I was eleven years old, my Uncle Anshel raced into our house just as my family was about to begin eating dinner.

"Meir and Rifka. Come over as quickly as you can and bring Yitzhak and Leah with you. The situation in Germany with Hitler has become worse for the Jews. I'm listening to the news coming from Warsaw. Come quickly."

When we got to their house, their living room was very crowded with other Jewish families. Everyone was silent and listening intently to the news announcer explaining the new laws announced by Hitler and the Nazis. Their new citizenship law defined Jews as a separate race and Jews would no longer be regarded as citizens of Germany, since they were now declared as racially impure and inferior. Intermarriages and sexual relations between Jews and people of German or related blood were now banned. The new citizenship law also specifically defined who would be considered a Jew. German people may need to present documents proving there was no Jewish family heritage.

All of the adults in my aunt and uncle's living room had horrified looks on their faces as they listened to the announcer's explanation of Germany's new racial laws. I understood most of the announcer's report. I sensed that life would be terrible and more difficult for the Jewish people who lived in Germany, when I saw the horrid look and tears flowing down some of the women's faces.

I started thinking: *Will our lives in Bolechov also become more difficult? Will we still be citizens?*

The newscast finally ended. My uncle turned off the radio when music started playing. No one spoke. Many of the women were still crying.

One man finally spoke up. "How could the Jews in Germany let this happen? They've lived in that country for hundreds of years and blended in with everyone. Many of the Jewish men served in the German army during the last war and even have their Iron Cross medals to prove it! Why didn't anyone stop Hitler?"

Another man interjected, "Everyone in Germany thought the Nazis were just a small marginal group with very little political influence. Hitler knew how to prey on people's fears and he used this to maneuver into the power he now has. It will be up to the rest of Europe to stop him. The question is, are any of Europe's leaders strong enough to stop him? Or are they afraid to confront Hitler, and will just go ahead to appease him? Appeasing Hitler could make things worse in Europe."

My father finally said something. "I think our biggest concern is to see how the Polish government and their offices react. Will they go ahead to enact similar laws as a way for Hitler to leave Poland alone? Should we expect our lives to be affected? We are already beginning to experience less cooperation from the Bolechov Polish officials. Those working in the government offices used to be very friendly toward us. Now they are very rude and often ignore our requests for dealing with issues that we present to them. So far, our children are safe going to the Tarbut Hebrew School. The elderly are the ones we need to keep an eye on. They may be viewed as easy victims to be bullied or physically attacked. We shouldn't let them walk alone on the streets. And I think all of us should avoid walking alone at night. Many of our streets and alleys are not well lit at night."

Many of the others agreed with my father.

A final comment was made. "We should ask the rabbis at both synagogues to have a joint congregation meeting to continue discussing all of this and form a Jewish Leadership Committee."

When my family returned to our house, my father had us all sit together. "Look. I know this all sounds very frightening to all of you. I am still on good terms with the town's marshal, Josef Spychalski. He still comes to the barbershop every week for his shave, moustache trim, and an occasional haircut. Of course, I never ask him to pay. As long as he and I are cordial with each other, we will be all right. If there will be some sort of governmental Jewish crackdown, I feel confident that he will give me advance notice. So, please don't let the news you heard tonight worry you. Leah and Yitzhak, your mom and I just want the two of you to continue being good students at school. Yitzhak, we are looking forward to your Bar Mitzvah

Day. It's now less than two years away. July 10$^{th}$, 1937 won't come soon enough!"

My father's consoling words were short-lived. There were reports circulating around the Bolechov Jewish community about Jews in the larger towns and cities being beaten up or even killed by their Polish and Ukrainian neighbors. There were also a few reports of Jews encountering verbal abuse in Bolechov.

I continued to excel at the secular school and at the Tarbut Hebrew School. I still hoped to be able to attend the high school in Stryi, even though my family would have to pay a high tuition fee. I often dreamed of becoming a medical doctor.

Four months before my Saturday, July 10$^{th}$, 1937 Bar Mitzvah, my father took me to my uncle's tailor shop on a Sunday afternoon, even though his shop was normally closed on Sundays.

"Yitzhak, I am so proud of you. The rabbi told me that you are also going to read from the Torah during your Bar Mitzvah ceremony. Do you know what an honor this is going to be for your mother and me? I've asked Uncle Anshel to make you a tailored suit, shirt, and a silk tie for this special occasion. I'm going to have him find the best material that he can obtain. He needs to take your measurements."

Uncle Anshel had me stand on a small platform. "Go ahead and step up there. Take off your shoes and stand up straight. This won't take me too long to measure you for a new suit and dress shirt. While I'm at it, I'm going to take your head size and your feet measurements. I'm going to go all the way to Lemberg to search for the material. While I'm there, I will also look for a matching hat and dress shoes for you."

42

"Remember, Anshel. Nothing but the best for my son! I want everyone to see my son, the mensch, read from the Torah. While you are in Lemberg, see if you can find a Judaica store and purchase the finest silk tallit and kippah for him."

Three weeks later, my father and I returned to my uncle's tailor shop for me to try on the shirt, tie, and suit for any needed altering. The shirt and tie were fine. The suit jacket and pants needed some adjusting.

"Come back next Sunday, Yitzhak. We'll see if everything fits you perfectly."

Sure enough, everything my uncle made for me fit just right. He even tied my tie with the perfect dress knot. "Here's the Fedora hat and the black leather shoes that I found for you. Put them on and look at yourself in the mirror. Do you see how your new hat and shoes match your black suit?"

As I stood on the platform, I found the courage to look at myself in the mirror.

*Was this really me?*

For the first time, I looked like a real gentleman and not like a schoolboy.

"Turn around, Yitzhak, so your father can take a good look at you."

"Anshel, put the tallit around his shoulder."

A minute or so later, my father proclaimed very loudly, "Here he is. My son. The man. The perfect mensch! I couldn't feel any prouder than I will be when the congregation sees my son. Thank you, Anshel, for what you have done for us."

He continued, "Yitzhak, I'm going to arrange for the town's photographer to take a photo portrait of you wearing your new Bar Mitzvah outfit so that we will always remember this special occasion."

During the Shabbat service on July 10th, I helped the rabbi remove the Torah from the Holy Ark and lay it open on the table in front of the ark. The rabbi opened the scroll for the service Torah reading. I didn't make any mistakes when I recited and chanted the Hebrew prayer said before the Torah reading. The rabbi read one section of the Torah portion and then had me recite and chant the rest. When I finished reading from the Torah, I recited and chanted the prayer said after the Torah portion was read. Next, I helped the rabbi roll the scroll's two ends together to secure it, place the traditional red velvet cover over the Torah, and place the Torah inside the ark. Once this task was finished and the ark was closed, the rabbi and I turned to face the congregation and he shook my right hand. Everyone stood up and applauded very loudly. Of course, the one clapping the loudest was my papa!

My family hosted a reception in the adjoining hall after the Shabbat service ended. I stood next to my father in the receiving line and everyone congratulated me by shaking my hand and also my father's. Many of the congregants kissed my mom on her cheek and also kissed the right hand of my sister.

There was a surprise family dinner prepared by Aneta and her daughter waiting for us when we got home. Apparently, Aneta's husband must have had the key to my uncle and aunt's house to get more chairs. Eleven chairs were squeezed together around our dining room table for my family, my aunt and uncle's family, and for Aneta, her husband, and Aneta's daughter and husband. Everyone who was a member of our family was there to celebrate my Bar Mitzvah with me! My father brought out the framed photo of me to show everyone the photo that was taken by the town's photographer for my Bar Mitzvah. My father declared, "Yitzhak is now a Jewish man!"

A few days whizzed by. I still felt like I was flying on a cloud from my Bar Mitzvah. One evening after dinner, my parents asked me to remain at the kitchen table. They wanted to have a serious talk with me.

"Yitzhak. Your mom and I want to talk to you about your future. As you can see with what is happening in Europe with Hitler and the Nazis, we want you to be prepared for your adult years. We know that you want to go to high school and eventually attend a university. It is possible that you may achieve this goal. But it is also possible that the world's situation may change for the worse and you may need to have a backup plan. The best backup plan for you is to learn a trade while you are still in school. This way you can earn the money that you may need. Your mother and I think that the best trade for you to learn is for you to become a skilled barber like me. After all, you've spent many years watching me and I think it will be very easy for you to quickly learn the needed barbering skills. I can show you and teach you everything, just like my father trained me. Your grandfather was also a barber.

"Since I'm still on good terms with the town's marshal, Josef Spychalski, I think he will be very willing to give you a work permit. We should get the permit now while he and I are still on good terms. The situation could change here in Bolechov in the future. Since school hasn't started yet, let's go first thing tomorrow morning to the town's magistrate building where his office is located. We may have to wait for him to arrive. His office is the place that issues the work permits. I think you will recognize him. He is the tall official who comes in every week in the late afternoon. You often watch me trim and wax his moustache into the curls on both sides of his mouth. I know he will recognize you too. Let me do all of the talking. I'll tell him I've already trained you and you will

45

start cutting the hair of the young boys who come into the barbershop with their father or mother.

"What do you think about this idea, Yitzhak? Want to become a barber like me?"

"Well, if both of you think this is best for me, why not? Let's do it. I think it will be fun to work beside you, Papa."

"Great. His office opens at 9 a.m. We'll leave here about 8:35 so that we can be first in line to see him. It should only take us 15 minutes to walk over there."

My father and I left promptly the next day and sat and waited in the chairs positioned outside the marshal's office. Thirty minutes later my father whispered in my ear, "Do you hear that thump-thumping sound? I think that is him walking down the hallway."

When a tall official looking, well-dressed man with a big moustache turned the corner and saw my father, he warmly greeted him. "Meir. It is good to see you. This is a surprise. What are you doing here with your son?"

"We came here to see you to get his work permit. I've been training him to become a barber and he is now ready to work with me in the shop. He will begin by giving the children their haircuts while I continue to show him how to give perfect shaves and trim moustaches like yours."

"Well, come on into the office and I'll fill out the form and sign it. Then, you will need to take the form to the office across the hall, pay the fee, and the clerk will stamp the permit. I'm glad to help you, young man. Your father is the best barber I've ever gone to. If he trained you, I know that your customers will be pleased. Now I will have another good reason to come to the shop and see the father-son team

46

actually working together. Here's the form. Please remember to display it in the shop to make it official."

I stood up and addressed the town marshal. "Thank you, Marshal Spychalski."

As my father and I exited the town's magistrate building, I turned toward him and said, "You were right, Papa. The two of you are very cordial with each other."

"This is what I've been trying to teach you, Yitzhak. You should always do your best to make a stranger feel welcomed and liked. This is a good way for people to respect each other, even if each comes from a different culture or way of life. Right now, there is tension among the Jewish, Polish, and Ukrainian people in our town. I try my best to still be friendly with everyone I meet."

"I will try my best, Papa. It's now up to you to train me to be a good barber just like you!"

# The New Barber, Yitzhak!
## Bolechov
## 1937 - 1938

As my father and I walked through the Rynek on our way home from the town marshal's office, I asked him very eagerly, "Now that I have the work permit, when can I get started?"

"I've been thinking about that, Yitzhak. I'm thinking that the easiest and fastest haircut style you could learn is what I call 'the clipper cut'. When you are in the barbershop watching me, you seem very fascinated with how I use the hand clippers. How about this? Let's go to the barbershop instead of going home. It's still early before any of my customers normally arrive. I can show you what I'm talking about with 'the clipper cut' and you can practice holding and using one of the hand clippers."

"Great idea, Papa!"

"After we get inside, just stay there and wait for me. I need to go home and get my metal barber's box and let your mom know where you are so she won't worry. If anyone comes in, tell them I'll be back in a few minutes."

When he returned to the shop, I took one of the hand clippers out of his box and started squeezing it with my dominant right hand. "Son, you will need to place the number one guard on the clipper before you use it on the lower sides and on the back of the head. Then, you place the number two guard on the hand clipper when you cut the upper sides and back of the head. For the top of the head, depending upon how much hair the person has, you will probably need to use the number three or four guard. The last step is to blend everything with a scissors and comb, or sometimes blend their hair with the thinning shears. That's all there is to it. It will take some practice for you to get the knack. Watch how I follow these steps with today's customers. It will be all right for you to stand close to me. I'll tell the customers that you are in training. I might as well begin promoting you as the new barber in town!"

At the end of the day, I asked my father to sit in the barber's chair so that I could demonstrate the steps that he showed me without actually cutting his hair.

"You caught on really quick, even though you will need more practice. Tomorrow, I'll let you practice using just the clipper on me. I could use a good trim! Just remember to release the clipper before raising it off the person's head. You will need to be careful that the clipper doesn't pull on their hair."

"Okay, Papa. I'd like to give it a try."

"Yitzhak, I've also been thinking about a really good way for you to get started and build your own clientele. Since school begins at the beginning of September, I have a good hunch that many parents, most likely the mothers, would like their sons to get a short haircut before school starts. I'm thinking we should open up on a Sunday and offer free clipper cuts to boys twelve and under. We can post a sign on the synagogue's bulletin board and in the barbershop's window advertising this event. You caught on very quickly. I think you will be ready in about a month. Let's go ahead and plan for Sunday, August 22nd, to be the day for this free haircut event for the young boys. I'll be going to Lemberg next Monday to purchase some barbershop supplies. While I'm there, I'll get you your own pair of scissors, a few combs, a barber's cape, and a cape to drape over your customers to prevent the cut hair from falling on them. We'll keep all of your equipment with mine inside my barber's metal box. There's enough room. In the meantime, you can use one of my clippers, the clipper guards, the thinning shears, and even the foldable hand mirror. Down the line, I'll show you how to safely use the hand razor for shaves and how to trim and shape beards and moustaches. But for now, let's just concentrate on the clipper cut for the young boys and let them become your first set of customers."

I think my father was really excited about me becoming a barber. He immediately went into high gear making all of the arrangements for my debut as a real barber on Sunday, August 22nd. He contacted one of his Ukrainian customers, who was a carpenter, and hired him to make a wooden barber's chair for me, since I wasn't tall enough to use his barber's chair. The carpenter shared his measurements with my Uncle Anshel. Being a tailor, my uncle offered to make the chair's seat cushion as his gift to me. When my father returned from Lemberg, he showed me the two drawings of the clipper cut that he found at the supply store. He thought that by attaching these to the two signs, the parents, seeing what a clipper cut looked like, would be very willing to have their sons get this free haircut style for school. After my father completed making the two signs, he attached them on the synagogue's bulletin board and in the barbershop window as planned.

I spent every day with my father in the barbershop during the rest of July and early August. Each evening, after our family ate dinner, my father went to my aunt and uncle's home to listen to the news on my uncle's radio. Being curious, one morning I asked him, "Papa, what's the latest news about the Nazis and Hitler?"

"Now, son, don't you worry about that right now."

"But Papa, when you return home, I hear you whispering to Mama about camps and Jews leaving Germany."

My father looked puzzled and didn't know how to respond to me. There was a long silence.

He turned closer to me and said very softly, "Come outside with me, Yitzhak. I'll tell you privately, but you must promise to keep this to yourself. Your sister, Leah, doesn't need to know any of this. I think you are now older and mature enough to handle knowing what is happening in Germany."

We walked into the garden behind our house, sat on a bench, and my father started his explanation.

"The Nazis now have camps where they send adults whom they arrested. Some of the radio reporters are calling them 'concentration camps'. Jews and those who oppose Hitler are being sent there without any trial. The radio reporters state that these people just disappear at night and are never seen again. There are also reports from people living close to these camps, that they often hear gunfire. Nobody knows exactly what is going on inside these camps. The news also mentions that many Jews are leaving Germany and moving to other countries like Holland, France, and Spain."

"Papa. Are Jews coming to Poland?"

"As far as we know, no. None are coming here."

He took a deep breath and continued. "Right now, I want you to just put your mind at ease. I won't let anything happen to you and your sister and our family. Just be happy that you are about to become a real barber and have your own customers. Make this your focus right now. Okay, Yitzhak? I am very proud of you."

"Yes, Papa."

Sunday, August 22$^{nd}$, 1937, approached very quickly. I overheard a number of my father's

51

customers and people at the synagogue express their enthusiasm about the free haircut event for their sons. Since my father knew the fathers of my Jewish friends, Zalman and Feivel, he received their permission for me to give Zalman and Feivel a clipper hair cut as practice for next Sunday's big event.

The day before they arrived, my father reminded me that I needed to be very talkative and prompt each customer to talk in order for them to remain calm during the haircut. My father kept repeating, "You want each person to be happy and to like you, so that they will become your repeat customer. You can do this, Yitzhak. Just be your friendly self."

When I finished cutting their hair and showed Zalman and Feivel what they looked like in the hand mirror, both replied, "Wow. You really are a good barber! I like my new haircut. Thanks, Yitzhak."

Their fathers both nodded to both my papa and me and expressed their thanks. Both fathers added, "My son will be back for another one of your haircuts, Yitzhak!"

The following Sunday was my big day. I had no idea how many parents would be bringing their sons. My father and I brought our kitchen table chairs to the barber shop, along with my aunt and uncle's kitchen table chairs, to have more seating just in case.

At 10 o'clock, when we displayed the 'Open' sign in the front window and opened the front door, there were three mothers and their sons already waiting for us. Within minutes of opening, people continuously filled the extra seats and lined up in front of the shop to wait for their son's haircut. Both my father and I were very busy giving clipper haircuts all day.

About 2 o'clock in the afternoon Town Marshal Spychalski, walked in. "Meir, as I was walking through the Rynek, I noticed a line of people in front of your shop. I wondered what was going on and if something was wrong. There are never people lined up at your shop on Sundays. I finally noticed the sign in the window about the free haircuts for the boys and just had to come in and see young Yitzhak at work. This is a great service you are offering, Meir. Okay, don't stop, Yitzhak, because I'm here. Keep going." And then he quietly left the shop.

I lost count of how many boys received their free haircuts that Sunday. The one thing that I did notice was my former Ukrainian and Polish volleyball teammates did not come. If they had showed up, I knew that I would need to remain calm and be friendly to them. I felt relieved that I didn't have to encounter them and cut their hair for free.

At 7 p.m., my dad turned the 'Open' sign over to display 'Closed'. When we finally finished our last haircut at 8 o'clock, my father and I finally sat down, feeling totally exhausted. "Papa. I'm glad that's over and the shop is closed tomorrow. My right hand needs a rest! I've never talked so much to people as I did today!"

"I'm also tired, my son. Let's go home. We'll come back in the morning to get the extra chairs."

When school finally started in September for the 1937-1938 school year, as I walked to and from the Hebrew school with my sister, mom, and Aneta, I was curious to see if the spirit in the town had changed. Just like the previous school year, people were walking along the streets very cautiously with frowns, and some with frightened looks on their faces. I got the impression that many of the Bolechov Polish and Ukrainian people were becoming more fearful of the Jewish majority. I hoped I was wrong. But I thought they were worried that the town's large Jewish population would cause the Nazis to march into our town and cause a lot of trouble.

The town's Jewish officials may have also noticed this growing tension. For the first time, the two synagogues and even the Jewish Hebrew School hired non-Jewish men to serve as security guards when the synagogues and school were in use. Once a service or class commenced, the front door was locked from the inside. The security guard had a key to open the door for an authorized individual. Those inside could still exit. This was just a precaution just in case someone wanted to cause trouble while anyone from our community was inside.

Then, later on during the school year, something tragic happened on Saturday, March 12th, 1938. My family and my Uncle Anshel's family were attending the Saturday morning Shabbat service at the synagogue. The synagogue's security guard entered the sanctuary, walked over to the rabbi, and whispered into the rabbi's left ear. The rabbi looked down to the floor with a very sad look. He continued with the service and then spoke to the congregation after the service's closing song.

"When you go home, even though it is Shabbat, it will be permissible for you to turn on your radio to listen to the news. If you don't have a radio, I will have one moved into our reception room and turned on for you to listen. The German army is marching into Austria and no one is stopping them. Hitler has accomplished his goal of annexing Austria. Please go home peacefully, quietly, quickly, and do not attract anyone's attention. Our security guard will remain outside until we all leave the building."

When we went to my uncle's home and he turned on his radio, the news reported that Hitler was riding in an open car through the streets of Vienna with crowds of people saluting him and loudly chanting, "Heil Hitler!"

We kept hearing the news announcer saying the word 'Anschluss'. My father explained that this was the German word for annexation and that Hitler has now expanded the German border to include all of Austria. Austria did not fight back. They just accepted him with open arms.

I spoke up and asked, "What will happen now to the Jewish people who live in Austria?

My parents and my aunt and uncle just looked at each other. Uncle Anshel replied, "Most likely, they will face the same restrictions and problems that the Jews in Germany are facing. This includes being arrested and sent to the camps."

As the months progressed, life for the Jewish people in all of Germany, including Austria, got worse. On Wednesday, August 17th, 1938, more restrictions were imposed on the Jews with new name restrictions. Jews now needed to choose a name from a government-approved list. Any Jew with a name not on the list needed to add an additional first name: Israel for the men, and Sara for the women. Each Jewish person was now required to report their new names to the government and list their new names on all business transactions.

My father thought this new restriction was implemented as a way to arrest more Jews and send them to the camps.

In late September during the evening of Thursday the 29th, my family joined my uncle's family to listen to the radio news report about a meeting in Munich, Germany. Italian Leader, Benito Mussolini, German Chancellor, Adolf Hitler, British Prime Minister, Neville Chamberlain, and French Premier, Edouard Daladier were meeting face to face. After entering their home and joining them at their dining room table, my Uncle Anshel told us these four leaders were discussing a peace settlement in order to avoid another large-scale European war.

I immediately asked, "Who is Mussolini and why is he meeting with these other European leaders? I've never heard of him."

Uncle Anshel explained, "He is an ally of Hitler and rules Italy very similarly to how Hitler rules Germany. The two of them formed a military alliance."

He continued, "I've been listening to the news for a couple of hours. Apparently, Hitler is demanding that Germany annex the western part of Czechoslovakia where a large number of German origin people live. This area is called the Sudetenland."

My mom spoke up and asked, "What do the Czechoslovakian people say about this? Do they want to become part of Germany? Why isn't someone from the Czechoslovakian government at the meeting? How can leaders from other countries make a decision about Czechoslovakia? Shouldn't the British and French leaders protect Czechoslovakia from Hitler?"

Uncle Anshel responded, "This is why they are meeting and trying to negotiate a peaceful solution with Hitler and his ally, Mussolini. The British and French leaders are trying to prevent Hitler from taking the Sudetenland by force. The Czechoslovakian government has no input. Apparently, both the French and British leaders believe that peace can only be achieved and a massive war prevented by allowing the transfer of the Sudetenland to Germany. They are trying to get Hitler to agree to take no military actions. No one wants another war like the last one, where thousands of soldiers and innocent people were killed."

My father finally added his opinion very angrily. "We always wondered if the European leaders would be strong and willful enough to stop Hitler. And now here they are bending over to appease Hitler's demands. What cowards they are! Do they really believe Hitler and trust him? Come on, don't they understand he's a mad man? How about all of the Jews who live in Czechoslovakia? What's going to happen to them? Isn't anyone brave enough to stop the Nazis' persecution of the Jews?"

"Papa, I'm scared. Will Hitler come after us?" This was the first time that my sister, Leah, ever spoke up in front of the whole family.

Since I was sitting next to her, I moved closer and put my arm around her. "Don't worry, Leah. Hitler is thousands of miles away from us. We'll be okay."

The next day, it was announced that the four leaders signed the Munich Agreement. The British Prime Minister, Neville Chamberlain, went back to England and proclaimed that peace had been achieved in Europe, while Hitler beamed with pride during a radio broadcast about his accomplishment expanding Germany's territorial boundary.

Six days later, on October 5th, 1938, the Nazis invalidated the German passports of all who were classified as Jews per the Nuremberg laws previously established. They now had to resubmit their passports to a passport office to be stamped with the letter "J". Most likely, this was done to prevent Jews from leaving Germany and its new territories.

That night, I couldn't fall asleep and tossed and turned all night in my bed. The following thoughts continuously spun around in my head:

*What else did Hitler and the Nazis plan that would further the persecution of the Jews?*

*Will daily life get any worse for them?*

*What will happen to the Jews, like us, who live in Poland?*

On Wednesday, November 9th, 1938, these questions were answered.

# Kristallnacht
## The Night of Broken Glass

November in Bolechov was the time of the year when you first noticed that the winter weather would soon arrive. Wednesday, November 9th, 1938, did not disappoint. On a typical day in November, the sky would be overcast with lots of clouds and only a jacket would be required to wear outside. But on this day, as soon as my mom, Leah, and I opened the front door in the early morning to walk to the Hebrew school, we encountered an unexpected blast of frigid air. All of us raced back inside the house to grab a thick sweater to wear under our jackets. The outside temperature felt like zero Celsius degrees *(32 degrees Fahrenheit)*, with dark threatening clouds hovering over us with the possibility of a downpour of rain.

My mom called out, "Hurry up, Leah and Yitzhak. Let's walk as fast as we can to get you to school before it rains."

Even when the school day ended and Aneta met us at the school gate, it felt very cold outside and that a heavy rain was still likely. Aneta dropped me off at the barbershop, and then she and Leah walked to our house.

When I entered the barbershop, I noticed my father was acting a bit grumpy.

"Bad day, Papa?" I asked.

"Not really. It just seems that all the customers that I've had today were in a bad mood for some reason and not talkative at all. This has been a very unusual day."

When the two of us returned home, Leah was setting the kitchen table, while my mom put the finishing touches to our dinner meal. None of us seemed to be in the mood to talk, and we all remained quiet throughout the meal.

Moments after finishing our meal, Uncle Anshel burst into our house through the back door from our garden and screamed very loudly at us, "Come quickly to listen to the radio. Come right now! Hurry!" And then he dashed out and left our back door open.

I thought: *Something horrible must be going on in Germany.*

When we got inside Uncle Anshel and Aunt Gital's home, we heard the Warsaw radio station's news announcer speaking very loudly, "Attention everyone! Tonight, the Nazi party has launched a highly organized massive action against the Jews."

Obviously, this statement got all of our attention, including Aunt Gital's 80-year-old mother, Feiga, who moved closer to the radio so that she could hear better.

Moments later the announcer added, "Gangs of the Nazi Youth Organization along with the brown-uniformed Nazi police are roaming the streets of Jewish neighborhoods throughout Germany, Austria, and the Sudetenland."

The eight of us sitting in the living room looked at each other with fright in our eyes.

The announcer continued. "They are breaking into Jewish homes, and vandalizing and looting them. Hundreds of Jewish families are being dragged out of their homes and beaten with thick hand clubs by these Nazis in all of the Nazi-controlled towns and cities. The Nazis are also killing many Jews. Thousands of Jewish-owned store windows are being shattered. Many windows and doorways are being painted with yellow Jewish stars and the word 'Jude' is painted in the middle of the six-pointed star."

Leah and Mindel started crying profusely and ran to the bathroom.

"Attention. The Nazis have now started to destroy the synagogues throughout Germany, Austria, and the Sudetenland by setting them on fire!"

Both my mom and Aunt Gital yelled out, "Oh no! No! No! Isn't anyone trying to stop this madness?"

As we continued to listen to the radio announcer report and repeat these horrific details, 80-year-old Feiga, who normally remains quiet when the family was together, stood up and started screaming, "Pogrom! Pogrom! Pogrom!"

Aunt Gital ran over to her. "Mom. Calm down. We'll be okay. Calm down." And Aunt Gital escorted Aunt Feiga back to the bedroom that she shared with Mindel. We could still hear Aunt Feiga continue to scream the word 'pogrom' a few more times.

Mindel and Leah were on their way back from the bathroom and heard Aunt Feiga's screams. Both of them were very alarmed by her acting this way. Mindel asked her father, "Why is she screaming? She never says anything. What is scaring her?"

Uncle Anshel replied, "When your Grandmother Feiga was a little girl, there was a tragic uprising against the Jewish people in Bolechov. Most likely, tonight's news on the radio reminded her of this uprising. These types of uprisings against Jews are called pogroms."

As soon as Uncle Anshel finished speaking to us, my father spoke up very sternly. "Anshel, Feiga has a good point. You and I both know when something against Jews happens elsewhere, the Bolechov Ukrainians and Poles use this as an excuse to terrorize us. This has happened to our families many times in the past, as our fathers and grandfathers have told us. The Bolechov Ukrainians and Poles are also hearing about what is going on right now against the Jews in Germany, Austria, and the Sudetenland. We should be prepared in case this news motivates them to take action against us. They might feel encouraged by these Nazi actions to go out tonight or tomorrow and vandalize the Jewish homes and businesses and possibly try to kill us like the Nazis are now doing.

"If you recall, our grandfathers built the cellars in our homes to serve as hiding places in case something like this would happen. I remember my grandfather telling me that his family often had to hide in the cellar during other pogroms. I know it is too late tonight to retrieve your sewing machine and remove other valuables from our shops. My barber's equipment is safe since I always bring my metal box home every night. I think it is best for us to all hide in our cellars at least tonight and all day tomorrow and tomorrow night. Our grandfathers were very wise to add a hidden window in our cellars for light and air. We need to reopen them so we can hide down there.

"Gital and Rifka, we will need you to fill some jars with drinking water and bring them down to the cellar and place a large open pot down in one of the corners that we can use as a temporary toilet. Both of our families should already have enough food stored down there. If we don't hear any noises in our homes and on the outside, let's agree to come out the day after tomorrow and check on each other.

"Just a reminder, Anshel. Remember to place the throw rug over the cellar door to conceal it! Not many people are even aware our houses have a cellar."

That was the plan that we followed. Leah and I were told to get a sweater and other clothes needed for a couple of days and bring them along with all of our blankets and pillows down to the cellar. My father kept a kerosene lamp in the cellar so we would have some light during the night. The only instructions he offered Leah and me were not to speak very loudly, try to get some sleep, and to remain silent if we heard any noises coming from our home upstairs and from the outside.

This was the first time my parents experienced the need for our family to go into hiding. At first it felt very scary. When I climbed downstairs into the cellar, I soon noticed how well organized and clean my mom and Aneta kept it. The jars of food stored on the shelves were not dusty. There were no spiders or cobwebs hanging anywhere. Nor was there any dirt on the concrete floor. I no longer felt reluctant to spread my blankets on the floor as my bed. As I looked around, I was impressed with how my ancestors constructed this cellar as a hiding place.

I could tell that Leah was very frightened when she reached the bottom step of the cellar staircase. I quickly raced toward her. "Don't worry. It will be all right. Stay close to me. Here, let me help you set up your blankets and pillow next to me."

I tried to get as comfortable as possible to sleep on the floor. Even so, I had trouble falling asleep. My mind kept racing with images of Nazis carrying torches, clubs, and guns as they marched through Bolechov setting homes and businesses on fire and dragging Jews out onto the streets. I finally dozed off since our upstairs and outside areas remained completely silent all night.

When Leah woke up the next morning, she asked, "Is it time for us to go upstairs yet?"

Our mom replied quietly, "Not yet. We need to stay down here one more day and night, just in case the vandals organize something. Here, Leah. Here's your toothbrush and some toothpaste. I'll pour you a cup of water and you can go into the corner over there and brush your teeth. You too, Yitzhak."

I thought that spending the whole day hiding in the cellar would be kind of boring. My mom prepared to keep all of us occupied by bringing down to the cellar her knitting supplies, my father's chess set, and clean bowls, spoons, forks, and knives, along with many jars filled with water. My mom taught Leah how to crochet, while my father showed me how to play chess. I even won one game. These activities filled the thirty-six hours we spent downstairs in the cellar.

During our second night of hiding, we still didn't hear any noises from the upstairs of our home, or any street noises, except for an occasional bark from a dog. As we agreed with Uncle Anshel, we left the cellar on Friday morning, not knowing the condition of our home and shop.

My father first stood on one of the crates to look out the opened window. He didn't notice anything unusual or disturbed and felt it was safe enough to climb the stairs and open the wooden cover and move the rug to the side. He opened the cover very slowly and looked around.

"Everything seems in place. Let's all get out of here."

He was right. Nothing in the house was disturbed.

My father instructed us to check all of the rooms in the house while he went over to Uncle Anshel and Aunt Rifka's home. About ten minutes later, he returned with Uncle Anshel.

"Meir, go outside and see if there are any Jewish stars painted on your door and walls."

We all went outside and noticed that every Jewish owned house on our street had big yellow stars painted on the doors and windows and some of the houses had the word 'Jude" painted in yellow.

Fortunately, it appeared that none of the homes encountered any additional damage.

"Anshel, it's going to take us some time to clean all of this. By some chance do you have any paint thinner?"

"Sorry, Meir, I don't. We should go over to see what our shops look like."

Sure enough, both the barbershop and tailor shop, along with the other Jewish shops, were painted with the same yellow markings. Fortunately, no windows were shattered and the shops were not broken into or vandalized. The big question to answer was where would my father, uncle, and the other Jewish business owners get the needed supplies to remove or cover these yellow painted markings?

Later in the afternoon, there was a knock on our home's back door. My father looked out the kitchen window and noticed it was Aneta and her husband, Ivan. He invited them to come inside and then asked, "What are you doing here? Aren't you worried someone would see you?"

Aneta replied, "That's why we walked through the narrow back alley to enter through your garden to come to your back door, so no one would see us. I peeked through your front window yesterday and noticed the carpet was covering the cellar door. So, I knew you were all safe in the cellar. You are going to need paint, brushes, and some rags to wipe off all of the yellow markings, aren't you?"

"Yes, Aneta."

"That's why I brought Ivan. If you give him a list of what you and your brother need, he'll get them for you. Just so you know, there are postings all over town not to do business with Jews. Ivan and I are here to help. We don't care what the government is doing. I think that it is awful what happened here in what used to be peaceful Bolechov."

"That's very thoughtful of the two of you to offer us this help and risk being seen."

"There is no need to worry about us, Meir. There are many Ukrainians and Poles who live here, like us, who have Jewish friends.

I knew that Aneta was regarded as a member of our family. Her thoughtfulness and caring for us just proved it!

The next day, even though it was Shabbat and we weren't supposed to do any work, my father used a straight razor to scrape off the yellow paint from the shop and house windows, while Uncle Anshel washed the windows. On Monday afternoon, Ivan brought the gallons of the white and brown paint along with the supplies that my father and uncle needed to cover the yellow markings on the outside walls. With me helping them with the painting, my father and uncle were able to reopen their shops the next day on Wednesday. They gave the leftover paint and brushes to Mrs. Gorbich who owned the candy store. She was very grateful and her daughter helped repair her small shop and house.

Somehow, most of the other Jewish shops along the Rynek also opened on Wednesday, November 16th.

However, there were some noticeable changes in Bolechov due to the actions of the anti-Semitic Polish government leaders who admired and appeased Hitler as an attempt to convince him to leave Poland alone. Aneta was correct. Notices were posted throughout the Rynek to order the Bolechov people to boycott Jewish businesses and the Jewish stalls during the Monday market. The Polish men who worked in the government offices were instructed by the Polish national government to begin wearing a black tie to work to show that they were also Nazi sympathizers. An 8 p.m. curfew for teenagers was also established.

Other Polish men, agitators wearing black ties, roamed through the Monday Rynek market urging Christians not to frequent the Jewish operated stalls. The Jewish business owners started worrying about a significant loss of business.

On the following Monday market day, my mother sent Aneta by herself with the shopping list. When she returned, Aneta told my mom she ignored the agitators who were roaming the Rynek market and they left her alone. Aneta also mentioned that she saw Jewish women operating their stalls and other Jewish women shopping in the market. She heard some derogatory remarks mentioned to the Jewish women, but for the most part, the agitators left them and the businesses alone. Aneta encouraged my mom to go with her to the market during the next market day.

The following week when I was at the barbershop after school, there was a series of knocks on the backdoor. I cracked open the door and saw Town Marshal Josef Spychalski standing outside, wearing a white shirt with a black tie.

"Is your father here, Yitzhak? I would like to speak to him if he is alone and no one else is inside except you."

"Come on in, Marshal Spychalski. There are no other customers inside."

"Hello, Meir. I was hoping I would find you alone in your shop so that I could talk to you.

"Please, Marshal Spychalski, sit down. Are you ready for a haircut or a shave?"

"Not today, Meir. I have something rather important to discuss with you. I know that you are well respected by the other Jewish business owners and those who attend your synagogue. The damage to the homes and shops with the yellow paint was done by a bunch of teenage hooligans. When the security officers learned they were doing this, they chased them away. I see that you and the others have already taken care of the damage and the shops have reopened. Good. As you know, the people of Bolechov depend upon the Jewish businesses and the factories for their daily livelihood.

"Being the town marshal, I have to follow the orders that I receive from the National Government in Warsaw. That's the reason for the posting of the Jewish business boycott notices and for the Polish officials to wear a black tie. I was ordered to post them and for me to wear this tie. The dilemma is, if there is a boycott of the Jewish shops and businesses, where else can our citizens shop and work? Many don't have the means to go shop or work elsewhere. Please spread the word among your friends that I will do my best to maintain order and peace in this town. Are you willing to let others know this and encourage them to try their best to continue living their lives here in Bolechov?"

"Yes, I can do that for you."

"Good. I do have one suggestion that you may pass on to the others. Most of the shops have a back door that opens to a rear alley. Your Polish and Ukrainian customers, and even your Jewish customers, may feel more comfortable and safe coming to the shops through the alley and entering through the back door. This way others may not see or hassle them. Maybe in a few months, things will calm down, and we can all return to a normal life."

"That's a good suggestion. I've also thought about using my shop's back door as an entrance."

"Good. Now, I'm going back to my office. Please spread the word. You are the only Jewish business owner that I will talk to. I have my superiors who oversee what I do and I have to be very careful. I know you understand this. If everything remains calm, I will be back in a week or so to see you for another haircut."

"My son and I look forward to seeing you soon."

Town Marshal Spychalski slightly cracked open the back door and peeked out. No one else must have been in the alley, and he quickly left the shop.

Being very curious, I asked, "Papa, do you think people will boycott our shop? Will we suffer any hardship or encounter any danger?"

"We'll just have to see how everyone responds to the boycott postings and seeing the men wearing the black ties. Marshal Spychalski is right. Where else can the Bolechov people shop and work? We own and operate most of the shops, factories, and farms. The Bolechov people depend on us. Your mom and I may have to make some adjustments to keep us safe. I think I should now accompany you and Leah to school in the morning. Aneta can meet the two of you after school. Since she is Ukrainian, I don't think any of the agitators will bother her. Let's just see what happens. I also think it is best for you and Leah not to go to the Rynek Town Square anymore to play with your friends. If agitators are there, something might happen to the two of you. It should be permissible to invite some of your Jewish friends to come and play at our house. I'll talk to your mom about this. I'll also check with the Hebrew school officials to see if they think it is still a good idea to allow their students to have recess outdoors when the weather is nice."

The next couple of weeks, customers started returning to the barbershop. Some of our regular Polish, Ukrainian and Jewish customers started to enter the shop through the back door. I even gave boys haircuts when I worked at the shop after school and on Saturday afternoons. Leah and I returned to the Hebrew school without experiencing any harassment and all of the students remained inside the building during recess. My family did see some men on the streets wearing black ties, staring at us, and snickering to each other. My mom decided to go with Aneta to the Monday market at the Rynek Town Square and didn't experience any hassles, except for an occasional rude comment made from someone walking near her.

We also heard reports from those attending the synagogue on Saturdays that Jews were being beaten and terrorized in the larger Polish towns and cities. Polish government officials were also told by their superiors to not have any Jewish friends. So far, nothing too tragic had happened to any of the Jews living in Bolechov.

I asked my mom about the word 'Kristallnacht' that Leah and I overheard at the synagogue. Some of synagogue congregants said this word when they described the November 9th actions taken against the Jews in Germany, Austria, and the Sudetenland. My mom told Leah and me that this German word meant 'The Night of Broken Glass' as a reference to the thousands of windows broken at the Jewish businesses and homes and the hundreds of lives that were lost.

I could sense the severe tension the people in Bolechov were now feeling. No one knew if there would be any more repercussions or restrictions enacted and enforced against us. I no longer felt at ease walking along the street. I knew I needed to keep an eye out all around Leah and me in order for us to avoid being hassled from any agitators who might threaten and harm us.

A new year, 1939, was approaching.

My mind was clouded with many unanswered thoughts and worries about the future:

*What else will Hitler and the Nazis do?*

*The radio news keeps reporting about the massive Nazi military and weapon buildup. Will another European war happen?*

*Will the Nazi army invade Poland, since Germany and Poland share a border?*

*Will Hitler and his Nazi government initiate more actions against the Jewish people and kill more of us?*

*What will happen to my family?*

# A New Restriction
## January 1939

On the first Sunday after New Year's Day, my father surprised me. "Yitzhak. Instead of going to your school tomorrow, how about going to Stryi with me? I need to get some supplies for the shop, and I thought that while we are there, we might as well walk over to the high school to inquire about their enrollment procedure and their tuition cost."

"Are you sure, Papa, that it's alright for me to miss a day of school? You always told me that the only time I could miss a day was if I was too sick to go."

"You are keeping up with your assignments and getting good grades. I think missing one day shouldn't be a problem for you to catch up with the rest of your class. Besides, I think it might be too risky right now for me to go by myself to the supply warehouse in Stanislavov or Lemberg with the current political tension from the Polish officials. Oh, I better stop saying 'Lemberg', since the Poles prefer calling that big city 'Lvov' or 'Lviv'. Anyway, there is a supply store in Stryi that is owned by a Jewish man named Solomon, and it is very close to the train station. Even though his prices are a little higher, I know he would appreciate more business from me. Plus, I think it is a good idea for you to know where his supply warehouse is located and for you to meet him. There may come a time when I will need you to go there on your own to buy supplies for the shop."

"Okay, Papa, if you think that this is best. Where is the Stryi high school located?"

"Do you remember me taking you and Leah to Stryi's town square?"

"Yes. That was a few years ago."

"Well, the high school is about a ten-minute walk from the square. We'll go to the school first, check it out, and then go to Solomon's warehouse."

My father and I took the 8:15 Monday morning train on a very cold, wintery day and arrived promptly at Stryi in about fifteen minutes. Stryi was a much larger town than Bolechov; about double the size and located along the north bank of the Stryi River. Similar to Bolechov, Stryi's Rynek Town Square was lined with shops and nearby warehouses. There was even a large synagogue located a few blocks from the town square.

"Stay close to me, Yitzhak. When we leave the train station, we have to walk along a very crowded main street for about twenty minutes to get to the high school. Most of the people walking this street ride the trains in the morning in order to get to work. It is best for us to not make eye contact with anyone. We need to blend in and not attract any attention."

He was right about the street being crowded with lots of people leaving the train station and even more people walking toward it. As predicted, in about twenty minutes, he pointed to a rather tall, four-story building that looked like a photo that I once saw in school of a Grecian or Roman temple with numerous columns going from the ground all of the way up to the roof! "Papa. Is that really the high school? It is so big. I've never seen a school look like this."

"That's it. Let's walk over there and go inside."

Once we opened the front door and entered the building, a heavy set, uniformed woman sitting in a chair noticed us and spoke with a stern and unwelcoming voice. "What brings you to Stryi High School Number One?"

73

"Madame, we are from Bolechov and I would like to enroll my son to attend this school beginning in the fall."

"You will need to go to the school's office. Go down the hall, turn left, and the office is the first door on the right."

The school office was easy to find. My father and I entered and walked up to the counter. One of the female clerks immediately noticed us, stood up from her desk, and came to the counter.

"Sir. How may I help you?"

"My son and I live in Bolechov. I would like to enroll him in your high school beginning next fall. We came here today to fill out the application form and learn about the tuition and other fees."

"What is your son's name and what school is he currently attending?"

"His name is Yitzhak Barkan and he attends the Bolechov Hebrew School."

"Oh, you are Jews! Jews can no longer attend this school. Sorry sir."

"Since when? I know of other Jewish families who enrolled their sons in this school."

"If they were here, they were dismissed along with all of the Jewish teachers. The Polish government now has new restrictions. They no longer permit Jews to attend or teach in public high schools. There is nothing I can do to enroll him. It is best that you two leave the school and return home."

"Let's go, Yitzhak. Let's get out of here."

I could tell by the tone of his voice that my father was very angry. He remained silent as we exited the building and made our way to the main street. After a long silence, he finally spoke to me with a consoling voice. "I'm sorry, Yitzhak, that you had to hear those words, 'Jews can no longer attend this school'. If I had known this before we left home, I wouldn't have bothered even coming here. This also means that Jewish students are being restricted from attending a university! I never thought I would see these types of restrictions being imposed on us."

"Don't worry, Papa, about me. You were very wise to help me become a barber. I can be just as successful as you and my grandfather and make a good living. I enjoy cutting hair. Yes, I'm disappointed. Maybe sometime in the future I will be able to study for a medical career."

My father now looked at me with a loving facial expression of pride. "How did my son become so wise? I'll tell you this. Since we still have to go to Solomon's warehouse, let's get you the additional equipment that you will need to learn the remaining barber skills, particularly how to give a good shave, prepare the shaving soap, and sharpen the straight razor."

"Really, Papa. You think I'm ready to learn how to use a straight razor? Do you think I'm ready to trim and shape moustaches too?"

"Yes. I might as well train you now for everything you will need to know in order to become a full-service barber. Let's go to Solomon's shop and get you everything that you will need."

"Papa. I brought some zloty bills with me. I can help pay for my equipment."

"No, Yitzhak. You hold onto them and save your Polish money. This will be my gift for you."

When we got to the supply warehouse, Solomon enthusiastically greeted my father, and my father introduced me.

"Ah, Meir, another barber in the family! It's nice to meet you, young man. Anytime you need any supplies or barber equipment, just come to see Solomon!"

After leaving Solomon's business, we needed to walk through the town's Rynek in order to get to the train station. As my father and I approached the town square, I noticed an unoccupied bench. "Papa, can we sit on the bench for a while before we go home?"

Once we were seated, I turned to look at him. I could tell he was deep in thought and possibly still upset at what happened at the school. "Papa, I'm also upset, but not with what happened at the school. I'm more worried about what is going on in the world right now and I'm having trouble sleeping again. When I listen to Uncle Anshel's radio, all I hear are the awful things Hitler is doing to start another war and his new restrictions on the Jewish people. I hear about the Nazi army, airplanes, tanks. New restrictions seem to be imposed on us every day. I have dreams about their soldiers invading and burning our town. You've told Leah and me how terrible the last European war was and how difficult life was for both your and Mom's families. I'm worried that the same thing will happen to us. Are we going to face bombs being dropped on us, and armies fighting and killing each other, here, in Bolechov? What will happen to us?"

There was a long pause before my father spoke.

"Yitzhak. You are right. War is awful and there is a lot of destruction and death. Let me just say this. Your mom and I will take every precaution to prepare for the worst, and if war comes, we will do our best to keep our family safe and alive. I am also worried that war is coming our way. Hitler is increasing Germany's military might. I don't trust him. He is power hungry, and I think he is looking to conquer all of Europe just like Napoleon tried to do over one hundred years ago."

He paused again.

"Let your mother and me worry about keeping our family safe. What I want you to do now is to focus on your schoolwork and learn the new barber skills. As for giving men shaves, I'll have to show you how to do this on my chair, since you will need to recline the back of the chair slightly backward. Enough talk. Let's go home and have some lunch. I'm sure you are as hungry as I am!"

Winter in Bolechov was not my favorite season. It was very cold with dark clouds hiding the sunlight practically every day. The only beauty one saw was occasional snow blanketing the peaks of the surrounding Carpathian Mountains.

During the following three winter months, the Polish government did not impose anything new that affected our daily lives. Leah and I continued attending the Hebrew school, and I earned and saved more money giving haircuts to the young boys. Aneta and our mom went shopping at the Rynek market on Mondays, while my father occasionally went to Stryi to purchase his needed supplies at Solomon's warehouse. My family regularly went over to Uncle Anshel and Aunt Gital's home on weekends and on some weeknights to listen to music and socialize with each other.

On Tuesday, March 14th, our daily lives faced a new challenge. Uncle Anshel invited my family to come over to his home after dinner and play a card game. As we listened to the music on his radio and played the card game, the music suddenly stopped for a special news report. The radio reporter announced Hitler's demand that the Czech government allow his German troops to have free passage to all of the Czech borders. If not, their capital city, Prague, would be bombed. Prague was located in an area of

Czechoslovakia that was not currently under German control.

Fifteen minutes later, the radio reporter once again interrupted the music playing on the radio station. He came back on the air to inform the listeners that Hitler didn't wait for an answer from the Czech government. The reporter announced that Hitler was now riding through Prague in his open car escorted by his army without any opposition from the Czech government or the Prague police.

Once the news report ended, my father spoke up. "See. I told you Hitler couldn't be trusted. Why would British Prime Minister Chamberlain and the rest of the European leaders think that Hitler would abide by their previous agreement? They were just being fooled and now Hitler is laughing at them. Do you think Hitler will now stop his aggression? Who will be next? Now that he has more control of Czechoslovakia, his army will be positioned along more of Poland's border. He now has his eyes on Poland! Poland will be next! You can bet on it!"

The next evening's radio report announced that the British and French governments were guaranteeing Poland's independence.

A few weeks later in April, Hitler announced that Germany was cancelling its non-aggression agreement with Poland.

It was obvious. The stage was now set for war. Poland was Hitler's next target!

After my mother woke up the next morning, got dressed, and went to the kitchen, she was surprised to find that Aneta had arrived early and already started preparing the family breakfast. My parents completely trusted Aneta and her family and gave her a key to our home many years ago.

I walked into the kitchen just as my mom was asking Aneta, "Why are you here so early? Is something wrong with your family?"

"Nothing is wrong with us. I'm sure all of you listened to last night's radio broadcast and learned that the German army is now positioned along more of Poland's border. I came early to speak privately with you and Meir before he left to go open the barber shop."

My mom continued, "Meir will be in the kitchen shortly. He's still getting dressed. Aneta, please sit down next to Yitzhak at the table and let me finish getting everything ready."

Leah was next to come into the kitchen. Minutes later, my father joined us. He seemed very surprised to see Aneta sitting at our kitchen table. My mom explained, "Aneta came early to talk with us about last night's radio broadcast."

My father asked, "What is it, Aneta, that is so urgent?"

"It's private, Meir. I should just speak with you."

"Rifka, how about you and Leah grab a warm sweater and go out into the garden to see if any of the vegetables are ripe enough to bring inside? Yitzhak, you stay here with me and listen to Aneta."

My mom understood my father's hint, so she and Leah went out to the garden in the back of the house.

"What's wrong, Aneta?"

"Meir, please don't tell anyone how you learned this. Even though my husband, daughter, son-in-law and I are Ukrainian, we do our best to maintain the peace in this small town and for everyone to get along as it has for hundreds of years, except, as you know for a few unfortunate instances. Your family and my family are the best of friends and I really and truly treasure our close connection."

"We feel the same as you, Aneta. I think you know that."

"Yes, I know. That's why I am here. I don't want anything terrible to happen.

"Let me explain. Last night after the broadcast ended, there was a gathering of many of the Ukrainian men inside our church's social hall. My husband, Ivan, and our son-in-law, Borysko, attended. When they came back home, they told me that these men agreed that the Ukrainians should cooperate with the German government and army if and when they arrive in Bolechov."

My father was surprised when I asked, "Why do they want to side with the Germans? I don't understand."

My father explained, "A long time ago, before this area was part of the Austro-Hungarian Empire, the Ukrainian people, who lived here at that time, had their own country. They lost their country to the Austro-Hungarians during a war. At the end of the Great European War in 1918, when the Austro-Hungarian Empire was defeated along with Germany, the Ukrainians were given back control of the country. Then, the next year, it was taken away from them and this area was given to Poland. The Ukrainian people have always wanted to regain control of their country. They now see a possible opportunity by siding with the Germans."

"Oh, I see, Papa."

Aneta continued, "I don't know what will happen if the Germans come here. You may want to let the word spread among the Jewish shop and business owners to prepare for a Ukrainian-led rebellion and violence toward the Jewish-owned businesses. I just don't want to see any rioting. And I don't want anything to happen to all of you."

"Thank you, Aneta, for the warning. I'll spread the word without mentioning you as the source. I greatly thank you on behalf of my family for looking out for us."

"Meir, all of you have always looked out for us too. We are all like one big family."

"Yes, we are Aneta. Please let Rifka know that she and Leah can come back inside. I'll share your information with Rifka later on after I come back from work."

My mom escorted Leah and me to school that morning. I really couldn't concentrate on my schoolwork all day.

My mind kept spinning with the question, *"When will the Nazis show up in Bolechov?"*

# The Molotov-Ribbentrop Pact
## August 23, 1939

The next four months dragged on very slowly. All of the people in Bolechov, particularly the large Jewish population, seemed to be very nervous and worried about when the German invasion would happen. When I walked to and from school, I saw adult men and women huddled together in small clusters on the streets, outside the various buildings, and in the Rynek. It seemed that the Polish, Ukrainian, and Jewish men and women formed separate groups to share their concerns and plans for a forthcoming German invasion.

Even at our synagogue on Saturday mornings before and after the service, people with worried faces huddled and talked with each other in whispered voices. I noticed my father and uncle speaking with groups of men. I assumed that they were sharing what they learned from Aneta about the Ukrainian men's plan to cooperate with the Germans. When my family and our relatives gathered together for lunch after the latest Shabbat service, my father and uncle shared with us the rumors that they heard from the other congregants about Germany's extensive preparation for a war. These rumors centered around the German military having more than two thousand tanks, over a thousand bombers and fighter planes, and at least one million soldiers. Another rumor shared with us was about the Polish army not having the number of men and modern military equipment needed to stop the German army. If these rumors were really true, how could the Polish army defend our country?

Then, on Friday morning, September 1$^{st}$, the Polish radio station announced that Hitler's army crossed the border and invaded Western Poland. Word about the invasion must have spread very quickly throughout the town. An announcement was made at my school for all of the students to immediately leave, because the school was going to close, with no explanation as to when we would return. As we all exited the building, our parents were waiting at the front gate to take us home. While going home at a very brisk pace, I noticed that businesses and factories had closed and people were rushing frantically to get home. It was obvious. Something very serious had happened.

Once my family, including my father, arrived at our house, my sister and I placed our schoolbooks on the kitchen table and we immediately raced over to my aunt and uncle's house to listen to the news report. The reporter stated that Hitler's army invaded Western Poland because of a Polish attack on a German radio station. The Polish government proclaimed that this attack claim was phony and that Hitler invented this false story as an excuse to invade Poland.

We were all stunned and looked at each other with horror in our eyes and thoughts about what the Germans could do to us.

My mom and Aunt Gital gave Leah and Mindel comforting hugs as the two girls cried excessively and screamed, "They're coming to kill us!"

With tears also flowing down both of my cheeks, I asked, "Papa, what are we going to do?"

"Listen, everyone. The Rynek Jewish business owners like Anshel and I have already agreed that if a war begins between Germany and Poland, we will keep our stores open in order to protect them from being damaged from rioting or looting by the Bolechov

Ukrainians who are German collaborators. The synagogue and the Hebrew school will remain closed for safety concerns. We feel it is best for a large number of Jews to not be at one location at the same time. This plan should prevent any attack on us while Poland is fighting Germany.

"Yitzhak, go with your uncle right now and help him move his sewing machine out of the store and bring it here so it won't get stolen. When we open our shops, Anshel and I will secure them from the front, while you, Yitzhak, guard our shops from the back alley. Here is a whistle for you to blow three times to signal to us that thugs are threatening our shops from the alley. The other Jewish business owners are also going to guard their shops. We also agreed to a rotation schedule to guard our shops during the evening and nighttime. We feel if we show an organized force, we will be left alone by these collaborators. Leah and Mindel, go with your mothers to help them prepare more food from the gardens to store in our cellars. We need to stock up with as much food as we can."

Later in the afternoon, Uncle Anshel took his radio to the shop and turned it on so that we could hear any updates about the invasion. On Sunday, September 3rd, the Warsaw radio station reported that Britain and France declared war on Germany in response to Hitler's aggressive action. A second European war had now begun. The reporter later announced that the Germans had easily broken through the border and were advancing into Poland with lightning speed and described their advance as a Blitzkrieg. Their fast-moving infantry was quickly heading toward Warsaw and Krakow, along with extensive bombing on these cities from its air force, called the Luftwaffe.

As horrendous as these reports sounded, surprisingly Bolechov remained very quiet that

Sunday. We didn't hear any rumbling from bombs, shootings, or airplane noises. There were also very few people walking along the town's streets and the Rynek was practically empty.

My father was correct with his prediction. The shops along the Rynek were left alone from vandals.

This all changed the next day, Monday, September 4th. Since there had been no threat to my family's shops, my father and uncle opened them, while I sat outside in the front. About 10 a.m., a battalion of Polish troops marched through Bolechov. Some of the infantry positioned themselves in front of the town hall, while the rest continued onward from the southern part of our town and headed northward. Shortly afterward, a steady stream of ragged-looking refugees flowed into the center city from the north in cars, bicycles, horse-drawn wagons, trucks, and on foot.

One man came up to me and asked, "Where is the grocery store?" I pointed to the grocery store located on the opposite side of the Rynek.

He then yelled out to the crowd of people surrounding him, "The grocery store is over there!" A surge of people followed him to the store. Within minutes, the shop owner closed and locked her door. I assumed she sold out all of her food supplies to these refugees.

Another man carrying a large sack of his belongings over his shoulder approached me. I asked him, "Where are all of you from and where are you going?"

"Oh, hello, young man. I think most of the people you see are Jews escaping from the center and southern part of Poland that is west of the Bug River. We are fleeing to safety by going south to either Hungary or Romania. Where can I get some food?"

"I don't know. The only grocery store that was open earlier today has now closed. I think they sold out of everything they had."

He then crossed the street to join the hundreds of refugees gathering in the Rynek.

My father was cutting a man's hair and must have heard all of the commotion coming from the outside. When his customer left, he came out of the shop to join me. We both noticed that the refugees, who had gathered in the Rynek, were gradually finding a place to sit to take a break from their long journey escaping from the Germans. The Rynek quickly turned into a large and crowded refugee camp.

As the day progressed, large numbers of refugees continued to arrive and clog the streets in the center of the town and in the Rynek. I noticed some tried to get past the Polish army guarding the town hall. "Papa, why are those people trying go inside the town hall?"

"Most likely, Yitzhak, they want to get some assistance from the Polish government officials to find food or get money to pay for their travel. They probably don't know that all of the trains are now reserved for the military."

The Bolechov Jewish leaders must have also taken notice of the vast number of Jewish refugees descending into the town. The next day, Tuesday, September 5th, with the help of women volunteers, including my mother and Aunt Gital, the Hebrew school opened the school's cafeteria and offered soup and temporary shelter to those who were destitute.

More refugees entered Bolechov during the next three days as the German army advanced farther into Poland. We also noticed that some of the existing and newly arrived refugees left Bolechov to continue their journey southward to Hungary or Romania, while others remained.

On Friday, September 8th, the radio announcer stated that the German army had surrounded Warsaw and this would be his last broadcast. My uncle quickly turned the radio's dial to a Stanislavov station, so that we could continue to keep track of the German advance.

The next day, Saturday, September 9th, the radio station and some of the newly arrived refugees confirmed that the German army had crossed over the Bug River that separated Eastern and Western Poland. The Germans quickly captured Lviv and were now advancing toward Stanislavov and Stryi. During the afternoon, an armed Polish garrison marched through Bolechov and headed toward these two cities to fight and hold back the German army.

Later that night, continuous loud rumbling noises woke all of us. Leah and I found our parents in the living room looking very concerned. My father peeked out of the living room window to see if he could determine what was causing these loud noises. "It looks safe everyone. Let's all go outside to see what is going on."

We weren't the only family who were awakened by these loud noises. My uncle's family and all of our neighbors were already standing out on the dirt street in front of their homes, looking upward and pointing to the flashing lights streaking across the sky, followed by loud thunderous noises.

Both Leah and I simultaneously asked our father, "Papa, what is going on?"

"It looks like the Germans are bombing Stryi with their tanks and possibly from their airplanes, while the Polish army is trying their best to protect the city."

Leah screamed and ran over to our mom. "Mama, I'm frightened. Hitler is going to kill all of us. Isn't he?"

My mom comforted her with a hug and said, "Let's go back inside. You don't have to stay out here any longer. Mindel, do you want to come inside with me?"

Aunt Gital added, "Mindel and I will go with you, Rifka."

My father, Uncle Anshel, and I must have remained outside for over an hour and finally went back inside to try to get some sleep.

On the following day, during the afternoon while we were guarding our shops, a Polish official, who escaped from Stryi, told us that the Polish army lost the battle at Stryi and that the German army now held a firm position along the northern bank of the Stryi River.

I thought: *When will the German army arrive in Bolechov? So far, there has been no battle here and no one has died.*

That evening, Aneta knocked on our kitchen door while we were eating dinner. She rarely came to our home on Sundays.

"Please don't let anyone know that I was here and that I told you this. There is a group of Ukrainian men who believe the German army will capture this city very soon. A few of them went to Stryi to speak with the leader of the German army. They want him to know that the Ukrainians are ready to collaborate with the Germans and that the German army should proceed to conquer Bolechov as soon as possible.

"I thought that you would want to know this so you can be prepared to protect your shop and home. You may need to once again hide in your cellar."

The next morning, on Monday, September 11th, my father and uncle once again guarded the front of their shops, while I sat in the alley. Nothing happened that day nor on the day after. The German army did not advance into Bolechov. Members of the Polish infantry were still in position guarding the town hall.

Two days later, on Wednesday, September 13th, another fleeing refugee confirmed that the Germans held their position along the Stryi River, and that it didn't appear that they were going to move forward to invade Bolechov. The Ukrainian men, who had previously spoken with the German army leader, must have realized that the Germans were not going to advance into our small town. An hour later, we witnessed a large group of Ukrainian farmers, obviously organized and encouraged by their leaders, storming through the town, carrying torches, yelling 'We own this town', and threatening to burn the stores and houses. Fortunately, my father must have contacted and organized a business owners' defense, just in case something like this would occur. The entire Rynek shop owners were lined up in front of their shops holding clubs and other wooden boards as weapons. Once this Ukrainian group of farmers noticed that the businessmen were prepared to defend from this type of anarchy, they retreated. The only thing we observed during this attempted riot was that some of the Polish officials and female clerks hurriedly left the town hall.

For the remainder of the week, the center of Bolechov was quiet. We no longer heard the sounds of battle coming from nearby Stryi. Since we didn't see any Polish soldiers retreating through our town, we assumed that they were either killed or taken as prisoners by the Germans.

More refugees, who had camped in the Rynek, left Bolechov to continue their journey southward. Since the grocery stores and butcher shops were depleted of their food supply, obtaining food became difficult. My mom and Aunt Gital were well-prepared for this situation and followed my father's advice and had already stocked up and stored more food in our cellars. The Hebrew school's cafeteria struggled to remain open and relied on food donations to offer only one bowl of soup and a slice of bread to the Jewish refugees who were staying there.

No one came to get haircuts or have any clothing altered by my uncle during the rest of the week.

The political situation changed drastically for Poland on Sunday, September 17th. While my father, uncle, and I were guarding our shops in the morning, my uncle continuously tried to locate a radio broadcast, since the Stanislavov's radio station went off the air many days ago. He finally found a Russian language station.

"Meir, since you understand Russian better than I, what is this announcer saying?"

My father waited until the announcer finished his report before telling us the latest news. As he listened to the report, my father's facial expression changed from a worried look to a joyful expression. "You're not going to believe this. I am stunned with this surprising news. The radio reporter announced that the Soviet Union's army crossed over the border and is invading into Eastern Poland. Apparently, there was some type of agreement between Stalin and Hitler. If this is true, the Soviet army will liberate Eastern Poland from the Germans and we will all remain safe."

The Polish government leaders in Bolechov, including the Town Marshal Josef Spychalski, either heard the broadcast or were notified by the Polish government. This Soviet advance meant that Poland was fighting both the German and Soviet armies.

As my father, uncle, and I sat in front of our shops, we saw a series of official cars race to park in front of the town hall. Those with families inside the parked cars had them wait, while the officials stormed inside the building. In a short time, Town Marshal Spychalski and the rest of the officials came out carrying boxes, placed them inside the trunks of their cars, and then quickly got into their cars and drove out of the town square at a fast speed. They headed south to leave Poland to escape to either Hungary or Romania. The Polish military guarding the town hall also retreated southward.

Bolechov was now left abandoned with no one in charge to protect it.

"Papa and Uncle Anshel. What's going to happen? Are the Ukrainians going to try to take control of our town?"

My father replied, "I don't know, Yitzhak. The Polish officials must have realized that they were unable to fight two armies at the same time. We'll just have to see how long it will take for the Soviet army to come here. In the meantime, the three of us and the other business owners will need to continue guarding our town."

The very next day, on Monday, September 18th, the town experienced a remarkable event during the late morning. A regiment of Soviet troops entered Bolechov from the south end of the town. This regiment was led by commanders riding beautiful horses followed by a large number of marching infantry soldiers. They proceeded slowly through the main street. Once my family and the townspeople, mainly the Jewish residents, realized what was happening, they all came out of their homes, lined the main street, and greeted the Soviets with loud cheers. Many threw flowers.

As my father was cheering, he turned to me and proclaimed, "We can breathe a sigh of relief that we will no longer feel threatened by the Germans! The Soviet army is a mighty army and not weak like the Polish army."

"I'm glad too, Papa!"

The infantry soldiers circled to protect and secure the Rynek and the town hall. Their commanders dismounted their horses, tied the reins to a railing, and quickly entered the office building.

Within an hour, the group of Ukrainian men, once again, paraded through the main streets around the Rynek to protest the Soviet control.

"Papa. What are these men trying to do?"

"I'm not sure. They might think the Soviets will retreat. But they will soon learn that the mighty Soviets are here to stay."

The Soviet infantry reacted very quickly to maintain peace by displaying their rifles and lining both sides of the main streets to not allow these Ukrainian protestors to enter the Rynek Town Square or the town hall. Surprisingly, a group of the Soviet soldiers also guarded the synagogues and the Ukrainian church to prevent the protestors from also entering those buildings. Seeing the Soviet army was now in control, the Ukrainian protesters soon retreated from the area.

My father, uncle, and the rest of the Rynek Jewish shop owners felt confident that the Soviet soldiers would maintain order and that we no longer had to guard our shops.

Three days later, on Thursday, September 21$^{st}$, notices were posted along the Rynek and on the walls of many businesses announcing that a Soviet military-controlled Bolechov municipal government had been established. The new mayor was Major Mikhail Orlov, and the new town marshal was Captain Pavel Novikov.

The next day, a tall bearded man with a thick curled moustache, looking very official with his black suit, white shirt, and black military-style boots, entered the barbershop in the early afternoon.

He announced himself with a loud and authoritarian sounding voice. "I'm Town Marshal Novikov. Who owns this shop?"

My father, unnerved by this loud formal greeting, offered his right hand for a handshake and spoke quietly, "I do, sir. My name is Meir Barkan, and this is my son, Yitzhak. We are the two barbers who work here."

As he shook my father's hand, the official responded, "Just the two of you, and no one else?"

"That's correct, Town Marshal Novikov."

"Well, that makes my job here much easier than I was anticipating. I was told that the Jews owned most of the shops in the middle of this town. I am here to inform you officially that you are now Soviet employees and the ownership of this shop has been nationalized."

My father responded with his calming voice, "Town Marshal Novikov. Have a seat in my chair. I can see that an important official like you could use a good shave."

"Well, I don't mind if I you do. This is very kind of you to offer me a shave. I haven't had one all week. "

As my father placed the protective neck strip and cape on him, my father initiated a conversation by asking, "Were you one of the officials who entered the town on Monday? You probably noticed the great reception you received from all of the town's Jewish businessmen and residents."

"Yes, I was one of the officials who rode into the town on a horse. I was very surprised we were greeted with such enthusiasm."

"We all feel that you are our liberators from the Germans."

"Well, you can really thank our supreme General Secretary of the Communist Party, Joseph Stalin, for his wisdom and leadership in making a pact with Hitler."

"Yes, I heard something about a pact on the radio. That was a big surprise."

"It was not only for you, but for the whole world! This is Stalin's genius to show the rest of the world that he can secretly establish a deal with Hitler."

"Well, tell me, Town Marshal Novikov, please explain to me as I do your shave, how did this all come about?"

"Last month, at the beginning of August, Stalin sent an invitation for the German foreign minister, Joachim von Ribbentrop, to come to Moscow to meet with our foreign minister, Vyasheslav Molotov. The two of them agreed to a non-aggression pact between our two counties. They also reached an agreement to divide Poland, with the Bug River serving as the dividing line. Germany would annex the section west of the Bug River, while the Soviet Union would annex the section east of the Bug River. The pact was approved by Hitler and signed in Moscow on August 23$^{rd}$. Stalin shook hands with Ribbentrop after the signing. Hitler's army jumped the gun by invading Poland on September 1$^{st}$. It took us a little longer to get our army organized. That's why the Soviet Union didn't enter eastern Poland until September 17$^{th}$. You did notice that as soon as we entered Eastern Poland, the German army retreated back to the other side the Bug River?"

"Yes, I learned that this week." My father continued with the shave.

"This is the greatness of Stalin. He established a buffer between the Soviet Union and Germany. No

94

other country's leader has accomplished anything like this with Hitler."

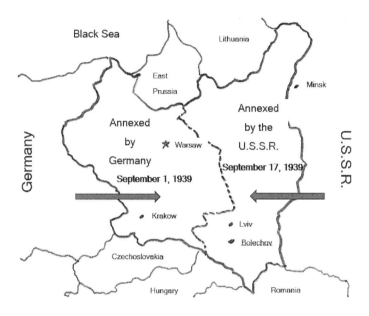

Molotov-Ribbentrop Pact
August 23, 1939
The Division of Poland

My father was almost finished with the shave when he asked, "How about I give your moustache a little trim to shape it and then wax it for you?"

"Sure. This will help me look my best as I go to the rest of the shops and businesses."

The town marshal continued. "How about this, Mr. Barkan? You could really help me. Now, that we have liberated your town, it is my duty for my office to issue every citizen an official Soviet identity card. How about you and your family being the first to receive them? I could use your help convincing the rest of the Jewish leaders to be as cooperative as you. I was told

95

that you helped organize a resistance to the Ukrainian agitators."

"Thank you for your offer. My family will gladly cooperate and be the first to receive the official cards."

"Good. You and your son need to come to the marshal's office first thing in the morning. Let's say at 8 a.m."

"Should I also bring my wife and daughter?"

"No. You can give me their information tomorrow. Where does your family live?"

"The four of us live in the small house behind the shop."

"Hmm. No extra room, I suppose for others."

"Not really, sir. Here let me wipe your neck with a towel and carefully take the cape off. Have a look in the hand mirror."

"Yes, I never looked better. I'm going to tell Mayor Orlov and the other officials to come to your shop. Keep in mind that eventually you and I will need to arrive at the monthly rent fee that you will pay us to work in this shop. Once we nationalize the bank, you will also need to exchange your Polish zloty currency to Soviet rubles."

"Yes, we can talk more when you come back to the shop. In about a week, you will probably need a haircut. But before you leave to go to visit more businesses, I noticed that you are missing a button on your shirt. Let me walk you over to my brother Anshel's tailor shop next door. I'm sure he can find and sew a replacement button on your shirt for you."

"That's a splendid idea! Do Anshel and his family also live in a small house behind his shop?"

"Yes, that is correct."

The new town marshal and my father left the barbershop with smiles on their faces.

96

About ten minutes later my father returned and said, "That my son is how you defuse a situation by making someone feel comfortable and respected by speaking to them with a calm and friendly voice. As you can see, he is now a satisfied, returning customer. But even more important, since the Soviets are now in control, we, as Jews, need to be in their good favor and show that we are willing to be cooperative. It doesn't matter that he may never pay for the service."

"Nice going, Papa. I am proud of you."

"Yitzhak, carefully remove our Polish work permits from the wall. We might need to show them tomorrow in order to receive our new Soviet identity cards and work permits. I bet Town Marshal Novikov will extend the same offer to Anshel and his family."

Sure enough, Uncle Anshel joined my father and me at the town marshal's office the next morning. We successfully and very quickly received the official Soviet identity cards and work permits. We didn't have to show or forfeit our Polish documents. Once we got home, my father saved all of our family's Polish documents in a secure place so that they wouldn't get lost or misplaced. The new Soviet identity cards indicated our occupation, place of employment, and the address of our residence, in addition to our name, age, and birth date. There was also a large J written on the card to indicate that we were Jewish.

My father added, "With the way we often live in different countries without ever leaving our kitchen table, you never know when these Polish documents will be needed. Today, we live in the Soviet Union. Tomorrow, who knows what country we will live in? Someday, we may need to prove that we were once Polish citizens!"

# A Serious Decision
## September 25, 1939 - June 22, 1941

On the following Monday, September 25th, 1939, the new town marshal had signs posted in the Rynck and on some of the walls of the businesses to announce that the primary schools will open the following week and that synagogues and churches could resume their religious services the coming weekend. This posted announcement seemed to ease my family's nervousness regarding the Soviet's control of our town.

Our regular Jewish customers started returning to the barbershop on that Monday for haircuts, shaves, and moustache trimmings. Hershel Birkenthal was one of them. I immediately recognized him. He owned and operated the local kosher butcher shop where my mom and Aunt Gital shopped every week.

As he entered our shop, my father greeted him very enthusiastically while motioning for him to sit in his barber's chair. "Hershel. It is good to see you. Have you opened your butcher shop?"

"Not yet, Meir. I'm waiting to get the needed beef and chicken from my local supplier. I'm expecting a delivery tomorrow. That's why I have the free time to come and see you for a haircut and shave."

While my father proceeded with the haircut, he continued their conversation by asking, "Have you met our new town marshal, Captain Pavel Novikov? He came to see me last Friday. I was impressed with his cooperative and receptive attitude."

"How so? I haven't met him yet."

"I got the impression that he won't impose too many restrictions on those of us who operate the family-run shops. I'm sure you are aware that the

Soviet Union is a communist country that nationalizes all businesses and claims to own everything, including our homes. After he announced himself, I offered for him to sit in my chair and get a haircut and moustache trim. I think he realized that he looked very unkempt and gladly accepted my offer without any hesitation. I also think he appreciated my gesture, since the tone of his voice softened. Before he left, he offered for my family to be the first to secure the new required Soviet identity cards. If you haven't met him yet, I suggest that you go to the town hall to initiate getting these cards for your family. Please tell him that I suggested this to you."

"Meir, do you think the Soviets will cooperate with us?"

"As long as they are in control, Bolechov's Jewish community should show our appreciation to the Soviets for keeping us safe from the Nazis. We can easily begin to show our appreciation by cooperating with them right away. Most likely, the local Ukrainians, who mainly work on the farms, and possibly some of the local Poles who work at the factories, will be their biggest headache to deal with. If Town Marshal Novikov and the other Soviet officials don't have to be concerned with any issues from the Jewish community, they shouldn't be too harsh on us with restrictions. After all, we are the majority in this town and they really need our cooperation."

"I like your attitude. Let them feel we are the helpful majority."

"Exactly. That's right. Please share this with others and suggest that they get their identity cards right away. Since you know more of the Jewish factory and farm owners, mention to them to initiate their contact with our new town marshal, instead of waiting for him to barge into their businesses. Their gesture of cooperation may allow them to stay on to help the Soviets manage the business operation. Town Marshal Novikov even asked me to help with his issuance of the identity cards. He told me that all of the Jewish families should mention my name to him. This will soften his attitude toward all of us and view us as loyal, cooperative citizens of Bolechov."

"Good idea. Will do. You and I, along with Anshel, need to circulate among the Jewish men before and after Saturday morning's service at the synagogue. This will be a good opportunity to spread the word."

After he left, my father and I were able to take a break and eat the lunch that my mom prepared for us.

While we were eating, I asked my father, "Papa, what does 'nationalization' mean? I heard Town Marshal Novikov say this word to you, and you also said it to Mr. Birkenthal."

"I guess the simplest way to explain this to you is that the Soviet government now owns everything and we are now their employees. That's why the new town marshal said to me that at some point he will need to decide on the amount of rent that I will need to pay in order for us to continue operating this shop."

"Oh. You mean you don't own the barbershop anymore. What about our house?"

"That too. But don't worry. The Soviets are more interested in taking over the large businesses like the leather tanning factory, the grain mill, and all of the farms. Small shops like ours will need to remain open. After all, you and I are the only barbers in Bolechov."

"I have one more question for you, Papa. Now that the primary schools will open and the Soviets are in control, do you think I can begin to attend the high school in Stryi?"

"Yitzhak, as much as your mom and I would like you to begin attending the high school, we need to be careful with spending money right now. We still don't know what will happen when the Polish money is converted into the Soviet rubles. It is best for us, as a family, to refrain from school tuition, books, and transportation expenses until we know more. Do you understand our reason for not sending you right now?"

"Yes, Papa. I think that the family will also need the extra money that I will earn from cutting hair. I understand. I know that I need to help us continue to live."

During the forthcoming months, daily life in Bolechov continued to return to being somewhat normal. In addition to the opening of the primary schools, the churches and the synagogues, Town Marshal Novikov posted new announcement signs on buildings and in the Rynek that anti-Jewish demonstrations and speeches against the Soviet control were forbidden and would be strictly enforced. My father felt this edict was to show his cooperation with the Jewish community and to maintain peaceful relations between the Jewish, Polish, and Ukrainian residents. He also explained to my sister, Leah, and me that Soviet strict enforcement meant sending those who violated their rules to a location in the far eastern area called Siberia as their harsh punishment.

As my father predicted, the factories, warehouses, and farms were immediately nationalized. Many of the Jewish owners were kept on to help operate them. Town Marshal Novikov and other Soviet officials often returned to the barbershop for haircuts, shaves, and moustache trims. My father never charged them, but some offered him a gratuity. During one visit, Town Marshal Novikov informed us that our monthly rent would be ten percent of the shop's monthly proceeds. My father thought this was a reasonable amount and voiced no objection.

The Ukrainian farmers, who formerly owned their farms, met the Soviet nationalization implementation with passive resistance by not working as hard as they used to. A lack of regular food supplies from the agricultural, cattle, and chicken farms resulted in a food shortage. Shops struggled to remain open and very few vendors set up their stalls during the Monday market at the Rynek. In order to solve the food shortage, the Soviets established a food rationing procedure. During one of our family Friday evening Shabbat dinners, my mom and Aunt Gital were very apologetic that they could only serve beet soup, known as borscht, and baked potatoes with the traditional challah bread. "We both waited in line for hours at the butcher shop. The butcher sold out very quickly."

My father responded, "Don't worry. Let me speak with Herschel. Maybe he and I can work something out where I can get some beef or chicken from him."

When the currency transfer occurred, the prices of food and services were cut in half. People raced to the stores and quickly depleted everything that was in stock. This left the stores with nothing to sell for weeks. Our earnings were also cut in half at the barbershop and we needed to gradually raise our price in order to make ends meet. My parents and my aunt and uncle were very wise for being conservative with their money and for stocking our cellars with food.

I understood my parents', Aunt Gital's, and Uncle Anshel's concern and focus regarding our family's livelihood. My sister, Leah, and cousin, Mindel, focused their attention on completing their school assignments and getting good grades. I felt that my focus for the family should be tracking and informing the family about Hitler's moves and, of course, earning as much as I could cutting hair.

"Mama and Papa, is it all right with the two of you if I go to Aunt Gital's and Uncle Anshel's home after dinner to listen to his radio?"

My mom responded, "Why do you want to listen to the radio so much, since Soviets are here to protect us from the Nazis?"

"Mom. It is too quiet right now in Bolechov. Everyone seems to be acting very contently. It just doesn't feel that the current situation with the Soviets will last. I think that Hitler has more tricks up his sleeve that could eventually affect us. Just look at how the Nazis are treating the Jews. This could happen to us!"

After a brief moment of silence, my father spoke. "If you want to keep track of him, go ahead. However, we don't need a daily report from you. Your mom and I have enough to worry about with trying to keep our family fed and safe. Just warn us when Hitler does something that you think will affect our family."

"Okay, Papa. Will do."

I was pleased that my parents were okay with me going next door every evening to listen to the daily evening news report on the radio. I gladly accepted the responsibility to serve my family in this capacity and to warn them when something very urgent happened. In order to keep track of Hitler's army's movements, I started keeping a diary-style notebook and entered what I learned each evening.

My first reports were to let the family know that Warsaw surrendered to the Nazis on Thursday, September 28th, and that the Polish government made their final surrender to Germany and the Soviet Union on Friday, October 6th.

Later, in November, I told my family that Hitler moved his attention away from Poland and advanced his army into Western Europe. My father was pleased with this news. "We can breathe a sigh of relief that Hitler will leave us alone while he terrorizes the Western European countries."

More countries were attacked and either surrendered or signed a peace treaty during the fall of 1939 and the spring of 1940. The Nazis were now in control of the eastern section of Czechoslovakia, Finland, the Netherlands, Belgium, Norway, Luxembourg, and Denmark.

On June 23rd, 1940, I reported to the family that Germany was bombing Paris, and then reported eleven days later that Hitler paraded through Paris, just like he did in Prague. I also shared that Hitler's Luftwaffe was bombing Great Britain. Again, both my father and uncle seemed relieved that Hitler's current attention was not on Eastern Europe.

This all changed during the fall when I mentioned to the family that Hitler's focus had shifted once again toward Eastern Europe. Romania and Hungary joined with the German led Axis allies. This caught my family's attention.

"Anshel. Hitler could soon be headed our way. Don't you agree?"

"I think you are right, Meir. How should we prepare, just in case? Now that Hungary and Romania are part of the German Axis, we can no longer think about escaping there."

Aunt Gital interjected by asking, "Don't you think that what we are hearing about Jews being rounded up and killed at concentration camps is really Soviet propaganda? I just can't believe civilized people would perform such inhumane acts. I know that my father was very proud of the Iron Cross that he earned during the Great War when he fought in the Austrian army. I still have it and will show it to the Germans if they get here!"

104

I could see my mother becoming outraged and annoyed with Aunt Gital. She finally spoke up. "We don't know what to believe these days. I agree with our husbands. We must begin preparing for the worst. If we need to flee somewhere, let's prepare to flee."

Gital replied. "Rifka, how can I flee anywhere? You know my mom is too frail and weak to leave the house. I can't leave her alone. I have to stay here regardless. Anshel, if you want to flee and take Mindel with you, then, just go!"

Mindel yelled back at her mother and started crying. "I don't want to leave you, Mama. Please, please don't send me away. I want to stay here with you and Grandma!"

Anshel replied to console Mindel, "Don't worry, Mindel. I'm not going anywhere. I will stay here with you, Mama and Grandma Feiga. Our family will always be together."

Then, he turned toward my father. "Meir, do you think that Aneta will hide us in her cellar?"

"Anshel, she has already put herself at risk by confiding with us the previous actions taken by the Ukrainian men. I don't want to put her and her family at any additional risk. No, I will not ask her. But if we decide to flee, I will let her know. I trust that she will keep our escape a secret from others and not tell anyone. "

My father continued. "I'm not sure where we could flee or hide. The Germans would eventually find us hiding in our cellars. We wouldn't last long trying to hide in the forest without any shelter or food."

The family debate about hiding or fleeing continued during the forthcoming weeks. My father was more inclined to consider fleeing than Uncle Anshel. The question was, 'where to flee'? If we crossed the former Polish-Soviet border without any authorization, we could risk being sent by the authorities to Siberia as prisoners.

When Yugoslavia and Greece surrendered to Germany in April 1941, I notified the family. Hitler's move into these countries made it very clear that his military force was moving closer toward us. Again, the four adults in my family debated whether to remain or flee, without reaching any agreement.

The worst scenario happened on Saturday, June $21^{st}$, 1941. Hitler broke the pact with the Soviet Union and ordered his army to invade Soviet-controlled Eastern Poland. The German army's invasion started the very next day by implementing their lightning Blitzkrieg military strategy that included massive Luftwaffe air attacks.

The German Invasion of the Soviet Union
1941-1942

For two days, Bolechov was at a standstill. My father and I sat in front of the barbershop and noticed that the center of the town was empty without any movement. There was complete silence, since the mill and factories were not operating. The synagogues, churches, and schools were also closed. It seemed like everyone in the town was staying home and waiting to see what the Soviet government and military would do to fight the German army.

*Would the Soviet army prevent the Nazis from conquering Eastern Poland and advancing into the Soviet Union?*

Since Bolechov and the larger cities in our area were located close to the east bank of the Bug River, the German army could attack us within days.

On Monday morning, June 23rd, I rushed over to my uncle's home to turn on the radio to listen to a news report. All I could hear was static as I turned the radio's tuning dial.

I kept thinking: *How close are the Nazis to Bolechov? What will we do when they march into or bomb our town?*

When my father and I opened the shop in the early morning and sat outside, there was still no sign of movement from the Soviet officials who had offices in the town hall or any presence of the Soviet military. This seemed rather odd, considering that the Nazis were headed in our direction. We did see a young man, who worked as an office clerk, posting signs announcing that the schools, synagogues, churches, and the Rynek Monday market would remain closed until further notice.

A few minutes later we saw Town Marshal Novikov exiting the town hall and very briskly walking toward our shop. My father greeted him and asked him to come inside and sit in his chair. Once he got inside, it became apparent he was in a hurry to speak quickly to my father and then leave. He remained standing.

"Meir. I got word early this morning from Moscow that Stalin's evacuation plan is about to begin."

My father looked very puzzled.

"Yes, this might sound to you like a big surprise. Again, our great leader, Joseph Stalin, has a brilliant plan already prepared. His evacuation plan is exactly what Russia did years ago when Napoleon tried to conquer all of Europe, and what we did when armies threatened to invade Russia during the Great War. We are evacuating by moving our superior military to the east, as well as our essential war effort factories. My assignment is to select specific families to join us with our evacuation. We will need more people to work at collective farms to produce the needed food for those that we move. I am offering you and your family the opportunity to escape with us to Soviet-controlled Uzbekistan and work at one of our collective farms. Do you want to go with us?"

My father looked a bit perplexed by his offer. "Thank you for including us, Town Marshal Novikov. When will this evacuation begin?

"We will secretly leave from the train station tomorrow evening at nine o'clock. If you want to go, you need to be at my office at eight o'clock tomorrow morning. I will fill out the official registration cards and travel permits that you and your family will need to show when you arrive at the train station evacuation centers, at the boat dock at Odessa, and when you arrive in Tashkent, Uzbekistan."

My father asked, "What about Anshel and his family? Can they also go with us?"

"He and his family can also go. However, you must not tell anyone else. There is only a limited amount of room on the trains. Our military, government officials, dignitaries, selected factory workers, and their families are our priority. I am adding you and your family and some of the other Jewish businessmen to show my appreciation for cooperating with the Soviet Union. Be on time at my office tomorrow morning and be prepared to be at the train station no later than 8:30 in the evening."

Town Marshal Novikov quickly turned around and exited the shop before my father could even thank him for his offer.

"Yitzhak, while I pack up all of our barber equipment and supplies, along with all of our official documents, go find Anshel and tell him to immediately come to our house. He may be inside his shop or he might be at his home. Go now, and hurry."

Within twenty minutes, my entire extended family, except for Aunt Feiga, gathered in my family's living room and waited for my father to return from the barbershop.

He finally raced into the house and placed his barber's box, equipment, and a folder of documents on the kitchen table.

"Listen, everyone. There is now an escape plan for us. Town Marshal Novikov offered all of us to be part of an evacuation plan. The Soviet Union is moving officials, dignitaries, their families, along with some military and factory workers. We can go with them to work on a collective farm located in Soviet-controlled Uzbekistan. It will be a long journey to get there by train and boat. If we want to go, we need to go to his office early tomorrow morning and obtain the needed official documents. We will have to be on the train that leaves tomorrow night!"

Aunt Gital was the first to comment. "Let me understand, Meir. Are you suggesting that we agree to go to a Soviet labor camp? How will that camp be safer for us than a German labor camp? Do you really trust the Soviets? Look at what they did to our ancestors years ago when their armed Cossacks came through to murder us?"

"Gital, I understand your concern. At this point, the Nazis are the ones treating the Jewish people harshly, not the Soviets. There have been no reports of Jews being dragged out of the homes and beaten by members of the Soviet government and their military like the Nazis have been doing. I feel we have a better chance of survival if we flee and agree to the Soviet's terms. Anshel, what are your thoughts?"

"Meir, if you think it is best for you and your family to flee with the Soviets, then go. I will give you all of the rubles that I have for you to take with you. They will be worthless to us once the Germans get here. Give me a jacket and I will sew the money inside the jacket's lining to keep it safe."

"Thanks, Anshel. You and your family may need valuables to offer as bribes to the Nazis. Rifka, please gather all of our jewelry and give them to Gital. Of course, Anshel and Gital, take from our home whatever you want and the food stored in the cellar. Do it quickly, because once people learn that we are gone, this house will be raided and looted. Just so you know, we will make the same offer to Aneta and her family."

The preparation for our escape commenced with great speed. Aneta arrived at our home about a half hour later and my mom informed her of our escape plan. The two of them, along with my sister, Leah, washed four empty glass jars and covers for us to use as drinking water containers. While Aneta started baking small bread rolls for us to take with us, my mom selected the clothing and bedding items that we would need, along with four large pillowcases for us to carry our belongings. She packed each pillowcase with a few small towels, soap, toothpaste, a toothbrush, and either a hairbrush or comb. My mother also selected a light jacket, a warm sweater, and comfortable walking shoes for each of us to wear. For my father and me, she found long sleeve cotton shirts, thick cotton pants, and a cap or us to wear on our heads. She also selected long-sleeve cotton housedresses, cotton stockings, and headscarves for Leah and her to wear on the train.

My father and I placed his barber equipment kit with all of our tools, including other barber supplies, and a satchel filled with our family's legal documents into his suitcase that he could keep locked. Later in the day, my mom and Aneta selected some stored food items from our cellar for us to take with us without our pillowcases being too heavy to carry.

My father and I left our house at 7:15 a.m. the next morning to get to Town Marshal Novikov's office area early enough to be the first in line. When we got there, a long line had been already formed. We waited and stood in line until 9:30 when we were finally called to go inside.

"Meir. I'm very pleased that you and your family decided to come with us. Let me start filling out the forms as you tell me the full name of each family member, their birth date, and place of birth. The forms will list your destination as Tashkent, Uzbekistan, and your assignment as collective farm workers. I will add barber to your card and your son's card. I'll list kitchen worker as the occupation for your wife and daughter. You are taking your barber's tools with you, aren't you?"

My father nodded affirmatively.

Within a few minutes, he gave us our sets of travel permits and registration cards, all stamped with an official Soviet seal. I noticed that he added a large J on all of the cards to indicate that we were Jewish.

"Remember to be at the train station early tonight and not tell anyone where you are going. The train will leave in darkness. I can't promise that you will have seats. There is a seating priority and, most likely, you will have to be as comfortable as you can in the baggage car. Keep in mind, there will be many stops and train transfers. Look for the official Evacuation Center at the stations and show them these cards. This is how you will receive your tickets for the next train or boat. Good luck to all of you. You'll like Tashkent. We call it the 'City of Bread!' Maybe we'll see each other again in the future."

My father thanked him, and we left the town hall very quickly to get home to help my mom, Leah, and Aneta complete the preparation for our nighttime departure. My mother found pieces of rope to tie around the top of the pillowcases to make it easier for each of us to carry them across our shoulders.

Before leaving to return to her home in the late afternoon to prepare and serve dinner to her husband, Aneta asked to speak to the four of us, "Please come back. I'll be waiting for you." She gave each of us a big hug and then left through the back kitchen door as tears flowed down her face.

Aunt Rifka and Uncle Anshel prepared dinner for all us. As we all sat down at their dining room table, we realized that this meal might be the last time we would be together as a complete family. It was a somber evening, and we all displayed very sad faces. No one spoke, for fear of sobbing.

Finally, my father, with tearing eyes, offered a prayer of hope. "Let us pray and ask God to help us all survive. And when this madness finally ends, we will be joined together once again."

We all replied, "Amen."

8 o'clock arrived very quickly and my family went back to our house. My father gathered us together into our living room. We formed a tight circle, held hands, and he said the following words. "Your mother and I have always told you, Yitzhak and Leah, that we will keep our family safe and survive. We are about to go on a very long and difficult journey into the unknown. But one thing is true. We are escaping, so that we can survive and continue to live. We are not cowards. We are survivors. We may face difficulties and hardships. Even so, we can handle whatever comes our way because we are a strong family. As long as we stay together, and love each other, we can face anything.

"Yitzhak, you will turn eighteen in a few weeks. Leah, you are already sixteen. The two of you are not young children anymore. You may be assigned to perform adult work at the collective farm. Your mom and I know that we can count on you to accept whatever faces us without any complaints.

"Is everyone ready to go and walk quietly in the dark to get to the train station?"

We all nodded our heads, and we quickly put on our jackets and head coverings.

"Then, let's go. Rifka, go ahead and turn off all of the lights. There is no sense locking the door and taking the house keys. Now, as we walk quickly to the train station, we need to be very quiet to not attract anyone's attention. I think very few people know that the Soviets are leaving tonight and that many people from Bolechov are leaving with them."

My father led the way through the dark alleys to get us to the street where the train station was located. It was a pleasant cool summer night with a light breeze. The sky was clear with visible stars and a moon that cast a dim light to help guide our way.

*As I left my home, possibly for the last time, and walked slowly through the silence and darkness to get to the train station, I realized the reality of our escape to a country that I never heard of before.*

*The Bolechov that I knew and loved as a child no longer existed. I am going far away from the Nazis, and where Hitler's persecution of the Jewish people won't reach us.*

*My father and mother are correct. We will all survive and live!*

# The Journey Begins
## June 24, 1941

Map Source: Nations Online Project

As my parents, my sister, Leah, and I quietly walked through the alley toward the train station, I felt a strange stillness. It was as if the entire town was fast asleep, including all of the household pets, chickens, and animals. It was eerie not hearing any sound, other than the soft touch of our shoes stepping onto the alley's dirt. This feeling of solitude continued as we crossed a main street and then walked through another alley that went between two of the town's large factories.

All of a sudden, I heard some noises that sounded like horses whinnying.

"Papa. What is that sound? Is it horses?"

"I hear it too, Yitzhak. It's hard to tell what it is in this darkness."

The whining sound got louder the closer we approached the train station's main street. Sure enough, when we got to the main street, we saw two horses attached to numerous horse-drawn wooden open wagons. They were lined up past the train station to our left and even more horse-drawn wagons to our right. All of these wagons were positioned to face toward the Rynek Town Square.

Leah asked, "Papa, what are all of these wagons doing here?"

"I don't know. I see that there is a long line of people up ahead. Why don't the three of you get in line and I'll try to find out what's going on?"

While we were standing still and waiting in the line, I took a good look around. I noticed that two Soviet soldiers were standing by each wagon, with one holding a rifle and a lit lantern. There was also a line of passenger cars alongside the wagons pointed in the same direction. This really raised my curiosity and concern for the purpose of all of these wagons.

My father returned to us about twenty minutes later. "The railway director, along with Town Marshal Novikov, are issuing wagon boarding cards to those with travel permits. Apparently, the train to Ternopil cannot get here. The Nazi Luftwaffe is bombing and attacking Lviv. The Lviv railroad station and the train tracks were all bombed. The Soviet army sent these wagons to take us to Ternopil, where we will board a train. The wagons that you see will join a longer convoy once we get to Stanislavov."

I asked, "What about all of these passenger cars?"

"I assume, Yitzhak, that the town officials, business owners, and those with their own vehicles will go ahead and drive to Stanislavov or Ternopil."

My mom then asked him, "Are we going there tonight?"

"It appears so. When we get to the front of the line, we should be able to get more answers."

The line slowly inched forward. We noticed that many people voiced loud angry remarks at the railway director and town marshal when they were denied a boarding card and could not flee with the Soviet army. I soon realized why my father tried very hard to cooperate with Town Marshal Novikov and win his favor. We were very fortunate to receive the official travel documents that will make our journey possible and, hopefully, with little interruption.

"Ah, Meir and family. Here are your boarding cards. You will be riding in wagon number eight. Look for the wagon with this number and show the boarding cards to the wagon's army sergeant and private."

"Town Marshal Novikov, when will we be leaving? How can we leave tonight in the dark?"

"Two of our master sergeants will lead the procession in one of our military cars with the headlights turned on to guide the way. Another two master sergeants will drive a car at the end. We need to leave tonight since our army is expecting us to arrive in Stanislavov tomorrow morning."

"That's good to know. Thank you Town Marshal Novikov, for all of your help."

My mom, sister, and I also thanked him.

My family walked between the wagons and passenger cars to look for wagon number eight. For some odd reason, the wagons were not lined up in a numerical sequence. When we got to the front of the convoy and didn't find it, we turned around and walked in the other direction. Our wagon was located three wagons from the end, and as the town marshal told us, two Soviet soldiers were standing next to it.

My father, being our family spokesperson, showed the soldiers our boarding cards. The older of the two spoke up. "We also need to see your travel permits. We need to confirm that all of you have official permission to travel with us."

After seeing our permits, the soldier continued, "Place your belongings in the back of the wagon.

117

You, Sir, I see you also have a small piece of luggage. Only one piece of baggage is allowed."

My father showed and pointed to our travel permits. He explained very politely, "You see, officer, my stamped travel permit and my son's stamped travel permit states that the two of us are barbers and we are being sent to be barbers. The town marshal told us to bring our barber tools. Our tools are in this small handbag. My son and I will gladly give you and your colleague a haircut during one of the rest stops."

"Really, you would do that for free?"

"Of course."

"Well, in that case, by all means put your bag in the cart. Thanks."

The younger soldier even helped my mother and sister climb into the wagon. Once the four of us were seated, I whispered to my father, "Papa. You really know how to get your way with kindness and cooperation. I'm really proud of you."

"Thank you, my son. All I ask of you is to follow my lead, and you should do well in life by getting along with others."

It took about an hour for those traveling in the wagons to get processed by the soldiers. A family of six, that we didn't recognize, squeezed into our wagon. Their father mentioned to us he was being sent to work at an ammunition factory.

When I observed Town Marshal Novikov getting into one of the passenger cars, I knew that we would depart shortly for our nighttime wagon ride to Stanislavov.

As our wagon started moving forward, I soon learned that sitting on a wooden bench was not going to be very comfortable. In order to remain in our seated position, we had to hold onto the wagon's sideboards. I could tell that Leah was also having difficulty getting adjusted to riding in the wagon. She asked my mom, "How are we supposed to get some sleep as we are being rocked forward and backward and from side to side?"

My father addressed her concern. "Leah. This journey may not be as comfortable as sleeping in your bed. Just remember that every day that we are together is a day that we stay alive and not killed by the Nazis. Just do your best to handle this. It may take us about three to four hours to get to Stanislavov. Most likely, there will be time to sleep and rest when we get there. After all, the army needs to stop to feed and water these horses."

"Okay, Papa. I will try my best."

The older soldier held the horse reins and gave the needed commands to the two horses, while the younger one served as his navigator. Our wagon soon got to the end of the street and turned right onto the town's main street adjacent to the Rynek Town Square. I was surprised that the noise from the procession didn't wake up anyone. No one came outside. The convoy soon left the center of the town and proceeded along the dirt road that led to Stanislavov. My father was the only one of our family who had ever been to that city. The moon and the front and rear cars' headlights cast enough light for me to see the road's surroundings. I found it interesting to view the farms, farmhouses, and barns that dotted the horizon. About a half hour later, all that was visible were the trees that lined both sides of the road and the shadow of forests in the distance. Somehow, I fell asleep by resting my head on my mom's right shoulder.

Hours later, I heard my mom's voice. "Wake up, Yitzhak and Leah. Stanislavov is in the distance. Here are your hats. Put them on to protect your faces from the sun."

Yes, the peeking sun revealed the skyline of a major city in the distance. I had never seen a city so large.

About an hour later, as the sun rose even higher and we could see the city's tallest buildings, the younger soldier's hand-held radio started beeping. He answered it and listened to a coded sounding message. Once the call ended, he turned around and announced to all of us, "We are not going to stop in the city center. The military convoy is waiting for us north of Stanislavov. I will know more when we arrive. The ride is going to get even bumpier. Just hold on as best you can."

The convoy turned onto a smaller country road. The soldier's warning was accurate. The wagon often swayed side to side as it meandered along. It took us another two hours to meet up with the other convoy that was waiting for us.

When our wagon finally came to a halt, the soldier informed us, "You might as well get out and get some rest. Don't go too far away. I don't know how long we will be here."

The younger soldier left his seat and offered his hand to my sister and smiled. "Let me help you get down, miss."

"Thank you, kind sir."

I noticed that both of them looked directly at each other with big smiling faces.

*Were they flirting with each other? The young soldier didn't look much older than me. This was the first time I noticed that Leah knew anything about flirting with young men.*

*It dawned on me. She is sixteen years old and now a young woman. Hmm. I may need to keep a brotherly eye on her. I wonder if my parents*

120

*have thought to talk to her about how to deal with flirtations from men?*

The four of us found a tree that offered shade from the sun. My mom retrieved her pillowcase and offered each of us a drink of water from a glass container and one of the small rolls that she and Aneta had baked.

About ninety minutes later, the older soldier gathered us up.

"Listen everyone. There has been a slight change of plans. The Nazi Luftwaffe is now bombing near Ternopil. The convoy will continue heading north. But as we approach Ternopil, we will once again ride along a narrow country road to connect to another main road that leads east to Kyiv. So, be prepared to ride for a long time. We may not get to our next rest stop and spend the night until near sunset. We will depart in about thirty minutes."

Then the soldier walked over to my father. "Sir, my colleague and I won't be able to take you up on your offer just yet. How about giving us a haircut when we stop for the evening?

"Sure, sergeant. It can wait for later."

When the officer walked away, Leah approached my father. "Papa. How did you know he was a sergeant and not a private?"

"He has a triangle on his military sleeve emblem, and the private does not. That's how you can tell."

"Oh, I see", was her response.

*Ah, I was right by her inquisitiveness. I could tell Leah does have some interest with this young private. Hmm.*

The sergeant was correct. After thirty minutes

passed, we boarded the wagon to continue to reach Ternopil.

Once the convoy traveled a short distance, the country road connected back onto the main road that headed north to Ternopil. As we traveled onward, we encountered large groups of people walking and carrying their belongings. Some were pulling or pushing carts with bags and suitcases, their children, or their elderly family members. When they saw the convoy, many of them started running toward us and screamed, "Stop! Stop! Take my child with you!"

I asked my father. "Papa. What's going on?"

"These people are refugees fleeing from the Nazis. Many may have come from Lviv or other towns and villages west of Lviv. Yes, it is frightening to see so many people trying to survive. All we can do is try our best to survive, like these people are attempting to do."

We saw a countless number of refugees as our convoy continued heading toward Ternopil. Many were camped alongside the road and begging others for food and water. It was heartbreaking actually seeing the affect that the Nazi invasion was having on so many people. I realized how fortunate my family was to be able ride in these wagons and flee from the Nazis. We could be like these people, who I see walking and begging.

Hours went by and the convoy was still heading north toward Ternopil on the main road. The railroad tracks were now visible, but there was no indication that any trains were operating.

As the convoy continued for about another hour, the private's hand-held radio started buzzing again. He listened to another coded message.

Once again, when he was finished, he turned to us. "Listen up. I was just informed that the Nazi Luftwaffe is bombing the railroad tracks up ahead and bombing west of Ternopil. All trains have ceased operating. Bombing the train station might be the Luftwaffe's next target. Therefore, it is confirmed that we will not stop in Ternopil. Instead, we will directly go to the main road that heads east to Kyiv and stop at a village to spend the night. A supply truck from the Ternopil station's Evacuation Center will meet us at this village. I'm not sure how long it will take us to get there. The master sergeant leading our convoy will soon find a safe place for us to stop for a quick fifteen-minute break. Again, when we stop, don't venture too far."

About ten minutes later, all of the wagons pulled over to the right side of the road where there were no refugees. When we stopped, the private got out of his front seat to help Leah climb down. I observed both of them smiling at each other again.

It felt good to take a short break to stand up and stretch from sitting on the wooden bench for hours. Like before, my mom made sure we all drank some water and ate a piece from one of her baked rolls.

As the convoy continued to go northward to get closer to Ternopil, I noticed a lot of black smoke in the distance. As we got closer to a small village, we could see that the Nazis bombed the railroad tracks. Later, there was more visible smoke in the distance, and we could see some flames stretching into the sky. Again, the railroad tracks at this village were bombed and the village's small train station was on fire.

More refugees, most likely from these villages, ran after us attempting to join our convoy. It was heartbreaking to know that we could not help everyone that we saw trying to find a safe place from the invading Nazis.

An hour later, Ternopil appeared in the distance. The private's information was correct. There were pillars of black smoke coming from the western side of this city.

When the convoy reached a village called Velyki Hi, the wagons turned right onto another road to circle around the east side of Ternopil. We quickly reached a paved main road that led to Kyiv. Since Ternopil was a very large city, even more people were seen fleeing on this paved road. Those riding in trucks and cars sped past us.

The convoy eventually pulled off the main road during the late afternoon onto a very narrow dirt road. I noticed a small sign. Smykivtsi was the name of the small village where we would spend the night. Small farms with quaint cottage-like, single story farmhouses formed a picturesque landscape.

The convoy stopped alongside a narrow river that flowed through the village. Smykivtsi was the perfect secluded place for us to stop and avoid being confronted by the fleeing refugees. It remained unscathed from the Luftwaffe's bombing maneuvers.

When we got out of our wagon with our belongings, the sergeant pointed to the supply truck parked in front of a church. To everyone's delight and surprise, members of the church greeted and led us to a small social hall, where they had already prepared vegetable soup and slices of bread. All of the soldiers joined us later, after they watered the horses at the river.

My mom pulled us aside and told us that before it got dark, she would give us a bar of soap and towel for us to wash ourselves at a secluded spot along the river. "We need to keep ourselves clean so we don't get body lice!"

After eating the soup and bread, we quietly left the social hall with our belongings, bathed in the river, and entered the church sanctuary to find an open pew to stretch out and instantly fall sleep.

# The Wagon Route Continues
## June 27, 1941 - July 24, 1941

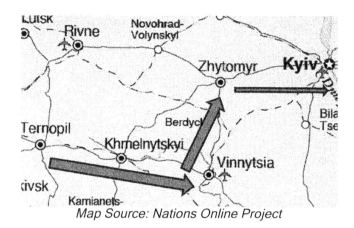

*Map Source: Nations Online Project*

The loud ringing from the Smykivtsi church bell tower woke up everyone. I stretched out on the church pew the best that I could, raised myself up, and saw that my mother and father were already awake. I asked them, "What's going on? Why are they waking us up? Are we about to leave?"

My father replied, "No, son. They're letting us know there are slices of bread and tea available in the social hall. I'm going to go in to see if any of the military officials are there and can tell us the details about our departure. Come with me and help bring back some bread and tea for all of us."

I followed my father into the social hall. A few of the sergeants were inside and we learned from them that our departure is scheduled for the following day, in order for more supplies to arrive.

After consuming the meager breakfast, my father and I took a stroll to see if we could find our wagon's sergeant and private, while my mother and Leah went to help the church volunteers in the kitchen.

"Yitzhak. I have a plan regarding the soldiers' haircuts. Don't act surprised with what I am going to say and do."

"Yes, Papa."

We found them at the supply truck sitting and chatting with the other soldiers.

"Are you two ready for your haircuts?"

They replied very enthusiastically, "Yes, sir!"

"While my son and I get our equipment, grab some crates from the truck that you can sit on. We'll be right back."

When my father and I returned, the two were already sitting on the crates and waiting for us.

"We're going to give both of you a short clipper cut. You will have short hair when we are finished. This type of haircut will help you feel cooler in the hot sun, and it will be easier for you to keep your head clean when you bathe or wash."

As we proceeded, some of the people escaping with us, along with other soldiers, surrounded us to see what we were doing. Many people from the convoy inquired if they could also get haircuts. My father responded, "A haircut will cost you one ruble or some food in exchange."

When a sergeant or private asked, my father told them, "I need to first speak with your commander in charge before my son and I can make any additional military personnel haircut commitments."

I now understood from my father's comments, that giving haircuts was going to be our method of providing food for our family while we were on this long journey.

An hour after finishing the two haircuts and cleaning up, a junior lieutenant approached my father. "I'm Lieutenant Gusev, in charge of this convoy's operation. I noticed the haircuts that you both gave to my two soldiers. Those short haircuts are a good idea. I like it. It will last them many weeks, and it will help them keep cool and clean. What will it take for you to give short haircuts to the rest of the soldiers on this convoy?"

"Thank you, lieutenant. My son and I are licensed barbers. My wife and daughter are traveling with us, so we are a family of four. How about this? Instead of paying our usual fee, we will gladly give your soldiers haircuts, probably a few at a time during the end-of-day rest stops, in exchange for furnishing my family with your military food rations."

"Well, sir. I can do that. But you must understand that all I can share with you are the canned goods that the military normally eats when they are away from camp or from a military base. Our supply truck is stocked with self-opening cans of tushonka meat stew mixed with vegetables, tea, water, condensed milk, and some black bread."

"Those will be enough to keep my family alive. You got yourself a deal, lieutenant. If you have some soap and a towel that I could use, I will gladly give you a complimentary shave. "

"Thank you. I will take you up on the shave offer. Just come to the supply wagon at each stop and see me. I'll give you the rations. Come with me now and I'll go ahead and give you some. I'm not sure what the church will be able to provide us this evening, with the limited food supply that we gave them when we arrived yesterday."

*Wow. My father is very clever making this bargain with the lieutenant to obtain food for us!*

When my father shared this food arrangement with my mother and sister, my mom surprised me with her question. "Oy vey, Meir. How are we going to keep Kosher? We have no idea what kind of meat will be in those tushonka cans!"

"Rifka, God will understand. God commands us to do our best to stay alive. Don't worry. We won't be punished for not keeping Kosher."

"Well, Meir, I also made some arrangements when Leah and I were helping in the kitchen. The church ladies are going to let me refill our water containers from their well before tomorrow's departure!"

The church bells woke us up, once again, the next morning. After eating a slice of bread and drinking some canned tea, it was time to board the wagons and continue the long journey to Kyiv. When we got to our wagon and placed our belongings in the back, I asked the private, "How far do you think we will go today?"

"This will depend upon how crowded the road will be with all of the people escaping to Kyiv. Our lieutenant thinks that we may be able to travel about one hundred kilometers (*sixty miles*) each day. If his estimate is correct, we should reach the large town, called Khmelnytskyi, later today. There are two other large towns that we should reach on the following days on our way to Kyiv. Even though the trains are not operating, official Evacuation Centers are in place inside the train stations at these larger towns, and they are supposed to have more supplies for our convoy. Kyiv is the place where you and your family will connect to a train. The lieutenant informed all of the soldiers during this morning's briefing, that our convoy should reach Kyiv in four more days."

He continued, "On our way, we will go through a series of small villages for our rest stops. We may have to spend the night at some of them. It will all depend upon the pedestrian and vehicle traffic. I'll keep everyone informed of our progress and plans, like I did the other day."

Our convoy was very long with twenty wagons, each carrying ten people and two soldiers, a military vehicle in the front leading the convoy, and the supply truck in the rear. When the convoy tried to reenter the paved, two-lane main road from the village, the road was already heavily packed with refugees walking, carrying sacks of belongings over their shoulders, or pulling carts. Others were attempting to ride their bicycles, while many others were riding in cars, horse-drawn carts, and trucks. The escalated number of refugees on this road created a heavy, slow moving traffic situation. When a vehicle came in the opposite direction, people had to move over to merge into the other lane. In order for our long convoy to enter the road, two of the soldiers from the leading car stepped out of the car and blocked and halted all of the traffic coming from both directions.

I became concerned about this very slow pace. *Reaching a daily distance of 100 kilometers was simply unrealistic.*

My assessment was correct. We only traveled less than thirty kilometers each day, and often had to spend the night in one of the small villages. When staying at a small village overnight became apparent, the military car leading the convoy maneuvered through the human and vehicle traffic to go ahead into the small village to find our resting spot. They also inquired if churches could open for us to sleep. Often, when the local farmers saw our convoy entering their village, many gathered fruit items, loaves of bread, and some offered stew or soup to sell to us at inflated prices. After witnessing my father and me giving the soldiers their haircuts, the locals were often willing to barter with my father with their food in exchange for their haircut. To everyone's disappointment, not all of the small villages where we stopped had churches that could open up for us. There were nights when we had to find an outdoor place to sleep.

It took the convoy four days to travel one hundred kilometers to reach the Khmelnytskyi train station on June 30th. The private was correct. There was an official Evacuation Center, even though there were no trains. Before we left our wagon, the sergeant and private informed us to take all of our belongings and documents with us. "You will need to check in at the Evacuation Center and show them your documents, including your wagon boarding card that will be re-validated. If you don't have your wagon boarding card anymore, go to the supply wagon and see the lieutenant. When we depart, you will need to show this validated boarding card to us, since there are other refugees at the station who may attempt to take your place."

We followed the same Evacuation Center check-in and validation procedure when we arrived at the other two large towns. It also took us two or three days to get to each of them, depending upon the distance. Before each stop, our wagon's two soldiers informed us of where the convoy would be located and when we should return. At all of these locations, our departure was delayed a day or two, due to the late arrival of military supplies.

Each train station's Evacuation Center was supposed to issue food ration coupons to documented evacuees. We all soon learned that this was not always the case. These centers were overcrowded with hundreds of documented and undocumented people attempting to flee eastward from the Nazis. My family was fortunate to find a corner inside each station where we could lay on the floor and place our pillowcase sacks to rest against the wall.

During the first day when we finally arrived at each of these large towns, my father went exploring to find a location for giving haircuts at a town square or park that was close to the station. Once he returned, the four of us followed him with all of our belongings. He always found someone who would agree to receive a free haircut. This attracted the attention of others. I convinced him to allow me to give children's haircuts at half price, along with trimming young girl's bangs or their hair length. Following his example, I gave a free haircut to a young boy in order to attract some business.

While we were busy giving haircuts and guarding our family's belongings, my father gave my mom some rubles for her and Leah to use to buy us some food and look for a place with clean drinking water to refill our drinking containers. At the end of the afternoon, the four of us returned to the train station, found a covered spot to lie down, eat what my mom and Leah purchased, and, then, do our best to get some sleep. If the station had a private place with running water at a sink, my mom insisted that we wash ourselves as best as we could, wash our undergarments, and change into fresh ones. My mom always found a spot where she could hang and dry the wet towels and clothes.

On July 2nd, when we arrived and stopped for the night at the local village, Medzhybizh, we learned from one of the village leaders, that the Nazis conquered Lviv, Ternopil, and Minsk. The following day, we learned that Stalin made a speech and announced his Scorched Earth Policy. He urged the Soviet citizens living in Leningrad, Stalingrad, and

Moscow to flee eastward. He ordered everyone, "Leave nothing for the enemy!"

When our convoy resumed the next day on July 4th from the small village, of Letychiv, we noticed that even more people, cars, and wagons were on the road fleeing to the east. The pace on the road was much slower due to the increase of people and vehicles.

I became concerned that Stalin's order to the Soviet citizens from these major cities to evacuate, would make it impossible for us to board a train to travel all the way to Tashkent.

*Would we have to ride in this uncomfortable wooden wagon for months and months in order to get there?*

Two more weeks transpired since the convoy left the small town located east of Ternopil. By July 5th, we had yet to reach the third large town, Zhytomyr, the closest large town to Kyiv!

*Will we ever get to Kyiv? How many people will be at the train station? Will their Evacuation Center be better organized than what we have experienced so far? Will we even connect to a train? When will we finally get to Tashkent?*

The convoy finally arrived in Zhytomyr on July 15th, and there were still five more small villages ahead of us before we would reach Kyiv. The four of us, along with the rest of the convoy escapees, were exhausted from this long and grueling experience. Many complained about the lack of food and water and having to sleep outdoors. Only four of the ten people riding in a wagon could lie down comfortably inside the wagon to sleep. Fortunately, summer was our dry season with very little rain, and we could sleep outside without any overhead structural cover.

My mom noticed many people scratching themselves and picking at their skin. She ordered us, "Stay away from those people. They have body lice. Continue washing yourselves as best as you can so that you will avoid getting body lice!"

The final small village before reaching Kyiv was called Sofivska. We arrived there on July 21$^{st}$. Fortunately, their local church's main sanctuary was open for those on our convoy to spend the night by either sleeping on the pews or on the floor. On the next morning, the convoy's commanding officer, Lieutenant Gusev, called everyone into the sanctuary so that he could deliver an official briefing about our expected arrival in Kyiv.

He raised his hands in order to get everyone's attention. Once there was total silence, he began his address.

"On behalf of our great Secretary General of the Communist Party, Joseph Stalin, and his superior Soviet army, we thank you for your cooperation. I understand that your local officials stated that a train would be your means of transportation. Riding in wooden wagons is not the most comfortable and my soldiers are trying their best to accommodate you. I know that all of you are anxious to get to Kyiv and finally begin your train journey.

"I received orders from the Kyiv military headquarters this morning. There is a change of plans due to the recent Soviet evacuation command issued by Secretary General Stalin. The trains in Kyiv will be used for the next few weeks to transport the Soviet military to outposts near Leningrad, Moscow, and Stalingrad. The military has immediate priority to use all available trains."

Someone yelled out, "What about us?"

Others responded, "Yeah, what about us?"

This loud outcry continued until the lieutenant raised his hands again to get everyone's attention.

"No need to worry. Let me reassure you that you and your families will not be abandoned. I already received clearance from headquarters to continue our convoy from Kyiv and take all of you to Kharkiv where you will definitely continue your journey to Uzbekistan by riding the trains. The employers at the factories and farms are eagerly waiting for your arrival."

After a few moments of silence, the lieutenant continued. "Our convoy will stop and drop you off tomorrow in front of the Kyiv train station. As you have done before, you will need to check with the Kyiv train station's Evacuation Center and show them your documents and get your wagon boarding card re-validated. The center will issue you food coupons to use at a soup kitchen area that is established for documented evacuees, like all of you. My soldiers and I will return in three days after another convoy arrives from Ternopil. This convoy will join us all the way to Kharkiv. We will meet you on July 27th at 9 a.m. at the same spot where we dropped you off. Please be there on time with your belongings and documentation. Come and see me if you have any questions or concerns. The Soviet army thanks you for your understanding and cooperation."

# Onward to Kharkiv
## July 27, 1941- August 5, 1941

*Map Source: Nations Online Project*

My family was not pleased at all with the lieutenant's report that our wagon convoy would continue to transport us instead of a train. We already spent nearly a month riding on a very uncomfortable wooden bench, sleeping on the floors and pews inside churches, occasionally sleeping outside during rather cool evenings, and having to eat nasty-tasting military canned food rations. More importantly than our level of discomfort riding inside the wagons, our biggest concern was the slow progress of our journey to get to Uzbekistan. The reports that we heard about the Nazi army's fast eastward progression through Poland were a frightening reality that could affect us.

Whenever one of us complained, my father always reminded us, "Every day that we are together, is another day that we are still alive!"

As the convoy rode through the streets of Kyiv during the late afternoon, I was surprised to see how huge a city it was. Since I was used to living in a very small town, Kyiv looked to me like it was at least one hundred times the size of Bolechov. It took our convoy about an hour to cross through the city to reach where the train station was located.

135

When we finally arrived, the convoy turned left and circled around a very large triangular-shaped square across from the train station's main entrance. There was a park inside the middle of this square. Once the convoy stopped, our wagon's private helped everyone get out and also helped all ten of us to retrieve our belongings.

Once again, I was surprised that my sister, Leah, initiated a conversation with him. "Are you sure that you will come back to get us and won't leave us stranded here?"

"Don't worry, miss. Our lieutenant values promptness and is a man of his word. We will be here waiting for you on the 27$^{th}$ at nine in the morning. I'll see you then. You can count on it."

After my family had all of our belongings, my mother, sister, and I followed our father into the park. He asked us to sit on one of the empty park benches, so that he could talk to us.

"As you can see, the Kyiv train station is immense with lots of people. Most likely it is jammed packed with Soviet soldiers waiting to board the trains and a massive amount of people crowded together. We will need to stay very close to each other and not get distracted and wander.

"The first thing we need to do is to find a place to sit in the waiting room. Since we will be here for three nights, I think it is best to find a place against a wall for us to try to be comfortable by lying on the floor, like we did at the previous train stations. I sincerely doubt that there will be space for us to lie down on any of the benches. Just follow me and let's stay close together.

"Once we get settled into our resting place, Yitzhak, you will go with me to find the Evacuation Center. I expect there will be a very long line. We all need to hold on tight to our belongings and avoid anyone attempting to steal from us."

My father was correct about the inside of the train station being very crowded and busy. There were five platforms to the left of the station's entrance with ten trains, one on each side of each platform. All of the platform areas were packed with soldiers who were waiting for their departure. Police guards were positioned on the platform area preventing civilians from trying to sneak onto the trains. It was very chaotic inside the station with frightened people screaming at the police guards to let them proceed to the trains.

We turned right and headed toward the waiting area. My father led the way, and we carefully managed to avoid stepping on the massive amount of people who were sitting on the floor. We found a vacant spot in a corner at the rear of the waiting room and placed our belongings against the wall in order for us to have enough space to lie down.

"Rifka and Leah, Yitzhak and I will wait here while the two of you find the women's restroom to clean up. We'll do the same, once you return. Also, see if you can find a place to refill our water containers."

While my father and I were waiting for them to return, we could hear two men standing next to us complaining back and forth to each other with very loud voices.

The taller of the two said, "You see all of these Jews. They are just cowards and fleeing in mass. Why are we the only ones fighting for our country? Why is the Soviet government even allowing them to flee?"

The other man responded, "You know, Hitler has the right idea. Just get rid of them, like our Cossacks did many years ago."

The taller man replied, "All of us would already be in the east, if it weren't for the Jews crowding all of the train stations. They are really the cause of this war and making all of us flee our homes and farms!"

The other man added, "Well, the Nazi army is moving very quickly across Poland. It won't be long until they take care of our Jewish Problem!"

My father turned toward me and whispered, "Don't make any eye contact with those men or anyone that speaks against the Jews. We don't want anyone to know we are Jewish, except the officials who notice the J written on our documents. As much as it angers us to hear these derogatory remarks, we need to remain safe. Slowly turn away from them."

It took the four of us about an hour to accomplish washing ourselves and changing into clean underwear, since the restrooms were crowded and very filthy.

When my father and I returned to the back area of the waiting room where my mother and sister were located, he said to me, "Yitzhak, let's go find the Evacuation Center. If the line is very long, I'll stay in the line while you go back and remain with your mom and Leah."

It turned out that the train station's ticket counter served as the Evacuation Center with two very slow-moving long lines: one for those with official documents, and the other for those with no documents. We got into the back of the line for those with official documents.

"Yitzhak, I'm not sure how long the Evacuation Center will remain open. It's already getting close to seven o'clock. If they close, I will stay here during the night in order to keep my place in line. Go ahead and go back to be with your mom and sister. When you wake up in the morning, come back to find me."

"Yes, Papa."

138

That was our plan, and he finally obtained our food vouchers from the Evacuation Center the following morning and returned to where we had spent the night. "Good news. Those of us in line with documents were processed first. There is a warehouse across the street where we can eat and also find a place to sleep. We don't have to wait in this waiting room for the next two days. Follow me. Bring all of the belongings, and I'll show you where it is located."

A two-story warehouse was located across the street from the station near the triangular square. From the outside, the warehouse looked like an abandoned building. There was no sign displayed on the outside to identify that it was a place for evacuees. A guard was stationed outside in front of the building to check and allow those with the required documents to enter. People were allowed to leave the warehouse and return, as long as they showed their documents to the guard upon their return.

The food offered was similar to what we experienced at other Evacuation Centers, mainly vegetable and potato soup, slices of bread, and black tea to drink. A sleeping area with cots was located on the second floor, along with a small medical center for those that felt ill.

Since the park in the middle of the triangular square was adjacent to the warehouse, my father and I went there during the two afternoons to earn some rubles by giving haircuts. In the mornings, my dad gave our earnings to my mom and Leah for them to purchase some additional food for us. So far on this journey, he and I were able to earn enough to not tap into the rubles that my father brought with him, along with those given to him from Uncle Anshel.

The two days at the Kyiv Evacuation Center went by very quickly. As promised, our convoy's wagon and the two soldiers were waiting for us on the 27th at the triangular square across the street from the train station. Our private told us that Kharkiv was located about 500 kilometers (*310 miles*) from Kyiv, and that it may take us at least a week to get there, depending upon the speed of the pedestrians and vehicle traffic.

As we climbed back into the wagon, the private smiled at Leah and greeted her. "See, I told you that I would be here waiting for you to return."

She replied, "Thank you, private. It is good to see you again."

This time, my father took notice of their interaction, and I could tell from his facial expression that he was not happy and very alarmed. The four of us sat together on the bench. My father sat on one side of Leah, and I sat on her other side. I overheard him telling her very quietly, "Leah, you should not be flirting with any young man that you don't know. You have no idea what their intention might be. They may try to get you to be alone with them. For your safety, it is best not to be overly friendly to that soldier. You are also Jewish. It is best for you to not tell your name to any young man that you don't know. There are many people who hate Jews and you could put yourself in great harm. Do you understand what I'm telling you? Your mother and I love you dearly, and we don't want anything dreadful to happen to you."

"Yes, Papa."

The convoy finally started to move very slowly on the road that led to Kharkiv. Like before, the road was packed with people walking, horse-drawn carts, trucks, and cars all moving very slowly. There were six small villages and one larger town for the convoy to go through before reaching Kharkiv. Some of these villages took longer to reach, due to them being more than a 30-kilometer distance from the previous village. An earlier than usual morning departure was needed to reach the villages, Boryspil and Berezan, before sunset. The small village, Yahotyn, was easier to reach in one day since it was only 28 kilometers from Berezan.

We left the village, Yahotyn, early in the morning to try to reach Pyrantan in one day. Pyrantan was 62 kilometers away from Yahotyn. Unfortunately, due to the slow traffic, our convoy had to find a place to pull over on the side of the road once it got too dark to proceed. Since there was not enough room in the wagon for everyone to lie down, many of the convoy passengers, like the four of us, had to find a place in an adjacent farm's field to spend the night. We reached Pyrantan the next day, and the convoy's lieutenant decided to stop there and try to find a church to open for everyone to spend the night.

We departed Pyrantan early the next morning and barely made it to Lubny before nightfall. On the next day, the convoy left Lubny and reached the large town, of Khorol, in the late afternoon. We stopped at a small park that was in front of the Khorol train station. The Khorol train station was a welcome sight, since everyone traveling with the convoy now knew there would be an Evacuation Center, with food possibly being available, and an indoor area where we could all sleep.

The Khorol train station was a small, one-story concrete building located on the western edge of the town. After retrieving our belongings, my family walked across the street, entered the train station, and was greeted by a smiling railway director.

"Good afternoon. Here are your train tickets. Your train is waiting for you at the platform. Just go through those doors in front of you to get to the platform located outside. Once everyone from the convoy has boarded, the train will take you all the way to Kharkiv, with one stop at Poltava, where more people will get onto the train. Watch your step as you go through the door and walk down to the platform."

The four of us were astonished. Leah was the first to speak. "Mama and Papa. Are we really going to get onto a train?" My parents affirmatively nodded. We also heard many cheers from the others riding with us in the convoy when they also learned that a train was waiting for us.

When we exited the train station and got outside, we actually saw that there really was a train waiting for us on the platform. A train official stood outside and guided us to our designated spot on the platform. Once we climbed the two steps to get inside the train car, we hurried to find an open, two-sided wooden bench where the four of us would sit together and then place our belongings underneath the bench. It took about thirty minutes for everyone from the convoy to be seated. There were loud cheers when the train pulled out of the station.

*Finally, we are riding on an actual train after nearly spending six weeks of sitting and bouncing around inside a wooden wagon!*

Poltava was 107 kilometers from Khorol. I estimated that the train was moving around 30 kilometers per hour when the train pulled into the Poltava train station around midnight.

The Khorol railway director was correct. There were a large number of civilians and Soviet military lined up on the Poltava station's platform, eager to get onto the train. Once the train stopped and the car doors opened, a sea of people poured into the train car expecting to find a seat. Unfortunately, those from our convoy had already taken all of the benches. The people from Poltava now entering the train scrambled to find an available open space to either stand or sit somewhere inside the train car. Somehow, a family of six squeezed onto the floor in between our bench and the one in front of us.

An hour later, the train left Poltava and proceeded to the next stop, Kharkiv, where everyone on board would need to obtain a transfer ticket at the Kharkiv's train station's Evacuation Center. I estimated correctly that our train would arrive in Kharkiv in five hours at around six o'clock in the morning on August 5th, 1941.

It took my family a total of ten days to get from Kyiv to Kharkiv.

# The Train Ride to
# Rostov-on-Don
## August 5, 1941 - August 28, 1941

*Map Source: Nations Online Project*

The sun started to rise behind the tall buildings in the eastern horizon. Since my father was awake, I asked him, "Papa, I'm starting to see some tall buildings in the distance. Are we approaching Kharkiv?"

He turned and looked out the window. "Yes, it must be Kharkiv that you're seeing."

"Do you know what time it is?"

He took out his pocket watch and told me, "It is five o'clock in the morning. We should arrive at the train station very soon. I think that I should wake up your mom and Leah to talk about our plans while we are at the Kharkiv train station."

144

After nudging both my mom and sister to get them to awake, he explained, "We should talk now about what we will do when we arrive at the train station. Kharkiv is the second largest city in Eastern Poland. I suspect that their train station will be as large as the one in Kyiv, with numerous platforms and trains, and will be just as crowded and chaotic. We will most likely see at least a hundred Soviet soldiers gathered on the platforms since they have priority in getting on these trains, even though evacuees, like us, have official travel documents. Like we did in Kyiv, when we depart from this train, tightly hold onto your pillowcase with your belongings and follow me into the waiting room. I'll look to see where it is as soon as we get off the train. Most likely, we will need to stay in Kharkiv for at least three days. Once we get situated in the waiting room and I obtain our train tickets, we'll look for a better place for us to sleep."

My mom affirmatively nodded her head, while both Leah and I responded, "Yes, Papa."

After a brief pause, Leah asked, "Is this what it will be like from now on when we ride on a train? These benches are worse to sit on than the bench on the wooden wagon. So many people are crowded into this train car, and many of them smell awful!"

My mom reminded us. "This is why I packed towels, soap, and extra underwear in everyone's pillowcase. We need to keep ourselves as clean as possible and also avoid getting body lice. We will need to find a place to wash when we arrive at every train station. The dirty and dusty condition of this train is awful. It looks like this train is meant for cattle and not people! There is still a very long journey ahead of us. So, yes, Leah, this is what it will probably be like for the remainder of our journey."

About a half hour later when I looked out the window, I saw more train tracks running parallel to

145

ours. This meant we were about to approach the station.

When the train finally stopped at the platform, my father was correct. The platform was jam-packed with soldiers carrying their rifles and duffle bags. My mother motioned to us to tightly grab the rope that she tied around our pillowcases, and patiently wait until the people sitting on the floor in front of us stood up and exited. As soon as the space was clear, my father rose first to lead us out of the train car. We squeezed through the soldiers waiting on the platform and slowly walked toward the waiting room that we could see in the distance.

I tapped my father's shoulder and mentioned, "Papa. I think this station is even bigger than the one in Kyiv, or at least it is further for us to get to the waiting room."

Once again, we had to proceed very carefully not to step on the people sitting or reclining on the waiting room floor. We eventually found a space toward the back section of the waiting room, placed our belongings next to the wall, and then took turns finding the restroom where we could clean up and, then, find a place to fill up our water containers.

After these chores were completed, my father and I walked through the station to locate the Evacuation Center. We looked everywhere and couldn't find it. The train station's ticket counter was not being used as the Evacuation Center. After searching the entire train station, my father asked a security guard who was guarding the platform's entrance gate. The guard told us to go to the Railroad Management Office located across the street from the train station and to the right of the square, known as Pryvokzal'na Square.

When we walked out of the station's front entrance, we immediately noticed a two-story gray concrete, squarish-looking office building across the street from the train station. My father showed our documents to the attending guard at the office's front door. Once we got inside, we saw the Evacuation Center sign in the distance. While Leah and my mom stayed in the waiting room, my father and I entered the back of the long line for those with the required documents.

"Yitzhak. It looks like I might be waiting in line all day and possibly overnight. I'll remain here as long as it takes to obtain our tickets. Go ahead and stay with your mom and Leah. Tell them where I am, and that I might need to be here for a long time."

"Okay, Papa."

When I left this office building, I was able to see the front of the train station. It was a magnificent-looking building with six Roman-style columns holding up the gabled roof over the entrance and a tall multi-story tower on each end. Once I got inside the station, I noticed a large map of Eastern Poland posted on the wall. Since there were no people standing in front of the map, I went over to examine it. It was a railroad map that showed where each train station was located. I quickly found Kharkiv on the map's right side. Arrows pointed out the train route from Kharkiv all the way to Rostov-on-Dov on the eastern side of the Sea of Azov. I was astonished to see how far Rostov was from Kharkiv, and that the train route went south from Kharkiv to reach the Sea of Azov. I also noticed that Rostov was located inside the Soviet Union.

This concerned me and I wondered. *How close are the Nazis to the villages and towns along this southern train route? What about the cities with ports and harbors along the Black Sea and the Sea of Azov? Are the Nazis bombing them?*

I was also curious to determine the number of train stations where we would stop. Most likely, since the Soviet soldiers have priority boarding, my family may have to wait at each train station for two or three days before getting a transfer ticket to go to the next station. I noticed there were five stations before we got to Rostov. Since the train to Kyiv only traveled at a speed of 30 kilometers per hour and if we experienced a two or three-day layover at each station, it might take us almost a month to reach Rostov!

My father returned from the Evacuation Center later in the afternoon and showed us our train tickets. The ticket listed Rostov as our final destination with three-day layovers and transfers at Dnipro, Zaporizhahia, Melitopil, Mariupol, and Taganrog. An August 8th, 8 p.m. departure was listed on our tickets. This meant that we needed to remain in Kharkiv for three more days.

Being curious about all of the stops at cities that I never heard before, I asked my father, "Papa, are the Nazis getting close to any of these cities?"

"That's a good question, Yitzhak. From Kharkiv, we will head south toward the Sea of Azov, where Melitopil is located. Once we change trains in Melitopil, we will follow the sea's coastline eastward to cross the border into the Soviet Union and arrive at Rostov-on-Don. I am aware that the Nazis are moving eastward across Poland and that the Luftwaffe is bombing Odessa's harbor on the northwestern part of the Black Sea. Most likely, bombing will occur along the sea at the cities with harbors. So far, we are fortunate that our travel has avoided any bombing. Let's pray that our luck continues.

"Now, follow me to the Evacuation Center that is across the street from the train station. They are supposed to have some food for us, and a place for us to sleep."

We spent the three days just like we did in Kyiv. During the afternoons, my father and I earned some money giving haircuts in the small park in front of the train station. In the mornings, while my father and I guarded our belongings in the Evacuation Center, my mother and sister searched the neighboring shops and market area to purchase non-perishable canned or sealed food items that we could take with us. My father suggested that we do our best to stock up on food, just in case the Evacuation Centers in the other cities do not provide meals.

This became our routine during all of the three-day layovers that we experienced in the other cities. As it turned out, my father was very wise for us to stock up on non-perishable food. No meals or lodging were provided at the Dnipro and Zaporizhazhia train stations.

We boarded each train in the evening and sat in the car with the two-sided bench seating. Starting with Kharkiv, my father had us stand in front of the platform gate two hours ahead of our departure time, in order for us to be able to sit together on a bench and not on the floor.

Once everyone had boarded and got situated inside the car, a train official entered and made an announcement at every station before the train departed.

He blew a whistle to get everyone's attention. When there was total silence, he announced, "The window shades need to be drawn down at all times. Since this train is traveling at night, it is necessary that inside light not be visible from the outside. There are reports that the German Luftwaffe airplanes are

149

bombing railroad tracks. Traveling at night and keeping the train in darkness should prevent the Luftwaffe from noticing this train. For your safety, we cannot allow the Germans to see any light coming from inside this train."

After a short pause, he continued. "In case there is an emergency and the train suddenly stops, grab your belongings, quickly and calmly depart the train, and run away from the train tracks. Find a place to lie face down on the ground. Everyone, please remain calm if you have to immediately leave the train. Chaos and confusion will only make things worse for everyone. Thank you for following these emergency instructions."

There was complete silence after the train official left our train car. Moments later, everyone on our train started speaking to each other very loudly. My father placed his arms around us to form a huddle and added, "If there is an emergency and we need to suddenly exit, I will go first, followed by Yitzhak. He and I will help you, Leah and Rifka, step off the train. Before you get off, toss your pillowcase on the ground below. You can grab it once you step down. Then, everyone follow me. We will run into a field on a farm and lie face down. Do you now know what to do?"

We all nodded affirmatively.

Fortunately, there were no emergency stops or bombings during the first three segments of our journey to Rostov. We reached the Melitopol train station in the morning of August 16th. Surprisingly, the train station was not located near the harbor. Three days later, we transferred to the train that would take us to Mariupol, which was located about 200 kilometers east of Melitopol, along the northern coastline of the Sea of Azov. Since our departure was scheduled for 9 p.m., I estimated that we would arrive at Mariupol around midnight.

Being concerned that the Nazis were more interested with bombing the harbors along the Sea of Azov, my father had us stand in front of the Melitopol train platform gate at 6 p.m., three hours before our departure. He explained, "I want us to do our best to sit as close to the train car's exit, in case the train makes an emergency stop."

This made me feel concerned and very nervous.

I wondered: *Did my father learn something about the Luftwaffe that he is not telling us?*

When the train finally departed for Mariupol, everyone in our car remained fairly quiet. Most likely, they were tired from waiting three days at many of the train stations. Even my sister and mother dosed off. Then, suddenly, after ninety minutes into our trip, explosions from the outside woke everyone up. The train came to a screeching halt. People panicked and started screaming. My father nudged all of us. "Grab onto your pillowcases. Yitzhak, grab mine. I will take my small suitcase with our tools and documents. Remember what I told all of you about getting off the train."

It didn't take too long for those sitting on the floor and in the benches in front of us to exit, while the screaming from others inside our train car continued. Minutes later, the four of us were off the train, and my father yelled, "Follow me. See that field in the distance with the tall crop of wheat? That's where we need to run. Let's go. We need to go far away from the railroad tracks to be safe. It looks like the train tracks ahead of us and Mariupol are being bombed!"

The four of us ran as fast as we could. When we reached the field, my father instructed us to go into the field and lie down beneath the crops. "This way the tall crops will hide us from the Luftwaffe!"

151

While lying face down in the field, I could see frequent flashes of light in the distant sky, followed by the roar of bomb explosions. Even though I dared not to look up, I estimated that the exploding bombs were at least five to ten kilometers away from us. I also heard the roar from airplane engines flying and bullets being fired. Apparently, our train remained invisible in the nighttime darkness, was not bombed, and bullets were not being fired at us. There were also steady flashes in the sky without any follow-up sound. I assumed the Nazi airplanes were bombing something more strategic in the far distance.

While all of this was happening, I heard screams from the other train passengers who were lying down near us. Obviously, everyone was scared that we would die from bombs exploding on top of us and bullets fired from the airplanes.

The bombing and the sound of bullets being fired lasted for about thirty minutes. Once it subsided and got quiet, my father told us to remain lying in the field and to try to get some sleep. "Since it is nighttime, we won't be able to see where we will walk. We might as well get some rest, and then see where we should go in the morning."

The streak of daylight from the rising sun woke us up. My mother reached into her pillowcase and retrieved her water container and slices of bread that she saved. "Here. All of you need to eat something and drink some water. Most likely, we will need to walk a great distance today."

We all stood up and looked around us. Our train was still on the tracks and had not been bombed. Not many people from our train remained. There were some of the passengers from the train walking alongside the tracks toward the direction of Mariupol, even though a small village could be seen in the distance. My father told us we should do the same. "If we follow the tracks, eventually we will get to Mariupol. Hopefully, their train station was not bombed."

After we walked for a while, the train tracks curved around a hill, and we could see smoldering gray smoke rising in the near distance. As we walked closer, we saw that a train that must have had an earlier departure was bombed, and most of the train cars were tipped over and lying off the track. The smoke was coming from the train's engine and was still on fire from the bomb that hit it. We saw dead people lying face up and face down on the ground, while some men were retrieving bodies out of the train cars.

Leah and my mom started crying and hugging each other when they saw the dead bodies.

My father spoke up. "All of you go over to the tree on the right and wait there. You might as well sit down. I'm going to see what happened, and if they need more help. Stay there until I get back."

"Papa, I should go with you."

"No, Yitzhak. Stay with your sister and mother. You need to comfort them. I'll come and get you if you are needed."

My father was correct. Leah, in particular, was visibly very frightened and started screaming. "They're going to kill us. I'm going to die!"

I sat next to her and hugged her tightly. "It will be alright, Leah. Don't worry. Remember what Papa keeps telling us. As long as we are together, we will remain safe."

"But the Germans are going to kill us", she kept repeating.

I did my best to keep her calm. "We'll be okay. Don't worry."

I looked ahead to see our father talking to the men who were retrieving the bodies. About thirty minutes later, he walked back to us.

"The bombing of this train and the bullets being fired were what we heard last night. If you look in the distance, it appears that the military base and the harbor in Mariupol were also bombed last night. Those who were riding in this train, that remained alive, have already left this area and are walking to Mariupol. The men that you see retrieving the bodies are from the local village, Manhush. They told me that we should continue to walk to Mariupol. I don't need to remain to help them, since they feel they have already removed the dead passengers and train's crew. So, let's continue our walk. The men told me that Mariupol is about twenty kilometers from here. We might as well walk slowly, since it might take us two days to get there.

"Yitzhak, stay alongside your sister and mother to try to comfort them. We will all see how war is gruesome and horrific."

As we slowly walked forward, we saw numerous dead bodies with blood protruding from bullet holes. Leah became very emotionally enraged when she saw a dead young girl holding onto her stuffed bear. It was an awful sight, and I held her closer against me so that she wouldn't see the girl anymore and the other dead bodies.

By the late afternoon, the four of us were very tired from walking. We noticed a large tree alongside the railroad tracks and decided to stop there to spend the night. Other passengers from our train, about twenty who were also walking to Mariupol, noticed us and asked if they could spend the night alongside us. We welcomed being with others, after witnessing the horrific sight caused by this bloody war. Two of the other families offered us some food. My mom pulled a can of stewed meat out of her pillowcase, to add to this makeshift family group meal. We also shared drinking the water from the container that I had in my pillowcase.

The next morning our group of people continued walking along the railroad tracks that led to Mariupol. As we entered the city from the west side, large plumes of smoke were visible. One of the men walking with us stated, "That must be the military base that was bombed last night."

We continued walking through the city and additional railroad tracks joined ours. We knew that we were getting closer to the train station. It was encouraging that no smoke was rising ahead of us. Our group reached the train station in the mid-afternoon on August 20th, and we all felt relieved when we saw that it was unscathed from being bombed.

We also noticed that a city garden was in front of the train station. The women and children from our group, along with my mother, sister, and me, joined others who were already situated in the garden. The men, including my father, went into the train station to learn if the station's Evacuation Center was open.

About an hour later, my father returned. "The Evacuation Center won't be issuing train tickets just yet. There is a large waiting room inside. Let's go there and find a spot against a wall to rest. The Evacuation Center official is recruiting men to work and help at the harbor. Apparently, help is needed to clear the damage. I'm going to go there tomorrow morning to work and earn more rubles. We might need the extra money to buy more non-perishable food for our journey."

I asked, "Papa, can I go with you and work?"

"No, Yitzhak. You should stay here and be with your mother and sister. You will need to watch our belongings, while your mom and Leah go to the market in the morning. I also don't want you to go on your own to give haircuts. I'm concerned that someone will steal our haircut equipment from you. Let's go and find a place to rest. Their restrooms are open, and we can get cleaned up and refill our water containers."

My mom interjected. "Don't worry, Leah and Yitzhak. I packed a deck of playing cards and your father's mini-chess set and board to keep you busy while we are waiting."

Being very concerned about our safety, I asked my father, "Papa. Is it safe for us to remain inside the train station? Won't the Nazi planes try to bomb it?

"Good questions. I asked the same questions to the train official at the Evacuation Center. He told me that the German infantry hasn't reached this region of the Sea of Azov, and that the Nazis are currently concentrating their military effort on capturing the port at Odessa. He believes that their Luftwaffe's attack the other night was to prevent the soldiers stationed at the Mariupol military base from being sent to defend Odessa. Let's see if we can find a place to rest near an exit door."

For the next three days, my father worked at the harbor and gave my mom his earnings, so that she and Leah could go to the market to purchase food for us to eat while we waited at the train station. I remained in the waiting room while they were gone to guard our belongings. It turned out that there wasn't much food available at the Evacuation Center.

When they returned from the market, my mom told me that I could take a walk through the train station and cross the street to walk through the city

156

garden. I was surprised that the train station wasn't too crowded with people escaping and soldiers waiting on the platforms. Most likely, our train was the last one to leave Melitopil, and the soldiers on the military base remained at the base, or were sent out to retrieve the dead bodies from the train that got bombed, and take those who got injured to a medical facility. Fortunately, the Mariupol train station was not bombed while we were there.

On the fourth day, August 24th, my father got in line early in the morning to try to obtain our train tickets to get to Rostov. He returned later in the afternoon and showed us our tickets. We would leave the next night at 9 p.m., and then transfer to another train at a city called Taganrog, that was located about 112 kilometers from Mariupol. Most likely we would have to wait another three days in Taganrog before departing for Rostov.

We left the Taganrog train station at 10 p.m. on August 28th and arrived in Rostov at 1 a.m. the next day. Since it was very late at night, my father led us from the platform to the train station's waiting room to find a spot to sleep.

My estimate was correct. It took us almost a month to get from Kharkiv to Rostov and the four of us were feeling extremely exhausted!

# Rostov to Krasnovodsk
## August 29, 1941- September 24, 1941

*Map Source: Nations Online Project*

"Wake up. Wake up, Yitzhak!"

I felt my father nudging my right shoulder.

"Time to get up. It's 11 o'clock in the morning, and you and I have things to do."

"Do I have to, Papa?"

I felt my mom rocking me back and forth. "Here, Yitzhak. I saved a slice of bread for you from yesterday. Eat and drink some water. You and Papa need to get cleaned up, and then find the Evacuation Center."

"Okay, if you say so."

Even though I was still groggy, I ate the slice of bread and drank some water. Then, I looked around the waiting room and asked my father, "Where did all of these people come from? It wasn't this crowded when we arrived here last night."

My father replied, "This morning I overheard a few of the men speaking to each other. Apparently, their train managed to leave Odessa during the night without being attacked by the Nazis. When their next train departed Melitopol, it was routed to a port city called Berdyansk due to the train tracks being bombed near Mariupol. These men commented that the Soviets sent cargo barges to bring them here from Berdyansk. They were annoyed and complained about their long walk from the Rostov port to get to this train station."

"Oh, I see, Papa. Last night when I saw that this station didn't have as many people as the other stations, I thought we would be able to leave here fairly soon and not have to wait for many days!"

"That's why you and I need to go find the Evacuation Center. Your mother and Leah will stay here and guard our belongings. Let's go. And bring your water container."

After getting cleaned up in the men's restroom and filling up our water containers at a drinking fountain, we started our search. This was the largest train station that we had seen so far. The waiting room, where we slept, was on one end of the station. As we proceeded through the center of the station with its very tall ceiling, I noticed another train route map that was posted on a wall.

"Papa, let's take a look at that map, okay?"

Similar to the map that I saw at the Kharkiv station, this map also had arrows pointing to cities that I never heard of before. There was one long arrow that pointed from Rostov-on-Don to a coastal city called Makhachkala.

I asked my father, "Papa, is this city on the coast of the Sea of Azov?"

"No, my son. That is the Caspian Sea. It looks like we will cross the Caspian Sea on a boat to reach a port in a city called Krasnovodsk. Once we get there, we will be in a Soviet-controlled Asian country called Turkmenistan."

"Really! A boat! That sounds exciting."

I took another close look and noticed that we will, most likely, transfer to trains at Pyatigorsk and Grozny. If we stayed three days in these cities and then one day on the boat, I estimated that it might take us another month to get to Turkmenistan.

"Let's go, Yitzhak. We need to get our travel tickets before all of these people wake up."

We first walked past six train platforms that could accommodate up to twelve trains. Oddly, there were no trains positioned alongside the platforms, and no people or soldiers were waiting. We continued walking to the opposite side of the station and noticed a long line of people.

"Yitzhak, you get in line while I walk ahead and take a look."

About thirty minutes later, my father returned. "As I thought. This is the line to obtain the tickets. I'll wait here. How about you take a look outside the station to see if there are a market, any shops, and a place for us to give haircuts? Then, go back and wait with your mother and Leah. If I don't return before you all go to sleep tonight, please bring me something to eat."

I did what my father asked and exited the train station. Once I got outside and walked a short distance, I turned around to look at the train station's exterior. I was correct. The Rostov train station was the largest one that we have been to. It was a huge concrete multi-story structure with three buildings connected to each side of the main entrance building. The main entrance building and the two end buildings on the far side were four stories tall. The two buildings adjacent to the main entrance were only three stories tall.

160

Being curious, I wondered: *Why are there so many buildings and floors?*

After taking one more view of the station, I turned around and looked at the surroundings. I thought the train station would be located along the coastline. Instead, it was located in the middle of an industrial area. Once I turned to the left and started walking a few blocks, I found a large park called the Nikolai Ostrovsky Recreation Park. There were lots of tall shade trees and many mothers were with their children playing in the park. Most likely these families lived in the homes across from the park's eastern entrance.

*This park will be the perfect place to give haircuts.*

Since I didn't find a market place or any grocery shops near the park, I walked to the eastern side of the train station and found the commercial street, Ulitsa Nansena, and a grocery store.

I walked back to the train station to tell my mother and Leah what I found, particularly the grocery store.

"Mama. How's our food supply? Do we have enough saved in case the Evacuation Center doesn't provide food? We may need to wait here for a long time. I can stay here with Leah, and I can tell you where the grocery store is located."

"Good idea, Yitzhak. Tell me where it is."

She left with an empty sack and didn't return until mid-afternoon. "Their food items were very expensive. I managed to purchase more self-opening canned meat stew and bread for us. I hope that it will be enough."

By 8 o'clock in the evening, my father hadn't returned. I went to find him and took a can of the meat stew and a fork to give to him. I found him standing in line, but a little closer to the Evacuation Center's ticket counter. "Papa, let me hold your place in line. I'm sure you need to go to the restroom."

Once he got back, I went back to spend the night with my mother and sister in the waiting room.

My father finally returned the next morning a little after 10 o'clock, and he showed us our tickets. We had to wait two more days before our train was scheduled to depart at 9 p.m. on September 1st. As my father and I predicted, we needed to transfer to another train at Pyatigorsk and at Grozny before arriving in Makhachkala. He reported, "There is some food available and a place to sleep on the floors above the Evacuation Center for those, like us, with official documents."

While we waited at the Rostov train station, my father and I gave haircuts at the park and gave our earnings to my mom so that she and Leah could go to the grocery store the next morning.

My family tried to follow the same routine when we arrived and waited at the Pyatigorsk and Grozny train stations. We had to spend four days at each station until we boarded the next available train. Pyatigorsk's Evacuation Center was located inside a large government building two blocks from the train station. To our amazement, they offered a good, nourishing menu consisting of noodle soup with meatballs, goulash, and tea. After experiencing a long seventeen-hour non-stop ride from Rostov to Pyatigorsk, while sitting on a wooden bench, having a good meal was very appreciated. There was a small grassy area near the Pystigorsk train station that served as a good place for haircuts.

The Grozny train station was much different. There was only one long outdoor covered platform. There was no waiting room, no town square, no market, and no shops nearby. Their ticket counter served as the Evacuation Center. The only place that we could find to sleep was at a small park about a block away. Stocking up on food turned out to be a good idea!

Shortly after departing from the Grozny train station in the evening of September 11th, a train official walked into our train car and blew his whistle to get everyone's attention.

"I'm here to inform you about disembarking from the train when you arrive in Makhachkala."

The train official waited until there was complete silence, and then he continued.

"When you disembark this train, you will exit the train station and walk to the left. You will wait in line to be processed at the Port Office. It is located behind the train station. Everyone, including children and infants, needs to be processed. Be prepared to show your travel documents. In order to be approved to enter Soviet Turkmenistan, a document check is required. Thank you for your cooperation."

After he left, I asked my father, "What happens to those who don't have official documents like we do?"

"No need to worry about that. We are very fortunate that Town Marshal Novikov issued us our documents. He made it possible for us to flee."

My family finally arrived in Makhachkala on September 12th in the late morning. As we stepped outside, we quickly noticed how hot it was. My mom ordered us to wear our hats to protect our head from the scorching sun, particularly since it appeared that we would be standing in line for a very long time.

It took us nearly four hours to reach the processing counter at the Port Office. When my father showed our documents to the port official, the official mentioned, "Your family is one of the few that I've seen today with the travel permits and the required official stamp. Did you notice all the hundreds of people gathering around the port? The majority of them don't have this type of document. I don't know how long they will need to wait at the port, since we only have two barges going back and forth to Krasnovodsk. I can get you on a boat at the end of next week on Friday, September 23$^{rd}$. The estimated departure will be at 10 a.m. I suggest that you get in line at the harbor gate no later than 8 a.m. It may take thirty hours for the barge to cross the Caspian Sea and arrive in Krasnovodsk. In the meantime, find a place to wait. Leninsky Park is about one kilometer away on the other side of the train station. Just walk along the main street and you will find it. You may want to wait there."

Yes, we were all pleased to get our tickets. However, we were not pleased with hearing that we needed to wait for eleven days!

As we left the Port Office, my mom spoke up. "Meir, I think that we should find that park. If you look around, hundreds of people are waiting on the beach in the direct sun. Some of them look very sickly, possibly from a lack of food and dehydration from a lack of water. I don't think staying on the beach around these possibly diseased people is a good idea."

My father agreed, and we turned around to walk past the train station and headed toward the park. While walking slowly with our belongings, we noticed more crowds of people sitting and sleeping on the sidewalks. We eventually found some shops and stopped in front of a small market stand. My mom went in to check it out while we waited. When she came out, she told us, "They have awfully expensive fresh fruit, vegetables, and canned food products. Let's continue and try to find the park".

After walking another thirty minutes, we entered the entrance to Leninsky Park. It was also crowded with people, who most likely, were also waiting to board a boat. Fortunately, we found a shaded area underneath a large tree where we could rest and wait.

Waiting eleven days to depart felt like an eternity. The only place for us to wash ourselves, our clothes, and refill our water containers was at the train station. My mother and Leah, and then my father and I, took turns each morning to walk forty-five minutes to the train station. Since the station didn't provide any food, we had to rely on our supply of canned food. My mom supplemented our food supply by purchasing the expensive food sold at the grocery store. Being afraid that we might catch a disease and become sick, she forbade my father and me to give haircuts to those who were waiting in the park and camped out on the street.

Finally, the morning of September 23$^{rd}$ arrived, and we walked back to the port and stood outside the harbor gate at seven o'clock in the morning. A long line had already been formed with about fifty people standing in front of us. After an hour passed, a long boat, with wooden crates stacked on top of each other and a few passengers, pulled into the dock. Being curious, I asked my father, "What kind of boat is that?"

"That's a cargo barge ship. It is called a barge because it is long with large open storage spaces on both ends. Do you see those large trucks on the dock? The wooden crates on the barge will be loaded onto those trucks."

"Well, Papa, is that the boat that we will get on? It looks like there are no seats for passengers!"

"Everyone will have to sit on the deck. Do you see the captain's covered cabin in the middle of the ship? Let's do our best to maneuver our way through the crowd, so that we can sit against one of the outside walls of the cabin. Stay close to me, just like you did when we entered and exited the trains, and I will lead the way."

As the deck and truck crews were loading the crates onto the trucks, I turned to Leah and whispered, "Leah, are you excited to ride on a boat? I know I am. This should be a thrilling experience for us to be sailing on the water."

"I am also excited, Yitzhak."

"Well, how about you and I ask Mama and Papa if they will let us stand against the rear railing so that we can watch the boat leave the harbor?"

"Okay. Let's ask."

By 10:30 all of the crates had been removed from the cargo barge and its passengers had departed. The line of people behind us had grown with at least three hundred standing in back of us. The man who issued us our boat tickets weaved his way through the line, walked up to the harbor gate, opened it slightly, and began to let ticketed passengers go up the ramp to get on board. We noticed that those in front of us raced to stand alongside the outside railing. My father's plan for us to sit on the deck alongside the captain's cabin worked. It took about ninety minutes for this cargo ship to be fully packed with passengers. Once all were on board, the ticket office official closed and locked the gate. In a short while, the captain blew the boat's loud horn two times to announce our departure.

Then, very politely I asked, "Mama and Papa, may Leah and I please go to the back railing so that we can see the boat's departure?"

My mom responded, "Go ahead. But be careful not to stand next to someone who looks sick. It should be all right for you to stand at the railing. There will be a breeze in the air as the boat crosses the water. Be careful not to lose your hats."

"Thank you. Leah, let's go!"

The two of us did our best not to be rude to others as we slowly wove through countless people standing and sitting on the boat's deck. It took a while to get to the back and squeeze to be at the rail to view the boat leaving the shore and sailing toward Soviet-controlled Asia.

As the barge departed, I asked Leah, "Doesn't it feel like we are going backward? As we move, we get further and further away from land."

"Yes, you're right, Yitzhak. It does feel like we are going backward. We can now see more of Makhachkala. Do you see the small homes in the distance on the left?"

"Yeah, there they are. I also see many trees in the distance too."

The city's harbor, buildings, and the green scenery kept getting smaller and smaller as the barge sailed away. Leah and I must have remained at the rail, admiring the distant view for at least an hour.

Leah commented, "You know Yitzhak. This is the first time that I can remember, when just you and I did something together. You were always busy playing volleyball with your friends, and later working with Papa at the barbershop. The only girl that I ever played with was our cousin, Mindel. We should do more things together."

I responded, "Yes, we should. You and I are no longer children, as Papa said. With us fleeing, we are going to have to do more to look out for each other."

"That would be nice. Can I ask you something?"

"Sure, Leah."

"Do you plan to always be a barber?"

"I'm not sure what my future will be like. I always dreamed about studying at a university to be a medical doctor. Maybe when this war ends, I will have the opportunity. What about you? Have you thought about your future?"

"Yitzhak, I think that I will become a typical Jewish woman by finding a man to love, marry and raise a family. I think that is my destiny."

I responded, "Will your husband be like that young soldier from the wagon that you flirted with?"

"Oh, stop that. I wasn't flirting. I was just being nice to him like Papa has always told us how to treat others."

With a slight laugh, I added, "I was just teasing you!"

After a brief pause, I continued, "You know, Leah, besides the two of us looking out for each other, we both need to look out for Mama and Papa. Even though they don't show it, they must be feeling very stressed and anxious about this escape. We should do more to help them. Look at how long Papa has been waiting hours by himself in those long lines. Mama is very worried about us having enough to eat, keeping our clothes and ourselves clean, and preventing us from getting sick. Now that we are older, you and I should find a way to help them, so that they don't have to do all of this on their own. I think that I can convince Papa to let me rotate with him to stand and wait in those long lines."

"You're right, Yitzhak. I can help Mama with washing and drying our clothes. Good idea, my brother."

"I love you, my sister."

"And I love you too, Yitzhak."

"How about the two of us going to the front of the boat tomorrow afternoon to see our arrival and what this new country looks like?"

"Yeah. Sounds like a plan!"

Leah reached out to hold my hand. I tightly held it, as we cautiously made our way back to where our parents were sitting.

Viewing sunset out on the water was just an awesome sight, with streaks of yellow, orange, and red blazing across the sky. The colors darkened and merged together at sunset until total darkness blanketed the entire sky. Once the sun disappeared from the horizon, the four of us felt very cold from the chilly air. My mom pulled out the sweaters and jackets that she packed inside our pillowcases so that we could stay warm and sleep during the night.

With Leah lying next to me, we both looked up at the nighttime sky and continued to hold hands. Since there were no clouds and the moon was not in view, the stars brightly sparkled. I never noticed that there were so many stars, since Bolechov always seemed cloudy during the night.

"Leah. Isn't looking at all of those stars just remarkable?"

"Yes, they are. I often wonder how far away the stars must be."

My father must have overheard us talking, and he added, "The stars are one of God's wondrous creations for us to enjoy and value."

All four of us didn't wake up until a few hours after sunrise. After eating a slice of bread and taking a drink of water, all four of us stood up to take a morning stretch. My father looked at his watch and informed us that we should arrive at Krasnovodosk in six to eight hours.

I asked, "Mama and Papa, is it okay with the two of you if Leah and I go to the front railing to watch our arrival?"

My mom answered, "Yes. Just come back to us before the boat gets close to the dock. We will need to be together when we depart the boat."

About five hours later, Leah and I saw a glimpse of land protruding up from the sea in the very far distance. Being very cautious again not to disturb anyone else sitting or standing, we made our way to the railing at the front of the barge.

It took over another hour before we could see any buildings in the distance. As the boat sailed further to the east, the view of land got closer and closer. We noticed that the boat was heading toward a wide bay.

"Leah, from what I can see, this new country is going to be quite different from what we are used to."

After another hour passed, Leah proclaimed with a surprising voice, "Yitzhak! I don't see any trees or anything green. All I see is a yellow ground!"

The man standing next to us at the rail explained, "That's because Turkmenistan is mainly a barren, sandy desert."

We both responded, "A desert!" Actually, we had no idea what this man was describing until the boat got even closer to the shoreline inside the bay.

"Yitzhak. You're right. This is going to be a different experience. What is our life going to be like being in a desert? How will we survive? I guess that little town on the left side of the bay is where we are going. It must be Krasnovodsk."

"Leah. It's time for us to go back to be with Mama and Papa. Let's go."

Another hour went by before the boat pulled into the harbor at one of the docks. We noticed that the harbor was far from the little town on the other side of the bay.

My father reminded all of us to follow his lead when we descended down the boat's ramp. "We need to stay close together. I think that there must be five hundred people on this boat. Most likely, there will be a long line departing and another long line for a document check at the port and at the Krasnovodsk train station."

Leah and I turned toward each other and once again held each other's hands. I whispered to her, "It's been nearly two months since we left Bolechov. Our future life into the unknown has now begun."

# Desert Survival:
## Krasnovodsk to Ashgabat
### September 24, 1941 - October 8, 1941

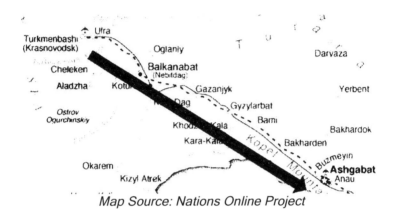

*Map Source: Nations Online Project*

The cargo boat's loud horn blew twice at 10 a.m., announcing that the boat was about to dock at the harbor. Those who were still sitting on the boat's deck quickly stood up and grabbed all of their belongings. Everyone was eager to depart.

A few minutes later, the boat's captain made an announcement by speaking in Russian and explained the departure instructions. When his announcement ended, my mom, Leah, and I quickly turned to my father and we asked, "What did he say?"

He turned to face us and responded, "When we depart the ship, there will be a document check by a government official. Those with Tashkent written and stamped on their official travel permit will be instructed to go directly to the train station. Everyone else will go to the Port Office for processing. It appears that passengers, like us, with the Tashkent stamp on their travel permit have received priority."

172

The line to descend from the boat to the bottom of the ramp moved very slowly. Being my curious self, I took another look around the harbor bay while we waited. On the right side of our boat's dock, I noticed in the distance that there were two very large elongated ships. They were both docked beside four tall round metal structures. I hadn't noticed them before when Leah and I were standing at the railing and looking at the horizon.

I pointed to them and asked, "Papa, do you know what kind of ships they are? They don't look like a cargo boat like ours."

"Yitzhak, I think those boats are oil tankers. Those round metal containers that you see in front of the dock must be storing oil to be pumped into each boat. I believe this country supplies oil to the Soviet army. If you look around the bay, you will see many industrial-type buildings and factories."

It took my family about an hour to descend all the way to the bottom of the ramp for the Turkmenistan government travel document check. When my father showed the official our documents, the official pointed to our left and spoke to my father in Russian. My father explained to us that we were instructed to follow the dirt road on our left and proceed to the train station. It looked like it would be a very long walk. I was surprised that very few people were being told to go to the train station. The majority of the passengers received instructions to walk straight ahead to the Port Office. I also noticed that people were exiting the Port Office from a side door and then walking on a different dirt road toward the town.

I asked my father, "Why are so many people going to the Port Office?"

He responded, "My assumption is that only those with the Tashkent stamp are being sent directly to the train station. Let's start walking while being careful to

173

hold onto the pillowcase with your belongings. It's going to be a long walk along the bay to get to the Krasnovodsk train station."

My father was correct with his assessment of the distance. It was a very long walk, and I often changed the position of the pillowcase across my shoulders. As anticipated, there was another long line at the train station that extended all the way out into the street. We moved forward very slowly. Since we didn't know if our father could represent all four us, we all waited together to be processed at the train station's ticket office.

As we got inside the building, we had a better view of the ticket office official's processing procedure. The line moved slowly because many passengers were arguing with the ticket office official and wouldn't leave the counter. Others were processed very quickly.

While we waited, the four of us continued to look around the inside of the station. My mom was interested to locate the restrooms, while my father looked for the waiting rooms. All four of us were horrified and shocked by seeing hundreds of people lying motionless on the floor. There was no room to even walk into the waiting rooms on either side of the ticket counter. The restroom areas were almost impossible to enter with so many people lying in front of the entrance.

My family was fortunate to have Tashkent officially stamped on our travel permits. The ticket office official smiled when my father handed him our cards. The official spoke to my father in Russian for a few minutes and handed him our train tickets. My father turned around and told us to follow him out of the train station, so that he could explain everything.

"The good news is, that since we are going to Tashkent, the Turkmenistan authorities received

174

orders from the Soviet Evacuation Council to provide those with the official stamp on their travel permit priority train tickets. All of the people that you see lying around are either waiting for a train, have Turkmenistan as their destination, or have no destination or travel permit. The bad news is there is only one train going back and forth between Krasnovodsk and their capital city, Ashgabat.

"We have tickets for the next train that will leave at 9 a.m. in three days, on September 27th. The official told me that we needed to be standing on their outdoor platform no later than 6 a.m. on the 27th. Since we have a third-class travel permit, we will have to exit the train at the Gazanjyk junction and wait another three days until Tuesday, September 30th, and transfer to the train that will take us to Ashgabat. There are already ticketed passengers from another train that will transfer onto our train in Gazanjyk. That's why we need to get off the train and wait another three days. From what he told me, Gazanjyk is a junction where two major train lines intersect and many people transfer to another train."

Leah interrupted. "Papa, that sounds crazy and very disorganized!"

"You're right, Leah. It is disorganized. Look at all the people who were sent to Turkmenistan by the Soviets who have no place to go. The Turkmenistan officials weren't prepared for the influx of so many people!

"There's more. There is no Evacuation Center at this train station. Since this station is located in an industrial area, there are no nearby shops or grocery stores. This means we are on our own for food and water while we wait for three days. With this train station already full of people, we will need to find a safe place outdoors to sleep. Rifka, how much food and water do we have?"

175

"I still have three cans of meat stew and some bread left. If I ration the portions, I can make it last three days. We are low on water and need to refill our water containers. Do you think the water from the restroom sinks is safe enough to drink?"

My father responded, "We will have to take the chance that their water is clean. Yitzhak and I will wait here while you and Leah go to the women's restroom. When you return, Yitzhak and I will do the same."

Our next task was to find a place to sleep. By the time we received our train tickets, used the restrooms, and refilled the water containers, it was already 4 p.m. As we continued to walk down the steps from the station's main entrance, we noticed there was a small park across the street. When we approached the park, it was already packed with people lying on the ground and along all of the adjoining streets and sidewalks. I've never seen so many people cramped together in one location.

We continued to follow my father and we walked along a side street to get to the back of the park. There were no empty spots to sit anywhere. Plus, my mom, being fearful of us contracting a disease or body lice, didn't want us near so many people. We continued to walk blocks away from the train station and the park until we found an alley alongside one of the factories where no people were lying. The four of us did our best to be as comfortable as possible. Fortunately, Turkmenistan had a dry desert climate and the temperature during late September was not excessively hot or cold, with no rain and only a slight wind in the air.

My father and I took a walk the next morning to see if there was a place in this industrial area where we could earn some money by giving haircuts to the local residents. When the two of us found an entrance to a textile-manufacturing factory, we noticed that the majority of the local men entering and leaving the factory had long beards and wore coverings on their heads that concealed the length of their hair.

I asked my father, "Why do the men look this way?"

"Oh, I forgot. This is a Muslim country and the people follow the Islamic religion. Muslim men and women wear head coverings just like many religious Jews. Having long beards is also part of their culture. I think that we can forget about giving them haircuts. As for those in the park, it is best for our health not to get near them. I still have enough rubles to last us a while. Let's go back and be with your mom and Leah and play a card game."

We passed the time as best we could and took turns walking to and from the train station to use their restroom facilities. My mom portioned the remaining canned food to last for the three days. On Saturday, September 27th, we arrived very early in the morning to stand and wait on the train station's platform. Surprisingly, exactly at 9 a.m. the train arrived. As passengers were leaving the train, we merged our way onto a third class designated train car and found a bench where the four of us could sit.

The Turkmenistan train car was in worse condition than the ones that we rode on in Poland. Our car appeared to be very old, dusty, and had a horrible smell. People jammed into the train car, many of them sitting on the floor. Most of them smelled from awful body odor.

The train departed for Gazanjyk thirty minutes later. When I looked out the window, it seemed like the train was traveling at a very slow speed. It took us nine hours to reach the Gazanjyk train station at 6:30 p.m.

As the train pulled into the station, I noticed that hundreds of people were already lined up on the outdoor platform, waiting to transfer onto our train. The four of us were crushed against those squeezing onto the train, and we had to force our way out of the train car. When we finally stood on the platform, we only saw a very small building that served as the train station. There was a small ticket window and some outdoor benches for people to sit. We didn't see any waiting rooms or restrooms.

My mom seemed frightened and asked, "Meir, where are we? There is no town. All I see are lots of train tracks with parked locomotives and unattached cargo train cars. Where are we going to wait for three days?"

I also felt frightened and confused. Most of the people who got off the train showed their transfer tickets to the train station's official and were instructed to remain on the platform to transfer to the next arriving train. Only about twenty of us, who were scheduled to transfer at a later date or time, were told to walk off the platform and wait in front of the small train station. Everyone who stood in front of the station stared at each other, wondering what to do.

My father tried his best to console us. "I think that we were left off in the middle of a railroad yard. I see some trucks traveling on a small highway up ahead in the distance. Let's walk there and take a look around."

The other passengers, who traveled with us and had later transfers, remained sitting on the ground in front of the train station. When the four of us reached the highway, all we found was barren desert sand with no shade trees. Occasionally, a truck passed by us. Some of the trucks honked their horns when they saw us. It became obvious. There was no place for us to go on this warm evening, and we had no food and only a limited supply of water.

*What are we going to do to survive these next three days in the desert?*

The only thing that we could do was either go back and sit in front of the train station, or sit alongside the highway. As we were pondering what to do, a truck stopped in front of us. I could tell from the man's head covering that he was Muslim. He loudly spoke some unfamiliar words out of the passenger window. My father stood up, walked over to his truck, and started speaking Russian to this man. The man in his truck raised his head up and down signaling that he understood my father. The two of them engaged in a lengthy conversation.

The man waited in his truck while my father returned to speak with us.

"I explained to this kind man that we have to wait three days for the next train. His name is Ibrahim. He just finished working at one of the oil refineries. He invited us to go with him to his home. He has a wife, a young son, and a young daughter. I accepted his offer. Don't worry. I feel that we can trust him. He knows that we have to be back here in three days to catch our train."

The four of us placed our belongings in the back of his truck. Then my mom, Leah, and I climbed into the back while my father sat in the front passenger seat. Ibrahim followed the highway through the desert. About thirty minutes later, I turned around and saw in the distance many canvas huts inside a green area that had tall, thin-looking trees. I once read in my geography class about an oasis in the middle of a desert with palm trees and a well full of water. This must be where we were headed.

179

Ibrahim honked his truck's horn when he pulled up and parked the truck in front of a very large canvas hut. As we got out of the truck and grabbed our belongings, his family came outside. He pointed and introduced each member of his family. His wife was Maryam, his son was Ahmed, and his daughter was Zara. His son and daughter looked like they were ten and eight years old, respectively. My father introduced us to Ibrahim's family, and we all smiled and nodded to each other. We all followed Maryam into their canvas hut. She signaled where we could place our belongings, and then we followed Ibrahim outside to the back of their hut. Ibrahim showed us how to use their outdoor shower. There was a cord to pull for water to gently descend down onto us. He also showed us where the outdoor toilet and sink were located. Within a few minutes, Maryam came out of their hut carrying a large wicker basket. She handed us towels, cotton garments to wear, clean headscarves for my mom and Leah, and a bar of soap. She motioned for us to place our dirty clothes into the wicker basket. While Leah and I took turns having our showers, my mom retrieved all of our remaining dirty clothes from our pillowcases and placed them into the basket. I overheard my father explaining to Ibrahim that my mom requested to wash our clothes. With my father and Ibrahim serving as interpreters, Maryam and my mom agreed to do this chore the next morning.

It felt great to wash in their shower, have a clean body, and to wear fresh clothes. Once all four of us were showered and dressed, Ibrahim motioned for us to sit in their hut with his family on a carpet around their round table for a dinner meal. Maryam placed in the center of the table a large platter of cooked fish, a bowl of rice, a plate of round flat bread, and a brass teapot. She gave each of us a plate, knife and fork, a cloth napkin, and a small glass for our tea.

Once Maryam, Ibrahim, Ahmed, and Zara were seated, Ibrahim picked up one of the flat breads and said a prayer. Then, he tore off a piece of the bread and handed each of us a piece to eat. My father, in turn, picked up another flat bread and recited the Hebrew prayer that my family said at the beginning of each meal. Apparently, Ibrahim, recognized the similarity of both meal prayer customs, and said the name, "Abraham." My father explained to us that both Muslims and Jews regard Abraham as their ancient father.

My family was just amazed by the hospitality Ibrahim's family offered us. At the end of the meal, Maryam brought out another platter of oblong-looking brown items and placed them on the table. My father recognized what these were, and told us they were a sweet-tasting fruit called dates.

"These are from their palm trees. Try one. You'll like the taste!"

After we were finished eating, my father showed us how to thank Ibrahim's family by placing our hands together in a prayer formation and then, bow. Ibraham's family thanked us in the same manner.

While my mom and Leah helped Maryam and Zara clear the table and wash the plates, eating utensils, and glasses, my father and I went with Ibrahim and Ahmed to get blankets and pillows that my family could use as bedding. Ibrahim showed us a good place in their hut where the four of us could sleep.

Once the dishes, glasses, and eating utensils were dry and placed on a kitchen shelf, my father mentioned to Ibrahim that the four of us were very tired and needed to get some sleep. Both of them bowed to each other, once again, with the prayer hand gesture.

Leah slept next to my mom, while I slept next to my father. He and I faced each other.

About fifteen minutes later, I whispered to him, "Papa, are you awake?"

He whispered back, "What is it, my son?"

"Papa, are all Muslims as nice and kind as Ibrahim and his family?"

"Yitzhak, when I was your age, I participated with a comparative religions class that was taught by our synagogue's rabbi. I learned that there are similarities among all religions. Jews have the five Books of Moses, also known as the Torah. Muslims have their own book written by their Prophet Mohammed. Christians have the teachings of Jesus and their own version of the Bible. They all teach people how to be kind and respectful to others. Yes, evil also exists among people with greed, hatred of others, brutality, and extreme political power. Just look at what is happening right now with Hitler.

"You will, most likely during your adult life, meet people from different religions, cultures, and countries. Many will look different to you. They may dress differently. Many may have a different skin color than you. Yitzhak, you should never be afraid when you meet someone who is different than you. If you smile and display kindness and respect to a stranger, most likely they will respond to you in the same manner. Does this make sense to you?"

"Yes, Papa."

"Good. Now, don't worry about anything. We are safe in Ibrahim's home. Go to sleep, my son."

"Good night, Papa."

The next two days with Ibrahim and his family were very enjoyable. After having breakfast with their family on the first day, my mom started washing our clothes placed in the large metal buckets that Maryam provided. Ahmed and Sara took Leah and me into another small canvas hut to show us their family's chicken coup with egg-laying chickens and how to feed them. Then they showed us the pen where they have sheep and how to obtain the sheep's milk. In the afternoon, we went with them to play a ball game with the other children from the other families that lived in this oasis. This was a new game for Leah and me. Two teams were formed to compete against each other by using only our feet to move and kick a ball into a goal. All of the parents, including my mom and dad, were the cheering spectators.

The next day, being Monday, Ibrahim drove Ahmed and Zara and six of the children from the other families to school on his way to work at the oil refinery. Before Ibrahim left, my father gave him some rubles to purchase canned food items for us at a local market or grocery store. After he left, my mom and Leah helped Maryam bake bread and prepare the food for the evening meal. While they were doing that, my father asked me to give him a shave. It had been a while since he last shaved. I used the soap that Maryam gave us to create the needed shaving lather.

In the evening, as our two families shared dinner together, my father and Ibrahim discussed the plans for our departure the next day. Ibrahim and all of the children from the oasis left at 9 o'clock in the morning. He didn't return home until 7 o'clock in the evening. Another father picked up all of the children at their school at 3:30 and brought them back to the oasis. Ibrahim apologized to my father that the only option was for him drop us off at the train station on his way to work in the morning. He would arrange with another father to take the children to school in the morning.

My father thanked Ibrahim for getting the canned food for us and making the children's school travel arrangements with the other father. My father also reassured Ibrahim that we were used to waiting many hours at a train station.

Before going to sleep, the four of us showered, changed into our clean clothes, refilled our water containers, and set aside the clothing that Maryam lent us to return to her in the morning.

The next morning was a bittersweet Tuesday. I grew very fond of Ibrahim's family and hated to leave them, knowing that I might never see them again. We all bowed to each other, and both my father and I extended our right hands to shake hands with all four of them. To our surprise, Maryam handed each of us a small paper bag that contained pieces of flat bread and dates.

When Ibrahim dropped us off at the train station at 9:30, my father offered him some rubles as a way of thanking him and his family for their hospitality. Ibrahim refused by gently holding my father's arm and pushing the hand holding the money back to my father. He and my father bowed again to each other. The four of us waved goodbye as he drove off to go to work.

The train station's ticket window was open and my father showed the official our tickets. I could tell that the two of them had a lengthy but friendly conversation. When their discussion ended, my father explained to us that there were other trains arriving prior to ours, and only those passengers with transfers to those trains will be allowed to wait on the outside platform. We would be allowed to go to the platform at 4 p.m. Until then, we would need to sit and wait outside with the others. There were already ten other people sitting and waiting for the same train as ours. An outdoor restroom out back was open. The good news was that our train would take us directly to the capital city, Ashgabat, without any transfers. We would arrive there after a nine-hour train ride at 4 a.m.

Our train arrived promptly at 6:30 p.m., and by racing inside the train car, we successfully secured a bench.

It was a very long nine hours sitting on this very uncomfortable hard bench inside a crowded and noisy train. Once again, the train car had a putrid smell.

There was no way anyone could get any sleep.

Throughout the long train ride, I kept wondering: *When are we ever going to get there?*

# Ashgabat to Bukhoro
## October 8, 1941 - October 24, 1941

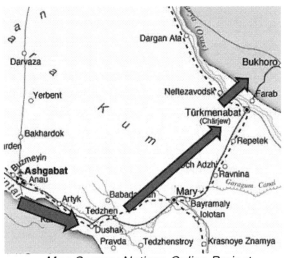

*Map Source: Nations Online Project*

Somehow, I managed to fall asleep and ignore all of the talking from inside our crowded train car. The screeching sound from the train's brakes and the sudden slowing of the train woke me up.

"Papa, why is the train stopping?"

While yawning, my father replied, "We are finally approaching the Ashgabat train station. It's time for us to get ready to get off this train. It's 4:30 in the morning. I'm not sure if their ticket office will be open this early. Let me be the first to get off so that I can take a look to see where we should go."

Since the bench where we sat was located in the middle of the train car, it took us about fifteen minutes to get off the train and onto the platform. I was surprised to see four indoor platforms that could accommodate up to eight trains. Since our train was the only one positioned at a platform this early in the morning, there were no people waiting to board a train.

I glanced around the station as my father led us through the platform gate and into the main section of the train station. It was very quiet inside, with no one walking around. The Ashgabat train station's tall ceiling in the main area reminded me of the other large train stations that I saw in Poland. This station was probably as large as the others since Ashgabat was the capital city of Turkmenistan.

My father stopped walking and turned around to speak to us. "Everyone must be sleeping, since I don't see anyone. Let's find the waiting room and go there in case there is a good place for us to lie down and get some sleep. I don't know about you, but I need to get some sleep before I can deal with the ticket procedure."

The waiting room was located to the right of the ticket counter and inside a large attached building. When we entered, we noticed many people were sleeping on the benches and on the floor. My mother whispered, "Look at the back corner. There's no one back there. Let's go there and be careful not to step on anyone. We don't want to scare anyone and wake them up."

Once the four of us placed our pillowcases against the wall and lied down on the floor, we went immediately to sleep.

I was the first to wake up. I looked around and noticed a large clock above the waiting room entrance. It was 11 a.m. I remained lying on the floor for another half hour. My father was the next one to wake up.

I asked him, "Shouldn't you and I see if the ticket counter is open and how long the line is?"

My father took out his pocket watch, opened it, and said, "Yes, you are right. Let me wake up your mom and sister and tell them where you and I are going."

Once we were all awake, my mom had us eat the bread and dates that Maryam packed for us as our breakfast and drink some water from our containers.

Before going to look for the ticket counter, my father and I cleaned up in the men's room and refilled our water containers. As we approached those standing in line in front of the ticket counter, my father noticed there was a stack of newspapers on a table against one of the walls.

"Yitzhak, while I stand in line, take a look at those newspapers and see if they have news reports on their front pages. It doesn't matter if they are out of date. While I'm waiting in line, I'd like to see if there are any reports about the war between Germany and the Soviet Union."

I returned with the whole stack. "Papa, they are all written in Russian. You'll have to take a look through them."

"Okay. I'll probably be here for the rest of the day. Go ahead and walk outside to see if there are shops and a place where we could give haircuts. I noticed that a lot of the people in the waiting room were not Muslim. We might be able to earn some rubles while we are here."

"Will do, Papa. Good idea."

When I left my father, I looked around this main section of the train station. Just like most of the

Polish train stations, there was a large map of Turkmenistan on one of the walls. The map showed where Ashgabat was located. Similar to the other train stations' maps, a large arrow showed the train route to Uzbekistan. The map's arrows showed that the train from Ashgabat to Bukhoro made two stops at Tedzhen and Turkenabat before reaching Bukhoro. I didn't realize that Uzbekistan was this close.

*Wow! After nearly three months of traveling in uncomfortable horse-drawn wagons, filthy crowded trains, and long delays at train stations, my family will finally reach our final destination!*

My excitement faded as I realized that we would encounter delays at all of the train stations between Ashgabat and Tashkent, Uzbekistan. Our current train ticket listed Samarqand, Uzbekistan as our next transfer train station where we will be re-ticketed. This city wasn't even on the map!

*It may take us at least another month or more to get to Tashkent!*

When I exited the train station, I noticed there was a small grassy area on the other side of a dirt street that had many vehicles going in both directions. The grassy area had a few benches. I saw many Muslim and non-Muslim people on the street's narrow sidewalk walking to and from a small shopping area just to the right of the grassy area. One of the stores looked like a grocery store.

I thought: *This could be a good place for my father and me to give haircuts.*

I quickly returned to the waiting room so that my mom and sister could get cleaned up in the women's room and refill their water containers.

My father returned to the waiting room six hours later and sat down to join us. "I have our train tickets. Once again, there is only one train that goes back and forth between this station and a city in Uzbekistan, called Bukhoro. Today's train to Bukhoro left earlier today. The next train that leaves in three days is already sold out. There were no seats or floor sitting tickets left. We will need to wait here until next Tuesday, the 14th. After we depart, we will need to wait three days at two small cities, before we finally reach Bukhoro."

My mom quickly interrupted, "Meir, what are we going to do for six days? We don't have enough food to last that long!"

I jumped into the conversation, "I think that I found a good place for us to give haircuts at a grassy area in front of the station. Plus, there is a small area of shops nearby, and one looks like a grocery store."

My father responded, "Good. We'll take a look at them later. In the meantime, there are two places where we can wait. We can remain and sleep here, or there is a large sports complex on the other side of the train station, where most people, who are also waiting, are sleeping on the field. I think that we should remain here, since we have a good spot in the waiting room. We are also indoors! I'm tired of having to sleep outdoors on the ground. Aren't you?"

We all nodded our heads in agreement.

He continued, "As for food, when the ticket office official saw that our travel permits had the official stamp, he gave me food coupons that we can use at the station's food counter. It is located on the other side of the ticket counter in a separate room. I checked it out. We can't take our belongings with us when we go there. So, we will have to take turns. Leah will go with me, and, Rifka, you'll go with Yitzhak. Staying here for six days shouldn't be that bad. If Yitzhak and I can earn some rubles, we can stock up on canned food, bread, and tea to take with us, just in case we get stuck again at another station."

There was a pause, and then Leah spoke up. "I suppose staying and sleeping here will be alright. Boring. But alright!"

I asked, "Papa, did you learn any news about the war from the newspapers that you read?"

He paused for a few moments before answering.

"Yes, I did. It is not good news. The Germans have already conquered Kyiv and Khorol. The paper stated that 30,000 Jews were murdered in Kyiv. The Soviet army is now fighting the Germans at Odessa and at the ports along the Sea of Azov. It's a good thing that we left Bolechov as soon as we did. The German army is now advancing toward Moscow and Leningrad."

My mom asked with tears flowing from both of her eyes, "Meir, if that many Jews were murdered in Kyiv, what happened to our family and the rest of the Jews in other areas of Eastern Poland?"

With panic in her voice she continued, "They must have been taken to camps and murdered!"

"I don't know what has happened, Rifka. The newspapers that I read didn't give reports about the Jews from other cities and towns in our area of Eastern Poland."

My mom continued to sob. "They're dead! They're dead! Those Nazis killed them all. I just know it!"

All four of us hugged her tightly to try our best to comfort her. Once she calmed down, my father continued.

"It doesn't look good right now for the Soviet army. Even though we are getting close to the Uzbekistan border, we still have a long way to go until we arrive in Tashkent. When we get there, we will be far away from the Germans. We made the right decision to flee. Here we are, still alive and together.

"Enough of the bad news. Rifka and Yitzhak, here are your food coupons. Go ahead and get something to eat. Leah and I will wait here until you get back."

I put my arm around my mother, and escorted her to the station's food counter.

The four of us settled into our typical train station routine for the next six days. After eating a simple breakfast and cleaning ourselves, my father and I set up our barber's station at the grassy area in front of the train station. To our surprise and delight, we did earn some rubles each day giving haircuts to the Soviets who lived in this capital city. When we were finished, we gave our earnings to my mom and Leah to spend at the small grocery store. We stocked up quite a large supply of canned food during those six days.

Our pillowcases were much heavier to carry when we finally boarded the train to Tedzhen at 2 p.m. on Tuesday, October 14th. Unfortunately, by the time we got inside the train car, all of the benches were filled with other passengers. The only space available was for us to sit on the floor and place our pillowcase belongings between our legs. It wasn't too bad. We could lean forward and rest against it.

The train arrived in Tedzhen seven hours later at 9 p.m. My father waited in line to obtain our train tickets, while my mom, Leah, and I found a place to lie down in the station's waiting room. Tedzhen also had a small park in front of the station where my father and I set up our barber station. It was a good thing we stocked up on canned food. There was no food offered at this station, nor was there a grocery store nearby.

From Tedhzen, the train to Turkenabat departed at 8 a.m. on Saturday, October 18th. Fortunately, we obtained a bench seat for the long, thirteen-hour ride.

We arrived in Turkenabat at 9 p.m. Luckily, their train station also had a park with a museum located across the street with shops to the left of the train station. My father and I earned more rubles, while my mom and Leah purchased more canned food, bread, fruit, and tea.

Three days later, the train from Turkenabat to Bukhoro departed at 11 a.m. on Tuesday, October 21st. This was a shorter ride and only five hours long. Before arriving in Bukhoro, a train official entered our train car to remind the passengers to have their travel documents ready to show the Uzbekistan government official at the platform exit gate.

The train arrived in Bukhoro on time at 4 p.m., and we stood in the long line for the document check. Those with the official stamp on their travel permit were sent directly to the ticket counter. Others, without the stamp or documentation, were told to either go to the waiting room or the park near the train station.

This Uzbekistan train station seemed more organized than the ones in Turkmenistan. Since our travel permits had the official Soviet stamp, we immediately received our train tickets to continue our travel through Uzbekistan to reach Samarqand. The ticket counter official told my father where the Evacuation Center was located and where we could sleep and eat some cooked food!

Our train was scheduled to depart Bukhoro in three days on Friday, October 24th, to travel to another Uzbekistan city called Navoi, where we would encounter another three-day wait. I estimated that we wouldn't reach Samarqand until the end of October!

I kept thinking: *When will we ever get to Tashkent?*

# Uzbekistan:
## Bukhoro to Tashkent
## October 24, 1941 - November 9, 1941

Map Source: Nations Online Project

My family took advantage of the opportunity to eat and sleep inside the Bukhoro Evacuation Center. When we first entered, my mom was the first to notice a few unoccupied long benches where we could sleep instead of lying on the floor. The four of us raced to claim our resting spots on these benches and to store our belongings underneath the bench.

My father and I left the train station the next morning to take a long walk. He was curious to see if setting up a haircut station at the park was possible. Once we exited the station, I noticed an unusual-looking concrete building that had a blue dome on the top.  Next to the building was a tall narrow circular tower.

I pointed to the concrete building and asked, "Papa, do you know anything about that building? I've never seen anything like it before."

195

"Yitzhak, that's a mosque where Muslim people pray. The circular tower is called a minaret. Before a prayer service begins, a mosque official makes a loud call to worship from the top of the tower to the Muslim people. We're going to see lots of mosques and minarets, since the majority of the people who live in Uzbekistan are Muslim."

"Oh, I see. So, the people living here are going to be like Ibrahim and Maryam?"

"Most likely they will be. However, each region has its own customs. The type of hair coverings and the clothes for the men and women may look slightly different here in Uzbekistan than the ones worn by the Muslim people we saw in Turkmenistan."

"Papa, does the inside of a mosque look like the inside of a synagogue or church?"

"I've never been inside one. I've only viewed some pictures when I took the comparative religions class. The only similarity to a synagogue that I recall learning was that men and women sit and pray in separate areas."

The park was located a few blocks away and behind the train station. Since the streets were unpaved, a plume of dust rose up into the air as a vehicle or a horse-drawn wagon passed by us. All of the men that we saw inside the vehicles, steering the wagons, and walking along the dirt street were Muslim men wearing head coverings and beards.

"Yitzhak, let's check out the people who are staying at the park to determine if earning some rubles will be possible."

When we got to the park, we quickly noticed it was jam-packed with unkempt-looking people, with many of them picking at their skin.

I quickly realized: *There are more people gathered at this park than what we witnessed at the Sea of Azov harbor at Makhachkala!*

"Yitzhak, let's turn around and go back to the train station. I don't think it is a good idea to walk through the park anymore."
"Okay, Papa."
When we returned to the Evacuation Center, my father explained what we saw to my mom and Leah. We all agreed to remain at the center and take turns walking outside in pairs without going anywhere near the park.

Our train was scheduled to leave the Bukhoro train station at 4 p.m. on the 27th and arrive in Navoi around 7 p.m. Once we arrived in Navoi, it wouldn't be necessary for my father to go to their ticket counter, since we already received all of the tickets that we needed to use to get to Samarqand.

On the afternoon of the 27th, my father kept an eye on the train station's platform area to determine when it would be best for us to stand and wait for our train's arrival. He gave us the signal at 2 p.m. to retrieve our pillowcase belongings and follow him to the platform area. By 3:30, the platform area was packed with people. When our train arrived at 4 p.m. and the train car doors opened, those waiting on the platform rushed and squeezed their way to get inside the train as the departing passengers were stepping out. Once we entered, there wasn't space for all four of us to sit together. My father and mother sat together on one bench, while Leah and I sat together on a bench a few rows in front of them.

After Leah and I got settled on our bench and placed our pillowcases underneath, Leah faced me and said, "You know, Yitzhak, you and I haven't had

197

any time alone since the boat ride. I really miss being with just you."

"I miss being with you too, Leah."

She continued by asking, "Did you think that Papa realized that we would be traveling for nearly five months?"

I replied, "When he and I received the official travel permits from Town Marshal Novikov, nothing was mentioned about how long our travel would be."

Leah asked me more questions. "I just don't understand why we have to wait three days at each train station. This makes no sense to me. What is going to happen to us when we finally arrive in Tashkent? Will we be able to stay together? How long will we stay there?"

"I don't know, Leah. You are asking good questions. I think that while we are waiting at Navoi, you should ask Papa these questions."

"Why me? Why can't you ask him?"

"It seems that I'm always the one asking him questions. It's your turn to speak up. Don't worry. I'll sit next to you. I think that you should initiate a family talk at the next station, since we should finally arrive in Tashkent fairly soon."

The train from Bukhoro arrived on time at the Navoi station at 7 p.m. We followed my father to the Navoi train station's waiting room. Luckily, we found another long bench where we could rest and sleep. My mom felt it was best for us to sleep somewhere indoors since she noticed the outside nighttime temperature in Uzbekistan was a cool 7 degrees Celsius (*44 degrees Fahrenheit*). I purposely sat next to Leah and gave her a poke to encourage her to ask her questions.

Once we all got settled, I gave Leah another poke and nodded to signal that this was a good time for her to initiate the family discussion.

She finally spoke up. "Papa, while we are sitting here, before we do anything, I think all of us should have a talk."

He replied, "What's on your mind, my daughter?"

"Lots of things. Did you think that we would be traveling for such a long time? It has almost been five months since we left Bolechov!"

"I really didn't know. I'm surprised, as I'm sure all of you are, that we had to wait for a number of days at each station. Even though our travel permits have the official stamp, others, like the military, dignitaries, and factory workers, received more priority than us.

"But on the good side, at least we have the official stamp. If not, we would need to wait like the hundreds that we see stranded at each station that don't have one. We could be stuck somewhere with no food or water, and with some dreadful disease! That's a good question, Leah. What else is on your mind?"

"Well, Papa, what will happen to us when we finally arrive in Tashkent? Will we be separated? Where will we go?"

He answered her with a very calming tone. "Those are more good questions, my sweet daughter. I'm thinking, that once we get off the train at the Tashkent station, there will be another document check. Our travel permits state that the four of us are to be sent to an agricultural farm. I anticipate that the document check official will give us our work assignment. I think all four of us will be sent to the same farm. It is possible that the farm may have separate dormitories for men and women. It is also possible that families will be housed together. We will just have to see what happens when we get to the farm."

My mom interrupted. "Meir, how long will we need to stay there? Will we ever get to go home? I miss being with our family. What will happen if the Nazis defeat the Soviets?"

He quietly replied to try to console my mom. "Rifka, I don't have the answers. Yes, it looks like the Germans are currently winning the war. I found a newspaper this morning at the Bukhoro train station. The Nazis have now taken Odessa and Kharkiv. Even so, we have to remember that the Russians have always had a strong army. When Napoleon moved his army into Russia, the world thought that Napoleon would defeat Russia. Napoleon's army retreated during the harsh Russian winter. During the Great War of the early 1900s, when the German army moved eastward toward Russia, they also eventually retreated. I believe the same thing will happen again. Once the Soviets win and the war ends, those sent eastward, like us, should be sent back to their hometown. The Russian winter is also about to begin. The four of us will just need to remain patient. We may find the work assigned to us at the farm to be difficult. But we will be safe and the days will be warm during the winter in Tashkent than in Russia. We should look forward to a happier future. Any other questions?"

No one spoke up.

My father continued, "Now, let's take turns getting cleaned up and refilling our water containers. Yitzhak and I will take a walk tomorrow through this station and then outside to see if there is an Evacuation Center and a place for us to give haircuts. I know that we are all exhausted from this very long trip. We are almost at the end of this journey. We depart in three days on Thursday, the 30th, at 7 p.m. to take the train to Samarqand, where we will receive our final train tickets. Hopefully, this time we will go directly to Tashkent without any transfers."

Even though there was a little park across the street from the Navoi station and a large park a block away, both of them were flooded with people. I think my father gave up the idea of giving any more haircuts. He gave my mom some rubles to purchase food at a small grocery store for us while we waited these three days.

On Thursday, October 30th, we promptly boarded the train at the Navoi station at 7 p.m. to go to Samarqand. This time, we found an open bench where all four of us could sit together. I was fortunate to sit next to the window and looked out while there was still daylight. All I saw was barren land. When it got dark, I looked up at the flickering stars in the clear sky during the remainder of the five-hour train ride and reflected on what the future had in store for us.

Once the train arrived at the Samarqand station at midnight, the four of us stood in line for the usual document check at the platform gate. When the train official viewed our travel permits, he explained to my father for us to go quickly to the ticket counter before it closed. Once he obtained our train tickets at the ticket office, we needed to walk two blocks to their Evacuation Center located inside a school. The official also told my father that we needed to keep a close eye on our belongings, since some theft incidents had occurred there. We got to this center at 1 a.m., just in time to find a place to sleep.

After we woke up the next morning, my father indicated he had some news to share with us. He spoke very quietly in order to not disturb those near us who were still sleeping. "I have some disappointing news. Like you, I was hoping that this time we wouldn't have to make any more train transfers. First, we won't leave this station until Sunday, November 2nd. Then, we are going to have to transfer trains again and wait three days at two more train stations in cities called Jizzakh and Guliston. It looks like we won't finally arrive in Tashkent until Saturday, November 8$^{th}$. I'm sorry. We'll just need to remain patient. We will finally get there!"

As much as I hated hearing that we still had to make two more stops before arriving in Tashkent, I knew that my father was correct about us doing our best to remain patient.

Since Leah was sitting next to me, I whispered, "Leah, don't be upset about having to wait again at two more stations. Papa is doing his best. We will get to Tashkent very soon."

I continued, "I'm very proud of you for speaking up the other day. Papa really respects your input and the questions that you asked. If something comes up in the future that is confusing or upsets you, don't hold back. We all want to listen to you."

"Thank you, my brother. I love you!"

When our train approached Jizzakh on Wednesday, November 5$^{th}$, I looked out the window and was surprised to see snow-capped mountains and lakes in the horizon instead of barren land. I also noticed that mature shade trees lined both sides of the city's streets. We spent the three days resting and eating inside the train station's service building. We also took walks along the tree-lined paved streets to enjoy viewing this scenic city with its many mosques and minarets. So far, Jizzahk was the most beautiful city I've seen since we arrived in Soviet-controlled Asia.

We left the Jizzakh station on Saturday, November 8$^{th}$, at 8 p.m. and arrived in Guliston at 11 p.m. We briskly walked as fast as we could to be the first from our train to find a place in the waiting room where we could sleep. When we woke up the next morning, my father took a walk through the station. He learned that there wasn't an Evacuation Center at this station. We were on our own to find something to eat while we waited for the three days inside the station's waiting room. My mom surprised us when she pulled out cans of food and some bread that she had saved.

There were two small grassy areas in front of the train station. We often took walks along the streets near the train station. Guliston was not as scenic as Jizzakh. The terrain was flat and barren with dirt streets and dust in the air. Even though mosques and minarets were visible, the city had a very drab appearance.

For some undisclosed reason, our train's departure time from Guliston on Monday, November 10th for Tashkent was delayed to 4 a.m. the next morning. Our new arrival time in Tashkent changed to 8 a.m. The delay actually worked in our favor, since most train stations' ticket offices and government offices didn't open until 8 a.m.

As the train slowly departed from the Guliston train station, I kept repeating these thoughts:

*What awaits us in Tashkent?*

*What will it be like working on a farm?*

*Is Tashkent really the "City of Bread" as many people have mentioned?*

# Arrival in Tashkent
## Tuesday, November 11, 1941

Once the door opened, we squeezed our way onto the train and managed to find an open bench for the four of us to sit together. As soon as the train left the Guliston Station, my mom and Leah quickly fell asleep. My father and I sat next to each other and both of us remained awake. After a while, I noticed that he frequently pulled out his pocket watch and looked at it. The frequency of this action was very unlike him. I never noticed him being so fidgety.

I quietly asked, "Papa, is something wrong or upsetting you? I've noticed that you keep looking at your pocket watch."

He didn't answer me at first. After a long pause, he confided with a despondent voice, "I'm thinking about Leah's questions. She raised some important issues and I really don't have the answers. I just don't know what will happen to us once we arrive in Tashkent and get to the document check. I'm worried that when the Soviet official notices that we are Jews, he may not immediately place us at a farm right away. If that happens, how will we survive? Where will we go? This train isn't going to be the only one arriving in Tashkent. The escapees arriving on the other trains may receive priority over us. I'm also worried that we may be separated from each other!"

I've never seen my father be so emotionally disturbed. He has always been our family's pillar of strength and optimism.

I tried my best to comfort him. "Try not to worry, Papa. Other officials along the way have treated us well, particularly when they saw the stamp on the

204

travel permits that we received from Town Marshal Novikov."

He drew me closer and placed my head on his right shoulder. "I hope you're right, Yitzhak. I hope you're right. Try to get some sleep, my son. Most likely we will stand in long lines when we arrive."

The rays from the rising sun streaking through the window woke me up. I looked past the other people sitting next to us to see outside. I could tell we were approaching Tashkent when I saw additional trains heading in the same direction as ours. My father was correct. Multiple trains from other areas of the Soviet Union were arriving at the same time as ours.

When our train slowed down even more, I noticed that father's eyes were closed and his lips slightly moved without making any sound.

I realized: *He is saying a prayer.*

The train's sudden and jerky stop woke up my mom and Leah. My father immediately grabbed all of us together into a tight huddle.

"We are here. We finally arrived in Tashkent. You will notice that a lot of people will be getting off numerous trains at the same time. It will be very crowded, and we need to stay close together. Don't get distracted. Stay focused and tightly hold onto your belongings. Are you ready to get off this train and face our next journey together?"

Both Leah and I energetically responded, "Yes, Papa!" My mom smiled at the three of us.

When I got off the train, I noticed that three trains arrived at the Tashkent station at the same time as ours. Each platform was packed with passengers who were lined up to show their documents to the train station's official at each platform's gate. Most of them

205

were carrying sacks of their belongings. As I stood in our line, I looked ahead to see how the train official was processing passengers. I noticed that those who showed a particular card to the official were allowed to immediately leave the station. Others were being directed by the official to get into another long line.

I pointed this out to my father and asked, "Do you have any idea what type of card those people are showing the train official?"

He responded. "My best guess is that their card is some type of Tashkent resident registration card."

Leah, then asked, "Papa, will we receive one of those cards?"

"We'll see."

About an hour passed before the train official processed us. Since we didn't have a Tashkent resident's card, the official pointed for us to stand in the other long line.

That line moved forward very slowly. When we got close enough to watch the processing procedure, we saw four Soviet uniformed officials sitting at a long table. Above the table was a sign written in Polish and in Russian. The sign explained that the officials sitting on the right would process those arriving from Eastern Poland, while the other two officials sitting on the left would process those arriving from the Soviet Union and other countries. Similar to the platform check, some people were directed by the officials to immediately leave the station very quickly, while others were processed slower and more intensively.

At least another hour passed before we stood in front of one of the officials who dealt with the arrivals from Eastern Poland.

With a very stern voice, the Soviet official asked, "Are all four of you arriving together?"

My father cordially replied, "Yes. We are one family, mother and father, son and daughter."

206

"Show me all of the travel permits. Only those with the official Soviet stamp on their permits will be processed today."

My father gave him the travel permits and pointed to the town marshal's stamp. The official carefully read each one.

"These are all in order. Good. I am going to fill out your official Tashkent identification registration cards. You will each receive one that has the official prospika registration stamp. Do not lose these cards. This is proof that you can remain in Tashkent. Each of you will need to show this card to your new employer, and any official, particularly the police, that requests seeing it. When you hear the word, 'prospika', you must show them this card. Do you understand?"

All four of us answered affirmatively.

It took the official some time to carefully fill out duplicate registration cards that listed our name, age, and where we were from. He also wrote a large letter 'J' on our cards. Since I was eighteen, I received my own card. Leah's name and age were written on the backside of my mother's card. The official told Leah to take my mother's card if she ventured out on her own. She would receive her own card on her eighteenth birthday. When he completed filling out all of the cards, he handed my father one set and filed the duplicate set into his official file box.

Then he told us, "You can now go to the Tashkent Executive Committee's Employment Office to receive your employment assignment. Turn left when you exit the train station and walk to the first wide street. Turn left again and walk to the next wide street called Nukus Street. Turn left once more onto Nukus Street and walk until you see the farmer's market called the Mirabad Bazaar on the right side. Walk straight through the Mirabad Bazaar. On the opposite side of the bazaar, you will see a gray multi-floor concrete building displaying the Soviet Union flag. This is the Soviet government office building. Go inside and tell the lobby clerk to point you to the Executive Committee's Employment office. Do you have any questions?"

My father replied, "No. Thank you for your help."

"Good luck to you. Welcome to Tashkent."

When we exited the Tashkent train station, all four of us stopped and looked with disbelief at the enormous number of impoverished looking people sitting on the ground very close to each other. We were horrified to see hordes of people covered with dust and dirt on their clothing and faces. Many were picking body lice off their skin. Others had open red sores on their bodies.

I immediately thought: *Tashkent doesn't look like the 'City of Bread' that Town Marshal Novikov mentioned. It looks more like the 'City of Disease'!*

When we slowly walked past them, many of their arms reached up to us as they begged in both Polish and Russian for something to eat and drink. Leah, my mom, and I moved closer to my father as he led us through the very narrow and dusty street with the crowds of people sitting on the ground. We also smelled an unusual odor coming from the camels and mules that trotted along on the street.

We easily found Nukus Street. All of the shops on the opposite sides of the street displayed the official Soviet Union hammer and sickle emblem on their entrance door, indicating that the Soviet government owned the shop. The Mirabad Bazaar looked quite different from the Rynek market of Bolechov. Instead of an orderly arrangement of the nice-looking stalls,

208

the ones in this market were shabby and not placed in any type of order. This market area seemed like a massive labyrinth of tight and twisted alleys. My father struggled to continue to find our way to the opposite end, as we encountered constant aggressive offers from the vendors to come into their stalls. Walking through the market was also difficult due to the large number of aggressive beggars approaching us.

The local Uzbek Muslim people who operated the stalls and those walking through the market looked very different than the Muslim people that we saw in Turkmenistan. The Uzbek men wore long white cotton kaftans and light brown cotton pants. Their head coverings were very colorful. Some were red, green, gray, or black. All had a black band going around the front and back of their heads. Some of their head coverings also had a square-shaped dome. The head coverings worn by the Uzbek men didn't cover up all of their hair. Hair protruded out of their head covering down to their ears. The only similarity to those from Turkmenistan was that the Uzbek men also had long beards.

When I saw the Uzbek men displaying some hair coming out of their head coverings, I immediately thought: *The Uzbek Muslim men might be willing to let us give them a haircut.*

Some of the Uzbek women wore long black veils to hide their faces. Others, particularly the younger women, wore long colorful embroidered dresses that reached their ankles. Their head coverings were also much different than the headscarves worn by the Turkmenistan women. The Uzbek women's head coverings were very colorful and matched or complimented the color of their long dresses. Another difference was that the front of their head coverings

209

had a stiff rim. We noticed that some of these women wore gold necklaces.

As we continued to make our way through the market, we saw exotic looking fruits being sold in the stalls. My father and mother identified them as honeydews, watermelons, cantaloupes, raisins, grapes, and apricots. There were all kinds of vegetables, fresh bread and butter, and bags of rice and nuts being sold. Many of the stalls were food stands with small wood-fired stoves and grills. They sold grilled meat with peppers and onions on skewers and served soup or some type of stew in small ceramic cups.

When we exited the market and crossed the street, the Soviet government building was facing us. We brushed off the dust from our clothing and entered. The lobby desk clerk told us to go up one level and wait in line to speak with the representative from the Executive Committee's Employment Office who was sitting at a desk in the hallway. Once again, we stood in line for about an hour before speaking to the representative.

I was not expecting to see an employment official wearing a Soviet military uniform. I could tell from the number of stripes on his sleeves that he was a sergeant.

Speaking in both Russian and Polish, he identified himself as Sergeant Orlov. After my father introduced us by speaking Polish, the sergeant asked in Polish to see our travel permits and prospikas.

After closely reviewing them, he inquired, "I notice that the travel permits state that you and your son are barbers."

My father replied, "Yes, we are. Let me show you our Soviet barber licenses." My dad quickly opened his barber's box to retrieve the licenses and showed them to the sergeant. "As you can see, we have our own tools."

The sergeant had a perplexed look on his face and then said, "Please take a seat on those four chairs down the hallway. I'll be back in a moment. I want to show your documents to my captain." He quickly went inside the office as we sat down on the chairs.

I asked, "Papa, do you think something is wrong?"

"I don't know, Yitzhak. Let's be patient and see what happens."

About ten minutes later, Sergeant Orlov returned with another Soviet officer. His uniform emblem identified him as a captain.

We all attentively stood up when the two of them approached us. The captain spoke to us in Polish. "I'm Captain Lebedev. I see that your documents show that the two of you are barbers, and all four of you were sent to Tashkent by your town marshal to work at one of our collective farms. I'm going to assign you to Kolkhoz Akkatay. I know their Soviet manager very well. We are in process of converting their fields to grow and harvest more wheat to help feed our military and the workers being sent here. This kolkhoz needs more workers and they can use all four of you. I'm marking on your official employment form for your wife and daughter to work in their bakery to help them increase their bread-making operation. Since you and your son are barbers and you have your own tools, the two of you will start working in their infirmary to cut the hair of the new arrivals and their current workers. You might also be assigned, on occasion, to help at their granary when you aren't giving haircuts. In addition, I'm going to mark on the employment form that Kolkhoz Akkatay will send the two of you to come to this building once a week to give our employees haircuts. How does this sound to you? Can you also give shaves and trim moustaches?"

My father responded, "We're very pleased with our work assignment, Captain Lebedev. Yes, my son and I can also give your employees shaves and trim moustaches. We can also cut women's hair, if you have women employees. For shaves, we will need you to provide the soap to make the needed shaving lather and to bring your own moustache wax. What about the towels that we will need for the shaves?"

"I'll mark on the employment form that the kolkhoz will provide and send some towels with you. They have a truck that comes to the market every morning to stock their stall with bread items. Their truck can bring you here on Wednesday mornings. In the late afternoon, their truck will take you back to the kolkhoz after they close the stall. We'll set up your haircut station in the upstairs restroom area, so that you can use the sink. There will be a broom and pan in there for you to use to clean the floor. Anything else?"

"No, sir. Thank you."

"You're welcome. I'm going to telephone the Soviet manager at the kolkhoz that you are here and explain to him your Wednesday and kolkhoz assignments. There are six others waiting outside for the Kolkhoz Akkatay truck. Go ahead and join them once Sergeant Orlov gives you the official employment forms. I'll see you and your son this coming Wednesday for my haircut, shave, and moustache trim." The captain quickly turned around, opened the office door, and went inside the office.

It took the sergeant about ten minutes to fill out our employment forms. When he handed them to my father, he said, "Now go to the front of the building and wait with the six others. A truck with an Akkatay sign on their windshield will arrive in about an hour. We'll have everything ready this coming Wednesday

212

for the haircuts. We've been waiting some time for skilled barbers to arrive!"

As we walked through the downstairs lobby, I turned to my father and asked, "Papa, did you ever expect that we would receive work assignments like these?"

"No, not at all. I wonder if this is the reason Town Marshal Novikov insisted that we bring our tools with us."

"Papa, I have one more question. What will we charge for their haircuts, shaves, and moustache trims?"

"I think that providing barber services is part of our regular Tashkent employment. I have a hunch we will only receive a meager gratuity for each service from the government employees. This may be a way for us to earn some extra money. We may not earn much from the farm since they are providing us with a place to live, eat, and work. Let us all be thankful that we are all still together."

When we got outside the government building, we saw the six others sitting on the building's front steps with their sacks of belongings. My dad approached them and asked in both Russian and Polish, "Are you waiting for the truck from Kolkhoz Akkatay?"

The four men answered affirmatively in Russian, while a man and woman answered in Polish. We all introduced each other with my father's translating assistance.

The four men told us that they were from Moscow. They all worked together as auto mechanics and the Soviets sent them to Tashkent to maintain and repair the farm equipment at a kolkhoz. When they mentioned that their names were Yankel, Schmuel, Natan, and Herschel, I asked my father to inquire if they were Jewish. The four nodded 'yes' and Schmuel told my father that many Jews fled from Moscow to come to Tashkent.

The man and woman were married, and their names were Marcin and Dominka. They were farmers from a village near Kyiv. They were sent by the Soviets to work as farmers at a kolkhoz.

About a half hour later, an old, open-bed truck, displaying the Akkatay sign on the passenger side window, pulled up in front of the Soviet government office. The driver was an Uzbek man. He asked all of us to show him our Soviet employment forms so he could verify that our names were on his list. Once he confirmed everything, he motioned to us where to place our belongings and to sit in the truck's rear bed.

The dusty dirt road that led out of the central area of Tashkent was very bumpy. The six of us turned around to face the front of the truck and raised our shirts or headscarves over our mouths and noses to avoid breathing in the stirred-up dust. I lost track of the direction we were going, since the truck made frequent turns onto other dirt roads. When the truck made another turn, we passed by a row of numerous mud huts that served as the living quarters for local Uzbek farmers and their families. Uzbek women were hanging up clothes behind the huts to dry in the sun. On the other side of the road, I viewed enormous fields of crops and some farm machinery being operated by their workers.

All of a sudden, our driver honked his truck's horn and pointed his left hand out of the truck window. I looked ahead. In the distance I saw a few tall, wooden structures, and a series of very large canvas tents.

*This must be Kolkhoz Akkatay where we will live and work.*

Within minutes, the truck pulled up and stopped in front of one of the large canvas tents. Two men came out to greet us. I surmised that the Uzbek man was the kolkhoz's foreman, and the man with a large curled moustache with an exposed full head of hair was the kolkhoz's Soviet manager. The ten of us climbed out of the truck's bed and grabbed our belongings. The kolkhoz manager greeted us by speaking in both Russian and Polish. "Welcome to Kolkhoz Aggatay. I'm Vladimir Petrov, the manager of this kolkhoz. This is our foreman, Rashid Umarov. Come with us to our infirmary. Since you have been on a rather long journey to get here, we need to spray you with disinfectant, cut your hair, and for you to take a good shower."

My father spoke up. "Mr. Petrov, my son and I were sent here to work as barbers. We have our own tools. We can begin right now to cut everyone's hair. I can show you our official employment forms."

"I don't need to see the forms. The employment office already called me and I know about the occupation of you and your son. I already planned for the two of you to begin working as barbers right away. By the way, it is not necessary for you to refer to me as Mr. Petrov. All of our workers call me Vladimir."

The infirmary was located inside one of the large canvas tents that I saw from the truck. The interior of the tent was divided into different sections with the largest one for medical purposes. The manager pointed to one of the small areas and told us that it would serve as our barber's station. When an Uzbek middle-aged woman approached the eight of us with two large bins, the manager explained, "All of your clothing needs to be washed. This is Soliha. She is in charge of our laundry services. She will give you a laundry pen. Clearly write your family name on all of

215

your clothing, including your sacks, pillowcases, and any other fabric items. After getting undressed, place your clothing and sacks in the designated bin. They will be washed tomorrow and returned to you. Soliha will issue you towels for your shower and a set of work clothes for you to wear in the meantime. She will show you where the men and women's changing areas, showers, and toilets are located.

"Meir, you and your son, Yitzhak, need to be the first to complete this process so that the two of you can give the others their haircuts."

My father asked, "How short should we cut everyone's hair?"

"Real short. The women should also have short hair, with some style. They will be wearing headscarves, as is the custom for women here in Uzbekistan.

"Any questions?"

My mom spoke up, "Yes, I have a question. What should we do with our glass water and food containers? Is there a place where they can be washed?"

He replied, "Keep them for now. Tomorrow, someone will show you where you can wash them in our kitchen. Now all of you follow Soliha. Rashid and I will see you in our dining area this evening."

Soliha gave each of us a set of work clothes and towels from the bin and showed where the changing rooms, showers, and toilets were located. The showers and toilets were located outside of the hut with canvas hangings to provide privacy. The outdoor showers were very similar to the one that we used at Ibrahim and Maryam's tent with a release cord for water to descend.

My father and I were the first of the men to be disinfected, showered, and dressed. He placed the case that stored our barber's tools and documents within his view in order to prevent it from being stolen.

As the two of us walked to the barber's station, he said, "Yitzhak, I want you to give the men the typical close clipper cut. When the women arrive, I'll go ahead and cut their hair since I have more practice cutting women's hair than you. While we wait for the others to come to the infirmary, go ahead and cut my hair and then I'll cut yours later on."

It took us about two hours to finish cutting everyone's hair. Leah and my mom sat in the infirmary and waited for us to finish. Once we were done and cleaned up the area from the cut hair, Soliha escorted us to the housing tent area. Three large tents were arranged in a circle, with additional outdoor restrooms placed in the middle. One large tent was designated for families and single adults with children. Single men and single women were assigned to separate tents.

The inside of our hut was arranged into separate compartments with canvas dividers hung from the ceiling. Married couples had one bunk bed, one four-drawer dresser, one stand with a kerosene lamp, and one cabinet. A family of four was provided with a larger compartment consisting of two sets of bunk beds, two four-drawer dressers, one stand with a kerosene lamp, and two cabinets. As we walked through the tent with Soliha, we were pleased to see that Marcin and Dominka were also assigned to live in our tent. Many of the compartments were empty. Apparently, the kolkhoz was expecting more workers to arrive.

Soliha escorted us into in our compartment and quickly left. My mom looked around and said, "There isn't much privacy. Others will hear what we say. I hope it is quiet at night so I can sleep!"

My father seemed pleased that we had our own area. He pointed to the cabinets. "Look. I can lock up and secure our documents and our barber's equipment box. I brought a lock and key. They're inside the box. I'll inquire about where I can obtain an additional lock to use on the other cabinet. There is plenty of room to store our belongings in these dressers."

He continued, "Yitzhak and Leah, the two of you will sleep on the top beds, while your mom and I will sleep on the bottom ones. I know that the two of you are used to sleeping in your own bedroom. We'll just have to get used to living in this arrangement. At least we are together and not in separate tents or being sent to different kolkhozes."

Leah and I gave a big sigh and said, "Yes, Papa."

Apparently, two other young married couples that were living in our tent overheard us speaking Yiddish. From outside our compartment, one of the men asked in Yiddish, "Where are you from?"

My mom pulled the canvas divider open to see who was there. It turned out these couples were also Jewish and lived in villages near Lviv. Their names were Dovid and Golda, and Feivel and Esther. They were sent by the Soviets to work as farmers. Both couples arrived in Tashkent six weeks earlier and didn't experience waiting many days at some of the train stations. I think my parents felt more at ease about being assigned to this kolkhoz knowing that there were other Jewish people living in our tent.

At 7 p.m., we heard a loud whistle. Leah, being alarmed, yelled, "What's going on?"

Feivel announced, "That's the whistle to let us know that it is time for all of us to go to their food canteen for our evening meal. Come with us and we'll show you where it is."

While walking to the canteen, Esther mentioned, "Don't expect much. They serve us the same food every day for lunch and dinner. The meal consists of slices of bread, a bowl of vegetable soup with potatoes and cabbage, and cups of tea to drink. Get in line with us. There should be a table where we can all sit together."

While we were waiting in the food line, I looked around the room. I was surprised to only see about thirty people. After we were all seated, I asked Dovid about the small number of people eating dinner. He responded, "Most of the Uzbek farmers return to their home at the end of the work day. They only eat lunch in the dining room. There are about a total of sixty workers. I think the Soviet manager, Vladimir, is expecting more workers will be placed here."

Being my curious self, I asked with a whisper, "Do we ever get a day off?"

"We usually don't work on Fridays. The Uzbek Muslims go to a mosque every Friday afternoon for prayers. There are also set times during the day when they are allowed to stop working and recite their prayers. The manager and foreman allow this. They feel permitting them to observe their religious practices keeps them focused to work hard."

I then very quietly asked him, "Do you and Golda and the other Jewish workers observe Shabbat?"

"No, we don't. Considering the hostility toward Jews in Europe, we all think it is best for us to remain as quiet as we can that we are Jews."

Once everyone in line was seated, the manager, Vladimir, clapped his hands to get everyone's attention. "Good evening, everyone. As you know, it is our custom to welcome the newcomers who are joining us at Kolkhoz Aggatay. Those that arrived today, please stand up."

When the eight of us stood up, Vladimir announced, "They will help us meet our new grain production quota. And by the way, we now have a father and son team of professional barbers. Please come to my office to sign up for your haircut. My secretary will coordinate their schedule. Rashid and I are getting our haircuts tomorrow, and we will be the first ones. Have a good rest tonight. Tomorrow begins a new week of productive work."

Everyone left the dining room at 8 p.m. to use the restrooms and prepare to go to sleep. Feivel reviewed with us the daily schedule. All lights inside the tents were turned off at 9 p.m. A wake-up whistle was blown at 6 a.m., breakfast was served at 7 a.m., and work began at 8 a.m. Lunch was served in two shifts. Non-Muslims were served at 12 noon. Muslims were served at 1 p.m., shortly after they finished their prayers.

My mom helped us prepare our bedding with the sheets, blankets, and pillowcases that were placed on each bed. My bed was above my father's, and Leah's was above my mom's.

Once we climbed in, my father tried his best to reassure and comfort us. "I know that being here is much different than our former life in Bolechov. It may take some time for us to get used to it. Do your best each day. We made the right decision to come here. The work may be hard, but we can do it as long as we are here together. We managed to endure all of the hardships that we faced during the five months spent riding in the wagon, on the trains, and waiting at all of the train stations. We can also handle working and living here. It seems that all of the workers respect Vladimir, the manager. I can tell that he has created a good working relationship with everyone. He doesn't act like a boss who is a tyrant.

"Get a good sleep tonight, my family. Your mom and I love you, Leah and Yitzhak. Tomorrow we will begin our new life."

Once he finished speaking, I said, "I love you, Papa and Mama."

Leah added, "I love you too!"

# Daily Life at the Kolkhoz
## November - December 1941

My mother was the only one who heard the 6 a.m. wake up whistle. I felt her shaking me. "Wake up, Yitzhak, wake up! It's time for you to get yourself ready for your first day of work!"

"Alright, mom." As I rose up, she shook Leah and my father to wake them up.

By seven o'clock, the four of us were ready to go to the canteen. After going through the food line, Dovid and Golda waved for us to join them at their table.

Golda greeted us as we sat down. "Are you ready to eat their wheat porridge for breakfast? It will taste better if you put a little sugar on it and then add some milk. You'll get used to eating it. This is what they serve us every morning."

As we were eating and drinking some tea, my mom asked Golda, "Do you know where the kitchen is located?"

"I'll show you where it is. It's in a separate area behind the canteen. It's actually easy to find. I'm surprised that you and Leah were assigned to work there. I've only seen Uzbek women working in the kitchen."

My mom replied, "We were told that this kolkhoz needed our help to improve their bread production for the Soviet army."

When the time got near 8 o'clock, my father motioned to me that we needed to leave the canteen and report to the infirmary. "Yitzhak and I will see all of you at lunch later on today." He and I returned our food trays, went back to our tent to retrieve the box with our barber supplies from the locked cabinet, and then headed to the infirmary.

Our kolkhoz manager, Vladimir, and foreman, Rashid, were already sitting in our area of the infirmary and waiting for us.

Vladimir greeted us when we entered. "Meir, I hope you and your family had a good rest last night after experiencing a rather long journey to get here."

My father responded, "Yes, we all had a very sound sleep. My wife woke the rest of us up when she heard the 6 a.m. whistle. So, I assume that you and Rashid are here to be the first ones to receive our services. What can we do for the two of you?"

Vladimir answered, "It has been many months since any of our workers, including the two of us, have had a good haircut. Some will also need a good shave. I know that I could also use a mustache trim. Rashid told me to tell you that in addition to cutting the hair that covers over his ears, he would like his beard slightly trimmed and shaped. He wants to show the other Uzbek men and women at lunch today what the two of you can do."

My father smiled at me and then explained, "We will gladly honor your requests. Both my son and I give a good shave, mustache trim, as well as a haircut. If anyone wants their mustache curled, they will need to bring their mustache wax with them. As for shaves, we will need some soap to make the lather, a large bowl of water, access to a sink, and some towels."

Vladimir repeated the needed supplies to Rashid, and Rashid left. "Rashid is going to get the soap, bowl, and towels from Soliha. He'll be right back. You can use the sink outside the shower area."

My father then asked, "Have many people signed up for their haircuts?"

223

Vladimir answered, "We have a total of ten people interested for today. How do you want them scheduled?"

"Let's do two per hour. I'll handle one, while Yitzhak will handle the other person."

"Great. I'll tell my secretary. She'll tell them that I have given them approval to leave their work assignment for an hour to come here. Rashid plans to take the two of you to the canteen during lunch today to introduce you to our Muslim workers. Soliha will be there and she can provide any needed translation."

When Rashid returned, my father and I placed our capes on both Vladimir and Rashid and proceeded to give them their requested services. Both beamed joyful smiles of approval when we dramatically removed their capes and they looked into our small mirror.

Vladimir enthusiastically proclaimed, "You two are going to be very busy once we show everyone what we now look like! Wow! I'm very impressed!"

He was correct. When Rashid introduced us to the Uzbek workers as the new barbers, we received a big cheer. As we were cleaning up our area at the end of the afternoon, Vladimir came into the infirmary and told us, "All of the slots for Thursday, Friday morning, Saturday, and Sunday are already filled. If we receive any new arrivals during the rest of the week, we'll just have to somehow squeeze them in. I'll make sure that Soliha provides your bowl and towels each day and the towels that you are taking with you on Wednesdays."

When my father and I got back to our area in the hut, we both climbed into our beds to get some rest before it was time to go to the canteen for dinner. We were very tired from standing on our feet for most of the day. My hands were also sore from gripping the hand clippers.

The 7 p.m. whistle woke us up. My father seemed concerned that my mom and Leah were not back from the kitchen. "Yitzhak. I have a hunch that your mom and Leah are meeting us in the canteen. Let's just go and see if they are there."

As my father anticipated, the two of them were already sitting at a table with Feivel and Esther. We joined them after we went through the food line.

Shortly after sitting down, I asked, "Mom and Leah, how was your first day?"

My mom responded, "Very tiring. Now, I know the reason Captain Lebedev assigned us to come here and work in the kitchen. This kolkhoz recently received new ovens to bake bread. The Uzbek women only know how to bake round bread in the wood-fired clay ovens that are kept outside. We had to show them how to use the rectangular pans, the use of yeast to make the dough rise, and bake the bread in the new ovens. The Uzbek women gasped when they saw Leah and me add a layer of twisted dough on the top, like we did when we baked challah. The bakery manager spoke some Russian that I could understand. She thought this type of braided bread would be a great addition to the bread sold at their market stall. She let me bring back four small rolls. Here. Take one and enjoy eating it!

"The Soviets also provided rectangular bags for packing the baked loaves. After the bread cooled, we packed all of the loaves. These will be the ones sent to the army. The kitchen has been ordered to immediately increase the bread supply shipments. Leah and I are going to be very busy.

"What about your day, Meir?"

He responded, "Just like you and Leah. We are going to be very busy, including Friday mornings."

"Leah and I were also told to report to work on Friday mornings in order for the kitchen to meet this new quota. While the bread was baking, I had time to wash out our water and food containers for you to take with you on Wednesdays."

I added, "I don't know about all of you, but with all of the work I did today, I'm hungry. Is this really what they are providing us to eat every day?"

Both Feivel and Esther nodded and said, "Get used to it."

Being inquisitive, my father quietly asked Feivel, "Do we get paid for working here?"

Feivel explained, "This is a collective farm. All of the workers are paid in cash at the end of the month when the kolkhoz financial office determines the monthly profit, after deducting the production expenses and administrative costs. Our monthly pay averages about one hundred rubles a month per worker, or a little over three rubles a day. As long as a worker is deemed productive by their supervisor, a worker will receive the same amount regardless of their job assignment. It isn't much and we can hardly afford to purchase anything at a market. Their prices are very high. The market's high prices are due to the demand from the massive number of evacuees and refugees in the city, along with the locals, who shop at the market. Others have told me that all of the food is sold out by the early afternoon every day!"

My father responded, "You're right, Feivel. One hundred rubles really don't sound like much. At least we don't have to pay any rent to stay here. The kolkhoz also provides us with some working clothes, and laundry service. They feed us what they can."

When my parents, Leah, and I returned to our tent area after dinner, we were very surprised to find all of the clothing and pillowcases that were placed in the bin were now clean, folded, and neatly placed on my

226

father's bed, along with another set of work clothing for each of us. Esther later explained that everyone was issued two sets of work clothes per week and that our dirty work clothes are to be placed in a bin in our tent.

The next day was even busier for my father and me in the infirmary. We each handled six men who all wanted haircuts, a beard trim, and a shave around their neck area. At the end of the workday, as Vladimir promised, Soliha gave us a stack of towels to take with us the next morning.

My father and I were very curious about giving haircuts the following Wednesday at the Soviet government building. We wondered if we would receive any gratuities. We also wondered what our clients would share with us during a conversation. My father made some suggestions. "Yitzhak, if a client asks about your name, just say 'Barkan' and refrain from saying 'Yitzhak'. It may be best to try to conceal that we are Jewish. We may receive better gratuities. If they bring up the war, don't ask any questions. Just let them talk. If we do learn anything important about the war, please don't share it with your mother. She is already too upset about the possibility that our family members are all dead."

"Okay, Papa. Will do. What about Leah, can I share any war news with her?"

"Just do it privately." Then he added, "I packed our barber's capes so that we would look like professional barbers to these government officials!"

The kolkhoz truck driver dropped us off at 7:30 a.m. in front of the Soviet government building and told us he would pick us up around 5 p.m. to take us back to Kolkhoz Aggatay. When we tried opening the building's entrance door, it was locked. A sign was posted on the door stating that the building would open at 8 a.m. While sitting on the front steps, my father and I had a great view of the vendors preparing their stalls for the market's opening.

The government office building guard unlocked the door promptly at 8 o'clock and intently questioned us about our purpose. Once my father explained to him that Captain Lebedev was expecting us, he let us come inside. We didn't see anyone in the upstairs hallway, so we went into the employment office and told one of the clerks who we were. Captain Lebedev must have heard our voices and came out of his office to great us.

"Good morning. You arrived promptly on time with all of your supplies. I assume the towels are inside the sack that you are carrying. I'll have to thank Vladimir for making all of the arrangements the next time that I speak to him. Did you have any difficulty getting inside the building?"

My father responded, "The guard at the front door asked us some questions."

"I have name badges for the two of you to wear when you come here. When you arrive next week, come to the employee's entrance at the rear of the building. The guard there will let you inside when he sees your badge. You can also go to our eating area in the basement to have lunch. We can't offer much, due to the food rationing, but you'll find something to eat and drink. It opens at 11:30. Let's go upstairs and I'll show you where the restroom area is that will serve as the barber station. Sergeant Orlov is up there with our custodian getting the area ready for you and the lather soap that you requested. Here's the hourly schedule that our office clerk organized for twelve men to receive haircuts, shaves, and moustache trims today. Sergeant Orlov and I will be the first ones."

My father commented, "Thank you for getting everything organized for us and allowing us to have lunch."

Captain Lebedev and Sergeant Orlov stared at us with awe when they saw my father and me put on our barber capes. After they sat down on their chair, we prepared them for their haircut by placing a cape over their clothing and wrapping some toilet roll paper around their neck to keep any cut hair falling on their skin.

Sergeant Orlov commented, "The two of you really are professional barbers, aren't you? It feels like we are actually inside a barber's shop, doesn't it, captain?"

The captain smiled and nodded his head in approval.

Once we began the haircuts, Captain Lebedev initiated a conversation with my father. "You may have noticed that Kolkhoz Aggatay is one of our smaller collective farms. Our government intentionally placed Vladimir to manage this farm. We've experienced some difficulty getting the local Uzbek people to work productively. Many of them still resent that the Soviet Union has taken control of the farms. We're allowing Vladimir some leeway with how he operates the kolkhoz. So far, the Soviet government is pleased with the productivity of his workers. In return, Vladimir has asked me to be very selective with placing new workers at this kolkhoz. He particularly requested that no children be sent there. He doesn't want to deal with the expense and management of operating a school. I felt that your family would be a good addition and that the workers would enjoy and be more motivated to work having access to barber services. Plus, I think your wife will prove to be a good asset with improving the quantity of bread produced in their kitchen with the new ovens. How do you like being there, so far?"

My father and I both nodded to show our approval and continued with their haircuts. In a little while, when Sergeant Orlov started talking about the war, my father stared at me as a reminder to remain quiet.

"It's a good thing that you and your family escaped when you did. If you had waited, you would never have been able to reach the Caspian Sea. At this moment, our army is fighting the Nazis at Stalingrad and along the entire northern coast of the Sea of Azov. We are probably going to have to recruit more soldiers if we are going to win this war."

After we finished and had them look at themselves in the mirror, both of them were very pleased. The captain said, "I know that I will be back in two weeks for another shave and I'll remember to bring my moustache wax next time. Thank you. Everyone will be very satisfied."

Both the captain and sergeant give us a ten-ruble bank note as our gratuity.

The other ten men also gave us ten-ruble gratuities after we completed giving them their haircuts, shaves, and a trim for those with moustaches. My father and I were thrilled to receive a total of 120 rubles for one day's work.

"Yitzhak, don't mention to anyone at the kolkhoz how much we earned today. We need to keep this a secret. Okay?"

"Yes, Papa."

Our last haircut ended at 4 o'clock, giving us enough time to shake out all of the capes, pack the capes and the used towels into our sack, brush off the chairs, clean out the sink, rinse our tools, and sweep the floor. On our way to the employee's entrance to leave the building, we stopped at the employment office and told the clerk we were finished and thanked her for organizing our day. She smiled and said, "We'll see you next week."

The truck driver picked us up a little after 5 o'clock, and we were resting in our beds by 5:30.

This became our weekly routine. Leah and my mom baked and packed loaves of bread every day, with the exception of Friday afternoons. My father and I gave haircuts every day, including the day at the Soviet Employment Office. The only exception was during Friday afternoons, due to the Muslims attending their Friday prayer service. As Esther warned us, the food provided in the kolkhoz canteen was the same every day with no variation.

My mother and the other women were concerned and complained that we were not getting the proper nourishment from this food. Esther and Golda, who had been living in the kolkhoz the longest, felt physically exhausted and blamed this on the lack of protein in the food. They were worried that we would all get sick from a lack of Vitamin A in the diet. Performing the same tedious and monotonous work for almost seven days a week added to our exhaustion.

By the end of December, my father told Leah, my mom, and me that he was going to speak with Manager Vladimir about the lack of protein in the food provided by the kolkhoz.

A few days later, after he and I finished completing our barber work and left the infirmary, my father mentioned, "Let's go see if Manager Vladimir is in his office."

His office was located inside the smaller tent near the kolkhoz's entrance. When we entered, we noticed he was sitting alone at his desk.

My father spoke up, "Vladimir. Do you have a moment to talk to me?"

"Sure, Meir. What's on your mind?"

"First, I want to thank you for allowing my son and me to go to the Employment Center on Wednesdays."

The manager responded, "Captain Lebedev called me and is very pleased with the services that

231

you and your son are providing those who work there. Is there something else?"

"Yes. I am concerned that since the canteen's daily menu does not include any protein, the workers will get excessively tired and may become ill. Is there any way to make the food more nourishing?"

"Meir, I share the same concern and have spoken to my Soviet supervisor about this issue. I understand what you are talking about. The problem is that all of the kolkhozes in Uzbekistan receive their food rations from the Soviet government authorities. The food that we offer is what they send us. When I asked about adding some meat, I'm told that there is a current meat shortage and the available meat is being sent to the military. The military is obviously our top priority."

My father then asked, "What about building a chicken coup inside one of the buildings and raising egg-laying chickens?"

"I've also asked about that. The authorities just paid for our wheat expansion equipment and the new ovens in the kitchen. My current assignment priority is to increase the amount of grain and bread to ship to the military. I'm told there is no available budget for us to raise chickens. Even though I see the need to improve the food, my hands are tied. I can't add any expense without their official approval."

My dad responded. "Then, let me ask you one more question, if you don't mind."

"Go ahead."

"When I'm finished cutting hair at the employment office on Wednesdays, will I be allowed to purchase food at the market and bring it back to the kolkhoz for my family?"

"It's up to you how you spend your own money. Yes, you can bring back food purchased at the market. I have no problem with you or anyone doing that. Just be aware, the prices at the market are awfully expensive. The Soviet government has no control over the market operation. Vendors set their own prices. The inflated food prices are due to the high demand and the limited supplies."

"Thank you, Vladimir, for our talk."

"Anytime, Meir. I'm always willing to speak with our workers. Say hello from me to your wife and daughter."

The next Wednesday, before we left the kolkhoz to go to the Employment Center, my father retrieved our gratuity earnings and an extra glass container from the locked cabinet. When we finished giving our haircuts and left the building, he and I searched for a food stall that had cooked meat or skewers of meat available for sale. We found one vendor that had a few skewers left to sell. He offered us a discounted price of 10 rubles per skewer, since these were his last ones. My dad didn't mind the price and purchased all three of them. He removed the meat and grilled vegetables from the skewer and put them inside the glass container.

When we returned to our tent, my father told my mom and Leah that he had a surprise and told my mom to get the four forks that she brought with us for our trip. Then he said, "Follow me outside and let's find a place where no one will see us."

No one knew that my family was privately and secretly eating food purchased from the market stall. We were afraid if others found out, they would become very angry and Vladimir would stop us from bringing back the food.

Needless to say, we were very joyful to see and taste the surprises that were inside that container!

# Unexpected Events
## 1942

In early January 1942, after my family finished eating dinner at the canteen and were returning to our hut, Leah whispered to me, "Yitzhak, let's go for a walk, just the two of us."

"Sure. It's been a while since we had some time alone."

When we told our parents that we were going out for a walk, my father reminded us, "Just make sure to be back before the lights get turned off at 9 o'clock."

Leah and I held hands and slowly strolled around the circle where all of the huts were located. I knew that something was on her mind since she remained silent and continuously looked down at the ground. Ten more minutes of total silence passed. I finally asked, "Leah, what's wrong? I can tell that there is something on your mind."

She stopped walking, broke into tears, and turned to face me. She replied with a forceful voice and thrusting hand gestures, "Yitzhak, I just can't take it anymore. We've now been here for more than six weeks and I'm ready to scream!"

While giving her a big hug, I responded, "Tell me, Leah. What's upsetting you? What are you finding to be so difficult?"

"Every day is the same. I do the same job in the kitchen every day. Other than Mama, there is no one else that I can talk to while I'm working. The only other women preparing and baking bread are the Uzbekistan women who are mom's age and I don't understand their language. There are no young women that I can talk to. The monotony of baking bread every day, six and a half days a week, is driving me crazy. At least you get out of here once a week. When you are cutting hair at the infirmary, you see different people every day. I just can't take another day of doing the same thing all of the time with no one to talk to!"

"Leah, I'm sorry that you are having a problem adjusting to this new life. Maybe you and I should regularly take a nightly stroll after dinner. Would that help you?"

"It might. I need someone to talk to. How long do you think we will be here? Did you hear anything about the war when you were cutting the Soviet men's hair? You and Papa never said anything to mom and me about the war."

"I'm sorry about that, Leah. Papa and I often hear the Soviet men talking about it. Papa asked me not to mention anything to Mama since she gets too emotionally upset thinking that our family members in Bolechov are all dead. If I tell you what I know, you must promise not to mention anything to her. We don't want to upset Mama."

"I promise, Yitzhak, not to say anything to her."

"Okay. Let's continue our walk and I'll share with you what I've learned so far.

"I think that you already know that the Nazis conquered Odessa and Kharkiv. The Nazi army has now advanced across the border into the Soviet Union. At the end of November, they conquered Rostov and destroyed their train station. In December the German and Soviet armies started fighting each other at Moscow. The biggest news is that the United States has now entered the war."

Leah asked, "How did that happen? I thought that the United States didn't want to get involved."

"Japan bombed Pearl Harbor in the Hawaiian Islands on December 7th. The Hawaiian Islands are a

U.S. territory. The United States declared war the next day."

"Well, Yitzhak, doesn't that mean that the war will end real soon and we can get out of here and go home sometime during this year?"

"Not so fast, Leah. It will take a while before the United States mobilizes their army and navy. Plus, the Nazis are now advancing into Northern Africa. Just like the Great War, it may take a long time to defeat Germany and their current Japanese and Italian allies. I heard a few of the Soviet officials mention that at the beginning of January, the Germans started sending their U-boats to the east coast of the United States. It may take a few years for this war to end."

Leah yelled, "A few years! Do you mean I'll be stuck here for a few years?"

"Shh. Be quiet, Leah, and calm down. We don't want anyone else to hear you. Being at this kolkhoz is still better than what might have happened to us if we all remained in Bolechov. You and I, along with Mama and Papa, need to make the best of it and remain patient while we are working here. At least the weather is warm and the sun shines most of the time in Tashkent."

"I suppose, my brother, that you are right. You and I will go for nightly strolls every day after dinner, eh?"

"Yes, Leah, I promise."

On a Monday morning at the beginning of February 1942, Manager Vladimir barged into the infirmary while my father and I were preparing for the day's haircuts.

"Meir, I'm sorry to interrupt you and Yitzhak. I just received this order from the Soviet Recruitment Office to give to you."

He handed my father the document and continued. "You are to report to their office today. They sent one of their official cars to take you and a few others from other kolkhoz farms to their office. The driver is waiting for you. Their office is in the same building where you go on Wednesdays."

"What do they want with me?"

"I don't know. You'll find out when you get there. You better get going. Yitzhak, you go ahead with today's haircuts. I'll have my secretary reschedule your father's appointments."

Manager Vladimir quickly left the infirmary. Feeling worried, I asked my father, "Papa, what do you think is going on? Should I go and tell Mama and Leah?"

"I don't know, my son, what this is all about. I don't want to alarm Mama so early in the day. I'm sure I'll be back here later today. I'll tell all of you what this is about when I return. If you happen to see them at lunch, just tell them I had an appointment at the Soviet office building. Okay?"

"Yes, Papa." I gave him a big hug before he left.

I was worried all day about my father. I kept thinking: *Why does the Soviet recruitment office want to see my father? The Soviet officials sent us here to work and not to fight in their army!*

He finally returned to the kolkhoz at 5:30 and walked into the infirmary as I was finishing the cleanup. He had a worried look on his face. I knew that something was wrong.

"Papa, you're back. What happened? What did they want with you?"

"I'll explain everything after we all have dinner. Let's go back to the hut and get cleaned up. Please don't say anything just yet to Mama and Leah."

237

When the four of us finished eating, he finally spoke up. "Let's all stay inside the canteen for a few minutes. Go ahead and return your food trays and then come back to sit at the table. I have some important news to share with all of you."

My mother looked at him very inquisitively. She could tell that something significant had happened. When we all returned and sat down at the table, she asked, "Meir, I can tell from the look on your face that something happened today. What's going on?"

"This morning, I received an official order to report to the Soviet Recruitment Office. The Polish Government is now in exile and located in London. Apparently, the Polish government officials reached an agreement with Stalin to form a Polish Brigade as part of the Soviet army to fight the Nazis. The command center of the Polish Brigade was recently moved to a small city called Yanghiyul. It is 20 kilometers from Tashkent. We passed through it on the train. The Polish Brigade is recruiting more Polish men from the Tashkent area to join this military brigade. Since I am a Polish man, I've been recruited to serve in the brigade."

My mom spoke with an alarmed voice. "But you aren't a young man. You're forty-four years old. Why you?"

"The recruitment officer thinks that I would be a good leader. He is sending me to be trained to lead one of the brigade's units. I leave next Monday for two weeks of training at their Yanghiyul base. I will return to the kolkhoz on the weekends. After the two-week training, the Polish Brigade units will be deployed. I don't know yet where my unit will be sent."

My mom pointed her right index finger at my father and in anger yelled at him. "I knew it. You should never have complained to Manager Vladimir about the food. He probably sees you as a troublemaker and told the recruitment office to recruit you. Yes, that is a convenient way for him to get rid of you. You and your big mouth! Why do you always have to be the one to speak up to reorganize everything? Now, what will happen to us when you're gone? How are we going to survive without you?"

I have never seen my mom get this angry with my father, at least not in front of Leah and me.

"Rifka, I don't think Vladimir had anything to do with it. I recall giving haircuts and shaves to some of the recruitment officers. That's how they probably knew I was from Eastern Poland. At least now I can actively help defeat the Germans and stop them from harshly treating the Jewish people. I want to do my share to help our people."

My mom continued her angry questioning. "You have heard many stories about how Jewish men are treated like slaves in the Soviet army. Why would you agree to doing this?"

"Rifka, please calm down. I really didn't have any choice. I was conscripted along with other Polish men. Yitzhak and Leah will be with you. He's now a grown man and can look after you and Leah."

Minutes of silence occurred without any of us reacting to my father's words.

Finally, he spoke up. "Let's get out of here and go back to our hut and get ready for bed. It's been a long day for all of us."

The following Monday morning, I watched my father pack up his toiletries and underwear and place them into one of the pillowcases. I asked him, "Papa, are you going to take any of your barber tools with you?"

He answered, "No, my son. You keep them for me and use them when you need to. Also, let me show you where all of our legal documents are kept in the locked cabinet. If for some reason, all of you are sent

239

to live somewhere else, secure the documents inside the barber's metal box and keep a close watch on it."

"Yes, Papa. I will take responsibility for not losing any of these documents. I know their importance if and when we move to another location. When you are ready to leave, let me walk with you to the truck that will take you to the Soviet office."

Once he finished packing, he gave Leah a big hug and said, "I love you, my lovely daughter."

My mom turned her face away from him when he tried kissing her. She was apparently still angry that he was leaving. Even so, he said, "I love you, Rifka."

When he and I got to the truck, we hugged each other and he said, "Don't worry. You'll see. I'll be back sometime on Friday. I love you, son."

"I love you too, Papa."

I stood there for a while and waved goodbye as the truck pulled out of the kolkhoz entrance area and onto the dirt road.

As promised, my father returned on Friday to our hut late in the afternoon wearing his green army uniform with a Polish Brigade patch sewed onto the top of each sleeve. He hadn't earned any stripes. Instead of carrying the pillowcase, he now carried an army issued duffle bag to store his belongings.

"See. I told you I would return today. I also brought some canned food items that you can store in the locked cabinet, just in case you need more nourishing food." He pulled a dozen cans out of the duffle bag and handed them to us to place in the cabinet.

He joined me giving haircuts in the infirmary during the weekend. Manager Vladimir's secretary quickly filled up his appointment schedule once many of the men learned that he was working that weekend.

Before he left on Monday morning, my mom asked him, "Do you know where you are being sent? Are you going to the front line and risk being killed? I'm worried, Meir, that I might never see you again." She started crying. "Meir, how can I live without you?"

My father tried his best to comfort her. "I'll be back, Rifka. Don't worry. I'll be back again on Friday."

This time the two of them hugged and kissed each other before he departed. Once again, I walked with him to the truck and waved goodbye.

Four days whizzed by very quickly with the anticipation of his Friday return. Leah, my mom, and I gave him a very cheerful and loving welcome when he walked into our hut. I was proud to see that one stripe was added to his uniform's sleeves.

My mom was the first to speak. "Meir, do you know where your unit is being sent? Do you know how we can write to you while you are gone?"

"Rifka, I don't know yet. The brigade officials won't tell us anything. They are afraid that there are German spies living in Tashkent. My unit may not know where we have been sent until we actually get there."

Then he pulled a card out of his pants right side pocket and handed it to my mom. "Here is an address card that we received to give to our family. All of you can write to me and mail the card to this address. Make sure that you include the words 'Polish Brigade' in the address so that your letter doesn't get mixed in with the Soviet army's mail. I should be able to write and mail a letter to all of you at least once a week. Please keep in mind that my letters may take a long time to get here. My letters will first be sent to the headquarters in Yanghiyul and then forwarded to Kolkhoz Aggatay."

My mom turned to me and said, "Here, Yitzhak. You keep this card and put it in a safe place."

Then I asked him about his stripe. "Papa, I see you now have one stripe. Don't you have to be at least a sergeant to lead a unit?"

"You are correct, Yitzhak. Once we get to our first location, I'll complete the leadership training and earn the sergeant's emblem. Enough talk about the army! Let's enjoy being together during this weekend."

The four of us woke up on Monday morning feeling very sad and concerned about my father's safety serving in the Polish Brigade. As she was getting dressed in the morning, my mom kept mumbling, "What will I do? What will I do?" I knew that she was very worried that my father might get killed.

He gave all of us a big hug and a kiss before he left the hut and walked to the kolkhoz entrance to meet his ride. "Please write so that I know that you are all doing well. I'll do the same as often as I can. Remember that I love you dearly, my family. Yitzhak, walk with me, okay?"

"Yes, Papa."

As he and I started walking toward the kolkhoz's entrance area, he put his right arm around me while carrying his duffle bag over his left shoulder. "Yitzhak, it's now up to you to be the man of the family and take good care of your mom and Leah. I know that I can count on you to do this. You have always been and will always be my good son. Your mom is very worried that something may happen to me and that I might not return. If something like that does happen, you will need to step in and help her stay both physically and emotionally healthy. You know how she gets when she is upset about something."

"Don't worry, Papa. I'll take good care of Mama, even if something happens to you."

"Good. Now, give your Papa one more hug before I leave."

I watched the car pull out of the kolkhoz entrance and waved goodbye. The movement of the car's tires sent a massive plume of dust into the air. The car was nowhere in sight when the dust finally cleared and settled.

I wondered: *Will I ever see my father again?"*

When my father got recruited, I was concerned that I would no longer be assigned to go to the Soviet office building and continue to give their employees haircuts. I was relieved when I walked into the employment office. Both Captain Lebedev and his secretary told me that they knew about my father's recruitment and adjusted the haircut appointments accordingly. Captain Lebedev even remarked, "Your haircuts, shaves, and trims are just as good as your father's. Of course, we want you to continue!"

Now that the brigade had left Tashkent, I asked the secretary how to mail our letters to him. I was very pleased with her helpful response. "Just bring them to me. I'll see to it that they get mailed. Since he is in the military, there is no mailing fee as long as you write the official address on the envelope."

"Thank you, I'll bring our first letter next week."

When I finished cleaning up the barber's station in the building's restroom at the end of the day, I wandered through the market to look for a stall that sold writing stationery, some pencils, and envelopes. It took me awhile, but I found one and the prices were not too expensive. Since I still had some rubles left from my gratuity earnings, I went to the stall that my father and I frequented to purchase some meat stew to take back to the hut. A young Uzbek man was working that day. He greeted me by saying, "Salam". Since this word was very similar to the Hebrew word 'Shalom', I knew he was saying 'hello' to me.

I quickly replied, "Salam."

When I pointed to the stew, he called it, "Palov". My family enjoyed eating this tasty stew because it was mixed with beef, carrots, onions, and dried raisins. At first, the young man must have thought I wanted to purchase only one cup. I took the glass container out of my sack, raised four fingers and showed him to place four cups of stew into the container. He smiled to indicate that he understood. I was delighted that he charged me less than what my father normally paid for the stew.

I showed my mom and Leah the purchased stationery and pulled out a sheet of paper and a pencil. "Now, each of us will write a message to Papa. I will take our letters with me next Wednesday. The employment office's secretary offered to mail them for me."

We never received a reply from him, even though we mailed four letters to my father.

My mom started to cry. "You see, Leah and Yitzhak, I was correct. I told you so. Something has happened to my Meir. I just can't live without him!"

I gave her a hug and responded, "Now, Mama. It's only been a month. He told us that it might take a long time for us to receive his letter. He's alright. I'm sure of it. Don't worry. We'll hear from him soon."

Even though we continued to send him weekly letters, two more months went by and we still hadn't heard from him.

At the beginning of April, there still was no letter. I was beginning to get worried that my mom was correct. Something must have happened to him.

On Monday, April 20th, as I was cleaning up my station at the infirmary, Manager Vladimir walked up to me and handed me a letter. I could tell from the handwriting that it was from my father.

I quickly finished cleaning and then raced to the kitchen. Leah and my mom were packing the loaves of baked bread when they saw me. Leah yelled out, "What are you doing here?"

I waved the letter in front of them. "See, a letter from Papa. He's okay, Mama! There's nothing to worry about. I won't open it until you come back to the hut."

The three of us were surprised to see the date, Tuesday, February 17th, written at the top of the letter. This date meant that it took two months for his letter to reach us! He didn't say much, other than he was well and completed his leadership training. There was no mention about where he was or where his unit will be employed. He did tell us that the brigade was being referred to as the 'Anders Army', since General Wladyslaw Anders was in charge.

Needless to say, my mom's worries about my father subsided. Her demeanor improved and she was more enthusiastic about baking bread in the kitchen. Leah, my mom, and I continued to send him weekly letters. We received another letter from him in May.

After not receiving anything else from him by August, my mom started worrying again and asked me to inquire when I went to the Soviet government building. The employment office secretary was very helpful. She explained, "You need to go to the brigade's headquarters office in Yanghiyul to file the inquiry. Their office is open on Fridays and you will need to take the train to get there. The headquarters office is located inside the police station and is easy to find. It is across from the large city park on

Samarkand Street and one long block from the train station. Show your work badge and your Tashkent registration card to the guard at the entrance. This may make it easier for you to be allowed inside."

I saved my gratuity earnings, purchased a round trip train ticket, and went to the headquarters office inside the Yanghiyul police station the next Friday afternoon. Manager Vladimir was kind enough to arrange a ride for me from the kolkhoz to the Tashkent train station during the mid-morning after giving some haircuts.

The work badge and the registration card did make it easier for me to get inside the Yanghiyul police station without too much questioning. The Polish Brigade's office was located in the third office on the right side of the main hallway. A uniformed man sitting at the counter was startled when he saw me. "How did you get in here? What do you want?"

I showed him my work badge and Tashkent registration card and said, "I'm here to file an inquiry about my father who is a sergeant in the Polish Brigade. It's been almost four months and we haven't received any letters from him."

"What's his name?"

"Meir Bakan."

"Meir. A Jew? And you're telling me that he is a sergeant? You're lying. That's all you Jews do, is lie."

I pulled out one of my father's letters. "See. Here is his name on the envelope. Sergeant Meir Barkan. You can also see that your office stamp is on this letter."

"Well, he must have good connections because very few Jews are in the Polish Brigade, let alone a sergeant. As far as we know, there have been no casualties reported from the Polish Brigade. All I can tell you is their units were deployed to join the British

246

Eighth Army. I can't tell you where, for security reasons. Is there anything else?"

"No, sir. I can now tell my family that he is alive. Thank you for your help."

I was very relieved to hear that my father was okay. I knew that this news would renew my mother's spirit.

It was a very long walk from the Tashkent train station to get back to the kolkhoz. Luckily, while walking on the first narrow dirt road that led out of the city's center, a truck stopped. The Uzbek man driving the truck signaled for me to get into the truck after I mentioned, "Salam. Kolkhoz Aggatay." He dropped me off at the kolkhoz's entrance. I remembered what my father taught me, when we stayed with Ibrahim and his family, with how to express my thanks to a Muslim individual. I nodded my head at the driver and placed my hands together in the prayer position. The driver did the same gesture to me and smiled.

Since it was dinnertime, I raced to the canteen. When I saw my mother, I gave her a big hug and with joy I said, "Mama, Papa's okay. I learned that he is okay. Isn't this great news?"

She replied, "So, where is he? Why haven't we heard from him?"

"His unit is now fighting with the British army. The official couldn't tell me where. The official did say that no casualties have been reported. This means that he is still alive, Mama and Leah. This is good news. We should write and send him another letter!"

While my family dealt with my father's conscription into the Polish Brigade, another serious event happened that affected all of us living and working at Kolkhoz Aggatay and those living in Tashkent. There was the outbreak of a contagious disease called typhus.

247

I first learned about this outbreak in early February when I gave a haircut to one of the men who worked in the Soviet health department office.

He asked me, "Barkan, does Kolkhoz Aggatay disinfect their new arrivals? What does your kolkhoz do with their clothes? Do they burn them?"

I replied, "We all get sprayed with disinfectant as soon as we arrive. Our clothes and all of our fabric belongings are placed into a bin to be thoroughly washed. Our hair gets cut and then we take a hot shower with soap. The kolkhoz gives us freshly washed work clothes to wear in the meantime. Why do you ask?"

"A disease called typhus caused from body lice is spreading throughout the city. Tashkent still has hundreds of unclean people living on the streets in crowded areas and spreading typhus. Many people are getting sick and dying."

I added, "When my family arrived here, we did see many dirty people begging on the streets and picking at their skin. Many of them had large red sores on their bodies. I haven't seen anyone like that at our kolkhoz, including our Uzbek workers."

"Good. I'm glad to hear that."

A few Wednesdays later, when I went to the Soviet government office, this health official walked into the restroom barber station and interrupted me from shaving one of the men.

"Barkan, you need not come here next week. Those who work here are being told to stay home so that my department can spray the entire inside of the building with disinfectant. Typhus is rampant and we need to take more preventative measures. We will begin examining everyone who comes to the entrance doors, including employees, before anyone can enter the building during this typhus epidemic. Thank you for your understanding and cooperation. My office is sending out instructions to all of the kolkhoz managers on how to prevent typhus from spreading. We are also closing the market tomorrow to spray disinfectant and move out the beggars. We are sending those living on the streets into the unused warehouses and other empty buildings."

When the stall market truck returned to Kolkhoz Aggatay that afternoon, Manager Vladimir and Foreman Rashid were standing in front of their office waiting for the driver, the two market stall workers, and me. As the four of us were getting out of the truck, both men approached us. With Rashid translating for the Uzbek driver and stall workers, Vladimir explained, "You may have heard about a disease called typhus spreading through Tashkent from body lice. We received new health prevention orders from the Soviet Health Department. When you return from the market every day, you will go directly to the infirmary to be disinfected and take a good shower. Soliha will wash your clothes and give you freshly washed work clothes to wear in the meantime. I've also been instructed to reorganize the canteen operation. I'll be holding meetings in each hut and with all of the Uzbek workers. Thank you for your cooperation keeping typhus from spreading here at this kolkhoz."

When I returned to my hut after my shower, Manager Vladimir was explaining the new disease prevention procedure to those living in our hut. "Typhus spreads from lice attacking unclean people being crowded together. Every worker, including me, will be required take a shower every day. The canteen meal hours will now be staggered with small groups eating at different times. The new schedule will be posted outside the canteen. Please check the schedule for when this hut will eat their meals. When you are in the canteen, sit at an empty table.

Everyone needs to spread out and not sit close to each other. The department supervisors will be told that their workers will be eating at different times, including the Uzbek workers. Tomorrow morning, please wear fresh work clothes and put your dirty clothes and all of your bedding into the bin to be thoroughly washed. We are also going to disinfect each hut, the offices, the kitchen, and the canteen. These new procedures are to prevent any of you from contracting and spreading typhus and from needing to be deloused. Are there any questions?"

Marcin raised his hand and asked, "What about the new employees who will be hired soon to help plant the spring wheat?"

"Good question, Marcin. The Soviet Employment Office will screen each new employee. In order to enter the Soviet government building, a prospective employee will be examined very thoroughly. When a new employee arrives here, they will be immediately disinfected, showered, and receive a short haircut. The only difference is that their old clothing will be burned to prevent any body lice from infesting this kolkhoz.

"Anything else?

"Since there are no further questions, I once again thank you for your cooperation."

Once my mother, Leah, and I returned to our compartment and sat down, I informed them about the new health procedures that were implemented at the government building, at the market, and when I return to the kolkhoz.

My mom added, "Now you understand my reason for us avoiding being close to the crowds of people at the train stations and the parks!"

Fortunately, with everyone diligently following these health prevention procedures, Kolkhoz Aggatay remained typhus free, even though outbreaks were rampant throughout Tashkent and some of the other kolkhoz farms.

Another health issue occurred during the spring of 1942. As Esther, Golda, and my mom warned, the lack of protein in the food served in the kolkhoz canteen took its toll on the health of many workers. Many went to the infirmary complaining about being malnourished and having a severe lack of energy. Others contracted respiratory issues caused by a weakened immune system.

Dominka, from our hut, and two men from the other huts complained and went to the infirmary about their inability to see well at night. When I returned to the Soviet government office the next Wednesday, I immediately went to the Health Department Office and asked the official what he knew about the cause of night vision problems at our kolkhoz. He replied, "This is caused from a Vitamin A deficiency. They will need to begin eating a lot of protein. There is also an old remedy about spreading oil from animal liver on their eyes. I'll call Vladimir and talk to him about this."

"Thank you, Sir."

A few days later, Vladimir held another series of meetings with those working at the Kolkhoz. He explained that he found an unofficial source to obtain a better quality of food to serve at the canteen. However, in order to pay for this extra expense, he needed to deduct five rubles per worker from their pay every week. No one voiced a complaint. Everyone realized the importance of adding protein to our diet in order to remain healthy. We also felt relieved that Vladimir finally addressed and found a solution to this issue.

His unofficial food source may have been with what is called 'The Black Market', meaning that the food was coming from a source not managed by the

Soviet government. Most likely, he had to bribe someone to obtain the food. No one asked how he arranged it. The food offered at the canteen changed. Eggs, slices or small chunks of meat, carrots, and more milk were provided. After a few weeks, everyone at the kolkhoz seemed more energetic and there were no more complaints about not being able to see during the night. I think Vladimir made this arrangement because of his concern fulfilling the Soviet ordered high quota of grain and bread produced by our kolkhoz. Of course, no one knew the secret of my family purchasing food from the market when I worked on Wednesdays at the government office.

In early June 1942, when I returned from the Soviet Government Office and got dressed after taking my shower, Manager Vladimir raced into the infirmary.

"Yitzhak, you have to immediately go with me to the apricot plantation that is next to us. The Uzbek man who lives and owns the plantation just called me. He is threatening to have your sister, Leah, arrested, along with one of our new kitchen workers, named Hershel Zimmerman. Hershel arrived last week and you gave him his haircut. You'll know him when you see him. We need to get over there right away."

"Vladimir, was he one of the ten people who were sent here to help with the wheat harvest?"

"Yes."

As we drove, I started thinking: *Leah's flirtatious nature with young men has returned and this time resulted with her getting into trouble!*

It didn't take us very long to drive to the neighbor's grove. When we arrived at the plantation,

252

we could see in the distance two Uzbek men standing in front of Leah and Hershel. They were sitting on the ground in front of an apricot tree. I immediately recognized Hershel as the lanky young man with the brown hair that I cut.

Manager Vladimir and the two Uzbek men had a lengthy conversation. He then translated in a very firm voice what they said. "The Uzbek owner of this plantation heard your loud voice, Leah. When they got here, they found you stuck in the tree and you couldn't manage to climb down. They helped you with their ladder and then the owner called me. What were the two of you doing here? They think you were trying to steal their apricots."

Hershel spoke up. "It's my fault Vladimir. I asked Leah to take a walk with me to show her an apricot. I saw this plantation the other day when I took a walk after I finished working in the bakery. The two of us found an apricot lying on the ground next to the fence. After Leah ate it and liked its sweet tangy taste, she wanted to taste more. That's when she climbed over the fence and went up the tree. I tried stopping her."

Vladimir responded, "Is this what happened, Leah?"

"Yes, sir. I'm sorry. I just got so excited after eating something so sweet and delicious."

"Leah and Hershel, you were trespassing on this man's property. He could call the police and have the two of you arrested."

Hershel asked, "Is there something that we can do to show the owner how sorry we are?"

"Yes, there is. I already told him that the two of you would work here on your free time on Friday afternoons to help with his apricot harvest. Your work here will begin this Friday and will end when the harvest is complete. Is this clear?"

Both Leah and Hershel answered, "Yes. How do we say 'I'm sorry' in the Uzbek language?"

"Just say 'iz-ur'".

Vladimir and the plantation owner spoke again for a few minutes and then he directed the three of us to get into his car. As he drove back to Kolkhoz Aggatay, I could tell that Vladimir was very angry when he said, "I've never had anyone from my kolkhoz ever trespass on someone else's property. I'm ordering the two of you to not mention this to anyone, ever! I don't want to encourage others to even think about trespassing. If the two of you ever do something like this again, I will dismiss you from the kolkhoz and you can just live on the streets in Tashkent. Do you understand?"

"Yes, sir."

After we arrived back at the kolkhoz, as Leah and I walked back to our hut, I gently pulled her aside to speak to her. With a quiet voice so that no one else would hear, I asked, "What were you thinking, Leah?"

"Yitzhak. Don't be angry with me. I've been telling you for months that I'm feeling lonely and I have no one to talk to, other than Mama, while I'm working in the bakery. Then, last week, Hershel arrived. He is a very nice and courteous man. Even Mama likes him. You should get to know him."

I responded, "That still doesn't explain why you climbed over the fence onto someone's property?"

"I know. That was a big mistake. I'm sorry."

"Leah. Is there anything romantically going on between you and Hershel?"

"No. We are just friends. Really, I swear. We are just friends. Let's go see Mama in the hut. She is probably worried about us."

When Leah and I walked into our compartment in the hut, my mom's worried face changed to a bright smile. "Where were the two of you? I was very concerned that something happened."

Leah and I looked at each other and then I explained, "Mama, Manager Vladimir asked to speak to Leah, Hershel, and me. He wanted to ask Leah and Hershel to start helping out at the neighboring apricot plantation on Friday afternoons. You do know Hershel, from the bakery, right?"

"Yes. He is a very polite young man and very helpful to everyone in the bakery. He washes and dries the pans and the equipment."

Leah must have said something to Hershel the next day at the bakery. While I was trimming an Uzbek worker's hair, Hershel came into the infirmary and started to speak to me.

"I'm on a short break, Yitzhak, and I wanted to apologize to you for getting Leah into trouble. When I asked her to take a walk with me to see the apricot grove, I really didn't expect her to act in such an excited way."

"Yes, Hershel. Leah can sometimes react that way."

"I would like for you and me to get to know each other and become friends. I know that you are busy right now. Could we have a talk this evening after dinner?"

"Sure, Hershel, that will be fine. I've known others with the name, Hershel. It will be easy for me to remember your name."

Hershel replied. "Thanks. I'll come to your hut after I get off work this evening."

Hershel and I had a long conversation. I learned that he was eighteen years old and how he got to Tashkent and assigned to work in the bakery.

"I come from an observant Jewish family. My parents and I fled from Kyiv once the Nazis invaded Eastern Poland. I worked in the bakery that my parents owned and operated. That's how I know so much about a bakery's operation. My parents and I

255

managed to get to Odessa. The Nazis bombed our ship shortly after it left the Odessa harbor and my parents drowned. I was strong enough to swim to the shore. Of course, all of our documents and belongings were lost. Since I had no documents, the Soviet authorities regarded me as an undocumented refugee and sent me to Siberia, along with hundreds of others. Once I got to Siberia and explained what happened, the officials believed me, issued a travel permit, and sent me to Tashkent. When I told the Tashkent Employment Office officials that I was a skilled baker, the manager of this kolkhoz accepted me to work here. I've survived on my own for many months. It is a wonderful experience for me to become friends with Leah and your mom. I hope that you and I can become good friends too."

I replied, "I'm sorry to learn that you lost your parents. Did other family members flee?"

"No. Our relatives decided to remain. As I was on my way to Siberia, a Soviet solder told me that the Nazis conquered Kyiv. I assume that the rest of my family members are now dead."

"Hershel, we also have relatives that did not flee with us. I assume that they are also dead. We are from a small eastern Polish town called Bolechov. It is near Stanislavov. You and I do have a similar Jewish background. Yes, it would be nice for us to be friends. Just don't get Leah into any more trouble! Okay?"

"I promise."

The other issue that my family faced was adjusting to the climate in Tashkent. Many people at the kolkhoz complained about it. In Bolechov, we were used to experiencing the changes in the weather during the four seasons. For our first few months, the weather in Tashkent was constantly warm and dry with sunny skies. The sameness of every day added to the monotony of everyone's daily life.

Just prior to plowing the soil and planting the spring wheat in March, severe rainstorms arrived. I finally understood the reason for the placement of raised wooden walkways that connected all of the huts and buildings at Kolkhoz Aggatay and the sandbags placed on the ground around all of the huts. The constant rain turned the dusty dirt roads and paths into a slippery mud. When it rained, your shoes could get stuck in the mud and pull off from your feet!

Work in the fields was cancelled during these rainstorms. The field workers who lived at the kolkhoz were ordered to stay inside the huts, except to go to the canteen. We all had to find some way to cover ourselves so that we wouldn't get soaked going to and from the canteen.

The daytime temperatures in June, July, and August soared and were very hot. The dust in the air turned into a gray powder. If you were outside long enough, you would come back to the hut covered in gray dust. Fortunately, my mom, Leah, Hershel, and I worked indoors. In order to avoid overheating, the work schedule for those working the fields was changed to begin at sunrise and end at lunchtime. When one walked outside, it felt like you were being baked inside an oven! I used some of my gratuity earnings to purchase floppy hats and umbrellas at the market for the four of us, including Hershel.

In early November, there were a few days when everything stopped at the kolkhoz. This was the first time that most of us ever experienced a severe dust storm. The wind was so strong that a thick blanket of dust was formed in the air. It was so thick that you couldn't see five feet in front of you. Once again, we needed to remain in our hut and keep the canvas entrance tightly sealed to prevent dust from entering.

Even when the wind subsided, the dust remained in the air for a few days. When the canteen reopened, we all needed to cover our noses and mouths to not inhale the dust.

The dust finally settled a week later. Everyone at the kolkhoz helped sweep and clean the dust out of the huts and buildings. Of course, all of our clothing and bedding needed to be washed.

Manager Vladimir later told me when I gave him a haircut, that the spring rain, the summer heat, and the fall dust storms were typical yearly Tashkent weather events. When he became the manager, one of his first projects was to install the raised wooden walkways to prevent mud from entering the huts and buildings.

Even though my mom, Leah, and I sent my father weekly letters, we hadn't' received anything from him since May. My mom started worrying about him again. She kept repeating, "He's dead. He's dead. I just know it. He's dead. What's the use in writing any more letters? He's dead."

As the months proceeded without any word from him, I was concerned about the decline of her mental state and her lack of motivation to work at the bakery. I tried my best to encourage her to stay strong for Leah's and my own benefit.

In September, I asked her, "Mom, would you like me to go back to brigade's headquarters once again to inquire about Papa?"

"Why go, Yitzhak? He's dead. I just know it."

"I'm going anyway. I'll go on Friday."

When I returned to the kolkhoz from the brigade's office, I reported to my mom and Leah, "Once again, no casualties or injuries have been reported. The Polish Brigade is still fighting together with the British. I was told that the British and the Polish Brigade were now in Persia. They were sent there to relieve the

Soviet army from occupying Persia. The Soviet army was needed elsewhere to fight the Germans."

Leah asked, "Is Papa fighting the Germans in Persia?"

"Nothing about the British Brigade being involved in a battle was mentioned to me."

Even with this report, my mom continued to constantly repeat, "He is dead. I just know it!"

Miraculously, a letter from my father arrived in December and Manager Vladimir gave it to me at the infirmary. I immediately opened it. The date written on the letter was September 12, 1942.

I raced to show the letter to my mom and Leah. He wrote that he was well and confirmed that his unit was now in Persia. He acknowledged receiving three of our letters and urged us to continue writing to him. The only detail that he stated was that the Polish Brigade was now called the Polish II Corps and that General Wladyslaw Anders was still the commander.

We all felt relieved, especially my mom. Her mood greatly improved.

# Life Continues at the Kolkhoz
## 1943 - 1944

I didn't realize that the world experienced a new calendar year until I went to the Soviet government's office building to give haircuts. When I checked in at the employment office counter, I saw a large clock hung on one of the walls. I hadn't noticed it before. A large changeable daily calendar was now placed underneath the clock. It displayed Wednesday, 06 January 1943.

I couldn't believe that my family had lived at the kolkhoz for over a year. We adjusted to the daily routine of meals, work, some free time during the evenings, and sleeping on bunk beds. My mom wasn't feeling any more stress and worry about my father after we received his letter in December. Leah stopped complaining about having no one to talk to since the arrival of Hershel. She seemed much happier going to the bakery every day. I was content with my job assignments and going to the market on Wednesdays after I finished cutting hair at the government building.

During December, I paid closer attention to the conversations regarding the war's progress during the Soviet employees' haircuts. I learned that the Soviets defeated the Italian troops near the Don River that flowed between Kharkiv and Rostov. These officials were very eager to brag about their army's victory. This news was very encouraging. The war could eventually come to an end.

My first haircut appointment on January 6th was with the official from the Health Department who had previously told me about the typhoid outbreak. He never sensed that I was Jewish, since I told him my name was Barkan and not Yitzhak.

As I started trimming the sides and back of his head with the hand clipper, he mentioned to me, "Barkan, you and your family are very fortunate that you were placed at the Kolkhoz Aggatay. Since the other kolkhozes are much larger than yours and many people are living there, they have experienced significant outbreaks of body lice and typhus."

I responded, "Our manager is well respected by those who work at our kolkhoz. We like that he regularly communicates with us. He treats us like we are one big team."

"Yes, he is a good manager and your kolkhoz always meets its monthly production quotas. You may have noticed that the streets of Tashkent are, once again, flooded with refugees. More and more undocumented refugees keep showing up every day. It has been increasingly difficult to find housing for all of them. The kolkhozes aren't hiring any more people and the factories only want to hire those sent to them specifically by the Soviet authorities. Just be careful, Barkan, not to get near any of those sleeping on the streets and avoid spreading any disease to your kolkhoz."

I replied, "Will do, sir. Thanks for informing me about the current situation in Tashkent."

When I returned to the kolkhoz later that day, after showering and changing into fresh work clothes, Manager Vladimir approached me.

"Yitzhak, I need to make a slight change with your work assignment. Since I'm not hiring any new employees, you won't have to give as many haircuts each week. Our granary now needs additional help. I'm assigning you to work the morning shift at the granary on Tuesdays, Thursdays, and on Friday mornings to prepare the harvested grain to be

261

transported to the mill in Tashkent. The grain is processed into flour at the mill, bagged, and then shipped by train to a distribution center east of Moscow. You can continue giving haircuts, trims, and shaves on Mondays, Saturdays, and Sundays."

I asked, "Which building is the granary?"

"It is the large concrete building on the eastern side of the kolkhoz that is raised up off the ground. All of the currently stored grain needs to be taken to the mill before the spring rainy season begins. You will start tomorrow. Some of the men from your hut also work there during the morning."

I responded, "When I arrived, The Soviet Employment Office official mentioned that I might be needed to work at the granary. I will do a good job there."

"Yitzhak, I know that I can count on you. You are a good employee."

When I returned to the hut, I told my mom and Leah about my new work assignment at the granary and the current refugee problem in Tashkent. Apparently, Dovid overheard me and asked, "Yitzhak, can I come inside to talk to you?"

"Yes, come on in."

"Feivel and I also work at the granary in the mornings. Come with us tomorrow morning after breakfast and I will introduce you to the manager, Akmel Abdullayeva. He speaks Polish. He allows us to call him Akmel. He's rather strict with the employees in order for the granary to meet its production quota. Just follow his instructions and he will leave you alone. Wear your work clothes and bring some water to drink while you are working there. You will need it."

"Thanks Dovid."

The next morning, as Dovid, Feivel, and I approached the granary, I asked them, "Why is this large concrete building raised off the ground?"

Feivel explained, "The grain needs to be kept very dry and being raised up prevents rodents and insects from getting inside. Since the rainy season is approaching, we need to empty the granary from all of the remaining grain and have it taken to the mill."

When we got inside the building, Dovid introduced me to Akmel. He was a very heavy-set, middle-aged Uzbek man with a very long gray beard and wearing a long white kaftan with a matching head covering. I didn't recall him ever coming to the infirmary to have his hair or beard trimmed.

"Vladimir told me to expect you today. Here is a set of work gloves. If you lose them, your pay will be docked to replace them. Do you see those men near the loading dock? You are to join them carrying the canvas sacks of grain and placing them inside the truck at the loading dock. The truck leaves every day at 2 p.m., except Fridays, to take the sacks of grain to the mill. Any questions?"

"No, sir."

"Good. Go and start loading the truck."

The four others loading the truck were husky, muscular Uzbek men. They just stared at me with a curious look when they saw me approaching. I think that they were surprised and leery that a much younger, rather thin, non-muscular, Polish, nineteen-year-old was assigned to work with them. When I smiled, nodded my head, and said, "Salam" to each of them, each man smiled back and said, "Salam" to me.

I didn't expect the canvas sacks of grain to be as heavy as they were. Wearing work gloves did make it manageable for me to lift and carry the sacks to the truck. The other four signaled when it was time to take our break. We stopped for five minutes every half hour for a rest and to drink some water. The five of us rotated going to lunch in order to continue loading the truck. Once the truck left the dock at 2 o'clock, we stacked the newly filled canvas sacks near the loading dock's door to load onto the truck the next morning. I noticed that Dovid and Feivel were two of the workers at the dispensary machine filling the canvas sacks with grain and then tying them.

Working two and a half days at the granary, three days at the infirmary giving haircuts, and one day at the government building giving the Soviet men haircuts kept me very busy. Once again, I lost track of the calendar. On Wednesday, February 3$^{rd}$, 1943, when I checked in at the employment office, a new announcement board had been installed below the clock and calendar. A sign in large bold print was fastened to the board announcing the German army's first surrender and defeat at Stalingrad on February 2$^{nd}$! Needless to say, that's all the men talked about that day when I gave them their haircuts, shaves, and moustache trims. Everyone in the building was very celebrative and joyful.

Manager Vladimir entered the canteen during dinner that evening. He proudly announced, with a loud and joyful voice, the Soviet army's victory. Everyone in the canteen cheered at this good news!

Leah was especially very excited to hear about the victory. When Hershel came to visit us at the hut after he finished eating dinner, Leah grabbed him and gave him a big kiss. "Isn't this great, Hershel? The war might end soon!"

I replied, "Not so fast, Leah. This was just one victory. It still may take a long time to push the Germans all the way back to Germany!"

Leah and Hershel kissing each other raised my curiosity. I thought: *I better keep a closer eye on the two of them to see if they are more than just 'friends'!*

During the forthcoming weeks, I tactfully asked if I could join them during their evening walks. Sure enough, the two of them were constantly holding each other's hands. Often, they hugged. At the end of our walks, the two of them kissed each other on the lips before Hershel left to go to his hut.

I knew that as her older, protective brother, I needed to have a talk with Hershel. A few weeks later, I noticed that Hershel's name appeared on my haircut list for a Monday afternoon appointment.

While prepping Hershel for his haircut, I started the needed conversation. "Hershel. Are you and my sister now more than 'friends'? I see the two of you regularly kissing and hugging each other. What's going on between the two of you?"

He replied, "I like your sister very much. She is very nice to me and we have great conversations. I feel that I can confide my deepest thoughts with her and I think that she feels the same way about me."

I continued my questioning. "Do you feel that the two of you are now 'boyfriend and girlfriend'?"

"I guess you can say that, Yitzhak."

"Hershel, Leah has never had a true boyfriend. She can be very flirtatious. My father asked me to watch over her while he was away. I know that she is very happy that you are working at the bakery and that she has someone around her age to talk to. I'm worried that she may somehow go too far with her flirtatiousness."

"You don't have to worry about that with me, Yitzhak. I will always respect her."

"I just don't want her to be taken advantage of, if you know what I mean, Hershel."

"I would never do anything like that. Honestly, I wouldn't."

"I have one request, Hershel. I don't mind if the two of you become romantically involved with each other. Even so, I want to have your word that you will not go somewhere private and secluded to be alone with her, even if she initiates and insists. You must make this promise to me. Do I have your word?"

"Yes, you have my word. You are a good brother and also my good friend. I come from a respectable Jewish family. I promise to always respect Leah."

"I also regard you as good friend, Hershel. I'm counting on you to keep Leah safe and away from any physical or emotional harm."

Later in February, the Soviet army continued being successful with pushing the Nazis westward. When I checked in at the employment office on Wednesday, February 10th, the bulletin board displayed a new message announcing that the Soviet army took control of the city of Kursk and was advancing westward. While I was giving haircuts that day, the topic of conversation was the current battle between the two armies at Kharkiv. Leah, Hershel, and my mom urged me to tell them about the war's progress when I returned each Wednesday.

Also in February, we received another letter from my father. This time the letter was dated December 4th, 1942. His unit was still in Persia and he wished us a Happy Chanukah. Of course, Leah, my mom, and I, sent him more letters. I felt fairly sure that Leah told my father about her boyfriend, Hershel. My letter informed my father that I was keeping a close eye on the two of them.

The fierce battle at Kharkiv continued for months. When I arrived at the employment office on Wednesday, August 25th, the message on the bulletin board stated that the Soviet army was finally victorious at Kharkiv on August 23rd, 1943. It seemed that everyone in Tashkent was feeling very optimistic that the Soviet army would continue being victorious.

Even with the joyful feeling in the air, a dark cloud penetrated into my family's life at the beginning of September. We had yet to receive another letter from my father since the last one we received was in February. My mom became fearful again that my father had been killed. She didn't eat much and lost her enthusiasm to continue working at the bakery. I became very worried about the decline of her physical and mental health. She started repeating again, "He's dead. I know he's dead. I just don't want to live without him!" She kept complaining that she was feeling too weak to work at the bakery and insisted on staying in bed.

When I inquired about the Polish II Corps at the recruitment office, I was told that their headquarters was no longer located in Yanghiyul. The only thing that I could do was to complete an inquiry request form and submit it to the recruitment office. The official said that he would submit my inquiry. Each week I checked as soon as I arrived at the government building. No further information was received regarding my inquiry.

Everyone at Kolkhoz Aggatay cheered when Vladimir announced on November 6th that the Soviet army recaptured Kyiv! This meant that the Soviet army was successfully pushing the German army westward and out of Eastern Poland! Even though this was great news, not knowing about my father was still a grave concern.

November passed without another letter from my father or a response to my inquiry. On Tuesday, December 28th, while I was carrying a sack to the truck, I noticed Manager Vladimir speaking with Akmet and pointing at me. Moments later, Vladimir said, "Yitzhak, stop what you are doing and come with me to my office."

My first thought was that I had done something wrong and I was in trouble. When we got inside his office, he said, "An official letter arrived today for your family. I thought that it would be best to give it to you and not your mother." He then handed me the letter.

The letter's envelope was addressed to 'The Family of Sergeant Meir Barkan' and was sent from the Polish II Corps Department in London, England. I asked, "Vladimir, do you know what this is about?"

"No, Yitzhak. You should open it."

The letter said:

To the family of Sergeant Meir Barkan:

We need to inform you that the Polish II Corps Fourth Unit, while fighting with the British Eighth Army in Italy on 04, December 2023, has reported Sergeant Meir Barkan as Missing in Action. We have no further information at this time.

My heart sank and I quickly sat down on one of the office chairs. I gave the letter to Vladimir for him to read. Then I asked, "How am I going to tell my mom? She is already beyond worry that he has been killed. I'm not sure she is physically and mentally strong enough to hear that he is missing. I'm sure you have been informed that she has complained about feeling too weak to work at the bakery."

Vladimir responded, "She should know about your father. I can have Dilara, our infirmary medical assistant, get her medical kit and accompany you to speak with your mother and sister. The two of you can retrieve Leah from the bakery and then go to the hut to show Leah and your mom the letter. If your mom reacts very negatively, the medical assistant will be there to assist."

"Thank you, Vladimir, for being so helpful and thoughtful".

My mom immediately noticed the medical assistant when Leah and I entered our hut's compartment. She was lying in her bed and Dilara helped her sit up. As she was getting up, she yelled, "What's wrong? What happened to my Meir?"

Dilara helped my mom calm down by taking some slow deep breaths. Leah and I sat on Leah's bed and I read the letter that stated my father was listed as 'Missing in Action'. As soon as I stated those words, my mom fainted and collapsed backward onto the bed's pillow. Dilara quickly examined her with a stethoscope and found she was still breathing. She retrieved some smelling salts from her medical bag and brought my mom back to consciousness.

Once my mom was awake, she complained with a hoarse weakened voice, "My chest hurts."

I was alarmed and asked, "Shouldn't we take her to a hospital?"

Dilara replied, "I don't think that is a good idea. She might get worse there. All of the Tashkent hospitals are overflowing with diseased people. It may also take many days until your mom would even be examined. I think that it is best for her to remain here, where it is quiet and safe, so that she can get some rest. I'll regularly check on her every day. If she

269

doesn't improve in a couple of days, I'll see if I can contact an available doctor. How old is your mom?"

I answered, "She is forty years old."

"Oh, she's young enough to recover quickly. Leah, go to the canteen, grab some straws and a glass to help your mom drink plenty of water. Your mom may be dehydrated. Do you have a water container?"

Leah nodded and said, "Yes, we have one."

"Good. Go fill it. I'll tell Vladimir that your mom will need Leah to attend to your mom and not report to the bakery. I'll check a few times a day to see if she is still feeling any more pain in her chest. You can bring her meals from the canteen. Let's see if she improves by allowing her to get some rest. I'll come back and give you a bedpan that your mom can use until she is strong enough to walk to the restroom. I'll also find a walking cane for her to use. "

Leah immediately left and I thanked Dilara for her help.

When Leah returned, she and I gently raised my mom up so that she could drink some water. She slowly sipped some water and then, in a hoarse whisper repeated, "Where's my Meir? Where's my Meir? I can't live without him. Just let me die."

Since Leah was going to remain with our mom, I decided that I should report to the employment office the next day and first go to the Soviet Army's Recruitment Office and show them the letter. I wanted to learn more about why the Polish II Corps was in Italy. As far as we knew, they were still in Persia.

The official told me, "The Polish II Corps was sent to join the British Eighth Army Division in Southern Italy to fight and defeat Mussolini's Fascist Italian army. There must have been a fierce battle at the front fortification line called the 'Gustav Line'.

"Yitzhak, 'Missing in Action' means that the army doesn't know what happened to your father. He could

270

have been injured and sent to a hospital. He could have been taken prisoner by the Italian army or his body couldn't be identified. You'll just have to remain patient. If you want, you can submit an inquiry form and I'll send it on. However, it may take months to receive any more information from the Polish government's London office. You may never receive a response."

I filled out the inquiry form and gave it to the Soviet official. He told me to come back in a month to learn if a response was received.

I saw the next new announcement on the employment office's bulletin board on Wednesday, January 12th, 1944. It stated in very large, bold print, that the Soviet army had crossed over the border and had now entered the rest of Eastern Poland. I was eager to share this news with my mom, Leah, and Hershel.

I thought: *This news may encourage my mom and improve her desire to live!*

After returning to the kolkhoz and taking my shower, I raced into the kitchen and found Leah and Hershel standing in front of the ovens. "Can the two of you take a short break? I have good news to share with you and mama!"

The two of them gave me a startled look and placed their oven mitts on the counter. I grabbed and tugged on one of Leah and Hershel's arms. "Hurry, let's go see mom." The three of us raced into the hut and quickly opened the curtain to our compartment to surprise her.

"What are the three of you doing here in the afternoon? Shouldn't all three of you be working?"

I spoke up very eagerly. "I learned some great news. We might be going home."

All three of them gave me a puzzled look and said, "Huh?"

"The Soviet army continues to win battles and has now pushed the German army out of the Soviet Union. The Soviet army crossed over the border between Eastern Poland and the Soviet Union. As they continue to successfully move the Nazis westward, we should be able to leave here and go home!"

Leah and Hershel joyfully hugged each other. Then Leah spoke, "Isn't that good news, Mama? We'll be leaving here. You now have a good reason to get well. It's time for you to get strong, get out of bed, and begin to take short walks with me so that you will be ready to go home!"

My mom replied, "I suppose you're right. I'm tired of using this bedpan. How about helping me up? I want to try taking some steps."

Hearing this good news worked. Numerous times a day, Leah helped my mom walk a little bit further while using her cane. Amazingly, within a week, my mom, with Leah's assistance and with the use of the cane, could walk to the restroom and shower area and then walk back to the hut. Within weeks, she was strong enough to walk to the kitchen. She also no longer complained about feeling any chest pain.

Vladimir found a chair for my mom to use in the kitchen. She learned to pace herself with preparing the bread dough to be baked in the ovens. By the end of February, she was able to work her regular hours while sitting in the chair.

I stopped at the recruitment center each month to learn if a response to my inquiry about my father was received. I was disappointed and concerned that there was no other information regarding my father. Since my mother and Leah never asked, I kept this disappointment to myself.

The Soviet army continued their successful assault pushing the Nazi army back to Germany. In March, the Soviet troops began an offensive attack to defeat the German army in the Belarusian area. In April, the Soviet troops began an offensive battle to liberate Crimea. The Soviet army recaptured the city of Sevastopol in May, and the Germans surrendered in Crimea. With each military success, it was clear that the tide had turned and the Soviet army was winning.

My mom's physical and mental health drastically improved when I told her on August 2$^{nd}$ that Stanislavov was liberated on July 27$^{th}$!

It became clear that returning home was a realistic expectation. Rumors about a return spread through our kolkhoz. Finally, on Tuesday, August 8$^{th}$, Vladimir held an afternoon meeting with all of the employees who were sent to Kolkhoz Aggatay by the Soviet Employment center.

"Thank you for meeting with me this afternoon. Beginning in the fall of 1943, the Soviet army was on the offense of pushing back the Nazi army. The rumor that the Nazi army has suffered many defeats is true. Their army has now retreated out of the Soviet Union and crossed the border into Eastern Poland. Their westward retreat continues as they are being defeated in Eastern Poland. Soon, they will be pushed all the way back to Germany!"

There was a loud applause.

"Let me continue. Many of you may be wondering if and when you will be able to return to your former city, town, or village. I just received today the official instructions from the Soviet Employment Center. Our great leader, Joseph Stalin, has proclaimed his 'Scorched Earth' Evacuation Policy has ended. He declared that it is now time to renew the country's socialistic economy and the livelihood of the Soviet people. The return to your former city, town, or village will be managed by following a specific timetable. The first to return will be those Soviet citizens who were issued official stamped employment travel permits from their former employer or a Soviet government official. Others who arrived in Tashkent without this official permit and were assigned employment by the Soviet Employment Center, along with those living independently in Uzbekistan, will remain in Tashkent for now and will be notified later about their return status."

He paused as members in the audience mumbled to each other.

He continued once their voices subsided. "I received more instructions today. Please listen carefully. Once I receive official clearance that your city, town, or village has been liberated and you are cleared to return to your former home, I will issue you an official return summons form to show to the train station's railroad director. The railroad director will issue you an official train travel permit and food vouchers. You will continue working your regular hours at Kolkhoz Aggatay until I contact you. Those who originally were from the Soviet Union, and not Eastern Poland, will be released immediately. Then, I will contact those of you from Eastern Poland when I get official word that you are to be released. When you arrive at your destination, you are to immediately report to the official municipal office to be processed. You will need to show them your official return summons and travel documents. Are there any questions?"

One man stood up. "What about those of us who are refugees and are not Soviet citizens?"

Vladimir answered, "I haven't received any official information regarding those of you who are classified as refugees. Until I do, you will continue working here, as assigned by the Soviet Employment Office. I didn't hire anyone without the office's approval. Anything else?"

No one stood up.

"Good. Thank you for listening and please return to work."

As Leah, Hershel, my mom, and I left the canteen, I brought the three of them close to me into a huddle.

I whispered so no one else could hear. "You know that he was talking about the three of us. We were sent here with the official stamped document. Once Bolechov is liberated, and this should happen very soon, we will be sent home."

Leah seemed alarmed and spoke up, "Yitzhak, I can't leave without Hershel. I want to stay to be with him."

Hershel immediately interrupted. "No, Leah. You must go while you have the chance to get out of here. I will find you. Don't worry. Yitzhak will give me the information on how to find you before you leave. I promise. I will find you so that we can be together. Besides, your mom will need your help with the train travel and getting settled once you arrive home."

I responded, "Thank you, Hershel. You are a thoughtful and kind individual. I will provide you with complete details on how to locate us. Everything will work out, Leah. You'll see."

That was our plan. We just needed to wait for Vladimir to tell us when we could officially leave.

The next day, I went to the Soviet government building to give haircuts. When I checked in at the Employment Center's counter, the office secretary enthusiastically said, "Yitzhak, take a good look at the announcement board!"

I looked up at it, and couldn't believe what I saw. 'The town of Bolechov was liberated today!' Then she said, "You and your family will be going home soon. We will all miss you, Yitzhak! We've enjoyed having you come here."

Of course, I couldn't wait to tell my mom and Leah the good news. The three of us hugged each other when I told them.

Then, my mom asked the question that I was trying my best to avoid answering, "Do you know what has happened to my Meir? Is he still listed as 'Missing in Action'? How can I go home without him?"

"Mom, I've been checking each month and there is no more information. I will give Manager Vladimir our Bolechov address and Aneta's address. If Papa returns to Kolkhoz Aggatay or if Vladimir receives an official response letter from the Polish II Corps, he will let Papa know how to find us and where to forward the response letter to us. Papa would want us to take care of ourselves. You know that. I'll continue to inquire about him when we get back to Bolechov."

This seemed to appease her for the moment. I was more worried about how she would endure the

276

long train trip, particularly walking long distances.

I knew that our return to Bolechov was near when I learned that Lviv was liberated on Wednesday, August 30th. On Sunday, September 3rd, Leah and I were contacted to report to Vladimir's office.

"Leah and Yitzhak, I received the official notice that the two of you and your mother are to report to the train station tomorrow morning after breakfast. Here are all of the documents that you will need to prove that you were officially released. You and your mother can quit working today to pack up all of your belongings. Foreman Rashid will drive the three of you to the train station in the morning. I greatly appreciate your hard work. I'm also very happy that your mom recovered and continued working as best as she could. I normally don't do this, but to show my appreciation, here are three canvas sacks and tie ropes from the granary. You can place all of your belongings in them. Please turn them inside out so that no one sees the Kolkhoz Aggatay marking. I don't have enough extras to give a sack to everyone."

I responded, "Will do, Vladimir, and thank you for the kindness that you displayed to me and my family while we were here. There is one favor that we want to ask you. I want to give you our home address in Bolechov and the address of one of our friends. If in case our father shows up here or if you receive an official letter from the Polish II Corps addressed to us, you will be able to tell our father where we are and where to send the letter."

"I was just about to ask you for this, Yitzhak."

"Thank you again, Vladimir."

"You're welcome. Good luck and I wish all of you a good future."

The next morning, Hershel accompanied my mom, Leah, and me to the front entrance where Foreman Rashid was waiting for us. As I started packing our belongings, including the barber box with the tools and all of our documents into the car's trunk, Leah and Hershel embraced and kissed. After a few moments, I gently pulled them apart and asked Leah to help my mom get into the car. My mom was heartbroken and very sad that she was leaving without my father. She kept repeating, "Where's my Meir? Where's my Meir? I can't live without him!"

As the car slowly pulled out of the dirt entrance to head to the main dirt road, we could hear Hershel yell, "I love you, Leah! I will come and get you. I promise!"

Tears flowed from both Leah and my mom. I was very worried how long it would take us to get from Tashkent to Bolechov. Facing another five months of travel was not what I wanted to endure ever again!

We arrived at the Tashkent train station twenty minutes later. Once inside, I had my mom and Leah sit on a bench in the lobby while I went to the ticket counter with our required documents. The ticket agent called for the station's railroad director to come to the counter. The director closely examined everything and then handed me three second-class tickets, our travel permits to show at the other train stations, and a packet of food vouchers to use on the trains. 'Direct Travel from Tashkent to Moscow' was printed on the tickets.

Being puzzled with the tickets' information, I asked, "Will we have to transfer to a different train at the local train stations?"

He replied, "You will go directly from one main station to the next one without any interruption. For example, from Tashkent, you will stay on the same train all the way to Moscow. The train will make many stops along the way. You won't have to get off to transfer to another train until you get to Moscow."

I asked the director, "How long will it take us to arrive in Moscow?"

"You should expect at least four days to reach Moscow." It may take you one month to arrive at Bolechov in Poland. Have a safe journey. Your train to Moscow will depart on platform three in two hours. "

*Wow! One month is surely better than five months!*

I purposely didn't tell Leah and my mom that we were issued second-class tickets. Leah and I helped my mom walk from the lobby to the platform ten minutes before our train's scheduled departure. When the train pulled up and stopped, I told them, "Follow me."

We walked to a second-class train car, showed our tickets to the boarding attendant, and the three of us entered a compartment that had upholstered seats and not a wooden bench! There was even a rack above our seats where we could place some of our belongings. I placed my sack and the case containing the barber's box under my seat for safekeeping.

Leah was the first one to notice. "Are you sure these are our right seats?"

"Yes. I think that we will ride more comfortably this time. We will stay on this train all the way to Moscow. I was told that we should arrive home in four weeks. That sure is better that our last train trip! Isn't that right, Mama?"

She smiled and nodded. "Yes, Yitzhak. This is better."

Leah asked, "Did I hear you correctly? We are going to Moscow?"

I replied, "Yes, we are. We are going home following a different route."

Ten minutes later our train departed from the Tashkent station.

When I heard the noise of the train rolling along the tracks, I started wondering: *What will we find in Bolechov?*

*Will our home, the barbershop, and our beautiful town be destroyed?*

*Will we learn the fate of Uncle Anshel and his family? Were they sent to a labor camp? Are they still alive?*

*Has anything happened to Aneta, her daughter, and their husbands?*

*What happened to my father? If he is still alive, will he know where to find us if our home was destroyed?*

These thoughts kept spinning inside my head until the sound of the train's wheels speeding on the tracks finally put me to sleep.

# The Return to Bolechov
## September 1944

The Tashkent Railway Director's estimate of us arriving at Bolechov in four weeks didn't seem realistic. I was anticipating that it would take longer to get there.

Three middle-aged men sat across from us all the way to Moscow. When we heard them speak Russian to each other, it became clear that it was best for Leah, my mom, and me to speak to each other in Polish, rather than Yiddish, to conceal that we were Jewish. Even so, when these Russian men heard us speak Polish and saw our sacks placed on the luggage rack above us, their indignant facial expressions made it clear that they thought we were refugees returning to Poland. I felt that it was best for Leah and my mom to go to the train's dining car with their food vouchers while I remained to guard our belongings, particularly the case with the barber's box that contained my tools and all of our documents. I didn't trust these Russian men.

We rode all the way from Tashkent to Moscow without having to transfer to another train along the way. Even so, sitting in the same seat for four days became very tiresome. The train made four stops, sometimes for at least two to three hours. The conductor allowed us to get off and reboard the train during those long stops. For us to not lose our seats I remained on the train while Leah and my mom got off to take a short walk and use the restrooms. I took my stroll and restroom break after they returned.

When our train departed from the first stop and gained full speed, I looked out the train car's window. It appeared that the train was not moving very fast. I was curious about this slow speed since our train car wasn't overloaded with passengers. When the train made its next stop, I took a short walk along the station's platform. I saw that there were at least five cargo cars attached behind the passenger cars. This must have been the reason for the train's slowness. I also noticed during the stops that the train stations seemed more orderly and organized. The platforms, lobbies, and waiting rooms were not packed with passengers and Soviet soldiers. Everyone was acting very calmly and not urgently pushing their way through the platform gates and racing to board the trains.

When Leah and my mom returned from the dining car the first time, they both complained, "The food is disgusting. It tasted like those military canned rations that we often ate." I agreed with them when I tasted the food, but at least it was free and available to us. It was best for us to save our money, not knowing what we would need when we arrived home.

The transfer at the Moscow train station went fairly smoothly. We arrived in the early morning on Friday, September 8th, and our departing train for Kyiv was scheduled to leave six hours later at 2 p.m. This was better than waiting three days and having to sleep on the floor inside a train station's waiting room. I was very pleased that once the station's ticket counter clerk examined our travel documents, he also issued us second-class tickets for compartment seats and food vouchers. He estimated that we would arrive in Kyiv in three days on Monday, September 11th, with numerous stops along the way. The ticket clerk also mentioned that the rail line between Moscow and Kyiv was recently repaired and restored between the two cities.

As our train neared Kyiv, I looked out the window and saw the scars caused by the war. Many war-torn houses in the villages and barns on the farms were completely destroyed or severely damaged. Destroyed military equipment was scattered across the land that was burned from bombs and battles. Our train slowed down even more and jerked side to side when it frequently changed tracks. I looked out again and noticed railroad workers repairing the tracks that had been bombed.

As our train entered Kyiv, I looked out the window again. The battle between the Soviet army and the Nazis resulted in numerous damaged buildings and debris spread across many of the streets. Work crews and large trucks were visible, clearing the streets from the rubble.

We arrived in Kyiv in the late afternoon on September 11th. As we walked along the platform, the outside wall of the station's waiting room had been bombed and a crew was busy clearing the scattered cement and bricks. Leah and my mom found an unoccupied bench in the lobby and sat there while I went to the ticket counter. When I showed our travel documents to the ticket counter agent, he said, "The train line from Kyiv to Lviv is still being repaired. The repair is almost complete and we should have the line reopened in two days. Come back to the counter the morning of the thirteenth."

I replied, "Where are the three of us supposed to go to wait until the thirteenth since the waiting room is closed?"

His response was, "I guess you can wait in the lobby."

When I explained the situation to my mom and sister, Leah suggested, "Why don't you check to see if the Evacuation Center is still open and if giving haircuts in the small park is possible?"

I didn't need to spend too much time looking outside. The two-story building across the street from the station that served as the previous Evacuation Center and the other businesses along the main street were damaged and unusable. The small park where I previously gave haircuts was now filled with military equipment and very few people were walking on this main street that I could approach for a haircut.

When I returned to the lobby and shared with them my findings, my mom said, "I saved some food from the kolkhoz kitchen and stored it in two of our glass containers. It still should be good enough for us to eat. We'll just have to make it last for the next two days."

The next day, late in the afternoon, the ticket agent came out into the lobby and confirmed that the track had been repaired and that the daily local train to Lviv would arrive the next morning. He also told us that our tickets and food vouchers would be ready to pick up at 9 a.m.

On Wednesday, September 13th, at 11 a.m. we departed from the Kyiv train station. This time we sat in a third-class passenger car with the wooden benches. Since this train was a local train, it made numerous stops and arrived in Lviv in two days on the morning of Friday, September 15th.

Our next train connection occurred in Lviv. We received tickets to board another daily local train that made frequent stops, which included Stanislavov and Stryi, before arriving at our final destination, Bolechov. The Lviv train station agent told us that we should expect long delays due to repairs and restoration of the train tracks. We finally left Stryi on Monday afternoon, the 18h of September, for a twenty-minute ride to reach the Bolechov train station.

As the train left the Stryi train station, my mind started spinning with many thoughts:

*With all of the reports of the Nazis murdering Jews in concentration camps, what happened to our relatives? Will we find any Jewish survivors?*

*After viewing the destruction from the bombs and battles at Kyiv, how much damage did Bolechov encounter?*

*How will the ethnic Ukrainians treat us, since we previously experienced many of them being German sympathizers?*

Similar to what I saw when the train approached Kyiv, work crews were busy repairing the train tracks between the Stryi and Bolechov train stations. To our surprise and delight, it only took us two weeks to travel from Tashkent to Bolechov. The train pulled into the station's platform at 2:20 p.m. on September 18th.

As Leah and I helped our mom cautiously step off the train and onto the platform, we noticed that sections of the train station's roof and walls were damaged from the war. My mom became frightened and loudly asked, "What have they done to my beautiful town?"

Since this was the very first local train to arrive in Bolechov in many weeks, the platform and the station's lobby area were crowded with many eager people. Some recognized us, pointed, and angrily yelled in both Polish and Ukrainian, "Look. Those dirty Jews are back! The Jews are back!" I recognized that some of the men who were yelling at us were my father's customers from the barbershop.

We continued to walk to the station's exit and others repeatedly yelled, "Cowards! Cowards! Shame

285

on you for being cowards! You should have died with the rest of the Jews! Why did you come back?  We don't want you here, you cowards!"

All three of us lowered our heads and made our way out of the station to reach the main street. I turned to Leah and my mom and suggested, "I think it is best for us to not walk to our home through the narrow alley by the factories.  It may be safer to just remain on the main streets."

As we proceeded to walk toward the Rynek Town Square, the town looked very desolate from the war. Many of the businesses and factories were damaged or destroyed.  We froze and stopped walking when we saw the condition of the Rynek area. The former scenic and thriving town square was terrifying to look at. The trees were barren and all of the wooden benches and market stalls were gone. There were no colorful flowers growing anywhere. Most of the surrounding businesses were completely destroyed, including my father's barbershop and Uncle Anshel's tailor shop. The windows of the synagogue and the adjoining Hebrew school were boarded up and visible scars from artillery fire appeared on their exterior walls. The Orthodox Christian Church was in the same damaged condition. The only building that did not encounter extensive damage was the town hall. There were a few official Soviet vehicles parked in front of it.

More people noticed us as they either walked by or rode in vehicles or horse-drawn wagons.  They also yelled loud hostile words and pointed at us. "Cowards! You should be dead! Go away you filthy Jews and don't come back!  The war was your fault!"

One young boy, who was walking with his mother, picked up a rock from the ground and threw it at us. Fortunately, the rock missed hitting us. The boy's mother quickly grabbed his arm and pulled him away.

The two of them turned and walked briskly in the other direction.

Tears flowed from my mom's eyes as she repeated, "What have they done? What have they done?"

In order for us to reach the street where we lived, we had to walk past my father's and my uncle's businesses. I immediately realized by seeing the barbershop's extensive damage, there was no way I could reinstate being a barber in Bolechov. The three of us were heartbroken to view my father and uncle's livelihoods completely destroyed.

When we turned right to begin walking toward our home, we froze again. The houses formerly occupied by the Jewish families were all severely damaged. Exterior doors were lying on the ground, windows were all smashed, and even some walls had huge holes. These houses were completely unlivable and beyond repair. When I suggested that we should turn around, my mom insisted, "No. I want to see what they did to my home!"

The three of us slowly approached our former house and stopped to face the home's front entrance. Leah suggested, "Mama, everything is destroyed. There's really nothing left. We should turn around and walk away."

"I don't care, Leah. I want to see what they did. Help me walk to the back of the house. I want to see what's left of my garden!"

When she saw that the garden was depleted of all living plants and that all of the furniture and other belongings left in the house were either destroyed or stolen, she finally said, "I've seen enough. Take me out of here."

I suggested, "Let's go to Aneta's home and see if she is still living there. I know that it is a long walk for you, Mama. We'll go slowly and if there is a place for you to sit and rest, we'll stop."

"No, Yitzhak. I don't want to stop and see any more of what has happened here. I can handle the long walk. I've walked to Aneta's house before and I can do it again."

In order to get to the street where Aneta's home was located, we had to walk through the Rynek Town Square and past the town hall. Her home was the tenth one on the left side of the street. Since large garden areas divided the homes on her street, it took a while to reach her house. I remembered that her one-story house was painted a bright yellow. Surprisingly, when we reached it, her house was still yellow, but not as vibrant as I remembered.

We opened the front wooden gate and walked to the front door. I knocked, not knowing if anyone would answer. No one came to the door. I knocked again and loudly yelled, "It's Yitzhak, Aneta!"

I finally heard some shuffling noises from inside the house. The front door opened slowly. Aneta's daughter, Maria, stood in front of us and yelled, "Mama! Come here quickly! A miracle has happened. Come and see for yourself!"

While Maria helped us enter the house, Aneta ran toward my mom with opened arms. "Rifka! You're here! I can't believe it. You are all here!"

After hugging all three of us, Aneta asked, "Where's Meir?"

My mom started to cry. Leah spoke up. "Maria, my mom needs to sit down. As you can see, she now needs a cane to walk."

Maria immediately responded, "Come. Let me help you, Rifka. Sit down in the comfortable chair in the living room. It has an ottoman for you to raise your feet. All of you come inside and sit. You must be

288

hungry and thirsty. Mom, there should be enough vegetables to make a good soup for all of us."

"Good idea, Maria. I'll start preparing the soup. Give them some water to drink and I'll also prepare some tea for all of us."

The three of us were relieved to know that Aneta and her daughter, Maria, were still alive and living in Bolechov. Once my mom and Leah were seated in their living room, I went into the kitchen and signaled to Maria that I wanted to speak privately to her. "Maria, my father is missing. It upsets my mom too much to talk about it. Please don't bring it up in front of her. I'll explain what happened to him later."

"Yitzhak, both my husband, Borysko, and my father, Ivan, are dead. I'm asking you the same thing. Please don't mention them in front of my mom. I have so much to tell you. It might be best if we took a walk tomorrow and, for the rest of today, just let the three of you get some rest from your long journey."

"That's a good idea. I'll let Leah know not to mention your father and husband and about going for a private walk with you tomorrow. Leah is now mature enough to know everything."

After the five of us ate the delicious vegetable soup and drank some tea, Aneta suggested that the three of us should get cleaned up and change clothes. Their shower was working and they handed us towels and clean clothes to wear.

We all relaxed the rest of the day and reminisced about the happy times that we previously shared together. Later, Maria offered to sleep with her mother, while Leah and my mom slept on the bed in her room. Their living room sofa was large enough for me to sleep on.

The next morning after we all had breakfast, Maria suggested, "Mom, why don't you and Rifka

289

spend the day together while Leah, Yitzhak, and I go for a walk?"

Aneta responded, "That's a good idea. Rifka, how about you and me wash clothes together like we used to do?"

Maria asked, "Do all of you have heavy coats and sweaters? Winter will arrive very soon."

The three of us shook our heads to indicate that we didn't.

"Don't worry. We have some that you can use and take with you. Leah, I'll also give you one of my headscarves to wear. I have one for you too, Rifka. Yitzhak, I'll give you one of my husband's hats. It should fit you. Leah, wear the headscarf, and, Yitzhak, wear the hat so that those who we pass will not recognize you. Let's leave in about fifteen minutes."

Tuesday, September 19th, was a cloudy and chilly morning with a slight cool breeze. The hat, headscarf, and the heavy sweaters that Maria gave us to wear kept us warm. As the three of us were leaving their house, Maria said, "I have something to show you at the end of our street where the Jewish cemetery is located."

When we approached the cemetery, Leah and I were shocked to see that the cemetery was all torn up. Gravestones were either broken or had fallen over onto the ground. I asked, "What happened here?"

Maria hesitated to answer and wouldn't look at us.

I asked again. "Please, Maria, tell us. Leah and I want to know."

With great hesitation and tears flowing from her eyes, she explained, "The Nazis, along with members of a Ukrainian gang, murdered the Bolechov Jewish people. The Germans called these massacres 'Aktions'. The final Aktion took place at this cemetery in March 1943. The remaining Jews were gathered together in this cemetery, ordered to completely undress, and then shot and killed. Their bodies fell into a mass grave that was dug in this cemetery."

After many moments of silence, Leah asked, "Are there any Jews left in Bolechov?"

"I've been told that there are about forty Jews who survived by hiding in attics, cellars, or bunkers in the forest. They remain very private due to the current hostility toward them from many of the Poles and the Ukrainians."

I interrupted, "I know what you mean, Maria. We were recognized as soon as we got off the train and people started yelling at us. A young boy even threw a rock at us!"

"I have more to show you and explain. Let's keep walking."

As we approached the Rynek Town Square, Maria stopped and said, "I'm sure you noticed how damaged and desolate our once beautiful little town has now become. Most of the damage that you see happened when the Soviet army returned and fought the Germans. After a few days of fierce fighting, the German army retreated along with all of their officials."

We continued walking and I asked, "What happened to the Great Synagogue and the Hebrew school?"

"The Soviets and later the Germans used those buildings, along with the Catholic Church, as warehouses to store their military supplies. Most of what existed inside the synagogue was destroyed, including your sacred scrolls."

Now that Maria was more composed and willing to tell us more details, I asked her, "What happened to our house? We walked there yesterday and saw that it was completely destroyed."

"It was just a coincidence that my husband and I planned to visit my mom the day after you left. As soon as we arrived, she asked us to go with her to retrieve the food stored in your cellar. When we got there, your Uncle Anshel, Aunt Gital, and cousin, Mindel, were in the cellar packing the jars. Between the six of us, we were able to clear out most of the items that were there. When we finished, we locked the door. The next day, when the Ukrainian thugs became aware that the Soviet officials had abandoned the town, they broke into and looted all of the empty houses, particularly those occupied by the Jewish families who had fled. Days later, many of these homes were damaged."

She continued to tell us more details while we walked further and approached the main bridge that crossed over the Sukiel River. "Those Ukrainian thugs enthusiastically greeted the Germans as soon as their army arrived to take over the town. Many of the Ukrainians, the German officials, and even some of the Poles moved into the abandoned homes that hadn't been trashed. They also moved into the homes that became vacant during the Aktions."

Maria stopped walking as soon as we crossed the bridge. "As you know, my family is ethnic Ukrainian. Even so, we were never supportive of the Germans and were completely outraged by the actions taken by these Ukrainian thugs. My father and husband made the decision to join the Polish Resistance when they saw how these thugs aligned with the Nazis. That night, the two of them fled into the forest to join the fight against the invading Nazis."

Leah asked, "What happened to your father and husband?"

"A few months later, one of the Polish men secretly came to our home during the night and told us that they were shot and killed in a battle. He wasn't sure where this took place. Of course, my mom was devastated with this news and just couldn't be left alone. That's when I decided to permanently move in with her. Let's keep walking. I have more to show you."

The three of us continued our walk out of the central part of the city and approached the surrounding forest.

I spoke up. "I remember when I was very young, I joined a few of my Ukrainian and Polish friends and went through this forest and climbed up a hill to view the city. Are we going to walk through the Taniava forest?"

"Yes, Yitzhak. That's where we are headed. I want the two of you to see what took place there."

As we walked through the forest, Maria asked about our father. This was when we explained to her that he was conscripted into the Polish Brigade, and later, was listed as 'Missing in Action' during a battle in Italy.

Maria responded, "I'm very sorry to learn about your father. Your mother must have been torn to pieces when she learned he was missing."

I replied, "Yes, she was. She fainted and we thought she had a heart attack. It took a number of weeks for her to recover. This is the reason that she now walks with a cane."

We stopped walking about thirty minutes later when Maria mentioned, "This is what I want to show you. Do you see that fallen tree in the distance? Let's go over there and sit on it."

Once we sat down, Maria asked, "Leah and Yitzhak, what do you see?"

Leah and I looked at each other and shrugged our shoulders. I finally answered, "I see a large, clear area that doesn't have any trees. The ground is barren and there are many ripples in the dirt. What is this?"

Maria started crying again and her voice cracked numerous times as she told us, "What you see is a very large mass grave. I believe that your aunts, Gital and Feiga, and cousin, Mindel, along with hundreds of other Jews were shot and murdered and their bodies are lying here in this covered pit."

She continued, "As I mentioned before, the Jews in Bolechov were murdered at different times in what the Germans called 'Aktions'. The first Aktion happened in October 1941, four months after the Nazis captured the town. The German police, along with the assistance of the Ukrainian thugs, rounded up about one thousand Jews, including the rabbis and many women who were just walking in the streets, and held them captive in the Rynek Town Square. Then, they were marched and locked inside the Catholic Church where they were tortured. When my mom and I heard women screaming we left our house and raced to the church to see what was happening. We were horrified to see German soldiers murdering babies up in the bell tower. Two days later, those in the church were taken to this place in the forest where they were shot and dropped into this pit. One of my Polish friends secretly witnessed this from the forest and later told me what happened."

Leah and I were horrified to learn how our relatives and others were tortured and murdered. Moments later, I asked Maria, "What about Uncle Anshel? Was he also murdered here?"

"As far as we know, my mom and I think he escaped and fled into the forest outside the eastern part of Bolechov when he realized that his wife, mother-in-law, and daughter were captured."

Then, Leah inquired, "Do you think that he may still be alive?"

Maria responded, "Yes, this is possible. He may have fled to join the Polish Resistance. We just don't know. He has yet to return."

I added, "Maria, when I begin inquiring more about the whereabouts of our father, I'll include Uncle Anshel. The two of them may still be alive."

Tears returned to Maria's face as she said, "It really hurts me deeply to talk about all of this knowing that many Ukrainians collaborated with the Nazis. Many of them believed that if they helped Germany win the war, the Germans would allow the Ukrainians to govern this country."

After about ten minutes of silence, Maria suggested, "Let's start walking back. There is more for me to tell you about the other Aktions that happened.

"A second Aktion occurred about a year later at the end of August 1942 and lasted three days. About fifteen hundred Jews were murdered, including children, and even more were sent to the Belzec death camp. Once again, the local Ukrainians assisted the Nazis. The bodies of those murdered were thrown into a pit dug in a cemetery.

"The third Aktion took place in December 1942. Those Jews who remained and previously placed together in a designated ghetto area were taken out during the night, shot, and buried in another pit in the cemetery. Weeks later, a fourth Aktion took place. Three hundred Jews were put into a cargo train and taken to a work camp. One more massacre happened at the Jewish cemetery near our house in March 1943. By August 1943, there were no Jews left. This is why there are currently very few Jewish people in Bolechov."

Maria finished telling these details when we crossed the bridge over the Sukiel River and reentered the center of the town. It became clear to me that there was no reason for Leah, my mom, and me to remain in Bolechov. "Leah, we shouldn't tell mom these details. I'm fearful that she will be so upset that her chest pains will return. Since we have to go to the municipal building to be processed, let's just explain to her that we need to be relocated somewhere else since our family home and business were destroyed."

Leah was obviously torn apart from learning about the murders of our relatives. In a very soft voice, she said, "Whatever you think is best, Yitzhak."

When we returned and entered Aneta's home, we heard Aneta sobbing from the bedroom where my mom and Leah had slept. We immediately knew something was wrong. We entered the bedroom and found my mom lying in the bed with Aneta holding a wet compress across my mom's forehead. My mom kept repeating very softly, "I can't go on. I don't want to live."

Being alarmed and concerned, I sat next to Aneta on the bed and asked her, "What happened?"

Aneta pulled out a handkerchief from her apron, dried her eyes, and in a slow whisper explained, "We were gathering up the clothes to wash and just having a conversation. Rifka asked me to tell her what happened to my husband and son-in-law. After I told her that Ivan and Borysko died fighting with the Polish Resistance, she asked about Uncle Anshel and his family. At first, I didn't want to answer, but she kept on insisting. When I told her that Gital, Feiga, and Mindel were murdered, she fell and started complaining about pains in her chest. I helped her stand up and slowly and carefully helped her get into the bed. I'm really scared. I'm sorry, Yitzhak. I shouldn't have told her anything."

I tried my best to console Aneta. "Don't worry, Aneta. She was eventually going to learn what happened to them. When she heard that our father was missing, she fainted and then complained about chest pains. Let's all remain quiet and calm so that she can get some rest."

I quietly asked my mom, "Mama, how are you feeling? Do you still feel any pain in your chest?"

She whispered, "It's not too bad. Just let me rest for a while and let Aneta stay with me."

Noticing that Leah was frantic, I walked her out of the bedroom along with Maria. "How about the two of you go ahead and finish washing our clothes? Maria, is the town magistrate or marshal's office still located in the town hall?"

"Yes, Yitzhak. The Soviet town marshal's office is still located there."

"Leah, you and I need to go there tomorrow with all of our documents. The three of us still need to be officially processed. We need to convince the town official to send us somewhere else where we can live and work. Okay? When we go to the office tomorrow, Mama can stay here with Aneta and Maria and get more rest. She needs to regain some strength in order to leave Bolechov."

Leah somberly responded, "Whatever you think is best, Yitzhak."

Leah and I went to the town hall the next morning and checked in at the town marshal's office. When we showed the clerk our official Soviet-issued return summons documents and travel permits, she said, "Have a seat and wait for Town Marshal Leonid Morozov. He should be here shortly."

An hour later, the clerk ushered us into his office. Town Marshal Morozov was very annoyed to see us and with a grumpy voice asked, "What are you doing here?"

I showed him the travel summons and permits from Tashkent. After closely examining them and negatively shaking his head back and forth, he yelled at us and slammed the papers onto his desk. "These are all wrong! Whoever filled these out sent you to the wrong place! You should have been sent to the oblast administrative center in Stanislavov, and not sent to Bolechov! Who sent you to Tashkent in the first place?"

When I showed him the documents that we received from the former Bolechov Town Marshal, Captain Pavel Novikov, he yelled more questions at us. "You are Jews! How could have he issued these to the two of you and your father and mother? Where are your parents?"

I showed him the letter that we received from the Polish II Corps about my father's disappearance and explained that my mom was resting from the long train journey.

"The three of you need to go to the Stanislavov administrative center's headquarters in their town hall to complete the repatriation process. Give me a few moments, and I'll issue you new authorization summons and travel permits. Show them to the ticket agent at our train station and he'll provide the train tickets. The Stanislavov office will process your return and provide the three of you with the official resident permits and make your housing arrangements. I still don't understand why you were sent here. Whoever sent you should have known that there is nothing left here for you Jews!"

I boldly asked, "Where is the town hall located in Stanislavov?"

"Their town hall is called the Ratusha. It is located in the center of the downtown Old City on Halych

Street. Just walk east on the main street from the train station. You can't miss it. It is an art-deco style tall building."

About twenty minutes later, I received the new documents for the three of us. As Leah and I entered the hallway outside his office, we overheard the town marshal say to the office secretary, "That's three more Jews that I won't have to deal with. Good riddance!"

I turned to Leah. "It's a good thing that we are getting out of here and leaving a place where we aren't welcome."

Leah and I agreed that we should let our mom rest for a few days and leave Bolechov on the following Monday, September 25th. Immediately after leaving the town hall, Leah and I walked to the train station to check the schedule. We learned that the daily train from Bolechov to Stanislavov departed at 9 a.m. and the ticket office opened at 8. Therefore, she and I decided that it was best for us to stand in line in front of the ticket office window by 7:30 on Monday morning.

Aneta and Maria helped us prepare for the next phase of our journey. They insisted on giving us additional winter clothing and coats that we would need, along with bread and jars filled with food. Somehow, we managed to stuff everything inside our canvas sacks.

While we were preparing for our Monday morning departure, I mentioned to Aneta and Maria, "I will write to you as soon as we are settled and give you our address. If by some chance our father and Uncle Anshel show up, you will be able to tell them where we are."

Leah immediately interrupted, "My boyfriend from Tashkent, Hershel Zimmerman, may also show up. I gave him your address in case he comes looking for me!"

Maria inquisitively looked at me. I winked back and nodded to indicate to her that I approved of Leah's romantic involvement with Hershel.

Maria responded, "I'll let all of them know where you are. I also want to go with you to the train station on Monday morning to give you a last goodbye. I don't know if my mom and I will ever see our good friends again. Let's all try our best to remain in touch with each other."

Saying goodbye to Aneta and Maria was very difficult. We all loved each other very much and felt that we were one family. Before leaving their home on that Monday morning, my mom mentioned to Aneta and Maria, "Thank you for everything you have done for me and my family for many years. I will always be grateful to you and remember the love that we share."

Maria accompanied the three of us to the train station and held on to my mom's left arm since she walked very slowly with her cane. We experienced no difficulty obtaining our train tickets. The train promptly arrived at the platform at 8:30 and the platform wasn't too crowded. The three of us gave Maria one last hug and kiss. I helped my mom and Leah board the train with all of our belongings.

Once they were settled on the bench, I went back to the train car's entrance door to give Maria one last goodbye wave. Both of us continued waving and crying sad tears as the train slowly departed from the station.

# Repatriation
## September 1944 - February 1945

As our train approached the Stanislavov train station at 10:30 a.m. on Monday, September 25th, I turned toward my mom and sister and suggested, "As we walk through the train station's lobby, I think it will be best for the two of you to find a place to sit down, guard our belongings, and wait for me. Since none of us have ever been to Stanislavov, I want to ask someone where their town hall is located and the easiest way to get there. Mama, I don't want you to have to walk very far."

While they sat on a lobby bench, I exited the train station and looked around in the distance for a tall, odd-shaped building. I was amazed at how large this city was. I became concerned that where we needed to go was not located in close proximity to the train station. Since I didn't see any building that resembled the description of the town hall, I went back inside to ask the ticket counter agent for directions.

"Young man, our town hall is located in the Old City section of Stanislavov on Halych Street. The easiest way to get there is to take streetcar number 24. You can get on this streetcar right in front of the train station. Ask the driver to let you know when to get off at the Melinchuka Street stop. Once you get off the streetcar, look for a two-story building with a round ball on the top. You can't miss it."

I asked, "Sir, what's the car fare?"

"A five-kopek coin is the fare for adults. Good luck, young man."

"Thank you, sir."

Both Leah and I helped my mom enter the streetcar and find a seat, and then I carried all of our belongings onto the streetcar and paid the fare.

When we got off at the stop at Melinchuka Street, we immediately saw the tall building with the round ball on the top. It was located in the center of a large square that may have previously served as a market area before the war.

We entered the town hall at 11:30. The magistrate's office entrance was located on the opposite end of the lobby. Of course, we had to wait in line to speak to an official. Thirty minutes later, a female official, wearing a gray, non-military official-looking uniform, escorted us into an office.

A middle-aged man, also wearing a similar gray uniform, was sitting behind his desk and asked us, "How can I help you?"

Representing my family, I answered, "We are here to complete our repatriation process. We are returning from Uzbekistan where we worked on a Soviet collective farm. I have all of our documents to show you."

He responded, "Let me review them."

I pulled everything out of the case that stored our documents. "Here are our original travel permits issued by the Bolechov town marshal, our Tashkent registration cards, our Tashkent employment permits, and our return summons forms that were issued at both Tashkent and Bolechov. We were first sent to return to Bolechov. As you can see, the current Bolechov town marshal sent us here. He told us that we should have been sent directly here and not Bolechov."

After reviewing everything very thoroughly, the official said, "Everything is in order. The Bolechov town marshal was correct. You should have been sent directly here since Stanislavov is the oblast administrative center. I will issue your Stanislavov registration cards and your new official work permits. I see that you are Jews. The Polish Committee of

National Liberation, in cooperation with the Soviet communist officials, anticipated that many Jews will return to Poland from the Soviet Union and will need assistance to begin a prosperous life to help rebuild Poland. The Office of Assistance to the Jewish People is located at the end of the hallway to the left of this office. Go there and they will help you secure a place to live and to find employment."

The three of us replied, "Thank you, Sir", as we left his office, and proceeded down the hallway to find the government's assistance office.

When we entered, a clerk told us to sit and wait for Mrs. Rotfeld to help us. About forty-five minutes later, a heavy-set woman, who appeared to be about the same age as my mom, came out of an office and welcomed us with a very jovial, Yiddish-sounding voice. "Please come into my office and tell me where you are from."

Once again, I showed all of our documents, including my barber's licenses, and explained how we were sent to Stanislavov.

Mrs. Rotfeld asked us, "Have any of you ever been to Stanislavov?"

All three of us shook our head and replied, "No."

She continued, "I think it might be best and more convenient if I placed you to live near the Old City. There are plenty unoccupied apartments available in this area. Even though these apartments and the buildings are older, not very fancy, and have basic furnishings, living there will suffice to help you get situated and begin your new life.

"Leah and Rifka, I see that the two of you worked inside the collective farm's kitchen. We are currently experiencing a staffing issue at our hospitals. In addition to our local residents with health issues, there is also a high demand from the people who are returning who need medical assistance. The two of

303

you should have no problem finding work in a hospital kitchen."

She wrote down the names and addresses of two hospitals and handed the list to Leah. "Yitzhak, you'll just have to walk through the main streets to see if an existing barbershop needs an additional barber. Show the shop's owner or manager both your Polish and Soviet barber licenses. Do you have your own barber equipment?"

I opened the case to show her.

"Good. If you have difficulty finding work, come back to see me. Now, I have to find an apartment where you will live. Let me see if one is available in the Old City and near the closest hospitals."

I interrupted. "Mrs. Rotfeld, as you can see, my mom requires a cane while walking. If possible, a ground-floor apartment will be best. Going up and down steps will be problematic for her. Plus, she needs to get some rest from this long trip before she can begin working."

"I understand, Yitzhak. Let me look through my list of available apartments and make some phone calls. While I'm doing this, you are welcome to use the restrooms in the hallway and ask the office clerk for a cup of water. This may take me awhile."

After another forty-five minutes passed, Mrs. Rotfeld, with her cheerful voice, announced, "I have good news for the three of you. I located a ground-floor two-bedroom apartment, not too far from here in the Old City. Your landlady, Mrs. Berkowicz, is getting everything ready for you. It is located near the intersection of Het'mana Mazepy and Sichovykh Stril'tsiv Streets. Let me add the apartment's complete address for you on the sheet that I gave you, Leah."

She continued, "Leah and Rifka, one of our main hospitals on the list is located at the intersection of Het'mana Mazepy and Sotnyka Martyntsya Streets. It

304

is not too far from your apartment building. I'll walk outside with all of you and show you where the apartment building and hospital are located.

"Let me also give you some food coupons to use at the grocery stores. You will also have a ninety-day grace period before you have to begin paying rent to Mrs. Berkowicz. Again, come back to see me if you need my assistance with anything.

"Do you have any questions?"

After a silent pause, she continued, "Let's gather your belongings and walk outside. Welcome to your new home in Stanislavov!"

Mrs. Rotfeld was correct. Our apartment building was not too far for my mom to walk there from the town hall. When we turned left onto Sichovykh Stril'tsiv Street, the building was the second one on the left-hand side of the street, 108 Sichovykh Stril'tsiv Street. Moments after ringing the building's doorbell, another middle-aged woman wearing a kitchen apron opened the door.

"Hello. You must be the Barkan family. Welcome. Come on in. I'm Mrs. Berkowicz. Follow me to apartment number four."

When we entered, the apartment looked exactly as Mrs. Rotfeld had described. There were two bedrooms. The larger one had two beds, two dressers, table and lamp, and closet. The smaller room had one bed, one dresser, table and lamp, and closet. The living area and kitchen were in one main room. The toilet and bathtub with a shower were located in a small area between the two bedrooms. The apartment was small, drab in appearance, and must have been vacant for a few years. The light green paint on the walls had faded and the wooden floors had scuffmarks with multiple scrapes. There were no area rugs on the floors, no pictures hung on the walls, and torn curtains and window shades.

Mrs. Berkowicz continued, "You'll find bedding and towels stored in the bedroom closets. The kitchen cabinets have some dishes, pots and pans, and eating and serving utensils. These should be enough to get you started. There is some tea and a kettle in the kitchen cabinet.

"I'm preparing a big pot of soup. Once it is ready, I'll bring you some for your dinner. I'm sure that you are all very hungry. I live in the apartment next to you in apartment number two. Don't be shy. Let me know if you need help with anything or have some questions. It's nice to have a family living in this apartment once again. Oh, before I forget, here are two keys to the apartment. It is best to lock the door behind you, since you are on the ground floor."

The first thing the three of us did was to place our belongings on the floor, sit down in the living room, take off our shoes, and relax for a while on the living room's sofa and chair after a very busy day. I could tell that my mom needed to rest her feet.

My mom looked around and commented, "Mrs. Rotfeld was correct. This apartment is rather drab. At least we will have some privacy and hopefully some peace and quiet!"

An hour later, Mrs. Berkowicz brought us the soup that she prepared and some slices of bread. After eating, we assembled the bedding onto beds. Leah and my mom shared the large bedroom, while I slept in the smaller bedroom. Even though it was only 7 p.m., we were exhausted and quickly fell asleep.

The next morning, we unpacked all of our belongings, took showers, and planned our first day of life in Stanislavov. Leah's plan was to walk to the closest neighboring hospital and apply for a job in their kitchen. I went exploring to look for work at a barbershop and to find a grocery store. My mom gave me a list of items to purchase at the grocery store. I took the food coupons and some of the rubles that I had saved. While we were gone, my mom cleaned the apartment by borrowing a broom, dustpan, cleanser, washrags, and an empty pail from Mrs. Berkowicz.

I decided to walk south along Het'mana Mazepy Street since it was fairly busy with many businesses on both sides. After walking a few blocks, I found a barbershop. I looked into the shop's front window and noticed two barbers giving haircuts and an unused barber's station.

When I walked inside, one of the barbers acknowledged me and said, "Have a seat. I'll be finished real soon."

I replied, "Are you the owner or manager? I see that you have an empty station."

"Yes, I'm the owner of this barbershop. Just wait. I can talk to you when I'm finished."

After his customer left the shop, I approached the owner and showed him my Polish and Soviet barber licenses and my new work permit. "I have my own tools. I see that you have an empty station and I'm interested in working here."

He examined the licenses very carefully, looked up at me, and then angrily yelled, "Your name is Yitzhak. You are a Jew! I thought all of you Jews were all gassed in the ovens. You are still alive and want to work here? I don't know why Stalin and his designated Polish communist officials are giving you Jews special treatment. No, I'm not hiring you! You dirty Jew! You Jews are all taking jobs away from us Poles. Get out of here and don't ever come back for a haircut. Get out!"

When he raised his fists at me, I felt very frightened by his anger and hurriedly got out of there. I was concerned that he was going to become violent and hit me. I walked very briskly further south to get out of his view. After catching my breath, I continued my walk along Het'mana Mazepy Street to search for another barbershop.

As I continued to walk along the street, I noticed a change in the architecture of the buildings. They didn't look as old as the buildings that I saw in the Old City and where our apartment building was located. Plus, their exterior wasn't darkened from soot or smoke.

I thought: *Maybe the Old City was where most of the fighting and bombing took place and not this area of Stanislavov.*

*I was curious to learn if the Old City was the former Jewish neighborhood.*

*Is this why Mrs. Rotfeld placed us to live near the Old City since we were Jewish?*

I crossed the next main street at the intersection and continued to walk further to the south, another six blocks. I discovered a large square with four-story office buildings with ground-floor storefronts. An industrial area was located on the opposite side of the square. It was a very busy commercial area with lots of vehicle and pedestrian traffic.

As I walked closer to the square, I saw another barbershop and it was much larger than the previous one. When I looked inside their front window, I noticed ten barber stations, with five on each side. Eight were in use and three men were sitting in the waiting room. I decided to go in and inquire about working there.

A female clerk at the front counter greeted me and asked, "Do you have an appointment?"

I replied, "No, I don't.  I'm a licensed barber and would like to speak with the shop's owner or manager."

"He's currently busy with a customer.  Have a seat in the waiting area and I'll let him know that you are here."

About thirty minutes later, a well-groomed, elderly gray-haired man with a moustache that had pronounced waxed curls approached me.  "I'm told that you are a licensed barber and are looking for work."

I stood up. "Yes, sir.  Here are my licenses and work permit.  I have my own tools."

After looking closely at the licenses and staring at me with an angry glare, he grabbed my right arm and said, "Come outside with me."

He pulled me out of the shop, handed the licenses and work permit back to me.  Then, with a very angry-sounding voice, he said, "I don't want to make a scene in front of my customers.  You are in the wrong neighborhood.  Jews aren't welcome here.  Never before, and especially now!  All of you Jews were the cause of the war that brought hardship to us Poles. We can rebuild this country without you. Don't come back here, ever again! Goodbye!"

It became clear. I entered a predominantly Polish neighborhood where the Jewish people weren't welcome and have always faced discrimination. Since I passed a few grocery stores and a market area, I walked back toward our apartment near the Old City to purchase the items on my mom's list.

When I entered our apartment and placed the bags of grocery items on the kitchen counter, I noticed that Leah was sitting in the living room.  "How did it go for you at the hospital?"

Leah replied, "I was surprised at how eager they were to hire me to work in the kitchen."

Being curious, I asked, "Did they say anything about you being Jewish?"

"Yitzhak, they never asked, nor did I tell them. I don't think it mattered to them. Mrs. Rotfeld was correct. The hospitals do need more workers. I inquired about Mama working there part-time. The employment official told me to have her apply. I begin working tomorrow! How did things go for you at the barbershops? Did you find a job at one of them?"

"No, I didn't. I must have walked into the wrong neighborhood. It became very clear that the Poles don't want Jews to come back to Poland. I was quickly ushered out of two shops, even though there were unfilled barber stations. Tomorrow, I'm going to walk in the other direction into the Old City. I also want to mail a letter to Aneta and give her our new address. In the morning, I'll ask Mrs. Berkowicz where the closest postal office is located."

"That must have been awful for you."

"It was. I was scared that I was going to be hit and knocked down. Jews in today's Poland are just going to have to be very careful."

Mrs. Berkowicz told me that a postal office was located near the town hall in the Old City and that it opened at 9 a.m. After mailing the letter to Aneta, I decided to walk southeast from the streetcar stop to see if I could find a business area with a barbershop. As I walked along the main street, I noticed many workers clearing debris and repairing many of the buildings. This part of the Old City looked like it had encountered the brunt of the battles with the Nazis and the workers were doing their best to revitalize it as quickly as possible.

After walking another five blocks, I noticed another town square in the near distance with a very large tall building that had a severely damaged roof and a missing top on its tall tower. Being curious to learn what this was, I walked closer to get a better view. When I stood directly in front of it, I still couldn't determine what it was. I turned and asked a woman who was walking by if she knew anything about the building.

She replied, "This was the large Jewish synagogue. It was severely damaged by the Nazis. It's been like this for a few years and is too dangerous to use. I don't know what will become of it. Apparently, the new Polish communist officials will have to make the decision."

It was confirmed. This area of Stanislavov was the former Jewish neighborhood. I continued my walk around the square. To my surprise, in the distance I saw people going in and out of shops. One was a small barbershop. Of course, I went inside.

There was only one barber inside giving a man a haircut and an empty barber station. I sat down in the waiting area for the barber to finish cutting the man's hair.

As soon as he finished the haircut and the customer left, I asked, "Are you looking for another barber to work here? I am a licensed barber and I have an official work permit. I also have my own tools."

"Do you have the license and work permit with you?"

"Yes. Here they are."

He reviewed the documents very closely. "I see that everything is in order. Yes, the shop is becoming busier since more people are being relocated to live in the Old City. I see that your name is Yitzhak. Are you a Jew?"

I replied, "Yes, I am Jewish. This doesn't need to be a problem. When I was cutting hair at the Soviet government building in Uzbekistan, I told my

311

customers that my name was Barkan to conceal that I was Jewish. I can do the same thing here at this shop."

"Hmm. That may be a good idea, at least at first. Many Polish people are very discriminatory towards the Jews and some are my customers. Even though I am Polish, I don't hate Jews. Plus, I'm noticing that more Jewish people are returning and being relocated to live in this neighborhood. I would like them to feel welcome and come here for their haircuts."

After a short pause, he handed back my work permit and licenses. "My name is Pawel Kacynski and the local officials from the Polish Liberation Committee accepted my business proposal and allowed me to open this shop last month after the repairs to the building were completed. I will need to begin paying rent next month. How soon can you start working?"

"Thank you, Mr. Kacynski. I can start tomorrow."

"Let me have you begin this Friday. So far, Fridays and Saturdays are my busiest days. The customers can be served much faster with a second barber in the shop. Let me see how you do this weekend. I open at 10 a.m. and usually don't close on Fridays and Saturdays until 8 p.m."

I replied, "The only supplies that I don't currently have are shaving lather soap, the paper neckbands, and moustache wax. At the government building I used paper from a toilet roll for the protective neckbands. Do you have plenty of towels?"

"You can use my supplies this weekend and I have plenty of towels. Take a look at the price list for services that is posted on the wall. I can pay you 80% of the revenue that you generate. Of course, you can keep your gratuities."

I graciously accepted the offer. "I will be here on Friday. How early should I arrive in the morning to help you prepare the shop?"

"Oh, that's nice of you to offer. How about being here at 9:15? And by the way, just call me Pawel and I'll refer to you as Barkan. Bring your licenses and work permit with you, just in case an inspector from the employment office shows up."

"Thanks again, Pawel. I'll see you on Friday."

I offered him my right hand and the two of us shook hands to seal the deal!

When I left Pawel's shop and walked a few blocks, I yelled, "Yes! I found a job! My new life will begin on Friday, October 1st!"

I was very eager to begin working on Friday morning and arrived at the shop at 9:10 a.m. Pawel was already inside, stocking a shelf with clean towels and organizing the day's supplies.

He was correct. The two of us were very busy with a steady stream of customers. I only had time for a very short lunch break on both days. When the last customer left on Saturday evening, I asked Pawel about working during the week.

He replied, "The shop is closed on Sundays and Mondays. The weekdays are a bit slow, since most of the men who come here work during the day."

I spoke up and suggested, "My father and I faced the same dilemma of slower business during the weekdays when we operated our shop in Bolechov. I am experienced with trimming women's bangs and the length of their hair. Plus, I am proficient with giving young boys a short clipper cut. Once we added these services for women and children, we had more customers during the weekdays. How about adding these services onto the fee list and posting all of the shop's services on your front window? My father even obtained photos of women's trims and boy's clipper cuts from a supply distributer and displayed them on the shop's front window. The signage and posters attracted more business for us during the week. What do you think of these ideas?"

He answered, "Yitzhak, your father was a genius, very clever, and wise businessman. Yes, let's do this beginning on Tuesday. I'm closed on Sundays and Mondays. You can help me add the new signage on the windows on Tuesday. I'll go to my distributor on Monday and inquire about the posters. If there is a demand, we can add Monday afternoons to our schedule."

Exactly as I predicted, the new signage of the shops services and posters attracted the attention of the women and mothers with young children. When they walked by the shop, most stopped to read the list of services provided and looked at the posters displayed on the shop's window. Many of them came inside and inquired about the fees. Within two weeks, enough new business was generated for me to work fulltime at the shop on weekdays and weekends.

Pawel regularly placed a copy of the daily Stanislavov newspaper on the small table in the waiting area for customers to read. When there was a break in between haircuts, I glanced through them to learn about the Soviet army's progress defeating the Nazis. I read that the Soviets captured Bucharest, Romania, arrived at a cease-fire with Finland, and that Soviet troops now occupied Estonia. Unfortunately, the war continued. The Soviets were still fighting the Nazis in Western Poland.

Later in October, a scruffy-looking new customer, who appeared to be around my age, entered the shop on a Tuesday late in the afternoon. He sat at my station and requested a complete haircut and shave service.

He seemed very eager to talk. "I just returned from Guryev, Kazakhstan to begin working again at a metal material producing factory. I used to work there before the Nazis invaded Eastern Poland."

Being curious and to generate more conversation, I asked, "What kind of products do they make?"

"Before the war, our factory produced the nails, screws, bolts, fasteners, and brackets for the construction industry. When the Nazis invaded Eastern Poland, the Soviets moved our factory operation and all of the workers to Guryev during the evacuation. Guryev is a port city on the west coast of the Caspian Sea. The factory manufactured and shipped ammunition to the army. Now that Stanislavov has been liberated, the Soviets relocated the factory operation back here after making a few repairs to the building. Our factory now provides the needed metal supplies for the construction companies to rebuild Poland."

I responded, "It must have been difficult for you to leave your family behind."

He didn't respond and remained silent. I immediately realized that this was a sensitive subject and that I should change to a different topic. "I recently returned from Uzbekistan."

"You did? What did you do there?"

"I was a barber and often worked at a collective farm granary."

A smile returned to his face as he responded. "I think that you and I have something in common. Where can we talk in private?"

"How about meeting me outside the shop shortly after I'm finished with your haircut and shave? You're my last customer today."

After he paid for the service and left the shop, I quickly cleaned up my station, told Pawel that I would be back in a few minutes, and went outside to talk to this man.

He was the first to initiate our conversation. "My name is Josef Lieber. That's Josef, spelled with an f, just like Stalin's first name. And you are?"

"I am called Barkan at the shop and not by my first name, Yitzhak."

He chuckled and responded, "You are trying to conceal that you are really Jewish, just like I am, right?"

I nodded and asked, "What is your real name?"

"In Yiddish, it is Yossel Lieberman. Yitzhak, when do you finish working tomorrow? My day at the factory ends at 4 o'clock in the afternoon and I can meet you here at the shop. You and I need to have a long talk."

"Josef, how about coming here around 6? I won't schedule an appointment after 5."

He nodded affirmatively. "I'll see you then."

The next afternoon the two of us walked from the shop to my apartment to meet my mother and sister. Along the way, Josef confided, "The first thing that I did when I arrived in Stanislavov was to go to my family's home. I found a Polish family living in our home. The wife told me that my parents, two sisters and all of my remaining relatives were murdered during one of the Nazi Aktions. Since the house was vacant, the Nazis allowed them to live there."

Josef became very emotional and paused to catch his breath. Then he continued. "Yitzhak, you are the first Jewish person that I have met since I returned. I finally know someone that I can talk to that understands what I am feeling. I feel that I now know someone that I can trust. When the factory relocated back to Stanislavov, I was placed, along with three other Polish single men who worked at the factory, to

316

live together in an assigned apartment. I need to conceal my Jewish identity from them. I don't mind working alongside with these Polish men. We are so busy producing the metal products that we have very little time to socialize. However, living with them is much different. They are often drunk and yelling very derogatory comments about Jews. They are often so loud that it is hard for me to get enough sleep."

Once again, Josef became emotional and paused to wipe his eyes. After about a minute, he spoke again, "I really miss my family and would enjoy getting to know you and your mother and sister. It would be a thrill for me to meet and get to know a Jewish family. Thank you for taking me to meet them."

My mother took an instant liking to Josef when she met him and proclaimed, "I now have two handsome sons!"

When Josef whispered to me that Leah was very beautiful, I felt the need to make him aware of Leah's hope that her boyfriend, Hershel, would miraculously appear.

Josef, Yossel Lieberman, and I quickly became good friends. For the first time since I left Bolechov, I have a Jewish friend.

Toward the end of October, my mom told Leah and me, "I feel well enough that I can walk to and from the hospital. Yitzhak, how about going with me to the hospital on Monday? Let me try to arrange to work in their kitchen with Leah only two or three days a week. We can use the extra money."

I responded, "Yes, Mama, I'll go with you, on one condition. You will quit if you ever feel that working in their kitchen is too much for you. Neither Leah nor I want you to risk having chest pains again."

She started working at the hospital's kitchen on Mondays and Wednesdays. Her first day was

317

Monday, October 30<sup>th</sup>. The hospital assigned her to work the same hours as Leah, so that the two of them could walk together to and from the hospital.

A month later, in the middle of November, Josef asked me, "Have you heard about the new CKZP?"

"No. What is it? What does CKZP mean?"

"It's a new national committee in Poland called the Central Committee of Jews in Poland. Everyone refers to it as the CKZP. In Stanislavov, it replaced the Office of Assistance to the Jewish People inside the town hall. The CKZP was formed to unite local groups of Jewish survivors, distribute food, provide health and employment assistance, and to promote the creation of socialistic business production. One of the men at the factory was furious that the Soviets and the new Polish Liberation Committee allowed the establishment of the national CKZP committee to help Jews. He even mentioned that a Polish worker protest march was being organized and urged others at the factory to participate. I think that the two of us should register as CKZP members."

"Are you sure about this? Won't this bring more attention to us?"

"Yitzhak, being registered may be a good way for you to get help learning what happened to your father and uncle. Meet me at the town hall next Monday after I get off work."

When Josef and I entered the CKZP office, the committee's director, Jakub Goren, greeted us and helped us register. To our surprise, he handed each of us a box that contained numerous small cans of vegetables and soups, packets of noodles and rice, small bags of flour, sugar, and salt, some toiletry items, and even a carton of eggs. He mentioned, "Come back every Monday afternoon to get a box. We restock supplies on Monday mornings. The CKZP will be holding monthly meetings here on the third Thursday evening at 7 o'clock. The two of you should attend."

I asked him about finding how to inquire about my father and uncle's disappearance. He told me that he would look into the matter and try his best to find out the names and addresses of the organizations or government offices that I should contact.

When we left the town hall, Josef told me, "Yitzhak, I can't take this box back to my apartment. If I do, my roommates will know that I am Jewish. Let's go to your apartment and I'll give your mother my box. I'm sure that all of you can make good use of these items."

"Thank you, Josef, for urging me to join the CKZP. I still think that my father and uncle are alive and the CKZP might help me find them."

Then Josef mentioned, "I'll understand if you aren't interested in going to the Thursday meetings with me. I know that you like to spend more time with your mom and sister. I'll go to their monthly meetings and tell you what I learn. I might learn what the Poles are planning that could impact the Jewish residents in Stanislavov."

My mom was thrilled with Josef's thoughtfulness and kindness with receiving his CKZP box. "Josef, you'll have to join us for dinner on a regular basis so that the four of us can be together. I'll do my best to prepare something nice for our Shabbat dinner on Friday evenings."

Josef accepted my mom's offer, joined us on most evenings, and became an integral member of our little family.

Our daily routine consisted of working at our jobs and being together as a family during the evenings. My mom managed to work at the hospital two days a week without any health issues. Leah continually reminded all of us, including Josef, that Hershel would arrive. I was busy at the barbershop. Our collective earnings were just enough to pay a nominal monthly rent to Mrs. Berkowicz and have enough to purchase food and some needed clothing. When a new Saturday market opened in front of the town hall, Leah and my mom went there to shop for fruit, vegetables, and chicken, depending upon the prices. On Mondays, Josef and I stopped at the CKZP office and often received another box of food items and toiletries. The director, Mr. Goren, told me he was still searching for the information regarding on how to find my father and uncle.

Beginning in January 1945, the daily newspaper reported that the Soviet army was making great strides in defeating the Nazis and pushing them farther out of Poland. When it was announced that the Soviet troops captured Warsaw on Wednesday, January 17th, it seemed like the whole city danced in the streets to celebrate this victory.

The joy of victory soon changed to a much more somber tone. Ten days later, on Saturday, January 27th, gruesome photos taken by the soldiers and officers who liberated the Auschwitz concentration camp the previous day shocked the world. The front page of Stanislavov's daily newspaper showed horrifying photos of dead bodies lying on the ground, the gas chamber, and the ovens with remnants of burned bodies. I reluctantly brought the shop's copy home to show Leah, Josef, and my mom.

With tears flowing, my mom cried out, "How could any human being do this to another human being? The Nazis who did this are monsters! Look at the photos of those who survived. They look like living skeletons!"

Leah screamed very loudly when she looked at the photos in the newspaper, "The Nazis could have done this to us!"

The weather turned much colder in February. We all made good use of the heavy coats and sweaters that Maria gave us. One evening in mid-February was excessively cold and windy, and I hurried home from the barbershop as quickly as I could. When I entered our apartment building, I overheard a loud conversation coming from inside our unit. I stood outside the door for a moment to try to recognize one of the voices. I thought the man's voice that I heard sounded familiar, but I wasn't sure. When I entered the apartment, I was surprised to see Hershel sitting on the sofa, hugging Leah, and engaging in a friendly conversation with my mom, Leah, and Josef.

As soon as Leah noticed me, she enthusiastically proclaimed, "See, Yitzhak and Josef. I told you that Hershel would come and find me!"

Hershel added, "It wasn't too difficult. I found Aneta's home and she gave me your address. Now, I am here!"

I asked him, "How were you able to leave Kolkhoz Aggatay so soon, since your documents were lost when the boat sank and you were listed by the Soviets as a refugee? I thought that refugees were going to be the last group allowed to leave Tashkent."

He responded, "Once Warsaw was liberated, rumors spread that a displaced persons' camp for refugees was going to be established there. I pleaded and convinced Manager Vladimir to issue me a return summons and send me to this displaced persons' camp. When I got to the Kyiv train station, I bought a ticket to Bolechov and then came here to see Leah. I would like her to go with me to Warsaw. Vladimir suggested that the Warsaw DP camp would send

321

Jewish refugees to Canada or South America. He also gave me a return summons document for Leah to go with me to the Warsaw DP camp. Since I know a great deal about operating a bakery, Leah and I could open and operate our own bakery business in our new country!"

Leah added, "Hershel and I will get married at the Warsaw DP camp. Mama, please say 'yes' that I can go with him. We have the opportunity to begin a new life together. You can see that we both love each other. Please say 'yes'."

My mom replied, "How can I say 'no'? I was nineteen, just like you are now, when I married your Papa. I can see that the two of you are in love. There isn't much left here in Poland and the Poles hate us. If you have the chance for a better life somewhere else, then you should go. This was what our ancestors faced when they were forced to leave Spain hundreds of years ago during the Inquisition."

Leah turned to me and asked, "Yitzhak, what about you? Since Papa put you in charge of our family, do I have your permission?"

"Yes, you do, as long as the two of you stay in touch with us and let us know where you are and how we can reach you. I'm not sure where Mama and I might be living in the future. The Polish officials could move us to another location in Stanislavov or to a different city. Aneta and her daughter, Maria, will always know where we are living."

"Thank you, Yitzhak. We promise to always stay in touch with you and Mama, and you too, Josef, since you are like my other brother. We'll also send you photos."

Then she asked, "Hershel, when should we leave?"

"We should depart the day after tomorrow on Saturday. This will give you time to gather your belongings, give notice at the hospital, and for me to purchase our train tickets to Warsaw and check the departure time. Most likely, we will need to transfer to a different train in Kyiv."

The morning of Saturday, February 24$^{th}$, was a bittersweet day for both my mom and me to see Leah leave us. My mom and I realized that we might never see her again, except in pictures that she will send. Since I had to work at the barbershop that day, I said my goodbyes and gave hugs to the two of them at the apartment.

"I love you, Leah."

"I love you too, Yitzhak."

"Hershel, always remember the promise that you made to me, that you will always take loving care of Leah."

"I promise, Yitzhak."

The day after Leah and Hershel left for Warsaw, Josef offered a great suggestion. "Yitzhak, your mom is going to miss Leah terribly and become very sad and lonely. She may need something to divert her sadness and find new joy. Would you consider letting me live with you and your mom on a permanent basis? It would make me feel that I am once again living with a loving Jewish family. Living here would also get me away from those loud, discriminating Polish men. I would also cover Leah's share of the rent and help with the food expenses. If you walk Mama to her job at the hospital, I can go to the hospital in the afternoon when I finish working at the factory and walk with her back to the apartment. What do you think about this idea?"

"Josef, this would mean that the two of us would share the bedroom with the two beds and move Mama into the single bedroom. Do you think that you and I would be good roommates?"

He responded, "Yes, I do. The two of us have a lot in common. Plus, you and I relate with each other as if we are brothers. Let's ask your mom."

Of course, she was thrilled with the suggestion that her 'two boys' were going to live with her. I think that she also liked the idea of having her own bedroom. Mrs. Berkowicz knew about Leah's departure and granted Josef permission to move into our apartment after he showed her his work permit and his factory's identification card.

Josef Lieber officially became a full member of the Barkan family on Wednesday, February 28th, 1945.

# Relocation to Dzierzoniow Lower Silesia
## March 1945 – August 1945

I left the barbershop on Friday, March 2$^{nd}$, 1945 a little early and walked to our apartment just as the sun was setting. This was the first Friday after Josef moved in with my mom and me. When I entered the apartment, my mom was busy preparing a pot of soup on the kitchen stove while Josef was setting the small table where we ate our meals. He placed an oval plate on the table that had a small white cloth covering a food item. This was the first time that my mom prepared something this special for our Friday Shabbat meal.

Being curious, I asked, "Mama, what is special about tonight?"

"Yitzhak, this is Josef's first Shabbat as an official member of our family! I know how much he misses his family and I thought that this would be a good time for the three of us to begin observing Shabbat in the true, traditional, Jewish manner."

"Well, Mama, what's under the cover?"

"Oh, Yitzhak, have you forgotten? Don't you remember that I always baked a challah on Fridays when we lived in Bolechov? Since I now have the flour, the eggs, and the needed condiments from the boxes you two brought home, I asked my hospital kitchen supervisor if I could have some yeast. I prepared and baked the challah this morning. We are also going to enjoy a good meal eating vegetable chicken soup with carrots and potatoes along with real pieces of chicken that I also brought home from the hospital!"

I replied, "Sounds great, Mama."

She continued, "Josef was a big help. On Wednesday, when we were walking home together, he showed me the location of a small shop that sold cheap used items. This was where we found the two small candlestick holders, the candles, and the loaf pan that I needed to bake the challah. We're about ready to eat, so go wash up."

A few minutes later, Josef and I sat down at the table. My mom remained standing, put a headscarf on her head, lit the two candles, closed her eyes, and waved her hands around the two candles a few times. The last time that I saw her announcing Shabbat's arrival in this manner was years ago.

Then she recited the Shabbat candle lighting Hebrew prayer, "Baruh, a-ta Adonai, Eh-lo-hey-nu me-lech ha-o-lam, a-sher ki-d'-sha-nu b'mitz-vo-tav, v'tzi-va-nu, l'had-lik-ner, shel Shabbat."

Joseph and I responded, "Amen. Good Shabbos."

As we were eating our meal, my mom enthusiastically announced, "I have some news to share with my two sons. The hospital's kitchen supervisor asked me to work an additional day since Leah is no longer working there. I told her that I wanted to first speak with my two sons. I feel that I can add Thursdays so that I can be home on Fridays to prepare for Shabbat."

I replied, "Mama, that would mean that you would work two days in a row on both Wednesdays and Thursdays. Don't you think that it will be too hard on you?"

"Yitzhak, you are a good son and very considerate. I think that I can do it. We really need the extra money. We are just getting by. Our rent and the prices on everything are much higher now that the currency changed from rubles back to Polish zlotys."

"Mama, just give it a try, but once you feel too tired and it is too much, you must quit. Do you agree?"

"Yes, Yitzhak. I'll stop if it becomes too much."

"Thank you, Mama."

She then pulled out an envelope from her apron and continued, "I have more to share with you. Here's a letter from Aneta. She wrote to tell us about Hershel coming to her home."

I replied, "Thank you, Mama. It's good to know that Aneta can reach us. I'll write back to her and let her know about Leah and Hershel getting married and going to the Warsaw DP camp with the intent to be relocated to a different country."

Josef interrupted, "Yitzhak, you have more letters to write. At last night's CKZP meeting, Jakub Goren, the committee's director, asked me to give you this piece of paper with the postal addresses of the American Jewish Joint Distribution Committee, also known as the JDC or The Joint, and the American Red Cross that recently opened offices in Warsaw. Both organizations are involved with tracking the whereabouts of the displaced Jewish people. Hopefully, they will find information about your father and uncle and send you their findings."

"That's great, Josef. Thank you. Yes, I'll write all of these letters this weekend and mail them on Monday."

Five weeks later on Thursday, April 5th, when I returned to the apartment after working all day at the barbershop, I found my mom lying in bed. Her hands were placed on her chest.

Being alarmed, I asked Josef, "What happened? Why is Mama in bed?"

He motioned for the two of us to leave her bedroom, close the door, and speak softly to each other in the kitchen. "Yitzhak, when I arrived at the hospital to walk home with Mama, she complained to me that her chest was hurting. The two of us walked very slowly to return to the apartment. Once we got inside, she asked me to help her get into bed so that she could get some rest before cooking dinner. She's asleep. I think we shouldn't disturb her."

I responded, "I was afraid that she took on way too much by working two consecutive days at the hospital's kitchen. How about helping me prepare dinner and some hot tea? Maybe she will eat when she wakes up."

She ended up sleeping the rest of the evening. The next morning after she woke up, I helped her walk to the toilet and then offered her some hot tea to drink and a slice of buttered bread. "Mama, I'm going to stay home from work. I'm worried about you."

"Don't be worried, my son. I'm okay. My chest doesn't hurt anymore. Once I fully wake up, I'll be ready to begin cooking for this evening. I insist that you and Josef should go to work. I'll see the two of you later."

Josef and I followed my mom's order to go to work. I was concerned all day about her being left alone in the apartment. The barbershop was very busy and my last customer didn't leave until 7:30 p.m. I quickly cleaned up my station, gathered the tools that I brought home every evening, and walked as fast as I could to get to the apartment.

When I entered, Mr. Goren, the CKZP director, and Josef were sitting in the living room. Both displayed very sad faces.

Josef wiped his eyes with his handkerchief and softly said, "Yitzhak, Mama died sometime during the day. I found her lying on the floor in her bedroom. Her cane was lying next to her. She may have fallen or had a heart attack. Her body had turned blue, so I knew that she had passed away. I went next door to get help from Mrs. Berkowicz. She wasn't home. I knew where Mr. Goren lived, so I went and brought him here. He was kind enough to wait here with me for you to get home from work."

I was shocked and didn't know what to do. "What do I do? Who do I call? How can I afford to bury Mama? How do I handle this? Jews aren't supposed to be cremated."

Mr. Goren stood up and gave me a big hug. "Don't worry. The CKZP can help you bury your mom in a simple, appropriate manner. We can provide the financial assistance for the burial and also place a small metal nameplate on top of the grave. The CKZP does have access to the Jewish cemetery located near the former synagogue that didn't encounter excessive damage from the Nazis. The Polish and Soviet officials do have one restriction. We aren't allowed to have a funeral service there. If no one is looking, we can at least recite the Hebrew Mourner's Kaddish.

"With your permission, I can have our volunteers prepare the grave at the cemetery tomorrow and bury your mom on Sunday morning."

As tears poured out of both of my eyes, I spoke with a cracked voice, "Thank you, Mr. Goren. Yes, please tell your volunteers to go ahead."

"One more thing, Yitzhak. I suggest that it will be best for you and Josef to keep your mom's bedroom door closed. Her body is completely covered. On Sunday, we'll come to the apartment to place your mom in a simple casket, and then we'll all go to the cemetery around 9 a.m. I'll report your mom's death as a natural cause to the Polish Liberation Committee. The two of you should stay as calm as you can this weekend. I'll see you on Sunday."

Josef and I both responded, "Thank you Mr. Goren."

When he left, I asked Josef, "What do you think I should do? Should I stay home tomorrow or go to work?"

"It might be a good idea, Yitzhak, for you to go to work to keep your mind occupied. All you can do here is stare at her bedroom door and cry. I'll stay here and let Mrs. Berkowicz know what happened."

When I told Pawel about my mom's burial being held at the Jewish cemetery the next morning, he asked for my permission to attend. I thought that this was very thoughtful and I agreed that he could be there.

The morning of Sunday, April 8$^{th}$, was a cloudy and dreary day. The warmth and brightness of spring had yet to arrive. Just as Mr. Goren explained, he and three CKZP volunteers promptly arrived at the apartment at 8 a.m. They placed my mom into a simple pine casket and then took the casket to the cemetery in their truck. Mr. Goren arranged for a car to take Josef and me, along with Mrs. Berkowicz, to the cemetery. When we arrived, Pawel was already there. Pawel, Mrs. Berkowicz, Mr. Goren, Josef, and I watched the volunteers lower the casket into the grave. Once the casket rested on the bottom of the grave, Mr. Goren led us with the recitation of the Hebrew Mourner's Kaddish prayer. Then all of the men, including Pawel, Josef, and me, took turns using the shovel to fill the grave with the dirt that had been unearthed.

Once the grave was completely filled, I stooped down, placed my hands on the dirt, and with more flowing tears, said, "Goodbye, Mama. I will always love you. I promise to keep looking for Papa and Uncle Anshel."

As we were leaving the cemetery, Mrs. Berkowicz approached Josef and me and mentioned, "I am deeply sorry about the loss of your mother. Don't worry about covering the total rent. I feel very safe having the two of you living next to me. I'll adjust your rent accordingly so that you can afford to remain in the apartment. Please don't tell the other residents that I did this."

Josef replied, "Thank you Mrs. Berkowicz for your kindness at this time of our grief."

After she walked away, I immediately gave Josef a hug. "I don't know how I would have handled this without you. I am very grateful that the two of us met, became friends, and are now sharing the apartment together."

"I feel the same, Yitzhak. I will miss your Mama! She reminded me very much of my mother."

I decided to join Josef and attend the monthly CKZP meeting on Thursday, April 19th. When the two of us entered the town hall, I followed Josef downstairs. I never realized that this building had a basement.

"Yitzhak, a lot of people are now attending these meetings. Director Goren and the other local CKZP leaders made the arrangements for the committee to use the downstairs meeting room."

Director Goren's address that evening was to raise everyone's awareness about the increase of hostility from the Poles toward the Jews living in Stanislavov.

"Please be vigilant when walking in the streets. If possible, avoid walking in the narrow streets and alleys that aren't well lit at night. Now that the Soviet army has liberated all of Western Poland, more Jewish people are being relocated from the Soviet Union and other places to live here. Many of the Polish residents are blaming us as the cause of the hardships that they are facing. The rise in prices is affecting everyone and they are also accusing the returning Jews of taking jobs away from them."

Josef turned toward me and whispered, "See, this is what I've been telling you. I still hear these comments from the Polish men at the factory. They don't want us here!"

I was pleased that I decided to participate with the CKZP for a different reason. At the beginning of May, I received a response from the Warsaw office of Jewish Joint Distribution Committee. Their letter stated that there was no further information from the Polish military officials about my father. His name and my uncle's name did not appear on the list of names at the Warsaw DP camp, and that they will continue their investigation. I felt reassured that I will receive more responses from them.

On Monday, May 7th, Josef was waiting outside the barbershop for me. With the increase of the Jewish people and Poles living in the Old City, Pawel trusted me to open the shop on Monday afternoons. After I locked up and went outside, I could tell by Josef's posture that he was very eager to tell me something.

"Yitzhak, have you heard? Germany surrendered unconditionally today! This was announced at the factory. That's how I learned about it. Isn't this great? The war in Europe has finally ended!"

I immediately placed my barber tool case on the ground, hugged him, and we both started jumping with great excitement.

"There's more, Yitzhak. It was announced at the factory that tomorrow will be a national holiday to celebrate V-E or Victory in Europe Day. People in Europe, the United States, and other countries are celebrating V-E Day tomorrow.

"There is going to be a big celebration at the town hall tomorrow at 10 a.m. Many of the main streets will be blocked from vehicles to accommodate the expected crowd of people. You and I should go out tomorrow and be part of the celebration."

Josef was correct. All of the Stanislavov businesses, factories, and shops closed so that the entire city could celebrate V-E Day. Josef and I left the apartment at 9 a.m. and found that Het'mana Mazepy Street was already flooded with people, holding Polish flags and celebratory posters, and marching toward the town hall. We inched our way into the crowd. People were hugging each other. Couples excitedly danced. It didn't matter if you were hugging or dancing with a stranger. This event was a day when people of all faiths and ethnicities were celebrating this victory together as one people.

As Josef and I managed to get closer to the town hall, he recognized men that worked with him at the factory. They all waved to Josef and he waved back. To my surprise, some of them approached Josef and they all hugged each other and loudly yelled, "Victory"!

I also saw some of my customers from the barbershop, waved to them, and also hugged those that I knew who were standing close to me. Somehow, Josef and I got separated when more people pushed their way through us.

The ceremony at the town hall started a little bit late, at 10:30, with a brass band playing loud patriotic music. The crowd continued cheering. I had no idea that a band even existed in Stanislavov.

The victory celebration continued for many hours into the afternoon. Around 3 p.m. I slowly inched my way through the crowd to walk onto the side streets to find my way back to the apartment.

Josef returned to the apartment close to 5 p.m. and proclaimed, "What a day!"

I responded, "Yes, it was. It was wonderful to see Poles and Jews celebrating together as one people. Do you think this coexistence will last?"

"I sure hope so, Yitzhak. We should pray that this peace between us lasts."

Instead of holding a formal meeting on Thursday, May 17th, the CKZP officials organized a social gathering in the meeting room to continue the victory celebration. This gave me the opportunity to thank Mr. Goren for connecting me with the Jewish Joint Distribution Committee and telling him that I received a response.

More Jewish people must have registered with the CKZP. All the seats in the town hall's downstairs meeting room were filled at the Thursday, June 14th, meeting. Many people had to stand along the walls.

After acknowledging all of the new enrollees, Mr. Goren went into a lengthy explanation about Jews being attacked during a pogrom two days prior at Rzeszów. Rzeszów was a very large city located in the southeast of Poland about 179 kilometers (*111 miles)* west of Lviv.

"Polish nationalists organized a hostile mass demonstration at Rzeszów to protest the growing number of Jews living in their city. Once again, the old medieval Christian myth that Jews kill Christians to use their blood in religious rituals has resurfaced and now being an excuse to attack Jews.

"A missing Polish girl was found in the basement of an apartment building where many Jews lived, including a kosher butcher. Militia arrived and claimed that the girl's blood was used for Jewish religious purposes. Hostile protestors clubbed the Jewish apartment residents and threw stones at them as the

334

police hauled the Jewish residents to the police station. What is even more frightening is that the local police and militia officials did nothing to stop the hostile crowd!"

After a long pause, he continued, "I want to remind you. Please be careful. Violent actions toward us may occur here. These blood libel accusations are being heard from some of our local Poles."

On Monday, July 9th, Josef shared with me some interesting and possible positive news when I returned from the barbershop in the early evening.

"Yitzhak, I don't know if this will be considered good news are not. There was an announcement at the factory today that the former Polish people who repatriated back to Poland can now renounce their Soviet citizenship and become Polish citizens."

"This sounds very puzzling to me."

"That's what I thought at first. On my way home from the factory I stopped at the CKZP office and asked Mr. Goren his opinion. He told me that he was learning the details and would inform everyone about it at Thursday's meeting. The two of us need to go to the meeting."

"Josef, did he tell you the procedure on how one becomes a Polish citizen?"

"This is one of the details that he is investigating."

I added, "This shouldn't be a problem for me. My father insisted that my family save all of our Polish documents in case we need them again. I still have all of mine. What about you?"

"I still have my Stanislavov travel permit and the Guryev, Kazakhstan resident permit. Both of them state that I am Polish. I think that these should be enough."

As promised, Mr. Goren explained at the meeting the new agreement between the Polish provisional government and the Soviet government.

"The new agreement is formally titled 'The Polish-Soviet Commission for Matters of Evacuation of Individuals of Polish or Jewish Nationality'. It establishes the right for eligible Poles to regain their citizenship. The national CKZP committee backs this initiative and encourages those eligible to do this to help rebuild and re-establish Poland as a thriving socialist country. Our cooperation with the Polish provisional government is essential for Jews to have a stronger voice in this country. Having Polish citizenship allows you to officially live and work in Poland and can prevent you from being sent to a displaced persons camp or a labor camp. Beginning Monday, this CKZP office will help you complete the process. Bring all the documents that you may have, such as a 1941 amnesty document, a Polish passport, military records, Polish school reports, any kind of Polish ID card, or a birth or marriage certificate. Please share this information with other Jewish people that you know who previously revoked their Polish citizenship in order to become Soviet citizens."

As we were walking home from the meeting, I asked Josef, "What do you think? Should we do this?"

"Yitzhak, since we have the needed documents, I think that we should go through the process to become Polish citizens as soon as possible. I don't trust the Soviets. Who knows? Stalin is very shrewd and could send Jews to a labor camp or even to Siberia at a whim. I'd rather live as a Polish citizen than suffer the hardships Jews reportedly face in the Soviet labor camps and Siberia. There may be other advantages to being a Polish citizen again. I don't know about you, but I don't see much of a future for us if we remain in Stanislavov. Hatred against Jews is escalating here. I want a better life. Don't you want to eventually marry a beautiful woman and have a family?"

"Yes, being married to a beautiful woman is one of my dreams. As for having children, I want them to experience a peaceful and happy childhood, have a good education, and have a prosperous career. I don't see any of that happening right now in Stanislavov. Life might be better living elsewhere. Okay, let's do it, Josef. I think more opportunities may open up for us as Polish citizens."

The following Monday morning, Mr. Goren was very pleased to see the two of us standing in line with our documents.

We later read in the Stanislavov newspaper about a major strategic decision regarding Poland's new postwar borders. The Potsdam Agreement between the United Kingdom, the United States, and the Soviet Union was ratified and announced on August 1st, 1945.

At the August 9th, CKZP meeting, Mr. Goren explained the details of this agreement.

"Poland's borders are now expanding westward due to Stalin's demand for the Soviet Union to retain the lands that the Soviet army captured from the Germans. Poland will now include and take control of Germany's eastern territories.

"The CKZP is very supportive for many reasons. Jewish participation in rebuilding the newly acquired territories and abandoned cities would allow for the redevelopment of the Jewish community and increase our influence with the Polish provisional government. By cooperating, the Polish government will be more sympathetic to us. Also, every Polish person, Jew and non-Jew, settling in these territories will be perceived as new. This may reduce the hatred that we, as Jews, face.

"Please keep attending our monthly meetings to learn more about Poland's plan for these new territories."

Four days later on Monday, August 13th, the Stanislavov newspaper featured the details of another pogrom against the Jews. This time it happened in Krakow. Jews returning to Krakow on the trains were targeted and murdered.

Josef and I had another long conversation when I returned to the apartment after closing up the barbershop.

After showing him the newspaper article about the Krakow murders, I said, "I strongly feel that the time has come for us to get out of here. Let's go see Mr. Goren tomorrow morning and find out when Jewish people are going to be sent to one of those abandoned cities. Maybe life will be better there and we won't face too much hatred from the Poles. The two of us can be part of the first group to go to one of those cities and help the CKZP prepare for the influx of Jews."

"That's a good idea, Yitzhak. We are young with plenty of energy. We can help develop and build a new Jewish community. If many Jews do go there, we'll meet many young Jewish women. Yes, let's go see him in the morning. I can be late for work."

Josef and I went to the CKZP office as planned the next morning at 8 a.m. and Mr. Goren was in his office. He was surprised to see us.

"Mr. Goren, Josef and I are very interested in being sent to one of the abandoned cities right away. We can help the CKZP prepare for the influx of the Jews and help build a new Jewish community. We

338

have no family ties here in Stanislavov. Is there a city where you can send us?"

He smiled at us and responded, "That's wonderful that the two of you are willing to help us. Yes, there is an abandoned city in Lower Silesia called Dzierzoniow. It is located along the Pilawa River and near the Czechoslovakian border. The German names of the city were Reichenbach or Rychbach. The Polish provisional government officials renamed it to honor the famous Polish priest, Johann Dzierzion, who lived in that area and is considered the father of modern beekeeping. From what I've been told, this city encountered very little damage and people can be easily resettled there immediately. The plan is for this city to become a thriving Jewish community and a manufacturing center. A German prison camp called Sportschule is located nearby. Jews from this camp are being relocated to Dzierzoniow along with Jews who returned to Poland and have obtained their Polish citizenship. How soon can the two of you leave Stanislavov?"

Josef and I nodded to each other and he answered, "We can leave in a few days. We will need to show an official document, such as a travel permit or new work permit, to show our employers and our landlady."

"I can easily obtain those documents for you. Come back to this office tomorrow to pick them up. I'll be able to give you more details tomorrow about your relocation to Dzierzoniow."

Both Josef and I replied, "Thank you, Mr. Goren."

He responded with great enthusiasm. "On behalf of the CKZP, thank you!"

When Josef and I were eating dinner that evening, I mentioned to him, "You know, Josef, the hardest thing for me about leaving Stanislavov is saying goodbye to both Mrs. Berkowicz and Pawel at the barbershop. Mrs. Berkowicz has been very kind and accommodating to all of us. Even though Pawel is Polish, he hired me, without questioning that I was Jewish."

"Yitzhak, I'm looking forward to showing the official documents to my boss at the factory. All he does is bark orders and demands to all of the workers. I'm looking forward to quitting. The sooner, the better!"

The travel documents that we received from Mr. Goren on Wednesday, August 15$^{th}$, stated that the two of us would leave Stanislavov four days later on Sunday, August 19$^{th}$. That gave us plenty of time to decide what to pack to take with us, and say goodbye to our employers and Mrs. Berkowicz.

When I told her that we were being assigned to another city, she responded with a sad look on her face. "It was nice having you two and your family living next to me. I will miss you. See me tomorrow and I will give you back some of your rent money that you paid for the full month."

I added, "Mrs. Berkowicz, I'm leaving my mom's clothing. I left it in her bedroom closet and chest of drawers. Either you or someone you know could use it."

"That's very thoughtful, Yitzhak. I really liked your mother."

At first, Pawel seemed surprised when I told him I was being reassigned to a new city. "Pawel, thank you for taking a chance with hiring me. I really appreciate your kindness, honesty, and coming to the cemetery when my mother passed away."

He responded, "I'm really going to miss you. You made it possible for me to build the business with your great ideas. I'm confident that you will do very well at the new city. Thank you, Yitzhak, for all of your help."

I packed all of my belongings in the canvas sacks that my mom and I used when we left Uzbekistan. In addition to all of my clothing and toiletries, I followed my mom's example. I carefully packed the four glass jars that we used as water containers and to store food, along with some tableware, the two Shabbat candleholders, and cups for drinking. I knew that I could manage to carry and walk with the two sacks and the case that contained my barber's box.

Of course, prior to the day of departure, Josef and I went to the cemetery to pay our respects and say our final goodbye to my mama.

Josef and I followed Mr. Goren's advice and arrived early at the train station's ticket counter before it opened at 8 a.m. We needed to show the ticket agent our official travel permits for Dzierzoniow to obtain our train tickets. The agent told us that we would transfer to another train in Lviv. That train would take us all the way to Dzierzoniow with stops at Rzeszów, Krakow, and Katrwicz. Mr. Goren also told us that other CKZP members will board the train at all of the stops and that CKZP officials would greet all of us at the Dzierzoniow train station. Our expected arrival was 2 p.m. the next day, on Monday, August 20th, 1945.

The train to Lviv departed the Stanislavov station at 9:30 a.m. I looked out the window to take one last look at the city where my mom is buried. I soon realized that my journey into the unknown has continued.

# A New Life in Dzierzoniow
## 1945 - 1946

Our train arrived in Dzierzoniow an hour late at 3 p.m. When Josef and I exited the train station, we immediately noticed a line of trucks parked along the curb on the main street with a CKZP card placed on each truck's dashboard. Josef turned toward me and said, "Yitzhak, they must be expecting to pick up at least fifty other people besides us."

As we approached one of the trucks, an official-looking man got out to greet us. "Hello. Welcome to Dzierzoniow. I'm from the local CKZP. Please show me your travel permits."

After he closely examined them, he continued, "Thank you. Go ahead and place your belongings in the back of the truck and have a seat on the bench. We need to wait here until everyone arrives. Six more people will ride with you in the back."

Josef was correct. There were about fifty arrivals. I commented to him, "This must be a very large city for trucks to transport us from the train station to the area where we will live."

We left the train station once the other arrivals were processed and seated in the trucks. As our truck crossed over the Pilawa River, I noticed the riverbank was lined with a greenbelt of small parks with huge green trees. Mr. Goren was correct when he told us that the Germans had left this picturesque city pristinely intact.

Our truck stopped at a very large square. The CKZP greeter came out of the truck and announced to the eight of us who were sitting in the back of the truck, "This is our main Rynek Square in the Old City where the Jewish community lived prior to the war. The big building that you see is the city's municipal

342

building. This is where the Dzierzoniow CKZP office is temporarily located. You will report here at 8 a.m. tomorrow for a breakfast meeting with our director, Avrom Landau. You will also pick up food packages, get your work assignment, and receive a monetary stipend. We're now going to drive to Zablowica Street where you will live. It is a block away from the Rynek."

Within minutes, all of the trucks had parked on Zablowica Street. The greeters announced to all of us, "These three-story apartments on this street are empty. Choose any apartment that you want. At least two single people or one married couple will occupy one apartment. You will find everything that you need, including some canned food items for your meal this evening and two sets of keys to the apartment on the kitchen counter. Have a restful evening. We look forward to seeing all of you tomorrow morning at 8 a.m."

Josef and I took a good look at the beige, green, and brown apartment buildings on the right side of the street. I asked him, "What color do you like?"

He responded, "Let's grab our bags and race over to the green building that is number six and move into an apartment on the second floor."

There were two apartments on each floor. We climbed up the stairway and selected apartment number four on the second floor. When we entered the apartment, Josef and I just stood in awe with what we saw.

"Josef, it looks like the former owners left everything as if they planned to return. Look at this fully furnished apartment with all of the gorgeous upholstered furniture and the wooden cabinets that are filled with curios and figurines! There is even drapery on all of the windows!"

The kitchen was filled with everything, including dishes, tableware, pots and pans. When we walked into the two bedrooms, we found clean sheets, an embroidered bedspread, covered pillows neatly placed on the beds, and clothing. Additional bed and bathroom linen and towels were stored in a linen closet. The metal bathroom fixtures glistened from its cleanliness. The CKZP representative was correct. We do have everything we need.

Within an hour, Josef and I were settled into our new home. We quickly plopped onto our comfortable beds and fell asleep.

The next morning, Josef and I were eager to meet the local CKZP director and the other representatives. Other groups of people must have arrived in addition to those on our train. There must have been at least 150 people attending the meeting.

"Greetings and welcome to Dzierzoniow. I'm Avrom Landau and I thank you for volunteering to help us re-establish a thriving Jewish community. Other groups have already arrived and begun their work. These include those who survived the Sportchule camp. We are expecting ten thousand Jews to be living here by the end of September along with the Poles who are coming here to work with us in the factories and at the farms. Your participation is vital to rebuilding our country from the devastation of the war.

"One of our first priorities is to reestablish the use of the old synagogue that was built in 1857 to serve as our new Jewish community center. The Nazis removed all of the pews for their Hitler Youth meetings and trainings. One broken window resulted in some water damage. With your help, it should be ready to use again in a few weeks, along with the school across the street.

"This morning you will meet and discuss your work assignment with the representatives sitting at the tables. They will also provide you with a food box that should suffice for this week. If you require any assistance, please come to my office. Once again, on behalf of the CKZP, thank you for your help."

Josef and I returned to our apartment at different times during the late afternoon. I was curious to learn his work assignment and share with him mine.

When I asked him, his face beamed. "I'm going to work with the crew who are restoring the synagogue and converting it to be the new community center. The CKZP representative thought that my knowledge regarding construction supplies and materials would be helpful with many of their restoration and construction projects. I am to report to the synagogue building tomorrow morning. It is located at the edge of the Old City and not too far of a walk from here. What about you?"

"When I showed the representative my barber licenses and told him that I brought my tools, he was thrilled. He told me that my barber skills are essential to improving everyone's personal hygiene and would complement the CKZP's goal of providing health care for children and adults. He told me that there is an abandoned barbershop on the corner of Koscielna and Spacerowa Streets near the Rynek Square. He asked me to go look at it and come back to see him. The barbershop is conveniently located two blocks away from our apartment. I looked into the shop's window and noticed four empty barber stations. I raced back to see him. I always dreamed of operating my own barbershop. He gave me the keys and told me that he would arrange for the water, the gas-powered water heater, and electricity to be turned on. He also told me to come back to see him if I needed supplies to clean the shop. He urged me to get the shop ready to open by next Monday! Do you think you can get me a small amount of black and white paint and a small paintbrush? I will need to make new signs and remove and discard the ones printed in German. I'm going to list my prices to be a bit lower than they were in Stanislavov. The lower price should entice new customers and build the business."

"Sure. I'll see what I can locate for you."

"Thanks".

Josef and I only saw each other for a brief moment during the mornings and in the evenings before we went to sleep. The two of us, along with all of the arrivals, were actively creating a new Jewish community. It seemed like hundreds of arrivals were moving into Dzierzoniow every day. As expected, the synagogue reopened by the middle of September. A sign with Yiddish lettering said, 'Community Center' and was placed above the front entrance! The CKZP and the newly established health and social organizations moved their headquarters to the community center. Cultural activities started being organized and held there. These included a Yiddish theater group and establishment of a new library. The Jewish presence in the city became very noticeable. Jews were strolling along the streets and standing and chatting with each other. Eventually, close to half of Dzierzoniow's population was Jewish with the highest percentage of Jews of any town in Poland. You often heard comments that Dzierzoniow was 'the Polish Jerusalem'!

When the main post office finally reopened at the Rynek, I quickly wrote and mailed letters to Aneta, the Jewish Joint Committee, and the American Red Cross to provide them with my new address. I was still hopeful that I would learn about my father and Uncle Anshel. I regularly went to shop at the new market that began operating on Mondays at the Rynek with stalls offering food items, particularly chicken, eggs, bread, and vegetables.

A rabbi from one of the displaced persons camps, named Rabbi Abraham Jakubicz, arrived in Dzierzoniow in February 1946. He quickly started organizing Saturday night social events for the Jewish community inside the synagogue's empty sanctuary area. He found enough musicians among the Jewish arrivals to form a band to play dance music. The first dance was scheduled for Saturday, February 23$^{rd}$.

Josef was very excited about going. "Yitzhak, we have to go to the synagogue on Saturday night. I've heard from the other Jewish construction workers that there are plenty of single women who are our age that are now living here. We need to go."

The two of us dressed in our best clothes and polished shoes and arrived at the synagogue around 8 o'clock in the evening. After retrieving a glass of non-alcoholic fruit punch, the two of us scoured the crowd to find single women who looked interesting. I saw two women sitting alone at a table on the other side of the room in the back corner. "Josef, I see two on the other side. They are sitting by themselves. Let's go ask them to dance before they are approached by other men."

When Josef and I got closer, we slowed down our walking pace to appear more gentlemanly to them. I approached the woman with blond hair, while Josef approached the one with brunette hair. Both accepted our offer to dance with us.

The band was playing a romantic slow song when the woman that I asked to dance stepped onto the dance floor with me. I gently placed my left arm around her waist and held her left hand with my right hand. She moved closer to me and placed her left cheek onto my right cheek. Following her lead, I moved closer to talk to her.

"I'm Yitzhak Barkan. What's your name?"

"I'm Gania Grossman, but just call me Jenny. Everyone calls me Jenny. When did you arrive in Dzierzoniow?"

"I got here last September. When did you arrive?"

"Oh, my friend and I got here about two weeks ago."

Just as Jenny finished speaking, the slow song ended and the band started playing a very loud swing dance song. The music was so loud that Jenny and I could no longer hear each other speak. I motioned for the two of us to leave the dance and go into the synagogue's lobby. Jenny nodded, held my hand, and followed me. The two of us spent the rest of the evening talking with each other. I was thrilled that a gorgeous woman around my age was interested in getting to know me. We both learned that we had many things in common and encountered similar life experiences during the war.

"Yitzhak, my parents insisted that I leave them and join the Soviet evacuation, even though I was their only child. My father was too ill to travel and my mother stayed to take care of him. I think that my mother bribed the magistrate to issue me the official travel permit. I later learned that my parents and all of my relatives were killed during the Nazi's Aktions in our small village, Rozdol. When I arrived in Tashkent, the authorities placed me at a kolkhoz to be their kindergarten teacher. Kolkhoz Pravda was very large and had many families with children. When I arrived in Dzierzoniow, the CKZP assigned me to be a pre-school teacher at the newly opened Jewish school across the street from this community center. Esther Rosenberg, who is dancing with your friend, was a primary school teacher at Kolkhoz Pravda. We lived in the same hut and became very good friends. She now teaches with me at the Jewish school. We were both sent back together from Uzbekistan and we share an apartment."

I told Jenny about my family's life at Kolkhoz Aggatay and my vocation as a barber. It turned out that her family's little village, Rozdol, wasn't too far from Bolechov.

Before we knew it, the band stopped playing at 10 p.m. and the dance ended.

"Jenny, may I walk with you and escort you to your apartment?"

"Oh, you don't have to. I just live up the street. Our apartment is very close to the school and synagogue."

I responded, "I would like to do this."

We both smiled at each other and Jenny commented, "You are a real gentleman, aren't you?"

As we slowly walked to her apartment on Ignacego Krassickiego Street, I asked, "Jenny, can I see you again? Since I work all day at the barber shop on Saturdays, Saturday evenings and any time on Sundays are good for me."

"Yitzhak, how about the two of us go on a picnic next Sunday afternoon at one of the parks along the river? If it is too cold, we can have our picnic inside in my apartment. I'll prepare everything."

"Jenny, that's a great idea."

When we reached her apartment, I accompanied her to the apartment building's front door. She turned around and, once again, moved very close to me. Jenny's beautiful face just shined as she initiated kissing me very gently and romantically. Then, she whispered in my left ear, "I look forward to being with you again next Sunday. Have a good week."

"You too, Jenny."

She unlocked and opened the door. The she turned around to look at me one more time with her adorable smile!

When I returned to my apartment and climbed into bed, I relived every moment that I spent with Jenny at the dance over and over again in my head. I never met a young girl or a young woman like her.

I kept thinking and asking myself: *Is Jenny really interested in getting to know me? Could the two of us become romantically involved?*

The next morning, Josef and I shared our experiences at the dance with Jenny and Esther. He really liked Esther and, like me, walked her home. The two of them made plans to see each other the following Friday evening.

I was excited all week about seeing Jenny again on Sunday afternoon. I was very surprised when she and Esther tapped on the barbershop window on Saturday afternoon and waved to me! When Jenny noticed me looking at her, she blew me a kiss and waved!

*Wow! She must really be interested in me!*

A florist shop recently opened near the barbershop. During the week, I placed an order for a bouquet of fresh flowers to give to Jenny on Sunday. When she opened her apartment door and saw the flowers, she greeted me with her bright smile and a long welcoming kiss.

It turned out that Sunday, March $3^{rd}$, was a sunny day and, while wearing a lined jacket, it was warm enough for Jenny and me to have the picnic at a park along the Pilawa River.

After we spread out the blanket that Jenny brought, sat on it, and started eating the sandwiches that she prepared, Jenny initiated our conversation.

"Yitzhak, I felt very sad when you told me that your relatives were also murdered during the Nazi Aktions, the death of your mother, and not knowing the whereabouts of your father and uncle. You must feel very lonely."

"I do miss all of them very much. Yes, I have lonely moments. I am very grateful that Josef and I became good friends. He was very helpful when my mother passed away."

Jenny responded, "I also feel all alone and lonely without any family, just like you. It was a miracle that Esther and I became good friends at Kolkhoz Pravda and were sent back together. Can I ask you a personal question, Yitzhak?"

"Of course. You can ask me anything. I trust you."

After a short pause, Jenny asked, "Have you always wanted to be a barber?"

"Jenny, when I was a young boy, I dreamed of becoming a medical doctor. But, as you probably know, Poland stopped allowing Jews to attend a high school and a university. When that dream vanished, my father urged me to become a barber like him and his father. It turned out that being a skilled barber and having all of the needed equipment allowed me to continue cutting hair in Tashkent and Stanislavov. Now, the CKZP has permitted me to open and operate my own shop here in Dzierzoniow. Since I offer trimming services to women, short haircuts for young boys, and a full service for men, the shop is so busy that two more barbers are now renting stations at the shop. I have one more empty station remaining and may fill it very shortly. Being a barber has allowed me to continue working, earn a living, and survive!"

351

"That's exactly how I feel, Yitzhak. Due to my young age, the Tashkent Employment Office assigned me to be the kindergarten teacher at the kolkhoz. When the CKZP reviewed my documents they immediately issued me a work permit that listed kindergarten teacher as my occupation. Being a teacher allows me to support myself and survive! You and I have so much in common. Will I continue to see you?"

Jenny and I agreed to spend every Saturday evening and Sunday afternoon together. Our lives soon merged and blended together and we became an inseparable couple. Every evening on my way home from the barbershop, I always stopped at Jenny's apartment to give her a goodnight kiss. Saturdays, when I was cutting hair at the barbershop, Jenny always brought me a food basket with my lunch. Of course, we were together every Saturday evening and all day on Sunday.

Rabbi Jakubicz continued to organize Saturday evening dances and occasional Yiddish theater performances from the community center's theater group. We attended all of these events, along with Josef and Esther, and the four of us became part of Rabbi Jakubicz's community center planning team. We became good friends with other young Jewish couples and singles. It felt wonderful to once again be part of a thriving Jewish community.

In March, the weather got warm enough for Jenny and me to continue having long strolls through the parks along the Pilawa River. A coffee shop opened across the street from the Rynek and we often met there in the early evening when I closed the barbershop. We became an inseparable couple.

*For the first time in my life, I fell in love with a beautiful woman who brings joy into my life.*

In April, Rabbi Jakubicz asked for volunteers to help organize a community Passover Seder to be held inside the synagogue on the evening of Monday, April 15th. Jenny and Esther quickly volunteered to serve as the lead organizers, while Josef and I, along with many others, served on the planning committee. Jenny and Esther immediately contacted the parents of the school's students for their family to attend the Passover Seder and to prepare and bring one of the food items from the list developed by the committee. The two of them also had their students create the table decorations. Each student used colored crayons and plain paper plates to draw a Seder plate with the food items that told the Passover story. These colorful plates were placed on each table. To everyone's surprise and delight, small groups of their students performed short skits about the Passover story. It was a delightful evening.

I was amazed at how much joy and happiness everyone experienced from the involvement of Jenny and Esther's students. Both of them and the children's parents beamed with pride as they watched their children perform. I realized that creating joyful and happy moments was an integral part of Jenny's personality. This made me love her even more!

This joyful life came to an abrupt halt when the ugliness of hating Jews, once again, resurfaced in Poland.

A political referendum in Poland was held on June 30th, 1946, to determine the public's mood and also to delay parliamentary elections. Since the Jewish people were now encountering a better life in Poland, they voted in favor of the communist's positions. The Polish nationalists opposed the referendum's positions. Polish anger resurfaced due to the communist government's support of Jews. On July 4th, a brutal attack on the Jews occurred in Kielce, a town located mid-way between Warsaw, Krakow, and Lublin. Forty-two Jews were brutally attacked and killed by Polish mobs in Kielce and many more were injured. Once again, there was no intervention from the police or military. The Jews living in Poland were caught in the middle of a political struggle between the nationalistic Poles and the communists who were aligned with the Soviets. The Kielce pogrom reminded all Jews that Poland was not going to be a permanent and safe place to live.

When we became aware of the Kielce pogrom, Jenny, Esther, Josef, and I had a long conversation at our apartment.

Josef started the conversation. "Should the four of us find a way to leave Poland? The Jewish men that I work with are saying that many Jews in Poland are fleeing through Czechoslovakia to reach the American zones in either Germany or Austria. They are saying that once you reach one of these zones, the authorities will send you to Palestine."

We all looked at each other being very puzzled as to how to respond.

After about five minutes of silence, Jenny replied, "I am tired of fleeing. I left my family and fled to Uzbekistan. Then I fled from Uzbekistan to come back to Poland. Aren't all of you fed up with having to flee? Yitzhak, you relocated three times since you returned to Poland!"

Esther responded. "If I am going to leave Poland, I don't want to just escape. I think it is best to find a way to first obtain official documents that will allow us to leave, and these documents must list a specific, final destination. I would feel more secure and safe by first having official documents. Look at what happened to the Jews who fled from the Nazis without any documentation. I don't want to live on the streets as a homeless person. I also don't want the Soviets to regard me as a criminal and send me to Siberia. Don't you agree that we should first obtain official documents? What about you, Yitzhak and Josef? What do you prefer to do?"

I responded, "I agree with you, Esther, that we should leave officially. Esther and Jenny, this may be too premature to mention this. If the four of us are going to officially immigrate to another country, it will be best for us to first be married! That way, we have a better chance for the authorities to keep us together as a couple and not separate us."

Jenny's eyes opened really wide and then she asked, "Yitzhak, are you proposing to me?"

"I guess I am, Jenny. Will you marry me? You know how much I love and adore you!"

Jenny quickly stood up and pulled me up out of my chair. She energetically proclaimed, "Yes, I would love to marry you, Yitzhak Barkan. I love you too. Let's go talk to Rabbi Jakubicz!" We then gave each other a long, passionate kiss.

Esther remained silent and stared at Josef. He knelt down by placing his right knee on the floor, took Esther's right hand, and said, "Esther, will you marry me?"

"Yes, I will Josef. Of course, I will marry you. I've been waiting for you to ask me!"

The next weekend when Jenny and I were strolling along the shore of the Pilawa River, Jenny stopped walking and asked, "Yitzhak, were you really serious that we should get married?"

"Yes, Jenny, I've been wanting to ask you for many weeks. I feel that you and I are a great loving team and that we would be very happy living together as a married couple. You bring a lot of joy into my life

355

that I have missed for many years. I always want to be with you! I really do!"

Jenny replied, "I feel the same about you. I have another question. Do you want to have children and raise a family?"

"Of course I do, Jenny. I'm just concerned that our children will suffer from the hatred that Jews are facing in Poland. It might be best to wait on having children until we can leave Poland. Living in Palestine might be a better environment to have a family than Poland. A thriving Jewish community would surround us there. If we have children, don't you want them to have the best opportunities that life can offer? I would want them to get a good education and to pursue a career of their choice."

"I feel the same way, Yitzhak. I think it is best for us to wait on raising a family and find a way for us to officially immigrate to Palestine. Let's go talk to Rabbi Jakubicz and plan our wedding."

Rabbi Jakubicz was very thrilled to learn that Jenny and I wanted to get married, as well as Josef and Esther's plans. He advised us to first go to the CKZP office to learn the legal procedures to obtain a marriage license and establish our living arrangements as a married couple. The four of us preferred to retain the use of our current apartments for each married couple. I won a coin toss. We agreed that Jenny and I would live together in my current apartment, and Josef and Esther would live together in her current apartment.

The CKZP office told us that there was no problem retaining our current apartments and that a marriage license application form could be obtained, submitted, and approved at the magistrate's office located in the town hall. We assumed that the authorities allowed us to continue living in our two-bedroom apartments since they probably anticipated that children would soon occupy the apartment's second bedroom!

The four of us decided to have a joint wedding. After consulting with Rabbi Jakubicz, the wedding was scheduled to take place inside the community center on Sunday afternoon, October 6th, at 2 p.m. This gave the four of us about two months to prepare for our big day and to invite our Jewish friends. I quickly mailed a note to Aneta and Maria to let them know about my wedding, even though I knew that they might not be able to afford to come.

A week prior to the wedding, I received a response from Maria. She regretted that she and Aneta could not attend. Aneta was too ill to travel and that she needed to remain home to take care of her mother. Maria also mentioned that she received another letter from Leah and Hershel. The two of them were sent to Canada from the Vienna DP camp.

Our big day arrived very quickly. All of our friends accepted the invitation and offered to prepare the food for the reception and a wedding cake. Josef and I saved up enough money for the reception, new suits for us to wear, and to purchase wedding rings for our brides and simple wedding bands for us.

When Jenny entered the room wearing a stylish white wedding dress, a veil, and carrying a bouquet of white flowers, she was the vision of joy, grace, and beauty. I felt very proud being the one marrying her. During the ceremony, we held hands very tightly, smiled at each other, and cried tears of joy.

After Rabbi Jakubicz announced that we were man and wife, Josef and I each stepped on a cloth-covered glass to break it and traditionally end the wedding ceremony. Everyone, including Rabbi Jakubicz, loudly yelled and cheered, "Mazel Tov"!!

Jenny and I were now Mr. and Mrs. Yitzhak and Jenny Barkan!

357

# Aliyah to Eretz-Israel
## 1947 - 1960

The CKZP's January meeting inside the community center was scheduled for 7 p.m. on Thursday, January 16th, 1947. The Dzierzoniow CKZP Director, Avrom Landau, was listed as the guest speaker on the agenda posted on the center's bulletin board. Since he was going to talk about the effect of the Kielce pogrom on the Jews living in Poland and the rumors about Jewish immigration to Palestine, Josef and I knew that Jenny and Esther would be interested and should attend the meeting with us.

The community center's meeting room was crowded that evening. All of the seats were taken with many people standing against the walls. Committee Director Landau's address was very direct with his official-sounding, stern voice. "It is true that hundreds of Jews, who aren't currently declared citizens of any country, are being sent from the displaced persons camps to Palestine and other countries. You may have also heard stories about Polish Jews crossing the border into Czechoslovakia to escape from the pogroms and the hostility that Jews are experiencing in Poland since the murders that happened at Kielce. They are escaping to try to get to one of these DP camps.

"As a result, the Soviets, along with the Polish Provisional Government, have intensified their border control in order to stop these illegal border crossings. The majority of the Jews living in Dzierzoniow have become Polish citizens, otherwise you wouldn't have been sent here. I need to remind you that a Polish citizen who is arrested trying to cross the border without a government issued exit permit or passport will risk being ineligible to receive one of these emigration documents in the future.

"The CKZP understands that you are concerned about your safety and welfare. So far, Dzierzoniow hasn't experienced a pogrom like those occurring elsewhere in Poland. If you are considering leaving Poland, the CKZP recommends that you wait until you can leave Poland through the legal process."

When the four of us left the meeting and were walking to our apartments, Esther initiated our conversation. "I was right. Mr. Landau confirmed what I've been telling you. It is best for us to legally leave Poland and not try to cross the border without any official documents."

I responded, "Jenny and I talked about having children. We decided to wait until we can officially leave Poland, so that our children won't face the hatred of Jews that exists in today's Poland."

Esther continued, "You may not know that my father's older brother, Chaim, lives on a kibbutz in Palestine. When he was in his twenties, he worked on a merchant ship. During one of the voyages, his ship docked in Haifa. He left the ship and remained there. I have an address for him and I'm going to try and contact him. It may be possible for him to be our sponsor so that Josef and I can move to Palestine. If we ever get there, it may be possible for the two of us to be your sponsors, Jenny and Yitzhak."

Jenny immediately answered, "That would be wonderful, Esther. Don't you think so, Yitzhak?"

"Yes. Thank you, Esther, for thinking of us. I recently learned that my sister, Leah, and her husband, Hershel, were sent to Canada from the Vienna DP camp. I will write to them as soon as our Bolechov friends send me their address.

"In the meantime, I'm going to subscribe to the local newspaper and have it delivered each day to the barbershop. I just hired a fourth barber and can afford this extra expense. Besides giving our customers something to read while they are waiting, I can keep track of what is happening elsewhere in Poland. When I was young, I often listened to my uncle's radio and kept track of what was happening with Hitler. Josef and Esther, when I spot something relevant in the newspaper, would you like to read it?"

Josef answered, "Yes. This will give the four of us something to talk about when we get together."

The four of us met at the coffee shop near the Rynek on a weekday evening three weeks later. After our coffee was served, Josef mentioned, "I don't think many of the Jews that live here are following the CKZP's advice to not flee. I've noticed that many of the Jewish men who worked with me at the distribution warehouse are no longer there. Have any of you noticed anything?"

Jenny replied, "Yes, I've also noticed that my kindergarten class has fewer students and that I don't see their mothers dropping them off and picking them up at the end of the day."

Esther confirmed that her class also had fewer students.

I replied, "Now that you mention this, the barbershop has had fewer customers during the past few weeks. I think that you are correct, Josef. Many of the Jews in Dzierzoniow are leaving."

The spring of 1947 didn't remain calm in Poland. The newspaper reported that, in many of the Polish cities, Jews were attacked at the markets and there was an increase in the occurrence of robberies and murders of Jews. Vandals marked numerous Jewish homes and apartment doors with anti-Jewish slogans. Anti-Jewish flyers were distributed on the major streets, including the main streets in Dzierzoniow.

The CKZP immediately advised the Jewish people to lock their doors and refrain from leaving their homes at night. The Polish students were given a survey to complete with the question, "Do you want to become friends with a Jewish child?" The newspaper reported that fifty percent of the Polish students answered "no".

On a warm and sunny April afternoon, the four of us had a picnic along the bank of the Pilawa River and discussed what the Jews of Poland were currently experiencing. We were frightened about the Polish government and the police not taking any preventive actions or arresting those committing these crimes. All four of us were becoming disillusioned with the communist Polish government and living in Poland. It was apparent to us that equality for Jews in Poland was not possible. We also noticed that fewer people were attending the Jewish community social events held at the community center. More were leaving Dzierzoniow.

Stalin's control of Poland escalated beginning in September 1947. The CKZP announced at their September 18th meeting that Stalin forced the President of the United States, Harry S. Truman, to recognize Soviet-controlled Poland as a new nation as part of a new agreement. The Polish communists immediately started nationalizing private businesses and properties.

The CKZP held a special meeting on Monday, December 1st, 1947. Everyone cheered following the announcement that the United National Assembly passed a resolution a few days prior on November 29th calling for the establishment of a Jewish state in Palestine. Once the cheers subsided, Director Landau cautioned everyone to be patient before a Jewish state would actually become a reality.

The newspaper stated that Stalin supported the creation of a Jewish state since he felt the country would adopt a socialistic structure and apply political pressure on the British government that controlled Palestine. On the other hand, new strict restrictions were initiated to prevent Jews from leaving Poland. Anyone termed a Zionist was considered a traitor. The four of us were feeling that Stalin trapped Jews to continue to work in Poland. Our desire to leave Poland faded away.

On May 14th, 1948, David Ben-Gurion, the head of the Jewish Agency, proclaimed the establishment and independence of the State of Israel, on the same day in which the British Mandate over Palestine expired. The return of our hope for a better future quickly extinguished when we learned that a war with the surrounding Arab countries had erupted. Director Landau was correct with his previous assessment about the speed of Israel becoming an independent country.

The situation worsened for the Jews living in Poland during the autumn of 1948. Stalin established a no exit policy and closed the Jewish Agency's Warsaw office and their emigration office. On December 15th, 1948, the new Polish Communist Party, the PZPR, officially called the Polish United Workers Party (*Polska Zjednoczona Partia Robotnicza*), was established and replaced the provisional government. All other political parties, including Zionist or religious political parties could no longer exist.

The Jewish existence in Poland looked very bleak. The noose tightened on us. Our plans of leaving Poland vanished. An application to obtain an official exit permit to emigrate from Poland was rarely granted.

On March 10<sup>th</sup>, 1949, the newspaper reported that the war between Israel and the neighboring Arab countries finally ended. A formal armistice was established between Israel, Egypt, Lebanon, and Jordan. The war lasted one year, three months, and ten days.

Even though Israel soon opened an embassy in Warsaw, the Jewish Distribution Committee (JDC) was expelled from Poland in order for Poland to continue restricting Jewish emigration.

It appeared that there was no way for Josef and Esther to leave Poland and join her Uncle Chaim in Israel. Even though I obtained Leah and Hershel's address in Montreal, Canada, there was no available path for Jenny and me to move there. Before they closed, I received another response from the JDC and the American Red Cross that there was no additional information regarding my father and uncle.

Stalin's grip on Poland tightened even more with additional centralization. In 1950, all schools, including Jewish schools, were nationalized along with a centralized healthcare system. The newspaper's headline on October 29<sup>th</sup>, 1950 announced the elimination of the CKZP. A new Soviet-controlled committee was formed to replace it called the TSKZ. The official name was the Socio-Cultural Association of Jews in Poland (*Towarzystwo Społeczno-Kulturalne Żydów w Polsce*).

In 1952 and 1953, more anti-Israel policies continued from Stalin. Israeli and Jewish emigration diplomats were expelled from Poland.

Suddenly, on March 5th, 1953, the newspaper's headline boldly announced the death of Josef Stalin. Shortly afterward, political reforms slowly swept through the Soviet-controlled Eastern Europe. The politicians called this "destalinization."

In the autumn of 1955, there was a slight thaw in the country's No Exit Policy with the cooperation of the Israeli minister in Poland. The PZPR's officials recommended allowing Jewish Polish citizens to emigrate to Israel if they were elderly or single people unable to work with no immediate family members left in Poland and if they had a next of kin living in Israel. This recommendation opened an increase to the possible expansion of future Jewish emigration. Many eligible Jews took advantage of this new opportunity and left Poland.

When Josef and Esther had dinner with us at our apartment, Jenny brought up the topic of emigrating and asked, "When will it be our turn?" We just stared at each other and wondered.

On October 8th, 1956, the newspaper announced that Wladyslaw Gomukla became the First Secretary of the Polish United Worker's Party and planned to initiate a more liberal and humanitarian policy for Jewish emigration. Rabbi Landau was still in charge of the community center at the old synagogue and announced that he was having a community meeting on Thursday, October 25th, at 7 p.m. Of course, Josef, Esther, Jenny, and I arrived early to get a seat.

"Shalom, everyone. I've been in touch with the local authorities and learned more about Gomukla's new aliyah Jewish emigration policy. His intent is to unite families and make it possible for Polish Jews to go to Israel. His government officials are working on the details for the official application procedure. It is clear that in order to be approved, you will need to forfeit your Polish citizenship and be considered as a foreigner. Arrangements are being made for the Jewish Distribution Committee, which many of you know as The Joint, to return to Poland to assist those eligible to leave Poland and immigrate to Israel. The JDC will help you prepare the needed documents to obtain exit permits, passports, visas, train and ship tickets, and financial assistance for those with a low income. I will contact the JDC when their Warsaw office reopens and invite a representative to come to Dzierzoniow. Please continue to check our bulletin board for more announcements."

The audience stood up, applauded, and then began talking very loudly. The four of us huddled together and Josef suggested, "Let's go to our apartment to talk so that we can hear each other."

Esther made some tea and the four of us sat at their kitchen table. I started the conversation, "Well, from what Rabbi Landau mentioned, the two of you should have no problem getting an exit pass to go to Israel. Esther, you're lucky that you have a relative living there."

Esther replied, "Yes, I'll send Uncle Chaim a letter and ask him to write back, stating that he will be our sponsor. I've saved all of his letters and envelopes and will use them to prove that I have a relative living there."

I responded, "The only thing that I can show are the letters about my father being listed as 'Missing' with the possibility that he may have found his way to Israel."

Josef spoke up, "I got the impression that First Secretary Gomukla is encouraging more Jewish emigration for Poland's national identity to become a nation of only Poles. I think that he is secretly doing this to get rid of all the Polish Jews. If I'm right, I think that you and Jenny will have no problems receiving an exit permit."

I responded, "We'll see what happens. Jenny and I will meet with the JDC representative. Like you, we have saved all of our documents."

On Monday, February 4th, 1957, Rabbi Landau posted that the JDC representative and two office assistants would be available for two weeks beginning on February 13th to assist those interested with applying for an exit permit. His announcement instructed those interested to make an appointment in advance at his office. Since Jenny and Esther's school used the community center for daily student activities, they regularly checked the bulletin board. When they read this announcement, they quickly signed up for appointments on Tuesday, February 14th, at 4 and 4:30 p.m., respectively. This time was convenient for them since their school day ended at 3:30 p.m. As manager of the barbershop, this appointment time was good for me. Josef needed to make arrangements to leave early from work that day.

Jenny and I were very excited and eager to meet with the JDC representative and we brought all of our documents to our appointment. I kept remembering what my father told me, "Save all of your documents. You may need to show them in the future." Today was one of those days.

The JDC office assistant greeted us. "Hello, I'm Golda Horowicz. I assume that you want to apply for an exit permit and leave Poland. The State of Israel is very pleased that Poland has eased the restrictions on Jewish emigration. Israel welcomes the Polish Jewish community. The Israeli government and the JDC will do its best to help you. I see that you have documents to show me. Let me review what you have."

After carefully reading everything, she handed us the exit permit application form. "Go ahead and fill it out. I see that you, sir, are a licensed barber, and you, madame, are a kindergarten teacher. Israel needs both of you. You can both work at a kibbutz. I also see that you, Yitzhak, think that your father, Meir, may be in Israel. Since we expect thousands of Polish Jews to apply, the JDC needs to prioritize the processing of applications. The first ones to be approved are those who have proof that a family member already lives in Israel. Please be patient with us. Your application will be processed, but it will not be dealt with immediately. You will have to wait. Is this your current address?"

I responded, "Yes."

"Good. We will send you notification when your application will be processed."

Jenny and I stood up and shook hands with the office assistance.

As we walked toward the community center's exit door, I asked Jenny, "Well, do you think that we will have the opportunity to go to Israel?"

"She seemed optimistic. You and I will need to remain hopeful, but I think that we will need to frequently inquire about our application's approval."

Josef and Esther's exit application was regarded as first priority since she had proof that her Uncle Chaim lived in Israel. A few weeks later, they received a notification letter that their departure date was set for Tuesday, April 2nd, and that all of their permits and transportation tickets would be sent to Rabbi Landau a week prior to their departure. They would take the train from Dzierzoniow to Rome, Italy's coastal port, Civitavecchia, board a ship to Cyprus, and then board another ship that would take them to Haifa in Israel.

As much as April 2$^{nd}$ was a joyful day for Josef and Esther, Jenny and I felt very sad about our closest friends leaving as we walked with them to the Dzierzoniow train station. I think that Josef must have noticed how Jenny and I were feeling and tried to humor us. "Do you remember what we always say at Passover, 'Next year in Jerusalem'? Well, that's what we will say to you when we learn that you are coming to join us. We'll send you our address and a sponsor letter as soon as we get settled."

As Jenny and I stood on the station's platform, we sobbed while waving goodbye as their train left the station and disappeared into the horizon.

In October, six months after Josef and Esther left, we inquired with Rabbi Landau about the progress of our application. After a year of not receiving an official notification letter, he suggested that we write a follow-up letter to the JDC Warsaw office. A month later, Rabbi Landau handed us a response stating that our application was still being processed.

Jenny and I did not receive a notification letter during 1958. We sent another inquiry to the JDC Warsaw office and received a response six months later that they received over fifty-one thousand applications and ours should be processed soon.

Rabbi Landau tried his best to assure us and not to worry. "It appears that the JDC is helping the approval for everyone who applied to go to Israel. You will eventually hear from them."

Finally, in the early evening of Wednesday, January 6$^{th}$, 1960, Rabbi Landau came to our home to show us our approved application form and give us our exit permits and transit information.

"You are scheduled to leave on Monday, April 4th, from the Dzierzoniow train station to go to Poland's northern port city, Gdynia. Since so many Jews are being sent to Israel, there are not enough trains available to take everyone by train to the Italian port. Apparently the Israeli government made arrangements to hire a ship from Panama called the Protea to transport over one thousand Polish Jews on each of their trips. Since your ship will sail across the Baltic Sea to reach the Atlantic Ocean and then enter the Mediterranean Sea, it is best to wait until April to avoid any serious winter weather conditions. The voyage will last thirteen days until you arrive in Haifa on Sunday, April 17th.

"This is good news, Rabbi. Jenny's smile is telling me that we can wait that long. This will give us enough time to sort through our belongings and decide what we will take with us. Thank you for all of your help."

"You're welcome. I am hoping that I will also receive good news from the JDC about my application."

April 4th couldn't come soon enough. Two days after Jenny and I received our notification, we already determined to take clothing and shoes for all seasonal weather, our documents and photos, my mother's Shabbat candlestick holders, and, of course, the case with all of my barber equipment and supplies. I also had time to write and send letters to Aneta and Maria, Josef and Esther, and Leah and Hershel to inform them that we were moving to Israel. Once I got settled in Israel, I planned to fulfill my promise to continue searching for my father and uncle.

Rabbi Landau was correct. The journey on the ship from Northern Poland all the way to Haifa seemed endless. We shared a third-class small cabin with another Jewish couple. A communal toilet was located in the hallway. Fortunately, there was a locked compartment where I could store the case with our documents and my barber's box. Even though it was April, it was still too cold, even with our winter coats, to stand or sit outside on the deck for a prolonged time during the first week on the Baltic Sea.

Once the ship entered the Mediterranean Sea with warmer weather, Jenny and I spent the days standing on the deck, looking out at the horizon, watching sunsets, and sharing our thoughts about what life would be like for us living in Israel. The two of us talked about having at least two children, a boy and a girl, and their possible names. I suggested that our son could be named Isaac to honor Jenny's deceased father. Jenny thought that since our life together was God's blessing our daughter's name could be Bracha.

After another six days, Jenny and I could see the Israeli coastline appear in the far distance. Once we noticed that our ship, the Protea, was getting closer to the Haifa port, we raced back to our cabin to gather up all of our belongings and prepare for our departure.

We descended the ramp and stood on Israeli ground and placed all of our belongings onto the ground. With joyful tears falling from our eyes, we gave each other a loving hug and kiss.

Moments later, I kept holding Jenny in my arms and said, "Jenny, our escape and journey has finally come to an end. We have now arrived in the Jewish homeland that really wants us. The land of Israel will be our family's new home!"

We picked up our belongings and walked into the Israeli immigration office to begin our new Israeli life together.

# Epilogue:
## Moishe's Promise
### Kiryat One, Israel
### 2012

While I was teaching my high school English class on a very chilly February afternoon, a clerk from the administration office quietly came into the classroom and handed me a pink message slip that read, "Moishe, go to your parents' apartment as soon as you're done teaching. Zaydie Yitzhak passed away."

I was very shaken and emotionally disturbed with this unexpected news. Even though I moved into my own apartment after I graduated from the university and secured my teaching job, I regularly stopped at my parent's apartment to spend time chatting with my grandfather. He looked healthy and continued wearing his dress clothes and tie every day. I saw no sign that he was ill or if something else was wrong.

I left school as soon as I could after the dismissal of my last class and drove to my parents' apartment.

When I arrived, the door to their apartment was open and I could hear my mom's voice coming from the living room.

My mom was the first one who noticed that I had arrived. She was standing next to my father and my sister, Shayna. Tears were flowing from my mom's eyes. She ran over to me and gave me a big hug. "Oh, Moishe. I'm so glad that you are here."

I looked over her shoulder and saw Zaydie lying in the recliner chair. The daily newspaper was opened on his lap and his black slippers were placed on the

371

floor beneath the chair. He looked like he was sleeping.

"What happened, Mom?"

My father spoke up. "The ambulance medical team was just here to examine him. They think that he died in his sleep from natural causes since there are no signs of physical pain or injury."

Mom chimed in. "When Shayna and I got here after we finished working and approached the front door of the apartment, we smelled something burning. He must have started to heat up the pot roast in the kitchen oven and then sat in the recliner to read the newspaper. It looks like he fell asleep while wearing his glasses. When I saw him, I shook him and he did not move or wake up. That's when I called for an ambulance to get here. Of course, I turned off the oven and removed the pot roast. The ambulance arrived in about five minutes and the medical team examined him."

My heart sank. My talks with Zaydie have come to an abrupt end.

My mom continued speaking to us. "Moishe and Shayna, you don't have to wait around for the funeral home to come."

Shayna and I looked at each other and we both spoke up. "We will stay until he is taken to the funeral home so that we can spend the remaining time with Zaydie and the two of you."

About thirty minutes later, I looked out of the living room window and saw the hearse pull up to the curb in front of the apartment building. "Mom. I think they're here."

"Moishe and Shayna. Do you want to give Zaydie your final kiss and say goodbye before he is taken to the funeral home?"

I didn't know how to respond about kissing someone who died.

*Should I kiss a dead body? Where?*

I looked at my mom and I could tell by her yearning facial expression that she wanted us to kiss him. Feeling somewhat reluctant, I leaned over and kissed him on the forehead. "Goodbye, Zaydie. I love you."

Shayna, and then my mother and father, followed my example and did the same.

The graveside funeral service was held three days later and was conducted by the rabbi from Zaydie's shul. He was buried in the grave next to Bubbie Jenny. Shayna's husband, Oded, and my girlfriend, Rachel, stood with us at his grave. About ten members from the shul also attended the service, and my parents invited them and the rabbi to come to our home afterward to begin the seven-day Shiva period. Both Shayna and I made the arrangements to take the seven days off from work. Many of our work associates, my parents' friends and their work colleagues visited us during Shiva.

The Friday after the Shiva period ended was our first Friday evening Shabbat family dinner with all six of us without our Zaydie. When dinner was over and the dishes were cleared off the dining room table, my mom asked, "Let's all sit in the living room and have some coffee. I have something to show everyone."

We all acknowledged her request and were curious to see what she wanted to show us.

After we were all seated and coffee was poured and served, mom said, "Wait right here. I have to go into Zaydie's bedroom and get what I want to show you."

Within minutes, my mom walked back into the living room carrying Zaydie's metal box.

She sat down and held up the box. "When I was going through Zaydie's belongings, I found this metal box placed on top of his dresser with this note taped to it.   The note says, 'Give this box to Moishe'. Moishe, do you know what this is?"

When she handed me the metal box, I replied, "Oh, Mom.  I do.  Haven't you ever seen this before?"

"No. Never. What is it?  I'm afraid to open it. Since he wanted you to have it, will you open it and show us what's inside?"

I remembered the promise that I made to Zaydie, that I would tell his story to the family when I felt the time was right.

I thought to myself: *Okay, Zaydie. I remember my promise.  I feel that now is the right moment for me to tell your story and show them what is saved in your box.  It is time for them to finally learn how your sister, mother, and you survived the Holocaust by fleeing from the German army, what happened to your father, and what happened to the rest of the family who remained and did not flee.*

"Let me begin. This metal box was originally his father's barber kit when his family lived in Bolechov. Bolechov is a small town that is located in what is now Western Ukraine..."

## Notes from the Author

The historic events mentioned in this book are true. Bolechov and the neighboring towns and villages of today's Western Ukraine were once part of the Austro-Hungarian Empire for many centuries. When World War I ended in 1918 with the defeat of Germany and its allies, including the Austro-Hungarian Empire, a Ukrainian state was established for a very brief period. In 1919, this area of today's Ukraine was incorporated into Poland.

My maternal grandmother, Nesha Recht Strahl, once commented that the name of the country changed after every war. Others joked that one could travel to Austria, Poland, Germany, Russia, and Ukraine without ever leaving your home!

On August 23, 1939, Germany and the Soviet Union signed a non-aggression agreement known as the Molotov-Ribbentrop Pact. Part of the agreement included their division of Poland. The German army invaded Western Poland on September 1, 1939, resulting in the onset of World War II. The Soviet army invaded Eastern Poland on September 17, 1939, and subsequently annexed Eastern Poland (today's Ukraine) into the Soviet Union. Many Jews living in Eastern Poland viewed the Soviets as liberators during this occupation. On June 22, 1941, the Nazi army moved eastward into Eastern Poland, breaking the pact, in order to fight and defeat the Soviet army.

Stalin and the Soviet Union government had already designed an evacuation plan, if needed. Evacuating the army, industries, and the population eastward was a military tactic, previously implemented by the Russian army during the

Napoleonic War and during World War I. Some historians refer to this tactic as the Scorched Earth Policy. As soon as the German army advanced into Eastern Poland on June 22$^{nd}$, 1941, the Soviet's evacuation plan to flee eastward to Soviet Asia, particularly to Uzbekistan, was immediately commenced, somewhat chaotically.

It is true that thousands of Jews fled eastward to join the Soviet evacuation by agreeing to become Soviet citizens as early as the 1939 German invasion into Western Poland. Others fled without documentation and were often sent to Siberia. The vast majority of the Eastern Polish Jews who decided to remain in their homes in 1941 were murdered by gunfire from the invading Nazis and buried in mass graves. Many Ukrainians collaborated and assisted the Nazis with the murders. These mass murders in former Eastern Poland are now referred to as the Holocaust By Bullets.

Members of my mother's paternal family faced this decision. Moshe Strahl and his family remained in Bolechov. Only Moshe and his son survived. The Nazis murdered his wife, mother, and daughters. Moshe's sister, Beilla Strahl Elner, her husband, Sucher Elner, and their four children fled to Uzbekistan and survived. It took them at least six months to arrive in Tashkent from Bolechov.

My cousin, Bracha, Beilla's granddaughter, participated at the Taniava Mass Grave Ceremony held in August 2010 and read a testimonial regarding her family.

The murderous Aktions in Bolechov did occur, though there is a discrepancy of the actual dates mentioned by different testimonial resources. The dates mentioned in this book are from the JewishGen website and the book, The Lost

The survivors: Beilla Elner and her four children:
Raya Rachel, Abraham, Luba, Tsipora Feiga

Moshe Strahl, his wife, mother, Sabina, and three
children (The women and girls were murdered.
Moshe and his son disappeared.)

Abraham Elner and Jenny
(Gania) Schindel
Wedding Photo (1956)

Other relatives who          Stanislavov,
were murdered          Soviet-controlled, Poland

The Polish Brigade fighting the German army was organized in cooperation with the Polish government in exile in Great Britain and the Soviet army. Many Polish men taking refuge in Tashkent, Uzbekistan, including some Jewish men, were recruited, trained for the Brigade, and sent to the front battle line.

In 1943, as the Soviet army pushed the German army out of the western part of the Soviet Union and Eastern Poland, those who had fled eastward were sent back to their place of origin.

During my conversations with Jewish organizations, synagogue leaders, and other Jewish people, many commented that they were unaware of the Jewish escape from Poland to the Soviet Union during World War II. There is very little written about this escape that I could find, except for the four books and websites listed in this book.

These books cite that between 1.2 and 1.6 million Jews are estimated to have fled from Poland to the

Soviet Union, beginning with the 1939 Nazi invasion. It is also estimated that fleeing to Uzbekistan saved 250,000 Jews.

Why is this aspect of the Holocaust rarely mentioned?

When speaking with others about the Holocaust, I've often heard the following: "Why remember the horrors of the past? It is just too painful to remember. It is better for me to focus on the joy of the present and the forthcoming future."

The book, Shelter from the Holocaust: Rethinking Jewish Survival in the Soviet Union, includes a chapter titled "The Layer of Silence" and offers an additional explanation. This chapter cites that many Holocaust survivors have feelings of grief, loss, and guilt that they survived while others close to them did not, particularly from survivors who learned their families and friends were murdered. Many survivors also felt their survival is of secondary importance to preserving the memory of the Nazis' murderous and gruesome genocide attempt to eliminate the existence of the Jewish people. These survivors feel that the ghettos, concentration camps, gas chambers, and the mass murders need to continue to remain in the forefront of the public's attention. Therefore, many survivors prefer to remain silent about the hardships they encountered during their escape.

Many of the details mentioned in this book about the family's travel experiences and their daily life in Bolechov and Tashkent were fictional. The reference books, and the testimony from those that I interviewed, revealed some information about the travel encounters and the daily life on an agricultural collective farm. Many experiences described in this book were based on this information.

The fictional characters of Yitzhak and his grandson, Moishe, were inspired by my relationship with my maternal grandfather, Isaac Strahl, who immigrated to the United States in 1903. When his wife, Nesha, died of a heart attack, Isaac moved from their apartment to live with my family. He and I shared a bedroom. Every day he would dress himself with a freshly ironed white dress shirt and freshly ironed dress slacks with perfect creases. He wore a tie and during the winter added a sweater vest. His black dress shoes glistened from his shoe polishing and he wore black slippers inside the house.

Isaac was a licensed barber and kept his barber tools in a black metal box that he stored in our bedroom closet. My nephew, Ryan, now has Isaac's metal box and his remaining barber tools to preserve for our family's future generations.

Similarly to Yitzhak, Isaac died in his sleep while resting in the reclining chair in our family's living room. He was dressed in his usual manner, slippers resting on the floor, and the daily newspaper opened and laying on his lap. He had already placed the pot roast in the oven to warm up for the family dinner. When the arriving doctor examined him, no signs of impairment were detected. Isaac fell asleep and died peacefully from natural causes.

Isaac was born on March 3rd, 1879, in Rozdol (a village near Bolechov). He died on February 4th, 1966, in Pittsburgh, Pennsylvania. He was 85 years old.

I miss my Zaydie!

Isaac Strahl

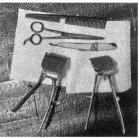

Isaac's barber box and some of his tools

# Suggested Discussion Questions

- Have you or has anyone in your family been in a situation similar to these characters?

- What do you think it meant for Yitzhak, Josef, and Yitzhak's mother to have a traditional Shabbat dinner for the first time in many years?

- If you had to permanently leave your life behind and flee, what would you take with you and why?

- Unlike today's air travel, what would a six-month travel experience by wagon and train, with lots of delays, train service cancellations, and sleeping on floors or outdoors be like for you?

- What is the author trying to accomplish by making some of the experiences, like the hours waiting in train stations, repetitious, even tedious?

- If you learned that the Nazis were arriving in a couple of days, would you or your family remain at your home or agree to flee with the Soviet evacuation? What are the reasons for your decision?

- How would your life be affected if you moved to an unfamiliar new country?

# *Suggested Bibliography and Websites*

## References:

Mendelsohn, Daniel (2013 Reissue) The Lost: A Search for Six of Six Million, Harper Perennnial

Edele, Mark; Fitzpatrick, Sheila; Grossman, Atina editors (2017) Shelter from the Holocaust - Rethinking Jewish Survival in the Soviet Union, Wayne State University Press https://www.wsupress.wayne.edu/books/detail/shelter-holocaust

Manley, Rebecca (2012) To The Tashkent Station: Evacuation and Survival in the Soviet Union at War, Cornell University Press; 1st edition

Tal, Haim (2009) The Fields of Ukraine: a 17-Year-Old's Survival of Nazi Occupation: The Story of Yosef Laufer, Dallci Press; English Edition

## Websites:

## Bolechow/Bolechov/Bolekhiv:

www.bolechow.org

https://sztetl.org.pl/pl/node/192026

https://yahadmap.org/#village/bolekhiv-bolekhov-bolechow-ivano-frankivsk-ukraine.621

https://www.jgaliciabukovina.net/110717/community/bolechow

https://www.jewishgen.org/yizkor/bolekhov/bol117.html

## Evacuation to the Soviet Union:

https://shtetlroutes.eu/en/bolekhv-putvnik/

https://soviethistory.msu.edu/1943-2/wartime-evacuation/

https://en.wikipedia.org/wiki/Evacuation_in_the_Soviet_Union

## Tashkent, Uzbekistan:

https://www.jewishgen.org/databases/holocaust/0136_uzbek.html (Jewish Refugees in Tashkent)

https://www.ushmm.org/online/hsv/source_view.php?SourceId=20492 (Registration Card Database of Jewish Refugees in Tashkent, Uzbekistan during WWII)

## Copyright Free Maps:

www.nationsonline.org

## Post World War 2 Poland:

www.jstor.org

https://www.sydneyjewishmuseum.com.au

https://www.academia.edu

# Acknowledgments

I want to acknowledge and thank Elaine Goldenthal, Abe Wagen, Adela Weinstein from the Phoenix Holocaust Association, and Al Guldner for their assistance.

Cousin Marlene, my longtime friend, David Kenney, and especially my Israeli cousins, Bracha Elner Alternovits and Eeki Elner, are thanked for their encouragement and support. My writing mentor and technology guide, Dave Hughes, is thanked for his guidance and assistance.

A big thank you goes out to my proofreading team: Barbara Nachman, Roger Lay, Debbie Donaldson, and Mary Louise Cohen. I could not have completed this project without their expertise and support.

And, of course, I thank my partner and my love, José Olagues, for his patience, love, encouragement, and proofreading assistance.

# About the Author

Sandor M. Lubisch is a retired high school English teacher, Professional Development Specialist, Arizona Master Teacher Mentor, and international education consultant. He serves as an advisory committee member for various Jewish and community non-profit organizations in Phoenix, Arizona.

Sandor previously researched and completed two family history books and published books regarding his challenging teaching and disc jockey careers.

His previously published novels are available from Amazon:

*Have I The Right?*

*My Own Sunrise*

sandorlubisch.com

Made in the USA
Columbia, SC
15 March 2024

df55acdc-7b8f-40a2-8ba4-616f7c723e13R01